THE PUREST FORM OF TROUBLE.

When he left the noble's house, a couple of hours later, Captain Deudermont found himself wandering not back to *Sea Sprite*, but along infamous Half-Moon Street, the toughest section of Luskan, the home of the Cutlass. He went in without hesitation, pulling up a chair at the first empty table. Deudermont spotted the big man before he even sat down. It was, without doubt, Wulfgar, son of Beornegar. The captain hadn't known Wulfgar very well and hadn't seen him in years, but there could be no question about it. The sheer size, the aura of strength, and the piercing blue eyes of the man gave him away. Oh, he was more haggard-looking now, with an unkempt beard and dirty clothes, but he was Wulfgar.

The big man met Deudermont's stare momentarily, but there was no recognition in the barbarian's eyes when he turned away. Deudermont became even more certain when he saw the magnificent warhammer, Aegis-fang, strapped across Wulfgar's broad back.

"Ye drinking or looking for a fight?"

FORGOTTEN REALMS

THE
SPINE OF THE WORLD

THE LEGEND OF DRIZZT.
BOOK XII

R. A. SALVATORE

THE LEGEND OF DRIZZT®
BOOK XII
THE SPINE OF THE WORLD

©1999 TSR, Inc
©2009 Wizards of the Coast LLC

Cover art by Todd Lockwood
Map by Todd Gamble
This Edition First Printing: April 2009
Originally Published in Hardcover in September 1999

9 8

ISBN: 978-0-7869-5107-9
ISBN: 978-0-7869-5472-8 (e-book)
620-23972740-001-EN

U.S., CANADA, ASIA,
PACIFIC, & LATIN AMERICA
Wizards of the Coast LLC
P.O. Box 707
Renton, WA 98057-0707
+1-800-324-6496

EUROPEAN HEADQUARTERS
Hasbro UK Ltd
Caswell Way
Newport, Gwent NP9 0YH
GREAT BRITAIN
Save this address for your records.

Visit our web site at www.wizards.com

MAERLON MOUNTAIN
TO HUNDLESTONE
GANDERLAY FARM
TO FIRESHEAR
ABANDONED LIGHTHOUSE
THE FIEFDOM OF AUCKNEY
N
W
E
S
CASTLE AUCK
The Sea of Swords
Auckney Harbor

The smaller man, known by many names in Luskan but most commonly as Morik the Rogue, held the bottle up in the air and gave it a shake, for it was a dirty thing and he wanted to measure the dark line of liquid against the orange light of sunset.

"Down to one," he said, and he brought his arm back in as if to take that final swig.

PROLOGUE

The huge man sitting on the end of the wharf beside him snatched the bottle away, moving with agility exceptional in a man of his tremendous size. Instinctively, Morik moved to grab the bottle back, but the large man held his muscular arm up to fend off the grabbing hands and drained the bottle in a single hearty swig.

"Bah, Wulfgar, but you're always getting the last one of late," Morik complained, giving Wulfgar a halfhearted swat across the shoulder.

"Earned it," Wulfgar argued.

Morik eyed him skeptically for just a moment, then remembered their last contest wherein Wulfgar had, indeed, earned the right to the last swig of the next bottle.

"Lucky throw," Morik mumbled. He knew better, though, and had long ago ceased to be amazed by Wulfgar's warrior prowess.

"One that I'll make again," Wulfgar proclaimed,

pulling himself to his feet and hoisting Aegis-fang, his wondrous warhammer. He staggered as he slapped the weapon across his open palm, and a sly smile spread across Morik's swarthy face. He, too, climbed to his feet, taking up the empty bottle, swinging it easily by the neck.

"Will you, now?" the rogue asked.

"You throw it high enough, or take a loss," the blond barbarian explained, lifting his arm and pointing the end of the warhammer out to the open sea.

"A five-count before it hits the water." Morik eyed his barbarian friend icily as he recited the terms of the little gambling game they had created many days ago. Morik had won the first few contests, but by the fourth day Wulfgar had learned to properly lead the descending bottle, his hammer scattering tiny shards of glass across the bay. Of late, Morik had a chance of winning the bet only when Wulfgar indulged too much in the bottle.

"Never will it hit," Wulfgar muttered as Morik reached back to throw.

The little man paused, and once again he eyed the big man with some measure of contempt. Back and forth swayed the arm. Suddenly Morik jerked as if to throw.

"What?" Surprised, Wulfgar realized the feint, realized that Morik had not sailed the bottle into the air. Even as Wulfgar turned his gaze upon Morik, the little man spun in a complete circuit and let the bottle fly high and far.

Right into the line of the descending sun.

Wulfgar hadn't followed it from the beginning of its flight, so he could only squint into the glare, but he caught sight of it at last. With a roar he let fly his mighty warhammer, the magical and brilliantly crafted weapon spinning out low over the bay.

Morik squealed in glee, thinking he had outfoxed the big man, for the bottle was low in the sky by the time Wulfgar threw and fully twenty strides out from the wharf. No one could skim a warhammer so far and so fast as to hit that, Morik believed, especially not a man who had just drained more than half the contents of the target!

The bottle nearly clipped a wave when Aegis-fang took it, exploding it into a thousand tiny pieces.

"It touched water!" Morik yelled.

"My win," Wulfgar said firmly, his tone offering no debate.

Morik could only grumble in reply, for he knew that the big man was right. The warhammer got the bottle in time.

"Seeming a mighty waste of a good hammer fer just a bottle," came a voice behind the duo. The pair turned as one to see two men, swords drawn, standing but a few feet away.

"Now, Mister Morik the Rogue," remarked one of them, a tall and lean fellow with a kerchief tied around his head, a patch over one eye, and a rusty, curving blade weaving in the air before him. "I'm knowin' ye got yerself a good haul from a gem merchant a tenday back, and I'm thinkin' that ye'd be wise to share a bit o' the booty with me and me friend."

Morik glanced up at Wulfgar, his wry grin and the twinkle in his dark eyes telling the barbarian that he didn't mean to share a thing, except perhaps the blade of his fine dagger.

"And if ye still had yer hammer, ye might be arguin' the point," laughed the other thug, as tall as his friend, but much wider and far dirtier. He prodded his sword toward Wulfgar. The barbarian staggered backward, nearly falling off the end of the wharf—or at least, pretending to.

"I'm thinking that you should have found the gem merchant before me," Morik replied calmly. "Assuming there was a gem merchant, my friend, because I assure you that I have no idea what you are talking about."

The slender thug growled and thrust his sword ahead. "Now, Morik!" he started to yell, but before the words even left his mouth, Morik had leaped ahead, spinning inside the angle of the curving sword blade, rolling around, putting his back against the man's forearm and pushing out. He ducked right under the startled man's arm, lifting it high with his right hand, while his left hand flashed, a silver sparkle in the last light of day, Morik's dagger stabbing into the stunned man's armpit.

Meanwhile, the other thug, thinking he

had an easy, unarmed target, waded in. His bloodshot eyes widened when Wulfgar brought his right arm from behind his hip, revealing that the mighty warhammer had magically returned to his grip. The thug skidded to a stop and glanced in panic at his companion. But by now Morik had the newly unarmed man turned around and in full flight with Morik running right behind him, taunting him and laughing hysterically as he repeatedly stabbed the man in the buttocks.

"Whoa!" the remaining thug cried, trying to turn.

"I can hit a falling bottle," Wulfgar reminded him. The man stopped abruptly and turned back slowly to face the huge barbarian.

"We don't want no trouble," the thug explained, slowly laying his sword down on the boarding of the wharf. "No trouble at all, good sir," he said, bowing repeatedly.

Wulfgar dropped Aegis-fang to the decking, and the thug stopped bobbing, staring hard at the weapon.

"Pick up your sword, if you choose," the barbarian offered.

The thug looked up at him incredulously. Then, seeing the barbarian without a weapon— except, of course, for those formidable fists—the man scooped up his sword.

Wulfgar had him before his first swing. The powerful warrior snapped out his hand to catch the man's sword arm at the wrist. With a sudden and ferocious jerk, Wulfgar brought that arm straight up, then hit the thug in the chest with a stunning right cross that blasted away his breath and his strength. The sword fell to the wharf.

Wulfgar jerked the arm again, lifting the man right from his feet and popping his shoulder out of joint. The barbarian let go, allowing the thug to fall heavily back to his feet, then hit him with a vicious left hook across the jaw. The only thing that stopped the man from flipping headlong over the side of the wharf was Wulfgar's right hand, catching him by the front of his shirt. With frightening strength, Wulfgar easily lifted the thug from the deck, holding him fully a foot off the planking.

The man tried to grab at Wulfgar and break the hold, but Wulfgar shook him so violently that he nearly bit off his tongue, and every limb on the man seemed made of rubber.

"This one's not got much of a purse," Morik called. Wulfgar looked past his victim to see that his companion had gone right around the fleeing thug, herding him back toward the end of the dock. The thug was limping badly now and whining for mercy, which only made Morik stick him again in the buttocks, drawing more yelps.

"Please, friend," stammered the man Wulfgar held aloft.

"Shut up!" the barbarian roared, bringing his arm down forcefully, bending his head and snapping his powerful neck muscles so that his forehead collided hard with the thug's face.

A primal rage boiled within the barbarian, an anger that went beyond this incident, beyond the attempted mugging. No longer was he standing on a dock in Luskan. Now he was back in the Abyss, in Errtu's lair, a tormented prisoner of the wicked demon. Now this man was one of the great demon's minions, the pincer-armed Glabrezu, or worse, the tempting succubus. Wulfgar was back there fully, seeing the gray smoke, smelling the foul stench, feeling the sting of whips and fires, the pincers on his throat, and the cold kiss of the demoness.

So clear it came to him! So vivid! The waking nightmare returned, holding him in a grip of the sheerest rage, stifling his mercy or compassion, throwing him into the pits of torment, emotional and physical torture. He felt the itching and burning of those little centipedes that Errtu used, burrowing under his skin and crawling inside him, their venomous pincers lighting a thousand fires within. They were on him and in him, all over him, their little legs tickling and exciting his nerves so that he would feel the exquisite agony of their burning venom all the more.

Tormented again, indeed, but suddenly and unexpectedly, Wulfgar found that he was no longer helpless.

Up into the air went the thug, Wulfgar effortlessly hoisting him overhead, though the man weighed well over two hundred pounds.

With a primal roar, a scream torn from his churning gut, the barbarian spun him around toward the open sea.

"I cannot swim!" the man shrieked. Arms and legs flailing pitifully, he hit the water fully fifteen feet from the wharf, where he splashed and bobbed, crying out for help. Wulfgar turned away. If he heard the man at all, he showed no indication.

Morik eyed the barbarian with some surprise. "He can't swim," Morik remarked as Wulfgar approached.

"Good time to learn, then," the barbarian muttered coldly, his thoughts still whirling down the smoky corridors of Errtu's vast dungeon. He kept brushing his hands along his arms and legs as he spoke, slapping away the imagined centipedes.

Morik shrugged. He looked down to the man who was squirming and crying on the planks at his feet. "Can you swim?"

The thug glanced up timidly at the little rogue and gave a slight, hopeful nod.

"Then go to your friend," Morik instructed. The man started to slowly crawl away.

"I fear his friend will be dead before he gets to his side," Morik remarked to Wulfgar. The barbarian didn't seem to hear him.

"Oh, do help the wretch," Morik sighed, grabbing Wulfgar by the arm and forcing that vacant gaze to focus. "For me. I would hate to start a night with a death on our hands."

With a sigh of his own, Wulfgar reached out his mighty hands. The thug on his knees suddenly found himself rising from the decking, one hand holding the back of his breeches, another clamped around his collar. Wulfgar took three running strides and hurled the man long and high. The flying thug cleared his splashing companion, landing nearby with a tremendous belly smack.

Wulfgar didn't see him land. Having lost all interest in the scene, he turned around and, after mentally recalling Aegis-fang to his grasp, stormed past Morik, who bowed in deference to his dangerous and powerful friend.

Morik caught up to Wulfgar as the barbarian exited the wharf. "They are still scrambling in the water," the rogue remarked. "The fat one, he keeps foolishly grabbing his friend, pulling them both underwater. Perhaps they will both drown."

Wulfgar didn't seem to care, and that was an honest reflection of his heart, Morik knew. The rogue gave one last look back at the harbor, then merely shrugged. The two thugs had brought it on themselves, after all.

Wulfgar, son of Beornegar, was not one to be toyed with.

So Morik, too, put them out of his mind—not that he was ever really concerned—and focused instead on his companion. His surprising companion, who had learned to fight at the training of a drow elf, of all things!

Morik winced, though, of course, Wulfgar was too distracted to catch it. The rogue thought of another drow, a visitor who had come unexpectedly to him not so long ago, bidding him to keep a watchful eye on Wulfgar and paying him in advance for his services—and not-so-subtly explaining that if Morik failed in the "requested" task, the dark elf's master would not be pleased. Morik hadn't heard from the dark elves again, to his relief, but still he kept to his end of the agreement to watch over Wulfgar.

No, that wasn't it, the rogue had to admit, at least to himself. He had started his relationship with Wulfgar for purely personal gain, partly out of fear of the drow, partly out of fear of Wulfgar and a desire to learn more about this man who had so obviously become his rival on the street. That had been in the beginning. He no longer feared Wulfgar, though he did sometimes fear *for* the deeply troubled, haunted man. Morik hardly ever thought about the drow elves, who had not come around in tendays and tendays. Surprisingly, Morik had come to like Wulfgar, had come to enjoy the man's company despite the many times when surliness dominated the barbarian's demeanor.

He almost told Wulfgar about the visit from the drow elves then, out of some basic desire to warn this man who had become his friend. Almost. . . . but the practical side of Morik, the cautious pragmatism that allowed him to stay alive in such a hostile environment as Luskan's streets, reminded him that to do so would do no one good. If the dark elves came for Wulfgar, whether Wulfgar expected them or not, the barbarian would be defeated. These were drow elves, after all, wielders of mighty magic and the finest of blades, elves who could walk uninvited into Morik's bedroom and rouse him from his slumber. Even Wulfgar had to sleep. If those dark elves, after they were finished with poor Wulfgar, ever learned that Morik had betrayed them. . . .

A shudder coursed along Morik's spine, and he forcefully shook the unsettling thoughts away, turning his attention back to his large friend. Oddly, Morik saw a kindred spirit here, a man who could be—and indeed had been—a noble and mighty warrior, a leader among men, but who, for one reason or another, had fallen from grace.

Such was the way Morik viewed his own situation, though in truth, he had been on a course to his present position since his early childhood. Still, if only his mother hadn't died in childbirth, if only his father hadn't abandoned him to the streets . . .

Looking at Wulfgar now, Morik couldn't help but think of the man he himself might have become, of the man Wulfgar had been. Circumstance had damned them both, to Morik's thinking, and so he held no illusions about their relationship now. The truth of his bond to Wulfgar, the real reason he stayed so close to him despite all his sensibilities—the barbarian was being watched by dark elves, after all!—was that he regarded the barbarian as he might a younger brother.

That, and the fact that Wulfgar's friendship brought him more respect among the rabble. For Morik, there always had to be a practical reason.

The day neared its end, the night its beginning, the time of Morik and Wulfgar, the time of Luskan's street life.

PART ONE

In my homeland of Menzoberranzan, where demons play and drow revel at the horrible demise of rivals, there remains a state of necessary alertness and wariness. A drow off-guard is a drow murdered in Menzoberranzan, and thus few are the times when dark elves engage in exotic weeds or drinks that dull the senses.

THE PRESENT

Few, but there are exceptions. At the final ceremony of Melee-Magthere, the school of fighters that I attended, graduated students engage in an orgy of mind-blurring herbs and sensual pleasures with the females of Arach-Tinilith, a moment of the purest hedonism, a party of the purest pleasures without regard to future implications.

I rejected that orgy, though I knew not why at the time. It assaulted my sense of morality, I believed—and still do—and it cheapened so many things that I hold precious. Now, in retrospect, I have come to understand another truth about myself that forced rejection of that orgy. Aside from the moral implications, and there were many, the mere notion of the mind blurring herbs frightened and repulsed me. I knew that all along, of course—as soon as I felt the intoxication at that ceremony, I instinctively rebelled against it—but it wasn't until very recently that I came to understand the truth of that rejection, the real reason why such influences have no place in my life.

These herbs attack the body in various ways, of course, from slowing reflexes to destroying coordination altogether, but more importantly, they attack the spirit in two different ways. First, they blur the past, erasing memories pleasant and unpleasant, and second, they eliminate any thoughts of the future. Intoxicants lock the imbiber in the present, the here and now, without regard for the future, without consideration of the past. That is the trap, a defeatist perspective that allows for attempted satiation of physical pleasures wantonly, recklessly. An intoxicated person will attempt even foolhardy dares because that inner guidance, even to the point of survival instinct itself, can be so impaired. How many young warriors foolishly throw themselves against greater enemies, only to be slain? How many young women find themselves with child, conceived with lovers they would not even consider as future husbands?

That is the trap, the defeatist perspective, that I cannot tolerate. I live my life with hope, always hope, that the future will be better than the present, but only as long as I work to make it so. Thus, with that toil, comes the satisfaction in life, the sense of accomplishment we all truly need for real joy. How could I remain honest to that hope if I allowed myself a moment of weakness that could well destroy all I have worked to achieve and all I hope to achieve? How might I have reacted to so many unexpected crises if, at the time of occurrence, I was influenced by a mind-altering substance, one that impaired my judgment or altered my perspective?

Also, the dangers of where such substances might lead cannot be underestimated. Had I allowed myself to be carried away with the mood of the graduation ceremony of Melee-Magthere, had I allowed myself the sensual pleasures offered by the priestesses, how cheapened might any honest encounter of love have been?

Greatly, to my way of thinking. Sensual pleasures are, or should be, the culmination of physical desires combined with an intellectual and emotional decision, a giving of oneself, body and spirit, in a bond of trust and respect. In such a manner as that graduation ceremony, no such sharing could have occurred; it would have been a giving of body only, and more so than that, a taking of another's offered wares. There would have been no higher joining, no spiritual experience, and thus, no true joy.

I cannot live in such a hopeless basking as that, for that is what it is: a pitiful basking in the lower, base levels of existence brought on, I believe, by the lack of hope for a higher level of existence.

And so I reject all but the most moderate use of such intoxicants, and while I'll not openly judge those who so indulge, I will pity them their empty souls.

What is it that drives a person to such depths? Pain, I believe, and memories too wretched to be openly faced and handled. Intoxicants can, indeed, blur the pains of the past at the expense of the future. But it is not an even trade.

With that in mind, I fear for Wulfgar, my lost friend. Where will he find escape from the torments of his enslavement?

— Drizzt Do'Urden

I

INTO PORT

"I do so hate this place," remarked Robillard, the robed wizard. He was speaking to Captain Deudermont of *Sea Sprite* as the three-masted schooner rounded a long jetty and came in sight of the harbor of the northern port of Luskan.

Deudermont, a tall and stately man, mannered as a lord and with a calm, pensive demeanor, merely nodded at his wizard's proclamation. He had heard it all before, and many times. He looked to the city skyline and noted the distinctive structure of the Hosttower of the Arcane, the famed wizards' guild of Luskan. That, Deudermont knew, was the source of Robillard's sneering attitude concerning this port, though the wizard had been sketchy in his explanations, making a few offhand remarks about the "idiots" running the Hosttower and their inability to discern a true wizardly master from a conniving trickster. Deudermont suspected that Robillard had once been denied admission to the guild.

"Why Luskan?" the ship's wizard complained. "Would

not Waterdeep have better suited our needs? No harbor along the entire Sword Coast can compare with Waterdeep's repair facilities."

"Luskan was closer," Deudermont reminded him.

"A couple of days, no more," Robillard retorted.

"If a storm found us in those couple of days, the damaged hull might have split apart, and all our bodies would have been food for the crabs and the fishes," said the captain. "It seemed a foolish gamble for the sake of one man's pride."

Robillard started to respond but caught the meaning of the captain's last statement before he could embarrass himself further. A great frown shadowed his face. "The pirates would have had us had I not timed the blast perfectly," the wizard muttered after he took a few moments to calm down.

Deudermont conceded the point. Indeed, Robillard's work in the last pirate hunt had been nothing short of spectacular. Several years before, *Sea Sprite*—the new, bigger, faster, and stronger *Sea Sprite*—had been commissioned by the lords of Waterdeep as a pirate hunter. No vessel had ever been as successful at the task, so much so that when the lookout spotted a pair of pirate cogs sailing the northern waters off the Sword Coast, so near to Luskan, where *Sea Sprite* often prowled, Deudermont could hardly believe it. The schooner's reputation alone had kept those waters clear for many months.

These pirates had come looking for vengeance, not easy merchant ship prey, and they were well prepared for the fight, each of them armed with a small catapult, a fair contingent of archers, and a pair of wizards. Even so, they found themselves outmaneuvered by the skilled Deudermont and his experienced crew, and out-enchanted by the mighty Robillard, who had been wielding his powerful dweomers in vessel-to-vessel warfare for well over a decade. One of Robillard's illusions had given the appearance that *Sea Sprite* was dead in the water, her mainmast down across her deck, with dozens of dead men at the rails. Like hungry wolves, the pirates had circled, closer and closer, then had come in, one to port and one to starboard, to finish off the wounded ship.

In truth, *Sea Sprite* hadn't been badly damaged at all, with Robillard countering the offensive magic of the enemy wizards. The small pirate catapults had little effect against the proud schooner's armored sides.

Deudermont's archers, brilliant bowmen all, had struck hard at the closing vessels, and the schooner went from battle sail to full sail with precision and efficiency, the prow of the ship verily leaping from the water as she scooted out between the surprised pirates.

Robillard dropped a veil of silence upon the pirate ships, preventing their wizards from casting any defensive spells, then plopped three fireballs—*Boom! Boom! Boom!*—in rapid succession, one atop each ship and one in between. Then came the conventional barrage from ballista and catapult, *Sea Sprite*'s gunners soaring lengths of chain to further destroy sails and rigging, and balls of pitch to heighten the flames.

De-masted and drifting, fully ablaze, the two pirates soon went down. So great was the conflagration that Deudermont and his crew managed to pluck only a few survivors from the cold ocean waters.

Sea Sprite hadn't escaped unscathed, though. She was under the power of but one full sail now. Even more dangerous, she had a fair-sized crack just above the waterline. Deudermont had to keep nearly a third of his crew at work bailing, which was why he had steered for the nearest port—Luskan.

Deudermont considered it a fine choice, indeed. He preferred Luskan to the much larger port of Waterdeep, for while his financing had come from the southern city and he could find dinner at the house of any lord in town, Luskan was more hospitable to his common crew members, men without the standing, the manners, or the pretensions to dine at the table of nobility. Luskan, like Waterdeep, had its defined classes, but the bottom rungs on Luskan's social ladder were still a few above the bottom of Waterdeep's.

Calls of greeting came to them from every wharf as they neared the city, for *Sea Sprite* was well known here and well respected. The honest fishermen and merchant sailors of Luskan, of all the northern reaches of the Sword Coast, had long ago come to appreciate the work of Captain Deudermont and his swift schooner.

"A fine choice, I'd say," the captain remarked.

"Better food, better women, and better entertainment in Waterdeep," Robillard replied.

"But no finer wizards," Deudermont couldn't resist saying. "Surely the Hosttower is among the most respected of mage guilds in all the Realms."

Robillard groaned and muttered a few curses, pointedly walking away.

Deudermont didn't turn to watch him go, but he couldn't miss the distinctive stomping of the wizard's hard-soled boots.

✗ ✗ ✗ ✗ ✗

"Just a short ride, then," the woman cooed, twirling her dirty blonde hair in one hand and striking a pouting posture. "A quick one to take me jitters off before a night at the tables."

The huge barbarian ran his tongue across his teeth, for his mouth felt as if it were full of fabric, and dirty cloth at that. After a night's work in the tavern of the Cutlass, he had returned to the wharves with Morik for a night of harder drinking. As usual, the pair had stayed there until after dawn, then Wulfgar had crawled back to the Cutlass, his home and place of employment, and straight to his bed.

But this woman, Delly Curtie, a barmaid in the tavern and Wulfgar's lover for the past few months, had come looking for him. Once, he had viewed her as a pleasurable distraction, the icing on his whisky cake, and even as a caring friend. Delly had nurtured Wulfgar through his first difficult days in Luskan. She had seen to his needs, emotional and physical, without question, without judgment, without asking anything in return. But of late the relationship had begun to shift, and not even subtly. Now that he had settled more comfortably into his new life, a life devoted almost entirely to fending the remembered pain of his years with Errtu, Wulfgar had come to see a different picture of Delly Curtie.

Emotionally, she was a child, a needful little girl. Wulfgar, who was well into his twenties, was several years older than she. Now, suddenly, he had become the adult in their relationship, and Delly's needs had begun to overshadow his own.

"Oh, but ye've got a few moments for me, me Wulfgar," she said, moving closer and rubbing her hand across his cheek.

Wulfgar grabbed her wrist and gently but firmly moved her hand away. "A long night," he replied. "And I had hoped for more rest before beginning my duties for Arumn."

"But I've got a tingling—"

"More rest," Wulfgar repeated, emphasizing each word.

Delly pulled away from him, her seductive pouting pose becoming suddenly cold and indifferent. "Good enough for ye, then," she said coarsely. "Ye think ye're the only man wanting to share me bed?"

Wulfgar didn't justify the rant with an answer. The only

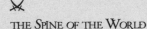

answer he could have given was to tell her he really didn't care, that all of this—his drinking, his fighting—was a manner of hiding and nothing more. In truth, Wulfgar did like and respect Delly and considered her a friend—or would have if he honestly believed that he could be a friend. He didn't mean to hurt her.

Delly stood in Wulfgar's room, trembling and unsure. Suddenly, feeling very naked in her slight shift, she gathered her arms in front of her and ran out into the hall and to her own room, slamming the door hard.

Wulfgar closed his eyes and shook his head. He chuckled helplessly and sadly when he heard Delly's door open again, followed by running footsteps heading down the hall toward the outside door. That one, too, slammed, and Wulfgar understood that all the ruckus had been for his benefit Delly wanted him to hear that she was, indeed, going out to find comfort in another's arms.

She was a complicated one, the barbarian understood, carrying more emotional turmoil than even he, if that were possible. He wondered how it had ever gone this far between them. Their relationship had been so simple at the start, so straightforward: two people in need of each other. Recently, though, it had become more complex, the needs having grown into emotional crutches. Delly needed Wulfgar to take care of her, to shelter her, to tell her she was beautiful, but Wulfgar knew he couldn't even take care of himself, let alone another. Delly needed Wulfgar to love her, and yet the barbarian had no love to give. For Wulfgar there was only pain and hatred, only memories of the demon Errtu and the prison of the Abyss, wherein he had been tortured for six long years.

Wulfgar sighed and rubbed the sleep from his eyes, then reached for a bottle, only to find it empty. With a frustrated snarl, he threw it across the room, where it shattered against a wall. He envisioned, for just a moment, that it had smashed against

Delly Curtie's face. The image startled Wulfgar, but it didn't surprise him. He vaguely wondered if Delly hadn't brought him to that point on purpose. Perhaps the woman was no innocent child, but a conniving huntress. When she had first come to him, offering comfort, had she intended to take advantage of his emotional weakness to pull him into a trap? To get him to marry her, perhaps? To rescue him that he might one day rescue her from the miserable existence she had carved out for herself as a tavern wench?

Wulfgar realized that his knuckles had gone white from clenching his hands so very hard, and he pointedly opened them and took several deep, steadying breaths. Another sigh, another rub of his tongue over dirty teeth, and the man stood and stretched his huge, nearly seven-foot, frame. He discovered, as he did nearly every afternoon when he went through this ritual, that he had even more aches in his huge muscles and bones this day. Wulfgar glanced over at his large arms, and though they were still thicker and more muscular than that of nearly any man alive, he couldn't help but notice a slackness in those muscles, as if his skin was starting to hang a bit too loosely on his massive frame.

How different his life was now than it had been those mornings years ago in Icewind Dale, when he had worked the long day with Bruenor, his adoptive dwarven father, hammering and lifting huge stones, or when he had gone out hunting for game or giants with Drizzt, his warrior friend, running all the day, fighting all the day. The hours had been even more strenuous then, more filled with physical burden, but that burden had been just physical and not emotional. In that time and in that place, he felt no aches.

The blackness in his heart, the sorest ache, was the source of it all.

He tried to think back to those lost years, working and fighting beside Bruenor and Drizzt, or when he had spent the day running along the wind-blown slopes of Kelvin's Cairn, the lone mountain in Icewind Dale, chasing Catti-brie. . . .

The mere thought of the woman stopped him cold and left him empty, and in that void, images of Errtu and the demon's minions inevitably filtered in. Once, one of those minions, the horrid succubus, had assumed the form of Catti-brie, a perfect image, and Errtu had convinced Wulfgar that he had managed to snare the woman, that she had been taken to suffer the same eternal torment as Wulfgar, *because* of Wulfgar.

Errtu had taken the succubus, Catti-brie, right before Wulfgar's horrified eyes and had torn the woman apart limb from limb, devouring her in an orgy of blood and gore.

Gasping for his breath, Wulfgar fought back to his thoughts of Catti-brie, of the real Catti-brie. He had loved her. She was, perhaps, the only woman he had ever loved, but she was lost to him now forever, he believed. Though he might travel to Ten-Towns in Icewind Dale and find her again, the bond between them had been severed, cut by the sharp scars of Errtu and by Wulfgar's own reactions to those scars.

The long shadows coming in through the window told him that the day neared its end and that his work as Arumn Gardpeck's bouncer would soon begin. The weary man hadn't lied to Delly when he had declared that he needed more rest, though, and so he collapsed back onto his bed and fell into a deep sleep.

Night had settled thickly about Luskan by the time Wulfgar staggered into the crowded common room of the Cutlass.

"Late again, as if we're to be surprised by that," a thin, beady-eyed man named Josi Puddles, a regular at the tavern and a good friend of Arumn Gardpeck, remarked to the barkeep when they both noticed Wulfgar's entrance. "That one's workin' less and drinkin' ye dry."

Arumn Gardpeck, a kind but stern and always practical man, wanted to give his typical response, that Josi should just shut his mouth, but he couldn't refute Josi's claim. It pained Arumn to watch Wulfgar's descent. He had befriended the barbarian those months before, when Wulfgar had first come to Luskan. Initially, Arumn had shown interest in the man only because of Wulfgar's obvious physical prowess—a mighty warrior like Wulfgar could indeed be a boon to business for a tavern in the tough dock section of the feisty city. After his very first conversation with the man, Arumn had understood that his feelings for Wulfgar went deeper than any business opportunity. He truly liked the man.

Always, Josi was there to remind Arumn of the potential pitfalls, to remind Arumn that, sooner or later, mighty bouncers made meals for rats in gutters.

"Ye thinkin' the sun just dropped in the water?" Josi asked Wulfgar as the big man shuffled by, yawning.

Wulfgar stopped, and turned slowly and deliberately to glare at the little man.

"Half the night's gone," Josi said, his tone changing abruptly from accusational to conversational, "but I was watchin' the place for ye. Thought I might have to break up a couple o' fights, too."

Wulfgar eyed the little man skeptically. "You couldn't break up a pane of thin glass with a heavy cudgel," he remarked, ending with another profound yawn.

Josi, ever the coward, took the insult with a bobbing head and a self-deprecating grin.

"We *do* have an agreement about yer time o' work," Arumn said seriously.

"And an understanding of your true needs," Wulfgar reminded the man. "By your own words, my real responsibility comes later in the night, for trouble rarely begins early. You named sundown as my time of duty but explained that I'd not truly be needed until much later."

"Fair enough," Arumn replied with a nod that brought a groan from Josi. He was anxious to see the big man—the big man whom he believed had replaced him as Arumn's closest friend—severely disciplined.

"The situation's changed," Arumn went on. "Ye've made a reputation and more than a few enemies. Every night, ye wander in late, and yer . . . our enemies take note. I fear that one night soon ye'll stagger in here past the crest o' night to find us all murdered."

Wulfgar put an incredulous expression on his face and turned away with a dismissive wave of his hand.

"Wulfgar," Arumn called after him forcefully.

The barbarian turned around, scowling.

"Three bottles missing last night," Arumn said calmly, quietly, a note of concern evident in his tone.

"You promised me all the drink I desired," Wulfgar answered.

"For yerself," Arumn insisted. "Not for yer skulking little friend."

All around widened their eyes at that remark, for not many of Luskan's tavernkeepers would speak so boldly concerning the dangerous Morik the Rogue.

Wulfgar lowered his gaze and chuckled, shaking his head. "Good Arumn," he began, "would you prefer to be the one to tell Morik he is not welcome to your drink?"

Arumn narrowed his eyes, and Wulfgar returned the glare for just a moment.

Delly Curtie entered the room just then, her eyes red and still lined with tears. Wulfgar looked at her and felt a pang of guilt, but it was not something he would admit publicly. He turned and went about his duties, moving to threaten a drunk who was getting a bit too loud.

"He's playing her like he'd pick a lute," Josi Puddles remarked to Arumn.

Arumn blew a frustrated sigh. He had become quite fond of Wulfgar, but the big man's increasingly offensive behavior was beginning to wear that fondness thin. Delly had been as a daughter to Arumn for a couple of years. If Wulfgar was playing her without regard for her emotions, he and Arumn were surely heading for a confrontation.

Arumn turned his attention from Delly to Wulfgar just in time to see the big man lift the loudmouth by the throat, carry him to the door, and none too gently heave him out into the street.

"Man didn't do nothing," Josi Puddles complained. "He keeps with that act, and you'll not have single customer."

Arumn merely sighed.

⚔ ⚔ ⚔ ⚔ ⚔

A trio of men in the opposite corner of the bar also studied the huge barbarian's movements with more than a passing interest. "Cannot be," one of them, a skinny, bearded fellow, muttered. "The world's a wider place than that."

"I'm telling ye it is," the middle one replied. "Ye wasn't aboard *Sea Sprite* back in them days. I'd not forget that one, not Wulfgar. Sailed with him all the way from Waterdeep to Memnon, I did, then back again, and we fought our share o' pirates along the way."

"Looks like a good one to have along for a pirate fight," remarked Waillan Micanty, the third of the group.

"So 'tis true!" said the second. "Not as good as his companion, though. Ye're knowin' that one. A dark-skinned fellow, small and pretty lookin', but fiercer than a wounded sahuagin, and quicker with a blade—or a pair o' the things—than any I ever seen."

"Drizzt Do'Urden?" asked the skinny one. "That big one traveled with the drow elf?"

"Yep," said the second, now commanding their fullest attention. He was smiling widely, both at being the center of it all and in remembering the exciting voyage he had taken with Wulfgar, Drizzt, and the drow's panther companion.

"What about Catti-brie?" asked Waillan, who, like all of Deudermont's crew, had developed a huge crush on the beautiful and capable woman soon after she and Drizzt had joined their crew a couple of years before. Drizzt, Catti-brie, and Guenhwyvar had sailed aboard *Sea Sprite* for many months, and how much easier scuttling pirates had been with that trio along!

"Catti-brie joined us south o' Baldur's Gate," the storyteller explained. "She came in with a dwarf, King Bruenor of Mithral Hall, on a flying chariot that was all aflame. Never seen anything like it, I tell ye, for that wild dwarf put the thing right across the sails o' one o' the pirate ships we was fighting. Took the whole danged ship down, he did, and was still full o' spit and battle spirit when we pulled him from the water!"

"Bah, but ye're lyin'," the skinny sailor started to protest.

"No, I heard the story," Waillan Micanty put in. "Heard it from the captain himself, and from Drizzt and Catti-brie."

That quieted the skinny man. All of them just sat and studied Wulfgar's movements a bit longer.

"Ye're sure that's him?" the first asked. "That's the Wulfgar fellow?"

Even as he asked the question, Wulfgar brought Aegis-fang off of his back and placed it against a wall.

"Oh, by me own eyes, that's him," the second answered. "I'd not be forgettin' him or that hammer o' his. He can split a mast with the thing, I tell ye, and put it in a pirate's eye, left or right, at a hunnerd long strides."

Across the room, Wulfgar had a short argument with a patron. With one mighty hand the barbarian reached out and grabbed the man's throat and easily, so very easily, hoisted him from his seat and into the air. Wulfgar strode calmly across the inn to the door and tossed the drunk into the street.

"Strongest man I ever seen," the second sailor remarked, and his two companions weren't about to disagree. They drained their drinks and watched a bit longer before leaving the Cutlass for home, where they found themselves running anxiously to inform their captain of who they'd seen.

⚔ ⚔ ⚔ ⚔ ⚔

Captain Deudermont rubbed his fingers pensively across his neatly trimmed beard, trying to digest the tale Waillan Micanty had just related to him. He was trying very hard, for it made no sense to him. When Drizzt and Catti-brie had sailed with him during those wonderful early years of chasing pirates along the Sword Coast, they had told him a sad tale of Wulfgar's demise. The story had had a profound effect on Deudermont, who had befriended the huge barbarian on that journey to Memnon years before.

Wulfgar was dead, so Drizzt and Catti-brie had claimed, and so Deudermont had believed. Yet here was one of Deudermont's trusted crewmen claiming that the barbarian was very much alive and well and working in the Cutlass, a tavern Deudermont had frequented.

The image brought Deudermont back to his first meeting with the barbarian and Drizzt in the Mermaid's Arms tavern in Waterdeep. Wulfgar had avoided a fight with a notorious brawler by the name of Bungo. What great things the barbarian and his companions had subsequently accomplished, from rescuing their little halfling friend from the clutches of a notorious pasha in Calimport to the reclamation of Mithral Hall for Clan Battlehammer. The thought of Wulfgar working as a brawler in a seedy tavern in Luskan seemed preposterous.

Especially since, according to Drizzt and Catti-brie, Wulfgar was dead.

Deudermont thought of his last voyage with the duo when *Sea Sprite* had put onto a remote island far out at sea. A blind seer had accosted Drizzt with a riddle about one he thought he had lost. The last time Deudermont had seen Drizzt and Catti-brie was at their parting, on an inland lake, no less, where *Sea Sprite* had been inadvertently transported.

So might Wulfgar be alive? Captain Deudermont had seen too much to dismiss the possibility out of hand.

Still, it seemed likely to the captain that his crewmen had been mistaken. They had little experience with northern barbarians, all of whom seemed huge and blond and strong. One might look like another to them. The Cutlass had taken on a barbarian warrior as a bouncer, but it was not Wulfgar.

He thought no more of it, having many duties and engagements to attend at the more upscale homes and establishments in the city. Three days later, however, when dining at the table of one of Luskan's noble families, the conversation turned to the death of one of the city's most renowned bullies.

"We're a lot better off without Tree Block Breaker," one of the guests insisted. "The purest form of trouble ever to enter our city."

"Just a thug and nothing more," another replied, "and not so tough."

"Bah, but he could take down a running horse by stepping in front of the thing," the first insisted. "I saw him do so!"

"But he couldn't take down Arumn Gardpeck's new boy," the other put in. "When he tried to fight that fellow, our Tree Block Breaker flew out of the Cutlass and brought the frame of a door with him."

Deudermont's ears perked up.

"Yeah, that one," the first agreed. "Too strong for any man, from the stories I am hearing, and that warhammer! Most beautiful weapon I've ever seen."

The mention of the hammer nearly made Deudermont choke on his food, for he remembered well the power of Aegis-fang. "What is his name?" the captain inquired.

"Who's name?"

"Arumn Gardpeck's new boy."

The two men looked at each other and shrugged. "Wolf-something, I believe," the first said.

When he left the noble's house, a couple of hours later, Captain Deudermont found himself wandering not back to *Sea Sprite*, but along infamous Half-Moon Street, the toughest section of Luskan, the home of the Cutlass. He went in without hesitation, pulling up a chair at the first empty table. Deudermont spotted the big man before he even sat down. It was, without doubt, Wulfgar, son of Beornegar. The captain hadn't known Wulfgar very well and hadn't seen him in years, but there could be no question about it. The sheer size, the aura of strength, and the piercing blue eyes of the man gave him away. Oh, he was more haggard-looking now, with an unkempt beard and dirty clothes, but he was Wulfgar.

The big man met Deudermont's stare momentarily, but there was no recognition in the barbarian's eyes when he turned away. Deudermont became even more certain when he saw the magnificent warhammer, Aegis-fang, strapped across Wulfgar's broad back.

"Ye drinking or looking for a fight?"

Deudermont turned around to see a young woman standing beside his table, tray in hand.

"Well?"

"Looking for a fight?" the captain repeated dully, not understanding.

"The way ye're staring at him," the young woman responded, motioning toward Wulfgar. "Many's the ones who come in here looking for a fight. Many's the ones who get carried away from here. But good enough for ye if ye're wanting to fight him, and good enough for him if ye leave him dead in the street."

"I seek no fight," Deudermont assured her. "But, do tell me, what is his name?"

The woman snorted and shook her head, frustrated for some reason Deudermont could not fathom. "Wulfgar," she answered. "And better for us all if he never came in here." Without asking again if he wanted a drink, she merely walked away.

Deudermont paid her no further heed, staring again at the big man. How had Wulfgar wound up here? Why wasn't he dead? And where were Drizzt, and Catti-brie?

He sat patiently, watching the lay of the place as the hours passed, until dawn neared and all the patrons, save he and one skinny fellow at the bar, had drifted out.

"Time for leaving," the barkeep called to him. When Deudermont made no move to respond or rise from his chair, the man's bouncer made his way over to the table.

Looming huge, Wulfgar glared down upon the seated captain. "You can walk out, or you can fly out," he explained gruffly. "The choice is yours to make."

"You have traveled far from your fight with pirates south of Baldur's Gate," the captain replied. "Though I question your direction."

Wulfgar cocked his head and studied the man more closely. A flicker of recognition, just a flicker, crossed his bearded face.

"Have you forgotten our voyage south?" Deudermont prompted him. "The fight with pirate Pinochet and the flaming chariot?"

Wulfgar's eyes widened. "What do you know of these things?"

"Know of them?" Deudermont echoed incredulously. "Why, Wulfgar, you sailed on my vessel to Memnon and back. Your friends, Drizzt and Catti-brie, sailed with me again not too long ago, though surely they thought you dead!"

The big man fell back as if he had been slapped across the face. A jumbled mixture of emotions flashed across his clear blue eyes, everything from nostalgia to loathing. He spent a long moment trying to recover from the shock.

"You are mistaken, good man," he replied at last to Deudermont's surprise. "About my name and about my past. It is time for you to leave."

"But Wulfgar," Deudermont started to protest. He jumped in surprise to find another man, small and dark and ominous, standing right behind him, though he had heard not a footfall of approach. Wulfgar looked to the little man, then motioned to Arumn. The barkeep, after a moment's hesitation, reached behind the bar and produced a bottle, tossing it across the way where sure-fingered Morik caught it easily.

"Walk or fly?" Wulfgar asked Deudermont again. The sheer emptiness of his tone, not icy cold, but purely indifferent, struck Deudermont profoundly, told him that the man would make good on the promise to launch him out of the tavern without hesitation if he didn't move immediately.

"*Sea Sprite* is in port for another tenday at the least," Deudermont explained, rising and heading for the door. "You are welcomed there as a guest or to join the crew, for I have not forgotten," he finished firmly, the promise ringing in his wake as he slipped from the inn.

"Who was that?" Morik asked Wulfgar after Deudermont had disappeared into the dark Luskan night.

"A fool," was all that the big man would answer. He went to the bar and pointedly pulled another bottle from the shelf. Turning his gaze from Arumn to Delly, the surly barbarian left with Morik.

⚔ ⚔ ⚔ ⚔ ⚔

Captain Deudermont had a long walk ahead of him to the dock. The sights and sounds of Luskan's nightlife washed over him—loud, slurred voices through open tavern windows, barking dogs, clandestine whispers in dark corners—but Deudermont scarcely heard them, engrossed as he was in his own thoughts.

So Wulfgar *was* alive, and yet in worse condition than the captain could ever have imagined the heroic man. His offer to the barbarian to join the crew of *Sea Sprite* had been genuine, but he knew from the barbarian's demeanor that Wulfgar would never take him up on it.

What was Deudermont to do?

He wanted to help Wulfgar, but Deudermont was experienced enough in the ways of trouble to understand that you couldn't help a man who didn't want help.

"If you plan to leave a dinner engagement, kindly inform us of your whereabouts," came a reproachful greeting as the captain approached his ship. He looked up to see both Robillard and Waillan Micanty staring down at him from the rail.

"You shouldn't be out alone," Waillan Micanty scolded, but Deudermont merely waved away the notion.

Robillard frowned his concern. "How many enemies have we made these last years?" the wizard demanded in all seriousness. "How many would pay sacks of gold for a mere chance at your head?"

"That's why I employ a wizard to watch over me," Deudermont replied calmly, setting foot up the plank.

Robillard snorted at the absurdity of the remark. "How am I to watch over you if I don't even know where you are?"

Deudermont stopped in his tracks, and a wide smile creased his face as he gazed up at his wizard. "If you can't locate me magically, what faith should I hold that you could find those who wish me harm?"

"But it is true, Captain," Waillan interjected while Robillard flushed darkly. "Many would love to meet up with you unguarded in the streets."

"Am I to bottle up the whole crew, then?" Deudermont asked. "None shall leave, for fear of reprisals by friends of the pirates?"

"Few would leave *Sea Sprite* alone," Waillan argued.

"Fewer still would be known enough to pirates to be targets!" Robillard spouted. "Our enemies would not attack a minor and easily replaced crewman, for to do so would incur the wrath of Deudermont and the lords of Waterdeep, but the price might be worth paying for the chance to eliminate the captain of *Sea Sprite*." The wizard blew a deep sigh and eyed the captain pointedly. "You should not be out alone," he finished firmly.

"I had to check on an old friend," Deudermont explained.

"Wulfgar, by name?" asked the perceptive wizard.

"So I thought," replied Deudermont sourly as he continued up the plank and by the two men, going to his quarters without another word.

It was too small and nasty a place to even have a name, a gathering hole for the worst of Luskan's wretches. They were sailors mostly, wanted by lords or angry families for heinous crimes. Their fears that walking openly down a street in whatever port their ship entered would get them arrested or murdered were justified. So they came to holes like this, back rooms in shanties conveniently stocked near to the docks.

Morik the Rogue knew these places well, for he'd got his start on the streets working as lookout for one of the most dangerous of these establishments when he was but a young boy. He didn't go into such holes often anymore. Among the more civilized establishments, he was highly respected and regarded, and feared, and that was probably the emotion Morik most enjoyed. In here, though, he was just another thug, a little thief in a nest of assassins.

He couldn't resist entering a hole this night, though, not with the captain of the famed *Sea Sprite* showing up to have a conversation with his new friend, Wulfgar.

"How tall?" asked Creeps Sharky, one of the two thugs at Morik's table. Creeps was a grizzled old sea dog with uneven clumps of dirty beard on his ruddy cheeks and one eye missing. "Cheap Creeps," the patrons often called him, for the man was quick with his rusty old dagger and slow with his purse. So tight was Creeps with his booty that he wouldn't even buy a proper patch for his missing eye. The dark edge of the empty socket stared out at Morik from beneath the lowest folds of the bandana Creeps had tied around his head.

"Head and a half taller than me," Morik answered. "Maybe two."

Creeps glanced to his pirate companion, an exotic specimen, indeed. The man had a thick topknot of black hair and tattoos all around his face, neck, and practically every other patch of exposed flesh—and since all he wore was a kilt of tiger skin, there was more than a little flesh exposed. Just following Creeps's glance to the other sent a shudder along Morik's spine, for while he didn't know the specifics of Creeps's companion, he had certainly heard the rumors about the "man," Tee-a-nicknick. This pirate was only half human, the other half being qullan, some rare and ferocious warrior race.

"*Sea Sprite*'s in port," Creeps remarked to Morik. The rogue nodded, for he had seen the three-masted schooner on his way to this drinking hole.

"He wore a beard just about the jawline," Morik added, trying to give as complete a description as he could.

"He sit straight?" the tattooed pirate asked.

Morik looked at Tee-a-nicknick as if he did not understand.

"Did he sit straight in his chair?" Creeps clarified, assuming a pose of perfect posture. "Lookin' like he had a plank shoved up his arse all the way to his throat?"

Morik smiled and nodded. "Straight and tall."

Again the two pirates shared a glance.

"Soundin' like Deudermont," Creeps put in. "The dog. I'd give a purse o' gold to put me knife across that one's throat. Put many o' me friends to the bottom, he has, and cost all o' us prettily."

The tattooed pirate showed his agreement by hoisting a bulging purse of coins onto the table. Morik realized then that every other conversation in the hole had come to an abrupt halt and that all eyes were upon him and his two rakish companions.

"Aye, Morik, but ye're likin' the sight," Creeps remarked, indicating the purse. "Well, it's yer own to have, and ten more like it, I'm guessin'." Creeps jumped up suddenly, sending his chair skidding back across the floor. "What're ye sayin', lads?" he cried. "Who's got a gold coin or ten for the head o' Deudermont o' *Sea Sprite*?"

A great cheer went up throughout the rat hole, with many curses spoken against Deudermont and his pirate-killing crew.

Morik hardly heard them, so focused was he on the purse of gold. Deudermont had come to see Wulfgar. Every man in the place, and a hundred more like them, no doubt, would pitch in a few more coins. Deudermont knew Wulfgar well and trusted him. A thousand gold pieces. Ten thousand? Morik and Wulfgar could get to Deudermont, and easily. Morik's greedy, thieving mind reeled at the possibilities.

2

ENCHANTMENT

She came skipping down the lane, so much like a little girl, and yet so obviously a young woman. Shiny black hair bounced around her shoulders, and her green eyes flashed as brightly as the beaming smile upon her fair face.

She had just spoken to *him,* to Jaka Sculi, with his soulful blue eyes and his curly brown hair, one strand hanging across the bridge of his nose. And just speaking to him made her skip where she might have walked, made her forget the mud that crept in through the holes in her old shoes or the tasteless food she would find in her wooden bowl at her parents' table that night. None of that mattered, not the bugs, not the dirty water, nothing. She had spoken to Jaka, and that alone made her warm and tingly and scared and alive all at the same time.

It went as one of life's little unrealized ironies that the same spirit freed by her encounter with the brooding Jaka inspired the eyes of another to settle upon her happy form.

Lord Feringal Auck had found his heart fluttering at the sight

39

of many different women over his twenty-four years, mostly merchant's daughters whose fathers were looking for another safe haven northwest of Luskan. The village was near to the most traveled pass through the Spine of the World where they might resupply and rest on the perilous journey to and from Ten-Towns in Icewind Dale.

Never before had Feringal Auck found his breathing so hard to steady that he was practically gasping for air as he hung from the window of his decorated carriage.

"Feri, the pines have begun sending their yellow dust throughout the winds," came the voice of Priscilla, Feringal's older sister. She, alone, called him Feri, to his everlasting irritation. "Do get inside the coach! The sneezing dust is thick about us. You know how terrible—"

The woman paused and studied her brother more intently, particularly the way he was gawking. "Feri?" she asked, sliding over in her seat, close beside him and grabbing his elbow and giving it a shake. "Feri?"

"Who is she?" the lord of Auckney asked, not even hearing his sister. "Who is that angelic creature, the avatar of the goddess of beauty, the image of man's purest desires, the embodiment of temptation?"

Priscilla shoved her brother aside and thrust her head out the carriage window. "What, that peasant girl?" she asked incredulously, a clear note of contempt sounding in her tone.

"I must know," Lord Feringal sang more than said. The side of his face sank against the edge of the carriage window, and his unblinking gaze locked on the skipping young woman. She slipped from his sight as the carriage sped around a bend in the curving road.

"Feri!" Priscilla scolded. She moved as if to slap her younger brother but held up short of the mark.

The lord of Auckney shook away his love-inspired lethargy long enough to eye his sister directly, even dangerously. "I shall know who she is," he insisted.

Priscilla Auck settled back in her seat and said no more, though she was truly taken aback by her younger brother's uncharacteristic show of emotion. Feringal had always been a gentle, quiet soul easily manipulated by his shrewish sister, fifteen years his senior. Now nearing her fortieth birthday, Priscilla had never married. In truth, she had never had any interest in a man beyond fulfilling her physical needs. Their mother had died giving birth to Feringal, their father passed on five years later, which left Priscilla, along with her father's counselor, Temigast, the stewardship of the fiefdom until Feringal grew old enough to rule. Priscilla had always enjoyed that arrangement, for even when Feringal had come of age, and even now, nearly a decade after that, her voice was substantial in the rulership of Auckney. She had never desired to bring another into the family, so she had assumed the same of Feri.

Scowling, Pricilla glanced back one last time in the general direction of the young lass, though they were far out of sight now. Their carriage rambled along the little stone bridge that arched into the sheltered bay toward the tiny isle where Castle Auck stood.

Like Auckney itself, a village of two hundred people that rarely showed up on any maps, the castle was of modest design. There were a dozen rooms for the family, and for Temigast, of course, and another five for the half-dozen servants and ten soldiers who served at the place. A pair of low and squat towers anchored the castle, barely topping fifteen feet, for the wind always blew strongly in Auckney. A common joke was, if the wind ever stopped blowing, all the villagers would fall over forward, so used were they to leaning as they walked.

"I should get out of the castle more often," Lord Feringal insisted as he and his sister moved through the foyer and into a sitting room, where old Steward Temigast sat painting another of his endless seascapes.

"To the village proper, you mean?" Priscilla said with obvious sarcasm. "Or to the outlying peat farms? Either way, it is all mud and stone, and dirty."

"And in that mud, a jewel might shine all the brighter," the love-struck lord insisted with a deep sigh.

The steward cocked an eyebrow at the odd exchange and looked up from his painting. Temigast had lived in Waterdeep for most of his younger days, coming to Auckney as a middle-aged man some thirty years before. Worldly compared to the isolated Auckney citizens—including the ruling family—Temigast had had little trouble in endearing himself to the feudal lord, Tristan Auck, and in rising to the post of principal counselor, then steward. That worldliness served Temigast well now, for he recognized the motivation for Feringal's sigh and understood its implications.

"She was just a girl," Priscilla complained. "A child, and a dirty one at that." She looked to Temigast for support, seeing that he was intent upon their conversation. "Feringal is smitten, I fear," she explained. "And with a peasant. The lord of Auckney desires a dirty, smelly peasant girl."

"Indeed," replied Temigast, feigning horror. By his estimation, by the estimation of anyone who was not from Auckney, the "lord of Auckney" was barely above a peasant himself. There *was* history there. The castle had stood for more than six hundred years, built by the Dorgenasts who had ruled for the first two centuries. Then, through marriage, it had been assumed by the Aucks.

But what, really, were they ruling? Auckney was on the very fringe of the trade routes, south of the westernmost spur of the Spine of the World. Most merchant caravans traveling between

Ten-Towns and Luskan avoided the place all together, many taking the more direct pass through the mountains many miles to the east. Even those who dared not brave the wilds of that unguarded pass crossed east of Auckney, through another pass that harbored the town of Hundelstone, which had six times the population of Auckney and many more valuable supplies and craftsmen.

Though a coastal village, Auckney was too far north for any shipping trade. Occasionally a ship—often a fisherman caught in a gale out of Fireshear to the south—would drift into the small harbor around Auckney, usually in need of repair. Some of those fishermen stayed on in the fiefdom, but the population here had remained fairly constant since the founding by the roguish Lord Dorgenast and his followers, refugees from a minor and failed power play among the secondary ruling families in Waterdeep. Nearing two hundred, the population was as large as it had ever been, mostly because of an influx of gnomes from Hundelstone, though on many occasions it was less than half of that. Most of the villagers were related, usually in more ways than one, except, of course, for the Aucks, who usually took their brides or husbands from outside stock.

"Can't you find a suitable wife from among the well-bred families of Luskan?" Priscilla asked. "Or in a favorable deal with a wealthy merchant? We could well use a large dowry, after all."

"Wife?" Temigast said with a chuckle. "Aren't we being a bit premature?"

"Not at all," Lord Feringal insisted evenly. "I love her. I know that I do."

"Fool!" Priscilla wailed, but Temigast patted her shoulder to calm her, chuckling all the while.

"Of course you do, my lord," the steward said, "but the marriage of a nobleman is rarely about love, I fear. It is about station, political alliances, and wealth," Temigast gently explained.

Feringal's eyes widened. "I love her!" the young lord insisted.

"Then take her as a mistress," Temigast suggested reasonably. "A plaything. Surely a man of your great station is deserving of at least one of those."

Hardly able to speak past the welling lump in his throat, Feringal ground his heel into the stone floor and stormed off to his private room.

⚔ ⚔ ⚔ ⚔ ⚔

"Did you kiss him?" Tori, the younger of the Ganderlay sisters, asked, giggling at the thought of it. Tori was only eleven, and just beginning to realize the differences between boys and girls, an education fast accelerating since Meralda, her older sister by six years, had taken a fancy to Jaka Sculi, with his delicate features and long eyelashes and brooding blue eyes.

"No, I surely did not," Meralda replied, brushing back her long black hair from her olive-skinned face, the face of beauty, the face that had unknowingly captured the heart of the lord of Auckney.

"But you wanted to," Tori teased, bursting into laughter, and Meralda joined her, as sure an admission as she could give.

"Oh, but I did," the older sister said.

"And you wanted to touch him," her young sister teased on. "Oh, to hug him and kiss him! Dear, sweet Jaka." Tori ended by making sloppy kissing noises and wrapping her arms around her chest, hands grabbing her shoulders as she turned around so that it looked as if someone was hugging her.

"You stop that!" Meralda said, slapping her sister across the back playfully.

"But you didn't even kiss him," Tori complained. "Why not,

if you wanted to? Did he not want the same?"

"To make him want it all the more," the older girl explained. "To make him think about me all the time. To make him dream about me."

"But if you're wanting it—"

"I'm wanting more than that," Meralda explained, "and if I make him wait, I can make him beg. If I make him beg, I can get all that I want from him and more."

"What more?" Tori asked, obviously confused.

"To be his wife," Meralda stated without reservation.

Tori nearly swooned. She grabbed her straw pillow and whacked her sister over the head with it. "Oh, you'll never!" she cried. Too loudly.

The curtain to their bedroom pulled back, and their father, Dohni Ganderlay, a ruddy man with strong muscles from working the peat fields and skin browned from both sun and dirt, poked his head in.

"You should be long asleep," Dohni scolded.

The girls dived down as one, scooting under the coarse, straw-lined ticking and pulling it tight to their chins, giggling all the while.

"Now, I'll be having none of that silliness!" Dohni yelled, and he came at them hard, falling over them like a great hunting beast, a wrestling tussle that ended in a hug shared between the two girls and their beloved father.

"Now, get your rest, you two," Dohni said quietly a moment later. "Your ma's a bit under the stone, and your laughter is keeping her awake." He kissed them both and left. The girls, respectful of their father and concerned about their mother, who had indeed been feeling even worse than usual, settled down to their own private thoughts.

Meralda's admission was strange and frightening to Tori. But while she was uncertain about her sister getting married and moving out of the house, she was also very excited at the prospect of growing into a young woman like her sister.

Lying next to her sister, Meralda's mind raced with anticipation. She had kissed a boy before, several boys actually, but it had always been out of curiosity or on a dare from her friends. This was the first time she really wanted to kiss someone. And how she did want to kiss Jaka Sculi! To kiss him and to run her fingers through his curly brown hair and gently down his soft, hairless cheek, and to have his hands caressing her thick hair, her face . . .

Meralda fell asleep to warm dreams.

⚔ ⚔ ⚔ ⚔ ⚔

In a much more comfortable bed in a room far less drafty not so many doors away, Lord Feringal nestled into his soft feather pillows. He longed to escape to dreams of holding the girl from the village, where he could throw off his suffocating station, where he could do as he pleased without interference from his sister or old Temigast.

He wanted to escape too much, perhaps, for Feringal found no rest in his huge, soft bed, and soon he had twisted and turned the feather ticking into knots about his legs. It was fortunate for him that he was hugging one of the pillows, for it was the only thing that broke his fall when he rolled right off the edge and onto the hard floor.

Feringal finally extricated himself from the bedding tangle, then paced about his room, scratching his head, his nerves more on edge than they'd ever been. What had this enchantress done to him?

"A cup of warm goat's milk," he muttered aloud, thinking that would calm him and afford him some sleep. Feringal slipped from his room and started along the narrow staircase. Halfway down he heard voices from below.

He paused, recognizing Priscilla's nasal tone, then a burst of laughter from his sister as well as from old, wheezing Temigast. Something struck Feringal as out of place, some sixth sense told him that he was the butt of that joke. He crept down more quietly, coming under the level of the first floor ceiling and ducking close in the shadows against the stone banister.

There sat Priscilla upon the divan, knitting, with old Temigast in a straight-backed chair across from her, a decanter of whisky in hand.

"Oh, but I love her," Priscilla wailed, stopping her knitting to sweep one hand across her brow dramatically. "I cannot live without her!"

"Got along well enough for all these years," Temigast remarked, playing along.

"But I am tired, good steward," Priscilla replied, obviously mocking her brother. "What great effort is lovemaking alone!"

Temigast coughed in his drink, and Priscilla exploded with laughter.

Feringal could take no more. He swept down the stairs, full of anger. "Enough! Enough I say!" he roared. Startled, the two turned to him and bit their lips, though Priscilla could not hold back one last bubble of laughter.

Lord Feringal glowered at her, his fists clenched at his sides, as close to rage as either of them had ever seen the gentle-natured man. "How dare you?" he asked through gritted teeth and trembling lips. "To mock me so!"

"A bit of a jest, my lord," Temigast explained weakly to defuse the situation, "nothing more."

Feringal ignored the steward's explanation and turned his

ire on his sister. "What do you know of love?" he screamed at
Priscilla. "You have never had a lustful thought in your miserable
life. You couldn't even imagine what it would be like to lay with
a man, could you, dear sister?"

"You know less than you think," Priscilla shot back, tossing
aside her knitting and starting to rise. Only Temigast's hand, grabbing hard at her knee, kept her in place. She calmed considerably
at that, but the old man's expression was a clear reminder to watch
her words carefully, to keep a certain secret between them.

"My dear Lord Feringal," the steward began quietly, "there is
nothing wrong with your desires. Quite the contrary. I should
consider them a healthy sign, if a bit late in coming. I don't doubt
that your heart aches for this peasant girl, but I assure you there's
nothing wrong with taking her as your mistress. Certainly there
is precedent for such an act among the previous lords of Auckney,
and of most kingdoms, I would say."

Feringal gave a long and profound sigh and shook his head
as Temigast rambled on. "I love her," he insisted again. "Can't
you understand that?"

"You don't even know her," Priscilla dared to interject. "She
farms peat, no doubt, with dirty fingers."

Feringal took a threatening step toward her, but Temigast, agile
and quick for his age, moved between them and gently nudged
the young man back into a chair. "I believe you, Feringal. You
love her, and you wish to rescue her."

That caught Feringal by surprise. "Rescue?" he echoed
blankly.

"Of course," reasoned Temigast. "You are the lord, the great
man of Auckney, and you alone have the power to elevate this
peasant girl from her station of misery."

Feringal held his perplexed pose for just a moment then said,
"Yes, yes," with an exuberant nod of his head.

"I have seen it before," Temigast said, shaking his head. "It is a common disease among young lords, this need to save some peasant or another. It will pass, Lord Feringal, and rest assured that you may enjoy all the company you need of the girl."

"You cheapen my feelings," Feringal accused.

"I speak the truth," Temigast was quick to reply.

"No!" insisted Feringal. "What would you know of my feelings, old man? You could never have loved a woman to suggest such a thing. You can't know what burns within me."

That statement seemed to hit a nerve with the old steward, but for whatever reason Temigast quieted, and his lips got very thin. He moved back to his chair and settled uncomfortably, staring blankly at Feringal.

The young lord, more full of the fires of life than he had ever been, would not buckle to that imposing stare. "I'll not take her as a mistress," he said determinedly. "Never that. She is the woman I shall love forever, the woman I shall take as my wife, the lady of Castle Auck."

"Feri!" Priscilla screeched.

The young lord, determined not to buckle as usual to the desires of his overbearing sister, turned and stormed off, back to the sanctuary of his room. He took care not to run, as he usually did in confrontations with his shrewish sister, but rather, afforded himself a bit of dignity, a stern and regal air. He was a man now, he understood.

"He has gone mad," Priscilla said to Temigast when they heard Feringal's door close. "He saw this girl but once from afar."

If Temigast even heard her, he made no indication. Stubborn Priscilla slipped down from the divan to her knees and moved up before the seated man. "He saw her but once," she said again, forcing Temigast's attention.

"Sometimes that's all it takes," the steward quietly replied.

Priscilla quieted and stared hard at the old man whose bed she had secretly shared since the earliest days of her womanhood. For all their physical intimacy, though, Temigast had never shared his inner self with Priscilla except for one occasion, and only briefly, when he had spoken of his life in Waterdeep before venturing to Auckney. He had stopped the conversation quickly, but only after mentioning a woman's name. Priscilla had always wondered if that woman had meant more to Temigast than he let on. Now, she recognized that he had fallen under the spell of some memory, coaxed by her brother's proclamations of undying love.

The woman turned away from him, jealous anger burning within her, but, as always, she was fast to let it go, to remember her lot and her pleasures in life. Temigast's own past might have softened his resolve against Feringal running after this peasant girl, but Priscilla wasn't so ready to accept her brother's impetuous decision. She had been comfortable with the arrangement in Castle Auck for many years, and the last thing she wanted now was to have some peasant girl, and perhaps her smelly peasant family, moving in with them.

✖ ✖ ✖ ✖ ✖

Temigast retired soon after, refusing Priscilla's invitation to share her bed. The old man's thoughts slipped far back across the decades to a woman he had once known, a woman who had so stolen his heart and who, by dying so very young, had left a bitterness and cynicism locked within him to this very day.

Temigast hadn't recognized the depth of those feelings until he realized his own doubt and dismissal of Lord Feringal's obvious feelings. What an old wretch he believed himself at that moment.

He sat in a chair by the narrow window overlooking Auckney Harbor. The moon had long ago set, leaving the cold waters dark and showing dull whitecaps under the starry sky. Temigast, like Priscilla, had never seen his young charge so animated and agitated, so full of fire and full of life. Feringal always had a dull humor about him, a sense of perpetual lethargy, but there had been nothing lethargic in the manner in which the young man had stormed down the stairs to proclaim his love for the peasant girl, nothing lethargic in the way in which Feringal had accosted his bullying older sister.

That image brought a smile to Temigast's face. Perhaps Castle Auck needed such fire again. Perhaps it was time to shake the place and all the fiefdom around it. Maybe a bit of spirit from the lord of Auckney would elevate the often overlooked village to the status of its more notable neighbors, Hundelstone and Fireshear. Never before had the lord of Auckney married one of the peasants of the village. There were simply too few people in that pool, most from families who had been in the village for centuries, and the possibility of bringing so many of the serfs into the ruling family, however distantly, was a definite argument against letting Feringal have his way.

But the sheer energy the young lord had shown seemed as much an argument in favor of the union at that moment, and so he decided he would look into this matter very carefully, would find out who this peasant girl might be and see if something could be arranged.

3

FINAL STRAW

"He knew you," Morik dared to say after he had rejoined Wulfgar very late that same night following his venture to the seedy drinking hole. By the time the rogue had caught up to his friend on the docks the big man had drained almost all of the second bottle. "And you knew him."

"He thought he knew me," Wulfgar corrected, slurring each word.

He was hardly able to sit without wobbling, obviously more drunk than usual for so early an hour. He and Morik had split up outside the Cutlass, with Wulfgar taking the two bottles. Instead of going straight to the docks the barbarian had wandered the streets and soon found himself in the more exclusive section of Luskan, the area of respectable folk and merchants. No city guards had come to chase him off, for in that area of town stood the Prisoner's Carnival, a public platform where outlaws were openly punished. A thief was up on the stage this night, asked repeatedly by the torturer if he admitted his crime. When he did not, the torturer took out a pair of heavy shears and snipped off his little finger. The thief's answer to the repeated question brought howls of approval from the scores of people watching the daily spectacle.

Of course, admitting to the crime was no easy way out for the poor man. He lost his whole hand, one finger at a time, the mob cheering and hooting with glee.

But not Wulfgar. No, the sight had proven too much for the barbarian, had catapulted him back in time, back to Errtu's Abyss and the helpless agony. What tortures he had known there! He had been cut and whipped and beaten within an inch of his life, only to be restored by the healing magic of one of Errtu's foul minions. He'd had his fingers bitten off and put back again.

The sight of the unfortunate thief brought all that back to him vividly now.

The anvil. Yes, that was the worst of all, the most agonizing physical torture Errtu had devised for him, reserved for those moments when the great demon was in such a fit of rage that he could not take the time to devise a more subtle, more crushing, mental torture.

The anvil. Cold it was, like a block of ice, so cold that it seemed like fire to Wulfgar's thighs when Errtu's mighty minions pulled him across it, forced him to straddle it, naked and stretched out on his back.

Errtu would come to him then, slowly, menacingly, would walk right up before him, and in a single, sudden movement, smash a small mallet set with tiny needles down into Wulfgar's opened eyes, exploding them and washing waves of nausea and agony through the barbarian.

And, of course, Errtu's minions would heal him, would make him whole again that their fun might be repeated.

Even now, long fled from Errtu's abyssal home, Wulfgar often awoke, curled like a baby, clutching his eyes, feeling the agony. Wulfgar knew of only one escape from the pain. Thus, he had taken his bottles and run away, and only by swallowing the fiery liquid had he blurred that memory.

"*Thought* he knew you?" Morik asked doubtfully.

Wulfgar stared at him blankly.

"The man in the Cutlass," Morik explained.

"He was mistaken," Wulfgar slurred.

Morik flashed him a skeptical look.

"He knew who I once was," the big man admitted. "Not who I am."

"Deudermont," Morik reasoned.

Now it was Wulfgar's turn to look surprised. Morik knew most of the folk of Luskan, of course—the rogue survived through information—but it surprised Wulfgar that he knew of an obscure sailor, which is what Wulfgar thought Deudermont to be, merely visiting the port.

"Captain Deudermont of the *Sea Sprite*," Morik explained. "Much known and much feared by the pirates of the Sword Coast. He knew you, and you knew him."

"I sailed with him once . . . a lifetime ago," Wulfgar admitted.

"I have many friends, profiteers of the sea, who would pay handsomely to see that one eliminated," Morik remarked, bending low over the seated Wulfgar. "Perhaps we could use your familiarity with this man to some advantage."

Even as the words left Morik's mouth, Wulfgar came up fast and hard, his hand going around Morik's throat. Staggering on unsteady legs, Wulfgar still had the strength in just that one arm to lift the rogue from the ground. A fast few strides, as much a fall as a run, brought them hard against the wall of a warehouse where Wulfgar pinned Morik the Rogue, whose feet dangled several inches above the ground.

Morik's hand went into a deep pocket, closing on a nasty knife, one that he knew he could put into the drunken Wulfgar's heart in an instant. He held his thrust, though, for Wulfgar did not press in any longer, did not try to injure him. Besides, there remained those nagging memories of drow elves holding an interest in Wulfgar. How would Morik explain killing the man to them? What would happen to the rogue if he didn't manage to finish the job?

"If ever you ask that of me again, I will—" Wulfgar left the threat unfinished, dropping Morik. He spun back to the sea, nearly overbalancing and tumbling from the pier in his drunken rush.

Morik rubbed a hand across his bruised throat, momentarily stunned by the explosive outburst. When he thought about it, though, he merely nodded. He had touched on a painful wound, one opened by the unexpected appearance of Wulfgar's old companion, Deudermont. It was the classic struggle of past and present, Morik knew, for he had seen it tear men apart time and again as they went about their descent to the bottom of a bottle. The feelings brought on by the sight of the captain, the man with whom he had once sailed, were too raw for Wulfgar. The barbarian couldn't put his present state in accord with what he had once been. Morik smiled and let it go, recognizing clearly that the emotional fight, past against present, was far from finished for his large friend.

Perhaps the present would win out, and Wulfgar would listen to Morik's potentially profitable proposition concerning Deudermont. Or, if not, maybe Morik would act independently and use Wulfgar's familiarity with the man to his own gain without Wulfgar's knowledge.

Morik forgave Wulfgar for attacking him. This time. . . .

"Would you like to sail with him again, then?" Morik asked, deliberately lightening his tone.

Wulfgar plopped to a sitting position, then stared incredulously through blurry eyes at the rogue.

"We must keep our purses full," Morik reminded him. "You do seem to be growing bored with Arumn and the Cutlass. Perhaps a few months at sea—"

Wulfgar waved him to silence, then turned around and spat into the sea. A moment later, he bent low over the dock and vomited.

Morik looked upon him with a mixture of pity, disgust, and anger. Yes, the rogue knew then and there he would get to Deudermont, whether Wulfgar went along with the plan or not. The rogue would use his friend to find a weakness in the infamous captain of *Sea Sprite*. A pang of guilt hit Morik as he came to that realization. Wulfgar was his friend, after all, but this was the street, and a wise man would not pass up so obvious an opportunity to grab a pot of gold.

✖ ✖ ✖ ✖ ✖

"You stink Morik get done it?" the tattooed pirate, Tee-a-nicknick, asked first thing when he awoke in an alley.

Next to him among the trash, Creeps Sharky looked over curiously, then deciphered the words. "Think, my friend, not stink," he corrected.

"You stink him done it?"

Propped on one elbow, Creeps snorted and looked away, his one-eyed gaze drifting around the fetid alley.

With no answer apparently forthcoming, Tee-a-nicknick swatted Creeps Sharky hard across the back of his head.

"What're you about?" the other pirate complained, trying

to turn around but merely falling face down on the ground, then slowly rolling to his back to glare at his exotic half-qullan companion.

"Morik done it?" Tee-a-nicknick asked. "Kill Deudermont?"

Creeps coughed up a ball of phlegm and managed, with great effort, to move to a sitting position. "Bah," he snorted doubtfully. "Morik's a sneaky one, to be sure, but he's out of his pond with Deudermont. More likely the captain'll be taking that one down."

"Ten thousand," Tee-a-nicknick said with great lament, for he and Creeps, in circulating the notion that Deudermont might be taken down before *Sea Sprite* ever left Luskan, had secured promises of nearly ten thousand gold pieces in bounty, funds they knew the offering pirates would gladly pay for the completed deed. Creeps and Tee-a-nicknick had already decided that should Morik finish the task, they would pay him seven of the ten, keeping three for themselves.

"I been thinking that maybe Morik'll set up Deudermont well enough," Creeps went on. "Might be that the little rat'll play a part without knowing he's playing it. If Deudermont's liking Morik's friend, then Deudermont might be letting down his guard a bit too much."

"You stink we do it?" Tee-a-nicknick asked, sounding intrigued.

Creeps eyed his friend. He chuckled at the half-qullan's continuing struggles with the language, though Tee-a-nicknick had been sailing with humans for most of his life, ever since he had been plucked from an island as a youth. His own people, the savage eight-foot-tall qullans were intolerant of mixed blood and had abandoned him as inferior.

Tee-a-nicknick gave a quick blow, ending in a smile, and Creeps Sharky didn't miss the reference. No pirate in any sea could handle a certain weapon, a long hollow tube that the tattooed pirate called a blowgun, better than Tee-a-nicknick. Creeps had seen his friend shoot a fly from the rail from across a wide ship's deck. Tee-a-nicknick also had a substantial understanding of poisons, a legacy of his life with the exotic qullans, Creeps believed, to tip the cat's claws he sometimes used as blowgun missiles. Poisons human clerics could not understand and counter.

One well-placed shot could make Creeps and Tee-a-nicknick wealthy men indeed, perhaps even wealthy enough to secure their own ship.

"You got a particularly nasty poison for Mister Deudermont?" Creeps asked.

The tattooed half-qullan smiled. "You stink we do it," he stated.

⚔ ⚔ ⚔ ⚔ ⚔

Arumn Gardpeck sighed when he saw the damage done to the door leading to the guest wing of the Cutlass. The hinges had been twisted so that the door no longer stood straight within its jamb. Now it tilted and wouldn't even close properly.

"A foul mood again," observed Josi Puddles, standing behind the tavernkeeper. "A foul mood today, a foul mood tomorrow. Always a foul mood for that one."

Arumn ignored the man and moved along the hallway to the door of Delly Curtie's room. He put his ear against the wood and heard soft sobbing from within.

"Pushed her out again," Josi spat. "Ah, the dog."

Arumn glared at the little man, though his thoughts weren't far different. Josi's whining didn't shake the tavernkeeper in the least. He recognized that the man had developed a particular sore spot against Wulfgar, one based mostly on jealousy, the emotion that always seemed to rule Josi's actions. The sobs of Delly Curtie cut deeply into troubled Arumn, who had come to think of the girl as his own daughter. At first, he had been thrilled by the budding relationship between Delly and Wulfgar, despite the protests of Josi, who had been enamored of the girl for years. Now those protests seemed to hold a bit of truth in them, for Wulfgar's actions toward Delly of late had brought a bitter taste to Arumn's mouth.

"He's costin' ye more than he's bringin' in," Josi went on, skipping to keep up with Arumn as the big man made his way determinedly toward Wulfgar's door at the end of the hall, "breakin' so much, and an honest fellow won't come into the Cutlass anymore. Too afraid to get his head busted."

Arumn stopped at the door and turned pointedly on Josi. "Shut yer mouth," he instructed plainly and firmly. He turned back and lifted his hand as if to knock, but he changed his mind and pushed right through the door. Wulfgar lay sprawled on the bed, still in his clothes and smelling of liquor.

"Always the drink," Arumn lamented. The sadness in his voice was indeed genuine, for despite all his anger at Wulfgar, Arumn couldn't dismiss his own responsibility in this situation. He had introduced the troubled barbarian to the bottle, but he hadn't recognized the depth of the big man's despair. The barkeep understood it now, the sheer desperation in Wulfgar to escape the agony of his recent past.

"What're ye thinking to do?" Josi asked.

Arumn ignored him and moved to the bed to give Wulfgar a rough shake. After a second, then a third shake the barbarian lifted his head and turned it to face Arumn, though his eyes were hardly open.

"Ye're done here," Arumn said plainly and calmly, shaking Wulfgar again. "I cannot let ye do this to me place and me friends no more. Ye gather all yer things tonight and be on yer way, wherever that road might take ye, for I'm not wanting to see ye in the common room. I'll put a bag o' coins inside yer door to help ye get set up somewhere else. I'm owin' ye that much, at least."

Wulfgar didn't respond.

"Ye hearin' me?" Arumn asked.

Wulfgar nodded and grumbled for Arumn to go away, a request heightened by a wave of the barbarian's arm, which, as sluggish as Wulfgar was, still easily and effectively pushed Arumn back from the bed.

Another sigh, another shake of his head, and Arumn left. Josi Puddles spent a long moment studying the huge man on the bed and the room around him and particularly the magnificent warhammer resting against the wall in the far corner.

⚔ ⚔ ⚔ ⚔ ⚔

"I owe it to him," Captain Deudermont said to Robillard, the two standing at the rail of the docked, nearly repaired *Sea Sprite*.

"Because he once sailed with you?" the wizard asked skeptically.

"More than sailed."

"He performed a service for your vessel, true enough," Robillard reasoned, "but did you not reciprocate? You took him and his friends all the way to Memnon and back."

Deudermont bowed his head in contemplation, then looked up at the wizard. "I owe it to him not out of any financial or business arrangement," he explained, "but because we became friends."

"You hardly knew him."

"But I know Drizzt Do'Urden and Catti-brie," Deudermont argued. "How many years did they sail with me? Do you deny our friendship?"

"But—"

"How can you so quickly deny my responsibility?" Deudermont asked.

"He is neither Drizzt nor Catti-brie," Robillard replied.

"No, but he is a dear friend of both and a man in great need."

"Who doesn't want your help," finished the wizard.

Deudermont bowed his head again, considering the words. They seemed true enough. Wulfgar had, indeed, denied his offers of help. Given the barbarian's state, the captain had to admit, privately, that chances were slim he could say or do anything to bring the big man from his downward spiral.

"I must try," he said a moment later, not bothering to look up.

Robillard didn't bother to argue the point. The wizard understood, from the captain's determined tone, that it was not his place to do so. He had been hired to protect Deudermont, and so he would do just that. Still, by his estimation, the sooner *Sea Sprite* was out of Luskan and far, far from this Wulfgar fellow, the better off they would all be.

✕ ✕ ✕ ✕ ✕

He was conscious of the sound of his breathing, gasping actually, for he was as scared as he had ever been. One slip, one inadvertent noise, would wake the giant, and he doubted any of the feeble explanations he'd concocted would save him then.

Something greater than fear prodded Josi Puddles along. More than anything, he had come to hate this man. Wulfgar had taken Delly from him—from his fantasies, at least. Wulfgar had enamored himself of Arumn, replacing Josi at the tavernkeeper's side. Wulfgar could bring complete ruin to the Cutlass, the only home Josi Puddles had ever known.

Josi didn't believe that the huge, wrathful barbarian would take Arumn's orders to leave without a fight, and Josi had seen enough of the brawling man to understand just how devastating that fight might become. Josi also understood that if it came to blows in the Cutlass, he would likely prove a prime target for Wulfgar's wrath.

He cracked open the door. Wulfgar lay on the bed in almost exactly the same position as he had been when Josi and Arumn had come there two hours earlier.

Aegis-fang leaned against the wall in the far corner. Josi shuddered at the sight, imagining the mighty warhammer spinning his way.

The little man crept into the room and paused to consider the small bag of coins Arumn had left to the side of the door beside Wulfgar's bed. Drawing out a large knife, he put his fingertip to the barbarian's back, just under the shoulder-blade, feeling for a heartbeat, then replaced his fingertip with the tip of the knife. All he had to do was lean on it hard, he told himself. All he had to do was drive the knife through Wulfgar's heart, and his troubles would be at their end. The Cutlass would survive as it had before this demon had come to Luskan, and Delly Curtie would be his for the taking.

He leaned over the blade. Wulfgar stirred, but just barely, the big man very far from consciousness.

What if he missed the mark? Josi thought with sudden panic. What if his thrust only wounded the big man? The image of a roaring Wulfgar leaping from the bed to corner a would-be assassin sapped the strength from Josi's knees, and he nearly fell over the sleeping barbarian. The little man skittered back from the bed and turned for the door, trying not to cry out in fright.

He composed himself and remembered his fears for the expected scene of that night, when Wulfgar would come down to confront Arumn, when the barbarian and that terrible warhammer would take down the Cutlass and everyone in the place.

Before he could even consider the action, Josi rushed across the room and, with great effort, hoisted the heavy hammer, cradling it like a baby. He ran out of the room and out the inn's back door.

⚔ ⚔ ⚔ ⚔ ⚔

"Ye shouldn't've brought 'em," Arumn scolded Josi Puddles again. Even as he finished, the door separating the common room from the private quarters swung open and a haggard-looking Wulfgar walked in.

"A foul mood," Josi remarked, as if that was vindication against Arumn's scolding. Josi had invited a few friends to the Cutlass that night, a thick-limbed rogue named Reef and his equally tough friends, including one thin man with soft hands—not a fighter, to be sure—whom Arumn believed he had seen before but in flowing robes and not breeches and a tunic. Reef had a score to settle against Wulfgar, for on the first day the barbarian arrived in the Cutlass Reef and a couple of his friends were working as Arumn's bouncers. When they tried to forcefully remove Wulfgar from the tavern, the barbarian had slapped Reef across the room.

Arumn's glare did not diminish. He was somewhat surprised to see Wulfgar in the tavern, but still he wanted to handle this with words alone. A fight with an outraged Wulfgar could cost the proprietor greatly.

The crowd in the common room went into a collective hush as Wulfgar made his way across the floor. Staring suspiciously at Arumn, the big man plopped a bag of coins on the bar.

"It's all I can give to ye," Arumn remarked, recognizing the bag as the one he had left for Wulfgar.

"Who asked for it?" Wulfgar replied, sounding as if he had no idea what was going on.

"It's what I told ye," Arumn started, then stopped and patted his hands in the air as if trying to calm Wulfgar down, though in truth, the mighty barbarian didn't seem the least bit agitated.

"Ye're not to stay here anymore," Arumn explained. "I can't be having it."

Wulfgar didn't respond other than to glare intensely at the tavernkeeper.

"Now, I'm wanting no trouble," Arumn explained, again patting his hands in the air.

Wulfgar wouldn't have given him any, though the big man was surely in a foul mood. He noticed a movement from Josi Puddles, obviously a signal, and half a dozen powerful men, including a couple Wulfgar recognized as Arumn's old crew, formed a semicircle around the huge man.

"No trouble!" Arumn said more forcefully, aiming his remark more at Josi's hunting pack than at Wulfgar.

"Aegis-fang," Wulfgar muttered.

A few seats down the bar, Josi stiffened and prayed that he had placed the hammer safely out of Wulfgar's magical calling range.

A moment passed, but the warhammer did not materialize in Wulfgar's hand.

"It's in yer room," Arumn offered.

With a sudden, vicious movement, Wulfgar slapped the bag of coins away, sending them clattering across the floor. "Are you thinking that to be ample payment?"

"More than I owe ye," Arumn dared to argue.

"A few coins for Aegis-fang?" Wulfgar asked incredulously.

"Not for the warhammer," Arumn stuttered, sensing that the

situation was deteriorating very fast. "That's in yer room."

"If it were in my room, then I would have seen it," Wulfgar replied, leaning forward threateningly. Josi's hunting pack closed in just a bit, two of them taking out small clubs, a third wrapping a chain around his fist. "Even if I did not see it, it would have come to my call from there," Wulfgar reasoned, and he called again, yelling this time, "Aegis-fang!"

Nothing.

"Where is my hammer?" Wulfgar demanded of Arumn.

"Just leave, Wulfgar," the tavernkeeper pleaded. "Just be gone. If we find yer hammer, we'll get it brought to ye, but go now."

Wulfgar saw it coming, so he baited it in. He reached across the bar for Arumn's throat, then pulled up short and snapped his arm back, catching the attacker coming in at his right flank, Reef, square in the face with a flying elbow. Reef staggered and wobbled, until Wulfgar pumped his arm and slammed him again, sending him flying away.

Purely on instinct, the barbarian spun back and threw his left arm up defensively. Just in time as one of Reef's cronies came in hard, swinging a short, thick club that smashed Wulfgar hard on the forearm.

All semblance of strategy and posturing disappeared in the blink of an eye, as all five of the thugs charged at Wulfgar. The barbarian began kicking and swinging his mighty fists, yelling out for Aegis-fang repeatedly and futilely. He even snapped his head forward viciously several times, connecting solidly with an attacker's nose, then again, catching another man on the side of the head and sending him staggering away.

Delly Curtie screamed, and Arumn cried "No!" repeatedly.

But Wulfgar couldn't hear them. Even if he could, he could not have taken a moment to heed the command. He had to buy some time and some room, for he was taking three hits for every one he was delivering in these close quarters. Though his punches and kicks were heavier by far, Reef's friends were no novices to brawling.

The rest of the Cutlass's patrons stared at the row in amusement and confusion, for they knew that Wulfgar worked for Arumn. The only ones moving were skidding safely out of range of the whirling ball of brawlers. One man in the far corner stood up, waving his arms wildly and spinning in circles.

"They're attacking the Cutlass crew!" the man cried. "To arms, patrons and friends! Defend Arumn and Wulfgar! Surely these thugs will destroy our tavern!"

"By the gods," Arumn Gardpeck muttered, for he knew the speaker, knew that Morik the Rogue had just condemned his precious establishment to devastation. With a shake of his head and a frustrated groan, the helpless Arumn ducked down behind the bar.

As if on cue, the entire Cutlass exploded into a huge brawl. Men and women, howling and taking no time to sort out allegiance, were just punching at the nearest potential victim.

Still at the bar, Wulfgar had to leave his right flank exposed, taking a brutal slug across the jaw, for he was focusing on the left, where the man with the club came at him yet again. He got his hands up to deflect the first strike and the second, then stepped toward the man, accepting a smack across the ribs, but catching the attacker by the forearm. Holding tightly Wulfgar shoved the man away, then yanked him powerfully back in, ducking and snapping his free hand into the staggering man's crotch. The man went high into the air, Wulfgar pressing him up to the limit of his reach and turning a quick circle, seeking a target.

The man flew away, hitting another, both of them falling into poor Reef and sending the big man sprawling once again.

Yet another attacker came hard at Wulfgar, arm cocked to punch. The barbarian steeled his gaze and his jaw, ready to trade hit for hit, but this ruffian had a chain wrapped around his fist. A flash of burning pain exploded on Wulfgar's face, and the taste of blood came thick in his mouth. Out pumped the dazed Wulfgar's arm, his fist just clipping the attacker's shoulder.

Another man dipped his shoulder in full charge, slamming Wulfgar's side, but the braced barbarian didn't budge. A second chain-wrapped punch came at his face—he saw the links gleaming red with his own blood—but he managed to duck the brunt of this one, though he still got a fair-sized gash across his cheek.

The other man, who had bounced off him harmlessly, leaped onto Wulfgar's side with a heavy flying tackle, but Wulfgar, with a defiant roar, held fast his footing. He twisted and wriggled his left arm up under the clinging man's shoulder and grabbed him by the hair on the back of his head.

Ahead strode the barbarian, roaring, punching again and again with his free right hand, while tugging with his left to keep the clinging man in check. The chain-fisted ruffian backed defensively, using his left arm to deflect the blows. He saw an opening he couldn't resist and came forward hard to land another solid blow on Wulfgar, clipping the barbarian's collar bone. The ruffian should have continued retreating, though, for Wulfgar had his footing and his balance now, enough to put all his weight behind one great hooking right.

The chain-fisted ruffian's blocking arm barely deflected the heavy blow. Wulfgar's fist smashed through the defenses and came crashing down against the side of the ruffian's face, spinning him in a downward spiral to the floor.

Morik sat at his table in the far corner, every now and then dodging a flying bottle or body, unperturbed as he sipped his drink. Despite his calm facade, the rogue was worried for his friend and for the Cutlass, for he could not believe the brutality of the row this night. It seemed as if all of Luskan's thugs had risen up in this one great opportunity to brawl in a tavern that had been relatively fight-free since Wulfgar had arrived, scaring off or quickly beating up any potential ruffians.

Morik winced as the chain slammed into Wulfgar's face, splattering blood. The rogue considered going to his friend's aid, but he quickly dismissed the notion. Morik was a clever information gatherer, a thief who survived through his wiles and his weapons, neither of which would help him in a common tavern brawl.

So he sat at his table, watching the tumult around him. Nearly everyone in the common room was into it now. One man came by, dragging a woman by her long, dark hair, heading for the door. He had hardly gone past Morik, though, when another man smashed a chair over his head, dropping him to the floor.

When that rescuer turned to the woman, she promptly smashed a bottle across the smile on his face, then turned and ran back to the melee, leaping atop one man and bearing him down, her fingernails raking his face.

Morik studied the woman more intently, marking well her features and thinking that her feisty spirit might prove quite enjoyable in some future private engagement.

Seeing movement from his right, Morik moved fast to slide his chair back and lift both his mug and bottle as two men came sailing across his table, smashing it and taking away the pieces with their brawl.

Morik merely shrugged, crossed his legs, leaned against the wall, and took another sip.

✕ ✕ ✕ ✕ ✕

Wulfgar found a temporary reprieve after dropping the chain-fisted man, but another quickly took his place, pressing in harder, hanging on Wulfgar's side. He finally gave up trying to wrestle away the powerful barbarian's arm. Instead he latched onto Wulfgar's face with two clawing hands and tried to pull the barbarian's head toward him, biting at his ear.

Yelping with pain, roaring with outrage, Wulfgar yanked hard on the man's hair, jerking his head and a small piece of Wulfgar's ear away. Wulfgar brought his right hand under the man's left arm, rolled it over and out, twisting the arm until breaking the hold on Wulfgar's shirt. He grabbed hard to the inside of the man's biceps. A twist turned Wulfgar square to the bar, and he drove both his arms down toward it hard, slamming the man's head against the wood so forcefully that the planking cracked. Wulfgar pulled the man back up. Hardly noticing that all struggling had abruptly ceased, Wulfgar slammed him facedown into the wood again. With a great shrug followed by a greater roar, Wulfgar sent the unconscious thug flying away. He spun around, preparing for the next round of attacks.

Wulfgar's blood-streaked eyes focused briefly. He couldn't believe the tumult. It seemed as if all the world had gone mad. Tables and bodies flew. Practically everyone in the place, near to a hundred patrons this night, was into the brawl. Across the way Wulfgar spotted Morik where he sat quietly leaning against the far wall, shifting his legs now and then to avoid whatever flew past them. Morik noticed him and lifted his glass cordially.

Wulfgar ducked and braced. A man, chopping a heavy board down at Wulfgar's head, went rolling over the barbarian's back.

Wulfgar spotted Delly then, rushing across the room, ducking for cover where she could and calling out for him. She was halfway across the inn from him when a flying chair cracked across the side of her head, dropping her straight down.

Wulfgar started for her, but another man came at the distracted barbarian hard and low, crunching him across the knees. The barbarian fought to hold his balance, staggered once, then another man leaped onto his back. The man below him grabbed an ankle in a two-armed hug and rolled around, twisting Wulfgar's leg. A third man rammed him full speed, and over they all went, falling down in a jumble of flailing arms and kicking legs.

Wulfgar rolled atop the last attacker, slamming his forearm down across the man's face and using that as leverage to try to rise, but a heavy boot stomped on his back. He went down hard, his breath blasted away. The unseen attacker above him tried to stomp him again, but Wulfgar kept the presence of mind to roll aside, and the attacker wound up stepping on his own comrade's exposed belly.

The abrupt shift only reminded Wulfgar that he still had a man hanging tough onto his ankle. The barbarian kicked at him with his free leg, but he had no leverage, lying on his back as he was, and so he went into a jerking, thrashing frenzy, trying desperately to pull free.

The man held on stubbornly, mostly because he was too scared to let go. Wulfgar took a different tact, drawing his leg up and taking the man along for the slide, then kicking straight out again, bringing his trapped foot somewhat below his opponent's grasp. At the same time, the barbarian snapped his other leg around the back of the man and managed to hook his ankles together.

A second thug jumped atop the barbarian, grabbing one arm and bringing it down under his weight while a third did likewise to the other arm. Wulfgar fought them savagely, twisting his arms. When that didn't work, he simply growled and pushed straight up, locking his arms in right angles at the elbows and drawing them up and together above his massive chest. At the same time, Wulfgar squeezed with his powerful legs. The man fought frantically against the vice and tried to cry out, but the only sound that came from him was the loud snap as his shoulder popped out of its socket.

Feeling the struggling ended down below, Wulfgar wriggled his legs free and kicked and kicked until the groaning man rolled away. The barbarian turned his attention to the two above who were punching and scratching him. With strength that mocked mortal men, Wulfgar extended his arms, lifting both the ruffians up to arms' length, then pulling them up above his head suddenly, at the same time rolling his legs up with a jerk. The momentum sent Wulfgar right over backward, and he managed to push off with his hands as he came around, landing unsteadily on his feet, facing the two prone and scrambling men.

Instinct alone spun the barbarian around to meet the latest charge, his fist flying. He caught the attacker, the chain-fisted man, square in the chest. It was a tremendous collision, but Wulfgar hadn't turned fast enough to get any defense in place against the man's flying fist, which hit him square in the face at the same time. The two shuddered to a stop, and the chain-fisted man fell over into Wulfgar's arms. The barbarian brushed him aside to land heavily, facedown, far, far from consciousness.

The blow had hurt Wulfgar badly, he knew, for his vision spun and blurred, and he had to keep reminding himself where he was. He got an arm up suddenly, but only partially deflected a flying chair, one leg spinning around to poke him hard in the forehead, which only heightened his dizziness. The fight around him was slowing now, for more men were down and groaning than still standing and punching, but Wulfgar needed another reprieve, a temporary one at least. He took the only route apparent to him, rushing to the bar and rolling over it, landing on his feet behind the barricade.

He landed face-to-face with Arumn Gardpeck. "Oh, but ye've done a wonderful thing this night, now haven't ye?" Arumn spat at him. "A fight every night for Wulfgar, or it's not a fun one."

Wulfgar grabbed the man by the front of his tunic. He pulled him up roughly from his crouch behind the bar, lifted him with ease, and slammed him hard against the back wall above the bottle shelving, destroying more than a bit of expensive stock in the process.

"Be glad your face is not at the end of my fist," the unrepentant barbarian growled.

"Or more, be glad ye've not toyed with me own emotions the way ye've burned poor Delly," Arumn growled right back.

His words hurt Wulfgar profoundly, for he had no answers to Arumn's accusation, could not rightly argue that he had no blame where Delly Curtie was involved. Wulfgar gave Arumn a little jerk, then set him down and took a step back, glaring at the tavernkeeper unblinkingly. He noticed a movement to the side, and he glanced over to see a huge, disembodied fist hovering in the air above the bar.

Wulfgar was hit on the side of the head, harder than he ever remembered being struck. He reeled, grabbing another shelf of potent whisky and pulling it down, then staggered and spun, grabbing the bar for support.

Across from him, Josi Puddles spat in his face. Before Wulfgar could respond, he noted the magical floating hand coming at him hard from the side. He was hit again, and his legs went weak. He was hit yet again, lifted right from his feet and slammed hard into the back wall. All the world was spinning, and he felt as if he were sinking into the floor.

He was half-carried, half-dragged, out from behind the bar and across the floor, all the fighting coming to an abrupt end at the sight of mighty Wulfgar finally defeated.

"Finish it outside," Reef said, kicking open the door. Even as the man turned for the street, he found a dagger point at his throat.

"It's already finished," Morik casually explained, though he betrayed his calm by glancing back inside toward the thin wizard who was packing up his things, apparently unconcerned by any of this. Reef had hired him as a bit of insurance. Since the wizard apparently held no personal stake in the brawl, the rogue calmed a bit and muttered under his breath, "I hate wizards." He turned his attention back to Reef and dug the knife in a bit more.

Reef looked to his companion, holding Wulfgar's other arm, and together they unceremoniously threw the barbarian into the mud.

Wulfgar climbed back to his feet, sheer willpower alone forcing him back into a state of readiness. He turned back toward the closed door, but Morik was there, grabbing his arm.

"Don't," the rogue commanded. "They don't want you in there. What will you prove?"

Wulfgar started to argue, but he looked Morik in the eye and saw no room for debate. He knew the rogue was right. He knew that he had no home.

4

A Lady's Life

"Ganderlay," Temigast announced as he entered the room to join Priscilla and Feringal. Both looked at the steward curiously, not understanding. "The woman you saw, my Lord Feringal," Temigast explained. "Her family name is Ganderlay."

"I know of no Ganderlays in Auckney," Priscilla argued.

"There are few families in the village whose names are familiar to you, my dear lady," Temigast replied, his tone somewhat dry, "but this woman is indeed a Ganderlay. She lives with her family on the south slope of Maerlon Mountain," he explained, referring to a fairly populated region of Auckney some two miles from the castle on a step-carved mountainside facing the harbor.

"Girl," Priscilla corrected condescendingly. "She's nowhere near to being a woman."

Feringal didn't even seem to hear the comment, too excited by the steward's news. "Are you certain?" he asked Temigast, jumping up and striding determinedly to stand right before the man. "Can it be?"

"The gir—the woman, was walking the road at the same time your coach rolled through," the steward confirmed. "She matches the description given by several people who know her and saw her on the road at the time. They all mentioned her striking long, black hair, which matches your own description of her, my lord. I am certain she is the eldest daughter of one Dohni Ganderlay."

"I'll go to her," Feringal announced, pacing back and forth eagerly, tapping one finger to his teeth, then turning fast, and then again, as if he didn't know where to go or what to do. "I will call the coach."

"My Lord Feringal," Temigast said quietly in a commanding tone that seemed to steady the eager young man. "That would be most inappropriate."

Feringal stared at him wide-eyed. "But why?"

"Because she is a peasant and not worthy of . . ." Priscilla began, but her voice trailed off for it was obvious that no one was listening to her.

"One does not go unannounced to the house of a proper lady," Temigast explained. "The way must be prepared by your steward and her father."

"But I am the lord of Auckney," Feringal protested. "I can—"

"You can do as you like if you desire her as a plaything," Temigast was quick to interrupt, drawing a frown from both Feringal and Priscilla, "but if you desire her as a wife proper, then arrange things properly. There is a way, my Lord Feringal, a manner in which we are all expected to act. To go against the etiquette in this matter could prove most disastrous, I assure you."

"I don't understand."

"Of course you don't," Temigast said, "but I do, fortunately for us all. Now go and bathe. If the young Ganderlay doe stood downwind of you she would run away." With that he turned

Lord Feringal toward the door and gave him a solid push to start him on his way.

"You have betrayed me!" Priscilla wailed when her brother was gone.

Temigast snorted at the ridiculous assertion.

"I'll not have her in this house," the woman said determinedly.

"Have you not come to realize that there's nothing short of murder you can do to stop it?" Temigast replied in all seriousness. "The murder of your brother, I mean, not of the girl, for that would only invite Feringal's wrath upon you."

"But you have aided him in this foolish pursuit."

"I have provided only what he could have learned on his own by asking questions of any peasant, including three women who work in this very house, one of whom was on the road yesterday."

"If the fool even noticed them," Priscilla argued.

"He would have discovered the girl's name," insisted Temigast, "and he might have embarrassed us all in the process of his undignified hunt." The steward chuckled and moved very close to Priscilla, draping one arm across her shoulders. "I understand your concerns, dear Priscilla," he said, "and I don't entirely disagree with you. I, too, would have preferred your brother to fall in love with some wealthy merchant girl from another place, rather than with a peasant of Auckney—or for him to forget the concept of love altogether and merely give in to his lust when and where it suited him without taking a wife. Perhaps it will yet come to that."

"Less likely, now that you have so aided him," Priscilla said sharply.

"Not so," Temigast explained with a wide smile, one that caught Priscilla's attention, for her expression changed to intrigue. "All I have done is heightened your brother's trust in me and my judgments. Perhaps he will hold fast to his notion of loving this girl, of marrying her, but I will watch him every step, I promise. I'll not allow him to bring shame to family Auck, nor will I allow the girl and her family to take from us what they do not deserve. We cannot defeat his will in this, I assure you, and your indignation will only strengthen Feringal's resolve."

Priscilla snorted doubtfully.

"Can't you hear his anger when you berate him about this?" Temigast demanded, and she winced at his words. "If we distance ourselves from your brother now, I warn you, the Ganderlay girl's hold over him—over Auckney—will only heighten."

Priscilla didn't snort, didn't shake her head, didn't show any sign of disagreement. She just stared at Temigast long and hard. He kissed her on the cheek and moved away, thinking that he should summon the castle coach at once and be on with his duties as emissary of Lord Feringal.

✕ ✕ ✕ ✕

Jaka Sculi looked up from the field of mud along with all the other workers, human and gnome, as the decorated coach made its way along the dirt lane. It came to a stop in front of Dohni Ganderlay's small house. An old man climbed out of the carriage door and ambled toward the house. Jaka's eyes narrowed slightly. Remembering suddenly that others might be watching him, he resumed his typically distant air. He was Jaka Sculi, after all, the fantasy lover of every young lady in Auckney, especially the woman who lived in the house where the lord's carriage had stopped. The notion that beautiful Meralda desired him was no small thing to the young man—though, of course, he couldn't let anyone else believe he cared.

"Dohni!" one of the other field workers, a crooked little gnome with a long and pointy nose, called. "Dohni Ganderlay, you've got guests!"

"Or mighten be they've figured you for the scoundrel you are!" another gnome cried out, and they all had a good laugh.

Except for Jaka, of course. Jaka wouldn't let them see him laugh.

Dohni Ganderlay walked over the ridge behind the peat field. He looked to those who yelled for some explanation, but they merely nodded their chins in the direction of his house. Dohni followed that movement, spotted the coach, and broke into a frantic run.

Jaka Sculi watched him run all the way home.

"You figuring to do some digging, boy?" came a question beside Jaka. When he turned to regard the toothless old man, the fool ran a hand through Jaka's curly brown hair.

The young man shook his head with disgust, noting the black peat encasing the old digger's fingers. He shook his head again and brushed his hair robustly, then slapped the man's hand away when it reached up to give another rub.

"Hee hee hee," the old man giggled. "Seems your little girlie's got a caller," he snickered.

"And an old one at that," remarked another, also more than willing to join in the play at Jaka's expense.

"But I'm thinking I might give the girl a try meself," the dirty old duffer at Jaka's side remarked. That drew a frown from Jaka, and so the old man only laughed all the harder at finally evoking some response from the boy.

Jaka turned his head slowly around, surveying the field and the workers, the few houses scattered on the mountainside, Castle Auck far in the distance, and the dark, cold waters beyond that. Those waters had brought him, his mother, and his uncle to this forlorn place only four years before. Jaka didn't know why they had come to Auckney—he had been quite content with his life in Luskan—except that it had something to do with his father, who used to beat his mother mercilessly. He suspected that they were running, either from the man or from the executioner. It seemed to be a typical tactic for the Sculi family, for they had done the same thing when Jaka was a toddler, fleeing from their ancestral home in the Blade Kingdoms all the way to Luskan. Certainly his father, a vicious man whom Jaka hardly knew, would search them out and kill his mother and her brother for running away. Or perhaps Jaka's father was already dead, left in his own blood by Rempini, Jaka's uncle.

Either way, it didn't matter to Jaka. All that he knew was that he was in this place, a dreadful, windy, cold, and barren fiefdom. Until recently, the only good thing about it all, in his view, was that the perpetual melancholy of the place enhanced his poetic nature. Even though he fancied himself quite the romantic hero, Jaka had passed his seventeenth birthday now, and had many times considered tagging along with one of the few merchants who happened through, going out into the wide world, back to Luskan perhaps, or even better, all the way to mighty Waterdeep. He planned to make his fortune there someday, somehow, and perhaps get all the way back to the Blade Kingdoms.

But those plans had been put on hold, for yet another positive aspect of Auckney had revealed itself to the young man. Jaka could not deny the attraction he felt to a certain young Ganderlay girl.

Of course, he couldn't let her or anyone else know that, not until he was certain that she would give herself over to him fully.

Hurrying past the coach, Dohni Ganderlay recognized the driver, a gray-bearded gnome he knew as Liam Woodgate. Liam smiled and nodded at him, which relaxed Dohni considerably, though he still kept his swift pace through the door. At his small kitchen table sat the steward of Castle Auck. Across from him was Dohni's ill wife, Biaste, whose beaming expression the peat farmer hadn't seen in a long, long time.

"Master Ganderlay," Temigast said politely. "I am Temigast, steward of Castle Auck, emissary of Lord Feringal."

"I know that," Dohni said warily. Never taking his eyes from the old man, Dohni Ganderlay made his way around the table, avoiding one of the two remaining chairs to stand behind his wife, dropping his hands on her shoulders.

"I was just explaining to your wife that my lord, and yours, requests the presence of your eldest daughter at the castle for dinner this evening," the steward said.

The startling news hit Dohni Ganderlay as solidly as any club ever could, but he held his balance and his expression, letting it sink in. He looked behind the words into Temigast's old, gray eyes.

"Of course, I have suitable clothing for Miss Meralda in the coach, should you agree," Temigast finished with a comforting smile.

Proud Dohni Ganderlay saw behind that smiling facade, behind the polite and respectful tone. He saw the condescension there and recognized the confidence within Temigast. Of course they could not refuse, Temigast believed, for they were but dirty peasants. The lord of Auckney had come a'calling, and the Ganderlays would welcome that call eagerly, hungrily.

"Where is Meralda?" the man asked his wife.

"She and Tori've gone to trading," the woman explained. Dohni couldn't ignore the weak trembling in her voice. "To get a few eggs for supper."

"Meralda can eat at a banquet this night, and perhaps for many nights," Temigast remarked.

Dohni saw it so clearly again, the wretched condescension that reminded him of his lot in life, of the fate of his children, all his friends, and their children as well.

"Then she will come?" Temigast prompted after a long and uncomfortable silence.

"That'll be Meralda's to choose," Dohni Ganderlay replied more sharply than he had intended.

"Ah," said the steward, nodding and smiling, always smiling. He rose from his chair and motioned for Biaste to remain seated. "Of course, of course, but do come and retrieve the gown, Master Ganderlay. Should you decide to send the young lady, it will be better and easier if she had it here."

"And if she doesn't want to go?"

Temigast arched a brow, suggesting he thought the notion that she might refuse absurd. "Then I will have my coachman return tomorrow to retrieve the gown, of course," he said.

Dohni looked down at his ill wife, at the plaintive expression on her too-delicate features.

"Master Ganderlay?" Temigast asked, motioning for the door. Dohni patted Biaste on the shoulders and walked beside the steward out to the coach. The gnome driver was waiting for them, gown in hand, and his arms uplifted to keep the delicate fabric from dragging in the dusty road.

"You would do well to urge your daughter to attend," Temigast advised, handing over the gown, which only made Dohni Ganderlay steel his features all the more.

"Your wife is sick," Temigast reasoned. "No doubt a meager existence in a drafty house will not do her well with the cold winter approaching."

"You speak as if we've a choice in the matter," Dohni replied.

"Lord Feringal is a man of great means," Temigast explained. "He has easy access to amazing herbs, warm beds, and powerful clerics. It would be a pity for your wife to suffer needlessly." The steward patted the gown. "We shall dine just after sundown," he explained. "I will have the coach pass by your home at dusk." With that, Temigast stepped into the coach and closed the door. The driver wasted no time in putting whip to horses to speed them away.

Dohni Ganderlay stood for a long while in the cloud of dust left by the departing coach, gown in hand, staring at the empty air before him. He wanted to scream out that if Lord Feringal was such a connected and beneficent lord, then he should willingly use his means for the welfare of his flock. People like Biaste Ganderlay should be able to get the aid they needed without selling their daughters. What Temigast had just offered him was akin to selling his daughter for the benefit of the family. Selling his daughter!

And yet, for all his pride, Dohni Ganderlay could not deny the opportunity that lay before him.

⚔ ⚔ ⚔ ⚔ ⚔

"It was the lord's coach," Jaka Sculi insisted to Meralda when he intercepted her on her way home later that same day. "At your own front door," he added with his exotic accent, a dialect thick with sighs and dramatic huffs.

Tori Ganderlay giggled. Meralda punched her in the shoulder and motioned for her to be on her way. "But I want to know," she whined.

"You'll be knowing the taste of dirt," Meralda promised her. She started for her sister but stopped abruptly and composed herself, remembering her audience. Meralda turned back to Jaka after painting a sweet smile on her face, still managing to glare at Tori out of the corner of her eye.

Tori started skipping down the road. "But I wanted to see you kiss him," she squealed happily as she ran on.

"Are you sure about the coach?" Meralda asked Jaka, trying very hard to leave Tori's embarrassing remarks behind.

The young man merely sighed with dramatic exasperation.

"But what business has Lord Feringal with my folks?" the young woman asked.

Jaka hung his head to the side, hands in pockets, and shrugged.

"Well, I should be going, then," Meralda said, and she took a step, but Jaka shifted to block her way. "What're you about?"

Jaka looked at her with those light blue eyes, running a hand through his mop of curly hair, his face tilted up at her.

Meralda felt as if she would choke for the lump that welled in her throat, or that her heart would beat so forcefully that it would pound right out of her chest.

"What're you about?" she asked again, much more quietly and without any real conviction.

Jaka moved toward her. She remembered her own advice to Tori, about how one had to make a boy beg. She reminded herself that she should not be doing this, not yet. She told herself that pointedly, and yet she was not retreating at all. He came closer, and as she felt the heat of his breath she, too, moved forward. Jaka just let his lips brush hers, then backed away, appearing suddenly shy.

"What?" Meralda asked again, this time with obvious eagerness.

Jaka sighed, and the woman came forward again, moving to kiss him, her whole body trembling, telling, begging him to kiss her back. He did, long and soft, then he moved away.

"I'll be waiting for you after supper," he said, and he turned with a shrug and started slowly away.

Meralda could hardly catch her breath, for that kiss had been everything she had dreamed it would be and more. She felt warm in her belly and weak in her knees and tingly all over. Never mind that Jaka, with one simple hesitation, had done to her exactly what she had told Tori a woman must do to a man. Meralda couldn't even think of that at the time, too entranced was she by the reality of what had just happened and by the promise of what might happen next.

She took the same path down the road Tori had taken, and her skipping was no less full of the girlish joy, as if Jaka's kiss had freed her of the bonds of temperance and dignity that came with being a woman.

Meralda entered her house all smiles. Her eyes widened when she saw her sick mother standing by the table, as happy as she had seen the woman in tendays. Biaste held a beautiful gown, rich emerald green with glittering gems sewn into its seams.

"Oh, but you'll be the prettiest Auckney's ever seen when you put this on," Biaste Ganderlay said, and beside her, Tori exploded in giggles.

Meralda stared at the gown wide-eyed, then turned to regard her father who was standing at the side of the room, smiling as well. Meralda recognized that his expression was somewhat more strained than Biaste's.

"But Ma, we've not the coin," Meralda reasoned, though she was truly enchanted by the gown. She moved up to stroke the soft material, thinking how much Jaka would love to see her in it.

"A gift, and nothing to buy," Biaste explained, and Tori giggled all the more.

Meralda's expression turned to one of curiosity, and she looked to her father again for some explanation, but, surprisingly, he turned away.

"What's it about, Ma?" the young woman asked.

"You've a suitor, my girl," Biaste said happily, pulling the gown out so that she could hug her daughter. "Oh, but you've got a lord hisself wanting to court you!"

Always considerate of her mother's feelings, especially now that the woman was ill, Meralda was glad that Biaste's head was on Meralda's shoulder, so her mother couldn't see the stunned and unhappy expression that crossed her daughter's face. Tori did see it, but the girl only looked up at Meralda and pursed her lips repeatedly in a mockery of a kiss. Meralda looked to her father, who now faced her but only nodded solemnly.

Biaste pulled her back to arms' length. "Oh, my little girl," she said. "When did you get so beautiful? To think that you've caught the heart of Lord Feringal."

Lord Feringal. Meralda could hardly catch her breath, and not for any joy. She hardly knew the lord of Castle Auck, though she had seen him on many occasions from afar, usually picking his fingernails and looking bored at the celebratory gatherings held in the town square.

"He's sweet on you, girl," Biaste went on, "and in it thick, by the words of his steward."

Meralda managed a smile for her mother's sake.

"They'll be coming for you soon," Biaste explained. "So be quick to get a bath. Then," she added, pausing to bring one hand up to her mouth, "then we'll put you in this gown, and oh, how all the men who see you will fall before your feet."

Meralda moved methodically, taking the gown and turning for her room with Tori on her heels. It all seemed a dream to the young woman, and not a pleasant one. Her father walked past her to her mother. She heard them strike up a conversation, though the words seemed all garbled to her, and the only thing she truly heard was Biaste's exclamation, "A lord for my girl!"

⚔ ⚔ ⚔ ⚔

Auckney was not a large place, and though its houses weren't cluttered together, the folk were certainly within shouting distance of each other. It didn't take long for word of the arrangement between Lord Feringal and Meralda Ganderlay to spread.

Jaka Sculi learned the truth about the visit of Lord Feringal's steward before he finished eating that same evening, before the sun touched the western horizon.

"To think one of his station will dip low enough to touch the likes of a peasant," Jaka's ever-pessimistic mother remarked, her voice still thick with the heavy peasant accent of their long-lost homeland in the Blade Kingdoms. "Ah, to the ruin of all the world!"

"Evil tiding," Jaka's uncle agreed, a grizzled old man who appeared to have seen too much of the world.

Jaka, too, thought this a terrible turn of events, but for a very different reason—at least he thought his anger had come from a different source, for he wasn't certain of the reason his mother and uncle were so upset by the news, and his expression clearly revealed that confusion.

"We've each our station," his uncle explained. "Clear lines, and not ones to be crossed."

"Lord Feringal brings dishonor to his family," said his mother.

"Meralda is a wonderful woman," Jaka argued before he could catch and hold the words secret.

"She's a peasant, as we all be," his mother was quick to explain. "We've our place, and Lord Feringal's got his. Oh, them folk will rejoice at the news, do not doubt, thinking to draw some of their own hope at Meralda's good fortunes, but they're not knowing the truth of it."

"What truth?"

"He'll use her to no good ends," foretold his mother. "He'll make himself the fool and the girl a tramp."

"And in the end, she'll be broken or dead, and Lord Feringal will have lost all favor with his peers," added his uncle. "Evil tiding."

"Why do you believe that she will succumb?" the young man asked, working hard to keep the desperation out of his tone.

His mother and uncle merely laughed at that question. Jaka understood their meaning all too clearly. Feringal was the lord of Auckney. How could Meralda refuse him?

It was more than poor, sensitive Jaka could take. He banged the table hard with his fist and slid his chair back. Rising fast to his feet, he matched the surprised stares of his mother and uncle with a glower of utter rage. With that Jaka turned on his heel and rushed out, slamming the door behind him.

Before he knew it he was running, his thoughts whirling. Jaka soon came to high ground, a small tumble of rocks just above the muddy field he had been working earlier that same day, a place affording him a splendid view of the sunset, as well as Meralda's house. In the distant southwest he saw the castle, and he pictured the magnificent coach making its deliberate way up the road to it with Meralda inside.

Jaka felt as if a heavy weight were pressing on his chest, as if all the limitations of his miserable existence had suddenly become tangible walls, closing, closing. For the last few years Jaka had gone to great lengths to acquire just the correct persona, the correct pose, and the correct attitude, to turn the heart of any young lady. Now here came this foolish nobleman, this prettily painted and perfumed fop with no claim to reputation other than the station to which he had been born, to take all that Jaka had cultivated right out from under him.

Jaka, of course, didn't see things with quite that measure of clarity. To him it seemed a plain enough truth, a grave injustice played against him simply because of the station, or lack thereof, of his birth. Because these pitiful peasants of Auckney didn't know the truth of him, the greatness that lay within him hidden by the dirt of farm fields and peat bogs.

The distraught young man ran his hands through his brown locks and heaved a great sigh.

⚔ ⚔ ⚔ ⚔ ⚔

"You best get it all cleaned, because you're not knowing what Lord Feringal will be seeing," Tori teased, and she ran a rough cloth across Meralda's back as her sister sat like a cat curled up in the steaming hot bath.

Meralda turned at the words and splashed water in Tori's face. The younger girl's giggles halted abruptly when she noted the grim expression on Meralda's face.

"I'm knowing what Lord Feringal will be seeing, all right," Meralda assured her sister. "If he's wanting his dress back, he'll have to be coming back to the house to get it."

"You'd refuse him?"

"I won't even kiss him," Meralda insisted, and she lifted a dripping fist into the air. "If he tries to kiss me, I'll—"

"You'll play the part of a lady," came the voice of her father. Both girls looked to the curtain to see the man enter the room. "Leave," he instructed Tori. The girl knew that tone well enough to obey without question.

Dohni Ganderlay stayed at the door a moment longer to make sure that too-curious Tori had, indeed, scooted far away, then he moved to the side of the tub and handed Meralda a soft cloth to dry herself. They lived in a small house where modesty was pointless, so Meralda was not the least bit embarrassed as she stepped from her bath, though she draped the cloth around her before she sat on a nearby stool.

"You're not happy about the turn of events," Dohni observed.

Meralda's lips grew thin, and she leaned over to splash a nervous hand in the cold bath water.

"You don't like Lord Feringal?"

"I don't know him," the young woman retorted, "and he's not knowing me. Not at all!"

"But he's wanting to," Dohni argued. "You should take that as the highest compliment."

"And taking a compliment means giving in to the one complimenting?" Meralda asked with biting sarcasm. "I've no choice in the matter? Lord Feringal's wanting you, so off you go?"

Her nervous splashing of water turned angry, and she accidentally sent a small wave washing over Dohni Ganderlay. The young woman understood that it was not the wetness, but the attitude, that provoked his unexpectedly violent reaction. He caught her wrist in his strong hand and tugged it back, turning Meralda toward him.

"No," he answered bluntly. "You've no choice. Feringal is the lord of Auckney, a man of great means, a man who can lift us from the dirt."

"Maybe I'd rather be dirty," Meralda started to say, but Dohni Ganderlay cut her short.

"A man who can heal your mother."

He could not have stunned her more with the effect of those seven words than if he had curled his great fist into a tight ball and punched Meralda hard in the face. She stared at her father

89

incredulously, at the desperate, almost wild, expression on his normally stoic face, and she was afraid, truly afraid.

"You've no choice," he said again, his voice a forced monotone. "Your ma's got the wilting and won't likely see the next turn of spring. You'll go to Lord Feringal and play the part of a lady. You'll laugh at his wit, and you'll praise his greatness. This you'll do for your ma," he finished simply, his voice full of defeat. As he turned away and rose Meralda caught a glint of moisture rimming his eye, and she understood.

Knowing how truly horrible this was for her father did help the young woman prepare for the night, helped greatly to cope with this seemingly cruel twist that fate had thrown before her.

⚔ ⚔ ⚔ ⚔ ⚔

The sun was down, and the sky was turning dark blue. The coach passed below him on the way to Meralda's meager house. She stepped from the door, and even from this great distance Jaka could see how beautiful she appeared, like some shining jewel that mocked the darkness of twilight.

His jewel. The just reward for the beauty that was within him, not a bought present for the spoiled lord of Auckney.

He pictured Lord Feringal holding his hand out of the coach, touching her and fondling her as she stepped inside to join him. The image made him want to scream out at the injustice of it all. The coach rolled back down the road toward the distant castle with Meralda inside, just as he had envisioned earlier. Jaka could not have felt more robbed if Lord Feringal had reached into his pockets and taken his last coin.

He sat wallowing on the peat-dusted hill for a long, long while, running his hands through his hair repeatedly and cursing the inequities of this miserable life. So self-involved was he that he was taken completely by surprise by the sudden sound of a young girl's voice.

"I knew you'd be about."

Jaka opened his dreamy, moist eyes to see Tori Ganderlay staring at him.

"I knew it," the girl teased.

"What do you know?"

"You heard about my sister's dinner and had to see for yourself," Tori reasoned. "And you're still waiting and watching."

"Your sister?" Jaka repeated dumbly. "I come here every night," he explained.

Tori turned from him to gaze down at the houses, at her own house, the firelight shining bright through the window. "Hoping to see Meralda naked through the window?" she asked with a giggle.

"I come out alone in the dark to get away from the fires and the light," Jaka replied firmly. "To get away from pestering people who cannot understand."

"Understand what?"

"The truth," the young man answered cryptically, hoping he sounded profound.

"The truth of what?"

"The truth of life," Jaka replied.

Tori looked at him long and hard, her face twisting as she tried to decipher his words. She looked back to her house. "Bah, I'm thinking you're just wanting to see Meralda naked," she said again, then skipped happily back down the path.

Wouldn't she have fun with Meralda at his expense, Jaka thought. He heaved another of his great sighs, then turned and walked away to the even darker fields higher up the mountainside.

"Fie this life!" he cried out, lifting his arms to the rising full moon. "Fie, fie, and fly from me now, trappings mortal! What cruel fate to live and to see the undeserving gather the spoils from me. When justice lies in spiked pit. When worth's measure is heredity. Oh, Lord Feringal feeds at Meralda's neck. Fie this life, and fly from me!"

He ended his impromptu verse by falling to his knees and clutching at his teary face, and there he wallowed for a long, long while.

Anger replaced self-pity, and Jaka came up with a new line to finish his verse. "When justice lies in spiked pit," he recited, his voice quivering with rage. "When worth's measure is heredity." Now a smile crept onto his undeniably handsome features. "Wretched Feringal feeds at Meralda's neck, but he'll not have her virginity!"

Jaka climbed unsteadily to his feet and looked up again at the full moon. "I swear to it," he said with a growl, then muttered dramatically, "Fie this life," one last time and started for home.

⚔ ⚔ ⚔ ⚔ ⚔

Meralda took the evening in stoic stride, answering questions politely and taking care to avoid the direct gaze of an obviously unhappy Lady Priscilla Auck. She found that she liked Steward Temigast quite a bit, mostly because the old man kept the conversation moving by telling many entertaining stories of his past and of the previous lord of the castle, Feringal's father. Temigast even set up a signal system with Meralda to help her understand which piece of silverware she should use for the various courses of food.

Though she remained unimpressed with the young lord of Auckney, who sat directly opposite her and stared unceasingly, the young woman couldn't deny her wonder at the delicious feast the servants laid out before her. Did they eat like this every day in Castle Auck—squab and fish, potatoes and sea greens—delicacies Meralda had never tasted before?

At Lord Feringal's insistence, after dinner the group retired to the drawing room, a comfortable, windowless square chamber at the center of the castle's ground floor. Thick walls kept out the chill ocean wind, and a massive hearth, burning with a fire as large as a village bonfire added to the coziness of the place.

"Perhaps you would like more food," Priscilla offered, but there was nothing generous about her tone. "I can have a serving woman bring it in."

"Oh, no, my lady," Meralda replied. "I couldn't eat another morsel."

"Indeed," said Priscilla, "but you did overindulge at dinner proper, now didn't you?" she asked, a sweet and phony smile painted on her ugly face. It occurred to Meralda that Lord Feringal was almost charming compared to his sister. Almost.

A servant entered then, bearing a tray of snifters filled with a brownish liquid Meralda didn't recognize. She took her glass, too afraid to refuse, and on Temigast's toast and motion, she raised it up and took a healthy swallow. The young woman nearly choked from the burning sensation that followed the liquid down her throat.

"We don't take such volumes of brandy here," Priscilla remarked dryly. "That is a peasant trait."

Meralda felt like crawling under the thick rug. Crinkling his nose at her, Lord Feringal didn't help much.

"More a trait for one who is not familiar with the potent drink," Temigast interjected, coming to Meralda's aid. "Tiny sips, my dear. You will learn, though you may never acquire a taste for this unique liquor. I haven't yet myself."

Meralda smiled and nodded a silent thank you to the old man, which relieved the tension again, and not for the last time. Feeling a bit light in the head, Meralda faded out of the conversation, oblivious to Priscilla's double-edged remarks and Lord Feringal's stares. Her mind drifted off, and she was beside Jaka Sculi—in a moonlit field, perhaps, or this very room. How wonderful this place would be, with its thick carpet, huge fire, and this warming drink if she had the companionship of her dear Jaka instead of the wretched Auck siblings.

Temigast's voice penetrated her fog, reminding Lord Feringal that they had promised to return the young lady by a certain hour, and that the hour was fast approaching.

"A few moments alone, then," Feringal replied.

Meralda tried not to panic.

"Hardly a proper request," Priscilla put in. She looked at Meralda and snickered. "Of course, what could possibly be the harm?"

Feringal's sister left, as did Temigast, the old steward patting Meralda comfortingly on the shoulder as he slipped past to the door.

"I trust you will act as a gentleman, my lord," he said to Feringal, "as your station demands. There are few women in all the wide world as beautiful as Lady Meralda." He gave the young woman a smile. "I will order the coach to the front door."

The old man was her ally, Meralda recognized, a very welcome ally.

"It was a wonderful meal, was it not?" Lord Feringal asked, moving quickly to take a seat on the chair beside Meralda's.

"Oh, yes, my lord," she replied, lowering her gaze.

"No, no," Feringal scolded. "You must call me Lord Feringal, not 'my lord.' "

"Yes, my—Lord Feringal." Meralda tried to keep her gaze averted, but the man was too close, too imposing. She looked up at him, and to his credit, he did take his stare from her breasts and looked into her eyes.

"I saw you on the road," he explained. "I had to know you. I had to see you again. Never has there been any woman as beautiful."

"Oh, my—Lord Feringal," she said, and she did look away again, for he was moving even closer, far too close, by Meralda's estimate.

"I had to see you," he said again, his voice barely a whisper, but he was close enough that Meralda heard it clearly and felt his breath hot on her ear.

Meralda fought hard to swallow her panic as the back of Feringal's hand brushed gently down her cheek. He cupped her chin then and turned her head to face him. He kissed her softly at first, then, despite the fact that she was hardly returning the kiss, more urgently, even rising out of his chair to lean into her. As he pressed and kissed, Meralda thought of Jaka and of her sick mother and tolerated it, even when his hand covered the soft fabric over her breast.

"Your pardon, Lord Feringal," came Temigast's voice from the door. Flushing, the young man broke away and stood up to face the steward.

"The coach is waiting," Temigast explained. "It is time for Lady Meralda to return to her home." Meralda nearly ran from the room.

"I will call for you again," Lord Feringal said after her. "And soon, to be sure."

By the time the coach had moved over the bridge that separated Castle Auck from the mainland, Meralda had managed to slow her heartbeat somewhat. She understood her duty to her family, to her sick mother, but she felt as if she would faint, or vomit. Wouldn't the wretch Priscilla have a grand time with that, if she found that the peasant had thrown up in the gilded coach.

A mile later, still feeling sick and aching to be out of all these trappings, Meralda leaned out the coach's window.

"Stop! Oh, please stop!" she yelled to the driver. The carriage shuddered to a halt, but even before it had completely stopped the young woman threw open the door and scrambled out.

"My lady, I am to take you to your home," Liam Woodgate said, leaping down to Meralda's side.

"And so you have," the woman replied. "Close enough."

"But you've a long dark lane before you," the gnome protested. "Steward Temigast'll have my heart in his hand if—"

"He'll never know," Meralda promised. "Don't fear for me. I walk this lane every night and know every bush and rock and person in every house between here and my own."

"But . . ." the gnome began to argue, but Meralda pushed past him, shot him a confident smile, and skipped away into the darkness.

The coach shadowed her for a short while, then, apparently convinced the woman was indeed familiar enough with this area to be safe, Liam turned it around and sped away.

The night was chill, but not too cold. Meralda veered from the road, moving to the dark fields higher up. She hoped to find Jaka there, waiting for her as they had arranged, but the place was empty. Alone in the dark, Meralda felt as if she were the only person in all the world. Anxious to forget tonight, to forget Lord Feringal and his wretched sister, she stripped off her gown, needing to be out of the fancy thing. Tonight she had dined as nobility, and other than the food and perhaps the warm drink, she had not been impressed. Not in the least.

Wearing only her plain undergarments, the young woman moved about the moonlit field, walking at first, but as thoughts of Jaka Sculi erased the too recent image of Lord Feringal, her step lightened to a skip, then a dance. Meralda reached up to catch a shooting star, spinning to follow its tail, then falling to her rump in the soft grass and mud, laughing all the while and thinking of Jaka.

She didn't know that she was in almost exactly the same spot where Jaka had been earlier that night. The place where Jaka had spat his protests at an unhearing god, where he'd cried out against the injustice of it all, where he'd called for his life to flee, and where he'd vowed to steal Meralda's virginity for no better reason than to ensure that Lord Feringal did not get it.

INSIDE A TIGHT FRAME

W here'd you put the durned thing?" a frustrated Arumn Gardpeck asked Josi Puddles the next afternoon. "I know ye took it, so don't be lying to me."

"Be glad that I took it," an unrepentant Josi countered, wagging his finger in Arumn's face. "Wulfgar would've torn the whole place apart to kindling with that warhammer in his hands."

"Bah, you're a fool, Josi Puddles," Arumn replied. "He'd a left without a fight."

"So ye're saying," Josi retorted. "Ye're always saying such, always taking up the man's cause, though he's been naught but trouble to yerself and to all who been loyal to ye. What good's Wulfgar done for ye, Arumn Gardpeck? What good ever?"

Arumn narrowed his eyes and stared hard at the man.

"And every fight he stopped was one he started," Josi added. "Bah, he's gone, and good enough for him, and good enough for all of us."

"Where'd ye put the warhammer?" Arumn pressed again.

Josi threw up his hands and spun away, but Arumn wouldn't let him go that easily. He grabbed the little man by the shoulder and whipped him around violently. "I asked ye twice already," he said grimly. "Don't ye make me ask again."

"It's gone," Josi replied. "Just gone, and far enough so that Wulfgar couldn't call to the thing."

"Gone?" Arumn echoed. His expression grew sly, for he understood Josi better than to think the man had simply thrown so wondrous a weapon into the ocean. "And how much did ye get for it?"

Josi stuttered a protest, waved his hand and stammered again, which only confirmed Arumn's suspicions. "Ye go get it back, Josi Puddles," the tavernkeeper instructed.

Josi's eyes widened. "Cannot—" he started to say, but Arumn grabbed him by the shoulder and the seat of his pants and ushered him along toward the door.

"Go get it back," Arumn said again, no room for debate in his stern tone, "and don't come back to me until ye got the hammer in hand."

"But I cannot," Josi protested. "Not with that crew."

"Then ye're not welcome here anymore," Arumn said, shoving Josi hard through the door and out into the street. "Not at all, Josi Puddles. Ye come back with the hammer, or ye don't come back!" He slammed the door, leaving a stunned Josi out in the street.

The skinny man's eyes darted around, as if he expected some thugs to step out and rob him. He had good cause for concern. Arumn's Cutlass was Josi's primary affiliation and, in a sense, his source of protection on the streets. Few bothered with Josi, mostly because he wasn't worth bothering with, but mainly because troubling Josi would shut down all routes to the Cutlass, a favorite place.

Josi had made more than few enemies on the street, and once

word spread that he and Arumn had fallen out. . . .

He had to get back in Arumn's favor, but when he considered the necessary task before him, his knees went weak. He had sold Aegis-fang cheaply to a nasty pirate in a wretched drinking hole, a place he visited as rarely as possible. Josi's eyes continued to dart all around, surveying Half-Moon Street and the alleys that would take him to the private and secret drinking hole by the docks. Sheila Kree would not be there yet, he knew. She would be at her ship, *Leaping Lady*. The name referred to the image of Sheila Kree leaping from her ship to that of her unfortunate victims, bloody saber in hand. Josi shuddered at the thought of meeting her on the very deck where she was known to have tortured dozens of innocent people to horrible deaths. No, he decided, he would wait to meet with her at the drinking hole, a place a bit more public.

The little man fished through his pockets. He still had all the gold Sheila had paid him for Aegis-fang and a couple of his own coins as well.

He hardly thought it enough, but with Arumn's friendship at stake, he had to try.

⚔ ⚔ ⚔ ⚔ ⚔

"It's wonderful to be with ye," Delly Curtie said, running her hand over Wulfgar's huge, bare shoulder, which drew a wince from the big man. That shoulder, like every other part of his body, had not escaped the battering at the Cutlass.

Wulfgar muttered something unintelligible and rose from the bed, and while Delly's hands continued to caress him, he continued to ignore the touch.

"Are ye sure ye're wantin' to leave already?" the woman asked in a seductive manner.

Wulfgar turned to regard her, stretching languidly on the rumpled bed.

"Yeah, I'm sure," he grumbled as he pulled on his clothes and headed for the door.

Delly started to call out after him but bit back her begging. She started to scold him but bit that back, too, understanding the futility of it and knowing that her own harsh words wouldn't cover her hurt. Not this time. She had gone to Wulfgar the previous night, as soon as Arumn closed his doors, which was not long after the fight had scuttled the Cutlass. Delly knew where to find the now homeless man, for Morik kept a room nearby.

How thrilled she had been when Wulfgar had taken her in, despite Morik's protests. She had let her guard back down again, for Delly had spent the night in Wulfgar's arms, fantasizing about escaping her miserable life with the heroic man. They could run away from Luskan, perhaps, and back to wild Icewind Dale, where she might raise his children as his proper wife.

Of course, the morning—or rather, the early afternoon—had shown her the truth of those fantasies in the form of a grumbling rejection.

She lay on the bed now, feeling empty and alone, helpless and hopeless. Though things between her and Wulfgar had been hurtful of late, the mere fact that the man was still around had allowed her to hold onto her dreams. If Wulfgar wouldn't be around anymore, Delly would be without any chance of escape.

"Did you expect anything different?" came a question from Morik, as if the rogue were reading her mind.

Delly gave him a sad, sour look.

"You must know by now what to expect from that one," Morik reasoned, moving to sit on the bed. Delly started to pull the covers up but remembered that it was just Morik, and he knew well enough what she looked like.

"He will never give you that which you truly desire," Morik added. "Too many burdens clouding his mind, too many remembered agonies. If he opened up to you as you hope, he'd likely kill you by mistake."

Delly looked at him as if she didn't understand. Hardly surprised, Morik merely smiled and said again, "He'll not give you that which you truly desire."

"And will Morik then?" Delly asked with open sarcasm.

The rogue laughed at the thought. "Hardly," he admitted, "but at least I tell you that openly. Except for my word, I am no honest man and want no honest woman. My life is my own, and I don't wish to be bothered with a child or a wife."

"Sounds lonely."

"Sounds free," Morik corrected with a laugh. "Ah, Delly," he said, reaching up to run a hand through her hair. "You would find life so much more enjoyable if you basked in present joys without fearing for future ones."

Delly Curtie leaned back against the headboard, considering the words and showing no practical response against them.

Morik took that as a cue and climbed into the bed beside her.

⚔ ⚔ ⚔ ⚔ ⚔

"I'll give you this part, me squeaky little friend, for your offered coins," the rowdy Sheila Kree said, tapping the flat of Aegis-fang's head. She exploded into a violent movement that brought the warhammer arching over her head to smash down on the center of the table separating her from Josi Puddles.

Suddenly, Josi realized with great alarm that there was only empty air between him and the vicious pirate, for the table had collapsed to splinters across the floor.

Sheila Kree smiled wickedly and lifted Aegis-fang. With a squeak Josi sprinted for and through the door, out into the wet, salty night air. He heard the explosion behind him, the hurled hammer connecting solidly against the jamb, heard the howls of laughter from the many cutthroats within.

Josi didn't look back. In fact, by the time he stopped running he was leaning against the wall of the Cutlass, wondering how in the Nine Hells he was going to explain the situation to Arumn.

He was still gasping to regain a steady breath when he spotted Delly moving fast down the road, her shawl pulled tight around her. She would not normally be returning to the Cutlass so late, for the place was already brimming with patrons, unless she were on an errand from Arumn. Her hands were empty, except for the folds of the shawl, so Josi had little trouble figuring out where she had gone, or at least who she had gone to visit.

As she neared, the little man heard her sobs, which only confirmed that Delly had gone to see Wulfgar and that the barbarian had ripped her heart open a bit wider.

"Are ye all right?" the man asked, moving out to intercept the woman. Delly jumped in surprise, unaware that Josi had been standing there. "What pains ye?" Josi asked softly, moving closer, lifting his hands to pat Delly's shoulders and thinking that he might use this moment of pain and vulnerability to his own gain, to finally bed the woman about whom he had fantasized for years.

Delly, despite her sobs and downcast expression, abruptly pulled away from him. The look she returned was not one of lust, not even of friendship.

"He hurt ye, Delly," Josi remarked quietly and comfortingly. "He hurt ye, and I can help ye feel better."

Delly scoffed openly. "Ye're the one who set it all up, aren't ye now, Josi Puddles?" she accused. "What a happy sot ye are for chasing Wulfgar away."

Before Josi could begin to answer, the woman brushed past him and disappeared into the Cutlass, a place where Josi could not follow. He stood out in the empty street, in the dark of night, with no place to go and no friends to speak of. He blamed Wulfgar for all of it.

Josi Puddles spent that night wandering the alleyways and drinking holes of the toughest parts of Luskan. He spoke not a word to anyone through the dark hours, but instead, listened carefully, always on the alert in these dangerous parts. To his surprise he heard something important and not threatening. It was an interesting story concerning Morik the Rogue and his large barbarian friend, and a hefty contract to eliminate a certain ship's captain.

ALTRUISM

W ell, Lord Dohni, I'll bow until my face blackens in the mud," one old peasant geezer said to Dohni Ganderlay in the field the next morning. All the men and gnomes who had gathered about Dohni broke into mocking laughter.

"Should I be tithing you direct now?" asked another. "A bit of this and a bit of that, the feed for the pig and the pig himself?"

"Just the back half of the pig," said the first. "You get to keep the front."

"You keep the part what eats the grain, but not the plump part that holds it for the meal," said a pointy-nosed gnome. "Don't that sound like a nobleman's thinking!"

They broke into peals of laughter again. Dohni Ganderlay tried hard, but unsuccessfully, to join in. He understood their mirth, of course. These peasants had little chance of lifting themselves up from the mud they tilled, but now, suddenly and unexpectedly, it appeared as if fortunes might have changed for the Ganderlay family, as if one of their own might climb that impossible ladder.

Dohni could have accepted their teasing, could have joined in wholeheartedly with the laughter, even adding a few witticisms of his own, except for one uncomfortable fact, one truth that nagged at him all the sleepless night and all that morning: Meralda hadn't wanted to go. If his girl had expressed some feelings, positive feelings, for Lord Feringal, then Dohni would be one of the happiest men in all the northland. He knew the truth of it, and he could not get past his own guilt. Because of it, the teasing bit hard at him that rainy morning in the muddy field, striking at raw nerves his friends couldn't begin to understand.

"So when are you and your family taking residence in the castle, Lord Dohni?" another man asked, moving right in front of Dohni and dipping an awkward bow.

Purely on instinct, before he could even consider the move, Dohni shoved the man's shoulder, sending him sprawling to the mud. He came up laughing, as were all the others.

"Oh, but ain't he acting the part of a nobleman already!" the first old geezer cried. "Down to the mud with us all, or Lord Dohni's to stomp us flat!"

On cue, all the peasant workers fell to their knees in the mud and began genuflecting before Dohni.

Biting back his rage, reminding himself that these were his friends and that they just didn't understand, Dohni Ganderlay shuffled through their ranks and walked away, fists clenched so tightly that his knuckles were white, teeth gnashing until his jaw hurt, and a stream of mumbled curses spewing forth from his mouth.

⚔ ⚔ ⚔ ⚔ ⚔

"Didn't I feel the fool," Meralda said honestly to Tori, the two girls in their room in the small stone house. Their mother had gone out for the first time in more than a tenday and a half, so eager was she to run and tell her neighbor friends about her daughter's evening with Lord Feringal.

"But you were so beautiful in the gown," Tori argued.

Meralda managed a weak but grateful smile for her sister.

"He couldn't have stopped looking at you, I'm sure," Tori added. From her expression, the young girl seemed to be lost in a dreamland of romantic fantasies.

"Nor could his sister, Lady Priscilla, stop mudding me," Meralda replied, using the peasant term for insults.

"Well, she's a fat cow," Tori snapped back, "and your own beauty only reminded her of it."

The two girls had a giggle at that, but Meralda's proved short-lived, her frown returning.

"How can you not be smiling?" Tori asked. "He's the lord of Auckney and can give you all that anyone would ever want."

"Can he now?" Meralda came back sarcastically. "Can he give me my freedom? Can he give me my Jaka?"

"Can he give you a kiss?" Tori asked impishly.

"I couldn't stop him on the kiss," Meralda replied, "but he'll get no more, don't you doubt. I'm giving me heart to Jaka and not to any pretty-smelling lord."

Her declaration lost its steam, her voice trailing away to a whisper, as the curtain pulled aside and a raging Dohni Ganderlay stormed into the room. "Leave us," he commanded Tori. When she hesitated, putting a concerned look over her sister, he roared even louder, "Be gone, little pig feeder!"

Tori scrambled from the room and turned to regard her father, but his glare kept her moving out of the house altogether.

Dohni Ganderlay dropped that awful scowl over Meralda, and

she didn't know what to make of it, for it was no look she was accustomed to seeing stamped on her father's face.

"Da," she began tentatively.

"You let him kiss you?" Dohni Ganderlay retorted, his voice trembling. "And he wanted more?"

"I couldn't stop him," Meralda insisted. "He came at me fast."

"But you wanted to stop him."

"Of course I did!"

The words were barely out of her mouth when Dohni Ganderlay's big, calloused hand came across Meralda's face.

"And you're wanting to give your heart and all your womanly charms to that peasant boy instead, aren't you?" the man roared.

"But, Da—"

Another smack knocked Meralda from the bed, to land on the floor. Dohni Ganderlay, all his frustration pouring out, fell over her, his big, hard hands slapping at her, beating her about the head and shoulders, while he cried out that she was "trampin' " and "whorin' " without a thought for her ma, without a care for the folks who fed and clothed her.

She tried to protest, tried to explain that she loved Jaka and not Lord Feringal, that she hadn't done anything wrong, but her father wasn't hearing anything. He just kept raining blows and curses on her, one after another, until she lay flat on the floor, arms crossed over her head in a futile attempt to protect herself.

The beating stopped as suddenly as it had begun. After a moment, Meralda dared to lift her bruised face from the floor and slowly turn around to regard her father. Dohni Ganderlay sat on the bed, head in his hands, weeping openly. Meralda had never seen him this way before. She came up to him slowly, calmly, whispering to him that it was all right. A sudden anger replaced his tears, and he grabbed the girl by the hair and pulled her up straight.

"Now you hear me, girl," he said through clamped teeth, "and hear me good. It's not yours to choose. Not at all. You'll give Lord Feringal all that he's wanting and more, and with a happy smile on your face. Your ma's close to dying, foolish girl, and Lord Feringal alone can save her. I'll not have her die, not for your selfishness." He gave her a rough shake and let her go. She stared at him as if he were some stranger, and that, perhaps, was the most painful thing of all to frustrated Dohni Ganderlay.

"Or better," he said calmly, "I'll see Jaka Sculi dead, his body on the rocks for the gulls and terns to pick at."

"Da . . ." the young woman protested, her voice barely a whisper, and a quivering whisper at that.

"Stay away from him," Dohni Ganderlay commanded. "You're going to Lord Feringal, and not a word of arguing."

Meralda didn't move, not even to wipe the tears that had begun flowing from her delicate green eyes.

"Get yourself cleaned up," Dohni Ganderlay instructed. "Your ma'll be home soon, and she's not to see you like that. This is all her hopes and dreams, girl, and if you take them from her, she'll surely go into the cold ground."

With that, Dohni rose from the bed and started for Meralda as if to hug her, but when he put his hands near to her, she tensed in a manner the man had never experienced before. He walked past her, his shoulders slumping in true defeat.

He left her alone in the house, then, walking deliberately to the northwest slope of the mountain, the rocky side where no men farmed, where he could be alone with his thoughts. And his horrors.

✕ ✕ ✕ ✕ ✕

"What're you to do?" Tori asked Meralda after the younger girl rushed back into the house as soon as their father had walked out of sight. Meralda, busy wiping the last remnants of blood from the side of her lip, didn't answer.

"You should run away with Jaka," Tori said suddenly, her face brightening as if she had just found the perfect solution to all the problems of the world. Meralda looked at her doubtfully.

"Oh, but it'd be the peak of love," the young girl beamed. "Running away from Lord Feringal. I can't believe how our da beat you."

Meralda looked back in the silver mirror at her bruises, so poignant a reminder of the awful explosion. Unlike Tori, she could believe it, every bit of it. She was no child anymore, and she had recognized the agony on her father's face even as he had slapped at her. He was afraid, so very afraid, for her mother and for all of them.

She came then to understand her duty. Meralda recognized that duty to her family was paramount and not because of threats but because of her love for her mother, father, and pesky little sister. Only then, staring into the mirror at her bruised face, did Meralda Ganderlay come to understand the responsibility that had been dropped upon her delicate shoulders, the opportunity that had been afforded her family.

Still, when she thought of Lord Feringal's lips against hers and his hand on her breast, she couldn't help but shudder.

⚔ ⚔ ⚔ ⚔ ⚔

Dohni Ganderlay was hardly aware of the sun dipping behind the distant water, or of the gnats that had found him sitting motionless and were feasting on his bare arms and neck. The discomfort hardly mattered. How could he have hit his beloved little girl? Where had the rage come from? How could he be angry with her, she who had done nothing wrong, who had not disobeyed him?

He replayed those awful moments again and again in his mind, saw Meralda, his beautiful, wonderful Meralda, falling to the floor to hide from him, to cover herself against his vicious blows. In his mind, Dohni Ganderlay understood that he was not angry with her, that his frustration and rage were against Lord Feringal. His anger came from his meager place in the world, a place that had left his family peasants, that had allowed his wife to sicken and would allow her to die, but for the possible intervention of Lord Feringal.

Dohni Ganderlay knew all of that, but in his heart he knew only that for his own selfish reasons he had sent his beloved daughter into the arms and bed of a man she did not love. Dohni Ganderlay knew himself to be a coward at that moment, mostly because he could not summon the courage to throw himself from the mountain spur, to break apart on the jagged rocks far below.

PART TWO

I have lived in many societies, from Menzoberranzan of the drow, to Blingdenstone of the deep gnomes, to Ten-Towns ruled as the most common human settlements, to the barbarian tribes and their own curious ways, to Mithral Hall of the Clan Battlehammer dwarves. I have lived aboard ship, another type of society altogether. All of these places have different customs and mores, all of them have varied government structures, social forces, churches, and societies.

WALKING DOWN A DARK ROAD

Which is the superior system? You

would hear many arguments concerning this, mostly based on prosperity, or god-given right, or simple destiny. For the drow, it is simply a religious matter—they structure their society to the desires of the chaotic Spider Queen, then wage war constantly to change the particulars of that structure, though not the structure itself. For the deep gnomes, it is a matter of paying homage and due respect to the elders of their race, accepting the wisdom of those who have lived for so many years. In the human settlement of Ten-Towns, leadership comes from popularity, while the barbarians choose their chieftains purely on physical prowess. For the dwarves, rulership is a matter of bloodline. Bruenor became king because his father was king, and his father's father before him, and his father's father's father before him.

I measure the superiority of any society in a different manner, based completely on individual freedom. Of all the places I have lived, I favor Mithral Hall, but that, I understand, is a matter of Bruenor's wisdom in allowing his flock their freedom, and not because of the dwarven political structure. Bruenor is not an active king. He serves as spokesman for the clan in matters politic, as commander in matters martial, and as mediator in disputes among his subjects, but only when so asked. Bruenor remains fiercely independent and grants that joy to those of Clan Battlehammer.

I have heard of many queens and kings, matron mothers and clerics, who justify rulership and absolve themselves of any ills by claiming that the commoners who serve them are in need of guidance. This might be true in many long-standing societies, but if it is, that is only because so many generations of conditioning have stolen something essential from the heart and soul of the subjects, because many generations of subordination have robbed the common folk of confidence in determining their own way. All of the governing systems share the trait of stealing freedom from the individual, of forcing certain conditions upon the lives of each citizen in the name of "community."

That concept, "community," is one that I hold dear, and surely, the individuals within any such grouping must sacrifice and accept certain displeasures in the name of the common good to make any community thrive. How much stronger might that community be if those sacrifices came from the heart of each citizen and not from the edicts of the elders, matron mothers, kings, or queens?

Freedom is the key to it all. The

freedom to stay or to leave, to work in harmony with others or to choose a more individual course. The freedom to help in the larger issues or to abstain. The freedom to build a good life or to live in squalor. The freedom to try anything, or merely to do nothing.

Few would dispute the desire for freedom. Everyone I have ever met desires free will, or thinks he does. How curious then, that so many refuse to accept the inverse cost of freedom: responsibility.

An ideal community would work well because the individual members would accept their responsibility toward the welfare of each other and to the community as a whole, not because they are commanded to do so, but because they understand and accept the benefits to such choices. For there are, indeed, consequences to every choice we make, to everything we do or choose not to do. Those consequences are not so obvious, I fear. The selfish man might think himself gaining, but in times when that person most needs his friends, they likely will not be there, and in the end, in the legacy the selfish person leaves behind, he will not be remembered fondly if at all. The selfish person's greed might bring material luxuries, but cannot bring the true joys, the intangible pleasures of love.

So it is with the hateful person, the slothful person, the envious person, the thief and the thug, the drunkard and the gossip. Freedom allows each the right to choose the life before him, but freedom demands that the person accept the responsibility for those choices, good and bad.

I have often heard tales of those who believed they were about to die replaying the events of their lives, even long past occurrences buried deep within their memories. In the end, I believe, in those last moments of this existence, before the mysteries of what may come next, we are given the blessing, or curse, to review our choices, to see them bared before our consciousness, without the confusion of the trappings of day-to-day living, without blurring justifications or the potential for empty promises to make amends.

How many priests, I wonder, would include this most naked moment in their descriptions of heaven and hell?

—Drizzt Do'Urden

LETTING GO OF
AN OLD FRIEND

The big man was only a stride away. Josi Puddles saw him coming too late. Squeamish Josi hunched against the wall, trying to cover up, but Wulfgar had him in an instant, lifting him with one hand, batting away his feeble attempts to slap with the other.

Then, *slam,* Josi went hard against the wall.

"I want it back," the barbarian said calmly. To poor Josi, the measure of serenity in Wulfgar's voice and his expression was perhaps the most frightening thing of all.

"Wh-what're ye lookin' t-to find?" the little man stuttered in reply.

Still with just one arm, Wulfgar pulled Josi out from the wall and slammed him back against it. "You know what I mean," he said, "and I know you took it."

Josi shrugged and shook his head, and that bought him another slam against the wall.

"You took Aegis-fang," Wulfgar clarified, now bringing his

scowl right up to Josi's face, "and if you do not return it to me, I will break you apart and assemble your bones to make my next weapon."

"I . . . I . . . I *borrowed* it . . ." Josi started to say, his rambling interrupted by yet another slam. "I thought ye'd kill Arumn!" the little man cried. "I thought ye'd kill us all."

Wulfgar calmed a bit at those curious words. "Kill Arumn?" he echoed incredulously.

"When he kicked ye out," Josi explained. "I knew he was kickin' ye out. He told me as much while ye slept. I thought ye'd kill him in yer rage."

"So you took my warhammer?"

"I did," Josi admitted, "but I meant to get it back. I tried to get it back."

"Where is it?" Wulfgar demanded.

"I gave it to a friend," Josi replied. "He gave it to a sailor woman to hold, to keep it out of the reach of yer call. I tried to get it back, but the sailor woman won't give it up. She tried to squish me head, she did!"

"Who?" Wulfgar asked.

"Sheila Kree of *Leapin' Lady*," Josi blurted. "She got it, and she's meanin' to keep it."

Wulfgar paused for a long moment, digesting the information, measuring its truth. He looked up at Josi again, and his scowl returned tenfold. "I am not fond of thieves," he said. He jostled Josi about, and when the little man tried to resist, even slapping Wulfgar, the barbarian brought him out from the wall and slammed him hard, once, then again.

"We stone thieves in my homeland," Wulfgar growled as he smashed Josi so hard against the wall the building shook.

"And in Luskan we shackle ruffians," came a voice to the side. Wulfgar and Josi turned their heads to see Arumn Gardpeck exit the establishment, along with several other men. Those others hung far back, though, obviously wanting nothing to do with Wulfgar, while Arumn, club in hand, approached cautiously. "Put him down," the tavernkeeper said.

Wulfgar slammed Josi one more time, then brought him down to his feet, but shook him roughly and did not let go. "He stole my warhammer, and I mean to get it back," the barbarian said determinedly.

Arumn glared at Josi.

"I tried," Josi wailed, "but Sheila Kree—yeah, that's her. She got it and won't give it over."

Wulfgar gave him another shake, rattling the teeth in his mouth. "She has it because you gave it to her," he reminded Josi.

"But he tried to retrieve it," Arumn said. "He's done all he can. Now, are ye meanin' to bust him up for that? Is that to make ye feel better, Wulfgar the brute? For suren it won't help to get yer hammer back."

Wulfgar glared at Arumn, then let the look fall over poor Josi. "It would, indeed, make me feel better," he admitted, and Josi seemed to shrink down, trembling visibly.

"Then ye'll have to beat me, as well," Arumn said. "Josi's me friend, as I thought yerself to be, and I'll be fighting for him."

Wulfgar scoffed at the notion. With a mere flick of his powerful arm, he sent Josi sprawling at Arumn's feet.

"He told ye where to find yer hammer," Arumn said.

Wulfgar took the cue and started away, but he glanced back to see Arumn helping Josi from the ground, then putting his arm around the trembling man's shoulders, leading him into the Cutlass.

That last image, a scene of true friendship, bothered the barbarian profoundly. He had known friendship like that, had once been blessed with friends who would come to his aid even when the odds seemed impossible. Images of Drizzt and Bruenor, of Regis and Guenhwyvar, and mostly of Catti-brie flitted across his thoughts.

But it was all a lie, a darker part of Wulfgar's deepest thoughts reminded him. The barbarian closed his eyes and swayed, near to falling over. There were places where no friends could follow, horrors that no amount of friendship could alleviate. It was all a lie, friendship, all a facade concocted by that so very human and ultimately childish need for security, to wrap oneself in false hopes. He knew it, because he had seen the futility, had seen the truth, and it was a dark truth indeed.

Hardly conscious of the action, Wulfgar ran to the door of the Cutlass and shoved it open so forcefully that the slam drew the attention of every one in the place. A single stride brought the barbarian up to Arumn and Josi, where he casually swatted aside Arumn's club, then slapped Josi across the face, launching him several feet to land sprawling on the floor.

Arumn came right back at him, swinging the club, but Wulfgar caught it in one hand, yanked it away from the tavernkeeper, then pushed Arumn back. He brought the club out in front of him, one hand on either end, and with a growl and a great flex of his huge neck and shoulders, he snapped the hard wood in half.

"Why're ye doin' this?" Arumn asked him.

Wulfgar had no answers, didn't even bother to look for them. In his swirling thoughts he had scored a victory here, a minor one, over Errtu and the demons. Here he had denied the lie of friendship, and by doing so, had denied Errtu one weapon, that most poignant weapon, to use against him. He tossed the splintered wood to the floor and stalked out of the Cutlass, knowing that none of his tormentors would dare follow.

He was still growling, still muttering curses, at Errtu, at Arumn, at Josi Puddles, when he arrived at the docks. He stalked up and down the long pier, his heavy boots clunking against the wood.

"Ere, what're you about?" one old woman asked him.

"The *Leaping Lady*?" Wulfgar asked. "Where is it?"

"That Kree's boat?" the woman asked, more to herself than to Wulfgar. "Oh, she's out. Out and running, not to doubt, fearing that one." As she finished, she pointed to the dark silhouette of a sleek vessel tied on the other side of the long wharf.

Wulfgar, curious, moved closer, noting the three sails, the last one triangular, a design he had never seen before. When he crossed the boardwalk, he remembered the tales Drizzt and Catti-brie had told to him, and he understood. *Sea Sprite*.

Wulfgar stood up very straight, the name sobering him from his jumbled thoughts. His eyes trailed up the planking, from the name to the deck rail, and there stood a sailor, staring back at him.

"Wulfgar," Waillan Micanty hailed. "Well met!"

The barbarian turned on his heel and stomped away.

✖ ✖ ✖ ✖ ✖

"Perhaps he was reaching out to us," Captain Deudermont reasoned.

"It seems more likely that he was merely lost," a skeptical Robillard replied. "By Micanty's description, the barbarian's reaction upon seeing *Sea Sprite* seemed more one of surprise."

"We can't be certain." Deudermont insisted, starting for the cabin door.

"We don't have to be certain," Robillard retorted, and he grabbed the captain by the arm to stop him. Deudermont did stop and turned to glare at the wizard's hand, then into the man's unyielding eyes.

"He is not your child," Robillard re-mind-ed the captain. "He's barely an acquaintance, and you bear him no responsibility."

"Drizzt and Catti-brie are my friends," Deudermont replied. "They're *our* friends, and Wulfgar is their friend. Are we to ignore that fact simply for convenience?"

The frustrated wizard let go of the captain's arm. "For safety, Captain," he corrected, "not convenience."

"I will go to him."

"You already tried and were summarily rejected," the wizard bluntly reminded him.

"Yet he came to us last night, perhaps rethinking that rejection."

"Or lost on the docks."

Deudermont nodded, conceding the possibility. "We'll never know if I don't return to Wulfgar and ask," he reasoned, and started for the door.

"Send another," Robillard said suddenly, the thought just popping into his mind. "Send Mister Micanty, perhaps. Or I shall go."

"Wulfgar knows neither you nor Micanty."

"Certainly there are crewmen aboard who were with Wulfgar on that voyage long ago," the stubborn wizard persisted. "Men who know him."

Deudermont shook his head, his jaw set determinedly. "There is but one man aboard *Sea Sprite* who can reach out to Wulfgar," he said. "I'll go back to him, then again, if necessary, before we put out to sea."

Robillard started to respond but finally recognized the futility of it all and threw up his hands in defeat. "The streets of Luskan's dockside are no haven for your friends, Captain," he reminded.

"Beware that every shadow might hold danger."

"I always am and always have been," Deudermont said with a grin, a grin that widened as Robillard walked up to him and put several enchantments upon him, spells to stop blows or defeat missiles, and even one to diffuse certain magical attacks.

"Take care of the duration," the wizard warned.

Deudermont nodded, thankful for his friend's precautions, then turned back to the door.

Robillard slumped into a chair as soon as the man had gone. He considered his crystal ball and the energy it would take for him to operate it. "Unnecessary work," he said with an exasperated sigh. "For the captain and for me. A useless effort for an undeserving gutter rat."

It was going to be a long night.

⚔ ⚔ ⚔ ⚔ ⚔

"And do you need it so badly?" Morik dared to ask. Given Wulfgar's foul mood, he knew that he was indeed taking a great risk in even posing the question.

Wulfgar didn't bother to answer the absurd question, but the look he gave Morik told the little thief well enough. "It must be a wondrous weapon, then," Morik said, abruptly shifting the subject to excuse his obviously sacrilegious thinking. Of course Morik had known all along how magnificent a weapon Aegis-fang truly was, how perfect the craftsmanship and how well it fit Wulfgar's strong hands. In the pragmatic thief's mind, even that didn't justify an excursion onto the open sea in pursuit of Sheila Kree's cutthroat band.

Perhaps the emotions went deeper, Morik wondered. Perhaps Wulfgar held a sentimental attachment to the warhammer. His adoptive father had crafted it for him, after all. Perhaps Aegis-fang was the one remaining piece of his former life, the one reminder of who he had been. It was a question Morik didn't dare ask aloud, for even if Wulfgar agreed with him the proud barbarian would never admit it, though he might launch Morik through the air for even asking.

"Can you make the arrangements?" an impatient Wulfgar asked again. He wanted Morik to charter a ship fast enough and with a captain knowledgeable enough to catch Sheila Kree, to shadow her into another harbor perhaps, or merely to get close enough so that Wulfgar could take a small boat in the dark of night and quietly board the privateer. He didn't expect any help in retrieving the warhammer once delivered to Kree. He didn't think he'd need any.

"What of your captain friend?" Morik replied.

Wulfgar looked at him incredulously.

"Deudermont's *Sea Sprite* is the most reputable pirate chaser on the Sword Coast," Morik stated bluntly. "If there is a boat in Luskan that can catch Sheila Kree, it's *Sea Sprite*, and from the way Captain Deudermont greeted you, I'll wager he would take on the task."

Wulfgar had no direct answer to Morik's claims other than to say, "Arrange for a different boat."

Morik eyed him for a long while, then nodded. "I will try," he promised.

"Now," Wulfgar instructed. "Before the *Leaping Lady* gets too far out."

"We have a job," Morik reminded him. Running a bit low on funds, the pair had agreed to help an innkeeper unload a ship's hold of slaughtered cattle that night.

"I'll unload the meat," Wulfgar offered, and those words sounded like music to Morik, who never really liked honest work.

The little thief had no idea where to begin chartering a boat that could catch Sheila Kree, but he much preferred searching for that answer, and perhaps finding a few pockets to pick along the way, to getting soggy and smelly under tons of salted meat.

⚔ ⚔ ⚔ ⚔ ⚔

Robillard stared into the crystal ball, watching Deudermont as the captain made his way along one wide and well-lit boulevard, heavily patrolled by city guards. Most of them stopped to greet the captain and offer praise. Robillard understood their intent though he couldn't hear their words through the crystal ball, which granted images only and no sound.

A knock on the door broke the wizard's concentration and sent the image in his crystal ball into a swirl of foggy grayness. He could have retrieved the scene immediately but figured that Deudermont was in no danger at that time, especially with the multitude of defensive spells the wizard had cast over the man. Still, always preferring his privacy, he called out a gruff, "Be gone!" then moved to pour himself a strong drink.

Another knock sounded, this one more insistent. "Ye must see this, Master Robillard," came a call, a voice Robillard recognized. With a grunt of protest and drink in hand, Robillard opened the door to find a crewman standing there, glancing back over his shoulder to the rail by the boarding plank.

Waillan Micanty and another seaman stood there, looking down at the docks, apparently speaking to someone.

"We've a guest," the crewman at Robillard's door remarked, and the wizard immediately thought it must be Wulfgar. Not sure if that was a good thing or bad, Robillard started across the deck, pausing only to turn back and shut his door in the face of the overly curious crewman.

"You're not to come up until Master Robillard says so," Micanty called down, and there came a plea for quiet from below in response.

Robillard moved to Micanty's side. The wizard looked down to see a pitiful figure huddled under a blanket, a tell-tale sign, for the night surely wasn't cold.

"Wants to speak to Captain Deudermont," Waillan Micanty explained.

"Indeed," Robillard replied. To the man on the wharf he said, "Are we to let every vagabond who wanders in come aboard to speak with Captain Deudermont?"

"Ye don't understand," the man below answered, lowering his voice and glancing nervously around as if expecting a murderer to descend upon him at any moment. "I got news ye're needin' to hear. But not here," he went on, glancing around yet again. "Not where any can hear."

"Let him up," Robillard instructed Micanty. When the crewman looked at him skeptically, the wizard returned the stare with an expression that reminded Micanty of who he was. It also demonstrated that Robillard thought it absurd to worry that this pitiful little man might cause mischief in the face of Robillard's wizardly power.

"I will see him in my quarters," the wizard instructed as he walked away.

A few moments later, Waillan Micanty led the shivering little man through Robillard's cabin door. Several other curious crewmen poked their heads into the room, but Micanty, without waiting for Robillard's permission, moved over and closed them out.

"Ye're Deudermont?" the little man asked.

"I am not," the wizard admitted, "but rest assured that I am the closest you will ever get to him."

"Got to see Deudermont," the little man explained.

"What is your name?" the wizard asked.

The little man shook his head. "Just got to tell Deudermont," he said. "But it don't come from me, if ye understand."

Never a patient man, Robillard certainly did not understand. He flicked his finger and sent a bolt of energy into the little man that jolted him backward. "Your name?" he asked again, and when the man hesitated, he hit him with another jolt. "There are many more waiting, I assure you," Robillard said.

The little man turned for the door but got hit in the face with a tremendous magical gust of wind that nearly knocked him over and sent him spinning to again face the wizard.

"Your name?" Robillard asked calmly.

"Josi Puddles," Josi blurted before he could think to create an alias.

Robillard pondered the name for a moment, putting his finger to his chin. He leaned back in his chair and struck a pensive pose. "Do tell me your news, Mister Puddles."

"For Captain Deudermont," an obviously overwhelmed Josi replied. "They're looking to kill 'im. Lots o' coin for his head."

"Who?"

"A big man," Josi replied. "Big man named Wulfgar and his friend Morik the Rogue."

Robillard did well to hide his surprise. "And how do you know this?" he asked.

"All on the street know," Josi answered. "Lookin' to kill Deudermont for ten thousand pieces o' gold, so they're sayin'."

"What else?" Robillard demanded, his voice taking on a threatening edge.

Josi shrugged, little eyes darting.

"Why have you come?" Robillard pressed.

"I was thinkin' ye should know," Josi answered. "I know I'd

want to be knowin' if people o' Wulfgar's and Morik's reputation was hunting me."

Robillard nodded, then chuckled. "You came to a ship—a pirate hunter—infamous among the most dangerous folk along the docks, to warn a man you have never met, knowing full well that to do so could put you in mortal danger. Your pardon, Mister Puddles, but I sense an inconsistency here."

"I thinked ye should know," Josi said again, lowering his eyes. "That's all."

"I think not," Robillard said calmly. Josi looked back at him, his expression fearful. "How much do you desire?"

Josi's expression turned curious.

"A wiser man would have bargained before offering the information," Robillard explained, "but we are not ungrateful. Will fifty gold pieces suffice?"

"W-well, yes," Josi stuttered, then he said, "Well, no. Not really, I mean. I was thinkin' a hunnerd."

"You are a powerful bargainer, Mister Puddles," Robillard said, and he nodded at Micanty to calm the increasingly agitated sailor. "Your information may well prove valuable, if you aren't lying, of course."

"No, sir, never that!"

"Then a hundred gold it is," Robillard said. "Return tomorrow to speak with Captain Deudermont, and you shall be paid."

Josi glanced all around. "I'm not comin' back, if ye please, Master Robillard," he said.

Robillard chuckled again. "Of course," he replied as he reached into a neck purse. He produced a key and tossed it to Waillan Micanty.

"See to it," he told the man. "You will find the sum in the left locker, bottom. Pay him in pieces of ten. Then escort Mister Puddles from our good ship and send a pair of crewmen along to get him safely off the docks."

Micanty could hardly believe what he was hearing, but he wasn't about to argue with the dangerous wizard. He took Josi Puddles by the arm and left the room.

When he returned a short while later, he found Robillard leaning over his crystal ball, studying the image intently.

"You believe him," Micanty stated. "Enough to pay him without any proof."

"A hundred copper pieces is not so great a sum," Robillard replied.

"Copper?" Micanty replied. "It was gold by my own eyes."

"So it seemed," the wizard explained, "but it was copper, I assure you, and coins that I can trace easily to find our Mister Puddles—to punish him if necessary, or to properly reward him if his information proves true."

"He did not come to us searching for any reward," the observant Micanty remarked. "Nor is he any friend of Captain Deudermont, surely. No, it seems to me that our friend Puddles isn't overly fond of Wulfgar or this Morik fellow."

Robillard glanced in his crystal ball again, then leaned back in his chair, thinking.

"Have you found the captain?" Micanty dared to ask.

"I have," the wizard answered. "Come, see this."

When Micanty got near to Robillard, he saw the scene in the crystal ball shift from Luskan's streets to a ship somewhere out on the open ocean. "The captain?" he said with concern.

"No, no," Robillard replied. "Wulfgar, perhaps, or at least his magical warhammer. I know of the weapon. It was described to me in depth. Thinking that it would show me Wulfgar, my magical search took me to this boat, *Leaping Lady* by name."

"Pirate?"

"Likely," the wizard answered. "If Wulfgar is indeed on her, we shall likely meet up with the man again. Though, if he is, our friend Puddles's story seems a bit unlikely."

"Can you call to the captain?" Micanty asked, still concerned. "Bring him home?"

"He'd not listen," Robillard said with a smirk. "Some things our stubborn Captain Deudermont must learn for himself. I will watch him closely. Go and secure the ship. Double the guard, triple it even, and tell every man to watch the shadows closely. If there are, indeed, some determined to assassinate Captain Deudermont, they might believe him to be here."

Robillard was alone again, and he turned to the crystal ball, returning the image to Captain Deudermont. He sighed in disappointment. He expected as much, but he was still sad to discover that the captain had again traveled to the rougher section of town. As Robillard focused in on him again, Deudermont passed under the sign for Half-Moon Street.

⚔ ⚔ ⚔ ⚔ ⚔

Had Robillard been able to better scan the wide area, he might have noticed two figures slipping into an alley paralleling the avenue Deudermont had just entered.

Creeps Sharky and Tee-a-nicknick rushed along, then cut down an alley, emerging onto Half-Moon Street right beside the Cutlass. They dashed inside, for Sharky was convinced that was where Deudermont was headed. The pair took the table in the corner to the right of the door, evicting the two patrons sitting there with threatening growls. They sat back, ordering drinks from Delly Curtie. Their smug smiles grew wider when Captain Deudermont walked through the door, making his way to the bar.

"He no stay long witout Wufgar here," Tee-a-nicknick remarked.

Creeps considered that, deciphered the words first, then the thought behind them and nodded. He had a fair idea of where Wulfgar and Morik might be. A comrade had spotted them along the dock area earlier that night. "Keep a watch on him," Creeps instructed. He held up a pouch he had prepared earlier, then started to leave.

"Too easy," Tee-a-nicknick remarked, reiterating his complaints about the plan Creeps had former earlier that day.

"Aye, but that's the beauty of it, my friend," said Creeps. "Morik's too cocky and too curious to cast it away. No, he'll have it, he will, and it'll bring him runnin' to us all the faster."

Creeps went out into the night and scanned the street. He had little trouble locating one of the many street children who lurked in the area, serving as lookouts or couriers.

" 'Ere boy," he called to one. The waif, a lad of no more than ten winters, eyed him suspiciously but did not approach. "Got a job for ye," Creeps explained, holding up the bag.

The boy made his way tentatively toward the dangerous-looking pirate.

"Take this," Creeps instructed, handing the little bag over. "And don't look in it!" he commanded when the boy started to loosen the top to peek inside.

Creeps had a change of mind immediately, realizing that the waif might then think there was something special in the bag— gold or magic—and might just run off with it. He pulled it back from the boy and tugged it open, revealing its contents: a few small claws, like those from a cat, a small vial filled with a clear liquid, and a seemingly unremarkable piece of stone.

"There, ye seen it, and so ye're knowin' it's nothing worth stealin'," Creeps said.

"I'm not for stealin'," the boy argued.

"Course ye're not," said Creeps with a knowing chuckle. "Ye're a good boy, now ain't ye? Well, ye know o' one called Wulfgar? A big fellow with yellow hair who used to beat up people for Arumn at the Cutlass?"

The boy nodded.

"And ye know his friend?"

"Morik the Rogue," the boy recited. "Everybody's knowin' Morik."

"Good enough for ye," said Creeps. "They're down at the docks, or between here and there, by my guess. I want ye to find 'em and give this to Morik. Tell him and Wulfgar that a Captain Deudermont's lookin' to meet them outside the Cutlass. Somethin' about a big hammer. Can ye do that?"

The boy smirked as if the question were ridiculous.

"And will ye do it?" Creeps asked. He reached into a pocket and produced a silver piece. Creeps started to hand it over, then changed his mind, and his hand went in again, coming back out with several of the glittering silver coins. "Ye get yer little friends lookin' all over Luskan," he instructed, handing the coins to the wide-eyed waif. "There'll be more for ye, don't ye doubt, if ye bring Wulfgar and Morik to the Cutlass."

Before Creeps could say another word, the boy snatched the coins, turned, and disappeared into the alleyway.

Creeps was smiling when he rejoined Tee-a-nicknick a few moments later, confident that the lad and the extensive network of street urchins he would tap would complete the task in short order.

"He just wait," Tee-a-nicknick explained, motioning to Deudermont, who stood leaning on the bar, sipping a glass of wine.

"A patient man," said Creeps, flashing that green-and-yellow toothy smile. "If he knew how much time he got left to live, he might be a bit more urgent, he might." He motioned to

133

Tee-a-nicknick to exit the Cutlass. They soon found a low rooftop close enough to afford them a fine view of the tavern's front door.

Tee-a-nicknick pulled a long hollow tube out of the back of his shirt, then took a cat's claw, tied with a small clutch of feathers, from his pocket. Kneeling low and moving very carefully, the tattooed half-qullan savage turned his right hand palm up, then, taking the cat's claw in his left hand, squeezed a secret packet on the bracelet around his right wrist. Slowly, slowly, the tattooed man increased the pressure until the packet popped open and a drop of molasseslike syrup oozed out. He caught most of it on the tip of the cat's claw, then stuffed the dart into the end of his blowgun.

"Tee-a-nicknick patient man, too," he said with a wicked grin.

8
Warm Feelings

Oh, look at you!" Biaste Ganderlay exclaimed when she moved to help Meralda put on the new gown Lord Feringal had sent for their dinner that night. Only then, only after Meralda had taken off the bunched-collar shift she had been wearing all the day, did her mother see the extent of her bruises, distinct purple blotches all around her neck and shoulders, bigger marks than the two showing on her face. "You can't be going to see Lord Feringal looking so," Biaste wailed. "What'll he think of you?"

"Then I'll not go," an unenthusiastic Meralda answered, but that only made Biaste fuss more urgently. Meralda's answer brought a frown to Biaste's gray and weary face, poignantly reminding Meralda of her mother's sickness, and of the only possible way to heal her.

The girl lowered her eyes and kept her gaze down as Biaste went to the cupboards, fumbling with boxes and jars. She found beeswax and lavender, comfrey root and oil, then she scurried outside and collected some light clay to put in the mixture. She

135

was back in Meralda's room shortly, holding a mortar she used to crunch the herbs and oil and clay together vigorously with her pestle.

"I'll tell him it was an accident," Meralda offered as Biaste moved to begin applying the masking and comforting salve. "If he fell down the stone stairs at Castle Auck, surely he'd have such bruises as to make these seem like nothing."

"Is that how this happened to you?" Biaste asked, though Meralda had already insisted that she hurt herself by absentmindedly running into a tree.

A twinge of panic hit the girl, for she did not want to reveal the truth, did not want to tell her mother that her loving, adoring father had beaten her. "What're you saying?" she asked defensively. "Do you think I'm daft enough to run into a tree on purpose, Ma?"

"Now, of course I don't," said Biaste, managing a smile. Meralda did, too, glad that her deflection had worked. Biaste took the scrap of flannel she was using to wipe the bruises and swatted Meralda playfully across the head. "It don't look so bad. Lord Feringal will not even see."

"Lord Feringal's looking at me more carefully than you think," Meralda replied, which brought a great laugh from Biaste and she wrapped her daughter in a hug. It seemed to Meralda that her mother was a bit stronger today.

"Steward Temigast said you'll be walking in the gardens tonight," said Biaste. "Oh, and the moon'll be big in the sky. My girl, could I even have dared hope for such a thing for you?"

Meralda answered with another smile, for she feared that if she opened her mouth all of her anger at this injustice would pour out and knock her mother back into bed.

Biaste took Meralda by the hand, and led her to the main room of the cottage where the table was already set for dinner. Tori was sitting, shifting impatiently. Dohni Ganderlay came in the front door at that moment and looked directly at the two women.

"She ran into a tree," Biaste remarked. "Can you believe the girl's foolishness? Running into a tree when Lord Feringal's a-calling!" She laughed again, and Meralda did, too, though she never blinked as she stared at her father.

Dohni and Tori shared an uncomfortable glance, and the moment passed. The Ganderlay family sat down together for a quiet evening meal. At least it would have been quiet, had it not been for the bubbling exuberance of an obviously thrilled Biaste Ganderlay.

Soon after, long before the sun even touched the rim of the western horizon, the Ganderlays stood outside their house, watching Meralda climb into the gilded coach. Biaste was so excited she ran out into the middle of the dirt lane to wave good-bye. That effort seemed to drain her of all her strength, though, for she nearly swooned and would have stumbled had not Dohni Ganderlay been there to catch and support her.

"Now get yourself to bed," he instructed. Dohni tenderly handed his wife over to Tori, who helped her into the house.

Dohni waited outside, watching the diminishing coach and the dusty road. The man was torn in heart and soul. He didn't regret the lesson he had given to Meralda—the girl needed to put her priorities straight—but hitting Meralda hurt Dohni Ganderlay as much as it had hurt the girl.

"Why'd Ma nearly fall down, Da?" Tori asked a moment later, the sound of the girl's voice catching the distracted Dohni by surprise. "She was so strong and smiling and all."

"She gave too much of herself," Dohni explained, not overly concerned. He knew the truth of Biaste's condition, "the wilting" as it was commonly called, and understood that it would take more than high spirits to heal her. Good spirits would bolster her temporarily, but the sickness would have its way with her in the end. It would take the efforts of Lord Feringal's connections to truly bring healing.

He looked down at Tori then and saw the honest fear there. "She's just needing rest," he explained, draping an arm across the young girl's shoulder

"Meralda told Ma she ran into a tree," Tori dared to say, drawing a frown from Dohni.

"So she did," Dohni agreed softly, sadly. "Why's she resisting?" he asked his youngest daughter impulsively. "She's got the lord himself fretting over her. A brighter world than ever she could've hoped to find."

Tori looked away, which told Dohni that the younger girl knew more than she was letting on. He moved in front of Tori, and when she tried to continue to look away, he caught her by the chin and forced her to eye him directly. "What do ye know?"

Tori didn't respond.

"Tell me girl," Dohni demanded, giving Tori a rough shake. "What's in your sister's mind?"

"She loves another," Tori said reluctantly.

"Jaka Sculi," he reasoned aloud. Dohni Ganderlay relaxed his grip, but his eyes narrowed. He had suspected as much, had figured that Meralda's feelings for Jaka Sculi might go deeper, or at least that Meralda thought they went deeper. Dohni knew Jaka well enough to understand that the boy was more facade than depth. Still, Dohni was not blind to the fact that nearly all of the village girls were taken with that moody young lad.

"She'll kill me if she thinks I told you," Tori pleaded, but she was cut short by another rough shake. The look on her father's face was one she had never seen before, but she was sure it was the same one Meralda had witnessed earlier that day.

"Do you think it's all a game?" Dohni scolded.

Tori burst into tears, and Dohni let her go. "Keep your mouth shut to your ma and your sister," he instructed.

"What're you going to do?"

"I'll do what needs doing and without answering to my girls!" Dohni shot back. He turned Tori around and shoved her toward the house. The young girl was more than willing to leave, sprinting through the front door without looking back.

Dohni stared down the empty road toward the castle where his oldest daughter, his beautiful Meralda, was off bartering her heart and body for the sake of her family. He wanted to run to Castle Auck and throttle Lord Feringal at that moment, but he dismissed the notion, reminding himself that there was another eager young man who needed his attention.

⚔ ⚔ ⚔ ⚔ ⚔

Down the rocky beach from Castle Auck, Jaka Sculi watched the fancy carriage ramble along the bridge and into Lord Feringal's castle. He knew who was in the coach even before watching Meralda disappear into the young lord's domain. His blood boiled at the sight and brought a great sickness to his stomach.

"Damn you!" he snarled, shaking his fist at the castle. "Damn, damn, damn! I should, I shall, find a sword and cut your heart, as you have cut mine, evil Feringal! The joy of seeing your flowing blood staining the ground beneath you, of whispering in your dying ear that I, and not you, won out in the end."

"But fie, I cannot!" the young man wailed, and he rolled back on the wet rock and slapped his arm across his forehead.

"But wait," he cried, sitting up straight and turning his arm over so that he felt his forehead with his fingers. "A fever upon me. A fever brought by Meralda. Wicked enchantress! A fever brought by Meralda and by Feringal, who deigns to take that which is rightfully mine. Deny him, Meralda!" he called loudly, and he broke down, kicking his foot against the stone and gnashing his teeth. He regained control quickly, reminding himself that only his wiles would allow him to beat Lord Feringal, that only his cleverness would allow him to overcome his enemy's unjust advantage, one given by birth and not quality of character. So Jaka began his plotting, thinking of how he might turn the mortal sickness he felt festering within his broken heart to some advantage over the stubborn girl's willpower.

✖ ✖ ✖ ✖ ✖

Meralda couldn't deny the beautiful aromas and sights of the small garden on the southern side of Castle Auck. Tall roses, white and pink, mingled with lady's mantle and lavender to form the main garden, creating a myriad of shapes and colors that drew Meralda's eye upward and back down again. Pansies filled in the lower level, and bachelor's buttons peeked out from hiding among the taller plants like secret prizes for the cunning examiner. Even in the perpetually dismal fog of Auckney, and perhaps in some large part because of it, the garden shone brightly, speaking of birth and renewal, of springtime and life itself.

Enchanted as she was, Meralda couldn't help but wish that her escort this waning afternoon was not Lord Feringal, but her Jaka. Wouldn't she love to take him and kiss him here amidst the flowery scents and sights, amidst the hum of happy bees?

"Priscilla tends the place, mostly," Lord Feringal remarked, walking politely a step behind Meralda as she made her way along the garden wall.

The news caught Meralda somewhat by surprise and made her rethink her first impression of the lady of Castle Auck. Anyone who could so carefully and lovingly tend a garden to this level of beauty must have some redeeming qualities. "And do you not come out here at all?" the woman asked, turning back to regard the young lord.

Feringal shrugged and smiled sheepishly, as if embarrassed to admit that he rarely ventured into the place.

"Do you not think it beautiful, then?" Meralda asked.

Lord Feringal rushed up to the woman and took her hand in his. "Surely it is not more beautiful than you," he blurted.

Bolder by far than she had been on their first meeting, Meralda pulled her hand away. "The garden," she insisted. "The flowers—all their shapes and smells. Don't you find it beautiful?"

"Of course," Lord Feringal answered immediately, obediently, Meralda realized.

"Well, look at it!" Meralda cried at him. "Don't just be staring at me. Look at the flowers, at the bounty of your sister's fine work. See how they live together? How one flower makes room for another, all bunching, but not blocking the sun?"

Lord Feringal did turn his gaze from Meralda to regard the myriad flowers, and a strange expression of revelation came over his face.

"You do see," Meralda remarked after a long, long silence. Lord Feringal continued to study the color surrounding them.

He turned back to Meralda, a look of wonder in his eyes. "I have lived here all my life," he said. "And in those years—no, decades—this garden has been here, yet never before have I seen it. It took you to show me the beauty." He came nearer to Meralda and took her hand in his, then leaned in gently and kissed her, though not urgently and demandingly as he had done their previous meeting. He was gentle and appreciative. "Thank you," he said as he pulled back from her.

Meralda managed a weak smile in reply. "Well, you should be thanking your sister," she said. "A load of work to get it this way."

"I shall," Lord Feringal replied unconvincingly.

Meralda smiled knowingly and turned her attention back to the garden, thinking again how grand it would be to walk through the place with Jaka at her side. The amorous young lord was beside her again, so close, his hands upon her, and she could not maintain the fantasy. Instead, she focused on the flowers, thinking that if she could just lose herself in their beauty, just stare at them until the sun went down, and even after, in the soft glow of the moon, she might survive this night.

To his credit, Lord Feringal allowed her a long, long while to simply stand quietly and stare. The sun disappeared and the moon came up, and though it was full in the sky, the garden lost some of its luster and enchantment except for the continuing aroma, mixing sweetly with the salty air.

"Won't you look at me all the night?" Feringal asked, gently turning her around.

"I was just thinking," Meralda replied.

"Tell me your thoughts," he eagerly prompted.

The woman shrugged. "Silly ones, only," she replied.

Lord Feringal's face brightened with a wide smile. "I'll wager you were thinking it would be grand to walk among these flowers every day," he ventured. "To come to this place whenever you desired, by sun or by moon, in winter even, to stare at the cold waters and the bergs as they build in the north?"

Meralda was wiser than to openly deny the guess or to add to it that she would only think of such things if another man, her Jaka, was beside her instead of Lord Feringal.

"Because you can have all of that," Feringal said excitedly. "You can, you know. All of it and more."

"You hardly know me," the girl exclaimed, near to panic and hardly believing what she was hearing.

"Oh, but I do, my Meralda," Feringal declared, and he fell to one knee, holding her hand in one of his and stroking it gently with the other. "I do know you, for I have looked for you all my life."

"You're speaking foolishness," Meralda muttered, but Feringal pressed on.

"I wondered if ever I would find the woman who could so steal my heart," he said, and he seemed to Meralda to be talking as much to himself as to her. "Others have been paraded before me, of course. Many merchants would desire to create a safe haven in Auckney by bartering their daughters as my wife, but none gave me pause." He rose dramatically, moving to the sea wall.

"None," he repeated. Feringal turned back, his eyes boring into hers. "Until I saw the vision of Meralda. With my heart, I know that there is no other woman in all the world I would have as a wife."

Meralda stammered over that one, stunned by the man's forwardness, by the sheer speed at which he was trying to move this courtship. Even as she stood trying to think of something to reply, he enveloped her, kissing her again and again, not gently, pressing his lips hard against hers, his hands running over her back.

"I must have you," he said, nearly pulling her off-balance.

Meralda brought her arm up between them, slamming her palm hard into Lord Feringal's face and driving him back a step. She pulled away, but he pressed in again.

"Please, Meralda!" he cried. "My blood boils within me!"

"You're saying you want me for a wife, but you're treating me like a harlot!" she cried. "No man takes a wife he's already bedded," Meralda pleaded.

Lord Feringal skidded to a stop. "But why?" asked the naive young man. "It is love, after all, and so it is right, I say. My blood boils, and my heart pounds in my chest for want of you."

Meralda looked around desperately for escape and found one from an unexpected source.

"Your pardon, my lord," came a voice from the door, and the pair turned to see Steward Temigast stepping from the castle. "I heard the cry and feared that one of you might have slipped over the rail."

"Well, you see that is not the case, so be gone with you," an exasperated Feringal replied, waving his hand dismissively, and turning back to Meralda.

Steward Temigast stared at her frightened, white face for a long while, a look of sympathy upon his own. "My lord," he ventured calmly. "If you are, indeed, serious about marrying this woman, then you must treat her like a lady. The hour grows long," he announced. "The Ganderlay family will be expecting the return of their child. I will summon the carriage."

"Not yet," Lord Feringal replied immediately, before Temigast could even turn around. "Please," he said more quietly and calmly to Temigast, but mostly to Meralda. "A short while longer?"

Temigast looked to Meralda, who reluctantly nodded her assent. "I will return for you soon," Temigast said, and he went back into the castle.

"I'll have no more of your foolery," Meralda warned her eager suitor, taking confidence in his sheepish plea.

"It is difficult for me, Meralda," he tried sincerely to explain. "More than you can understand. I think about you day and night. I grow impatient for the day when we shall be wed, the day when you shall give yourself to me fully."

Meralda had no reply, but she had to work hard to keep any expression of anger from appearing on her fair face. She thought of her mother then, remembered a conversation she had overheard between her father and a woman friend of the family, when the woman bemoaned that Biaste likely would not live out the winter if they could find no better shelter or no cleric or skilled healer to tend her.

"I'll not wait long, I assure you," Lord Feringal went on. "I will tell Priscilla to make the arrangements this very night."

"I haven't even said I would marry you," Meralda squealed a weak protest.

"But you will marry me, of course," Feringal said confidently. "All the village will be in attendance, a faire that will stay in hearts and memories for all the lives of all who witness it. On that day, Meralda, it will be you whom they rejoice in most of all," he said, coming over and taking her hand again, but gently and respectfully this time. "Years—no, decades—from now, the village women will still remark on the beauty of Lord Feringal's bride."

Meralda couldn't deny she was touched by the man's sincerity and somewhat thrilled by the prospect of having as great a day as Feringal spoke of, a wedding that would be the talk of Auckney for years and years to come. What woman would not desire such a thing?

Yet, Meralda also could not deny that while the glorious wedding was appealing, her heart longed for another. She was beginning to notice another side of Lord Feringal now, a decent and caring nature, perhaps, buried beneath the trappings of his sheltered upbringing. Despite that, Meralda could not forget, even for one moment, that Lord Feringal, simply was not her Jaka.

Steward Temigast returned and announced that the coach was ready, and Meralda went straight to him, but she was still not quick enough to dodge the young man's last attempt to steal a kiss.

It hardly mattered. Meralda was beginning to see things clearly now, and she understood her responsibility to her family and would put that responsibility above all else. Still, it was a long and miserable ride across the bridge and down the road, the young woman's head swirling with so many conflicting thoughts and emotions.

Once again she bade the gnomish driver to let her out some distance from her home. Pulling off the uncomfortable shoes Temigast had sent along with the dress, Meralda walked barefoot down the lane under the moon. Too confused by the events—to think that she was to be married!—Meralda was barely conscious of her surroundings and wasn't even hoping, as she had after her first meeting, that Jaka would find her on the road. She was taken completely by surprise when the young man appeared before her.

"What did he do to you?" Jaka asked before Meralda could even say his name.

"Do?" she echoed.

"What did you do?" Jaka demanded. "You were there for a long time."

"We walked in the garden," the woman answered.

"Just walked?" Jaka's voice took on a frightful edge at that moment, one that set Meralda back on her heels.

"What're you thinking?" she dared ask.

Jaka gave a great sigh and spun away. "I am not thinking, and that is the problem," he wailed. "What enchantment have you cast upon me, Meralda? Oh, the bewitching! I know miserable Feringal must feel the same," he added, spinning back on her. "What man could not?"

A great smile erupted on the young woman's face, but it didn't hold, not at all. Why was Jaka acting so peculiar, so love struck all of a sudden? she wondered. Why hadn't he behaved this way before?

"Did he have you?" Jaka asked, coming very close. "Did you let him?"

The questions hit Meralda like a wet towel across the face. "How can you be asking me such a thing?" she protested.

Jaka fell to his knees before her, taking both her hands and pressing them against his cheek. "Because I shall die to think of you with him," he explained.

Meralda felt weak in her knees and sick to her stomach. She was too young and too inexperienced, she realized, and could not fathom any of this, not the marriage, not Lord Feringal's polite and almost animalistic polarities, and not Jaka's sudden conversion to lovesick suitor.

"I . . ." she started. "We did nothing. Oh, he stole a kiss, but I didn't kiss him back."

Jaka looked at her, and the smile upon his face was somehow unnerving to Meralda. He came closer then, moving his lips to brush against hers and lighting fires everywhere in her body, it seemed. She felt his hands roaming her body, and she did not fear them—at least not in the same manner in which she had feared her noble suitor. No, this time it was an exciting thing, but still she pushed the man back from her.

"Do you deny the love that we feel for each other?" a wounded Jaka asked.

"But it's not about how we're feeling," Meralda tried to explain.

"Of course it is," the young man said quietly, and he came forward again. "That is all that matters."

He kissed her gently again, and Meralda found that she believed him. The only thing in all the world that mattered at that moment was how she and Jaka felt for each other. She returned the kiss, falling deeper and deeper, tumbling away to an abyss of joy.

Then he was gone from her, too abruptly. Meralda popped open her eyes to see Jaka tumbling to the ground, a raging Dohni Ganderlay standing before her.

"Are you a fool then?" the man asked, and he lifted his arm as if to strike Meralda. A look of pain crossed his rugged face then, and he quickly put his arm down, but up it came again, grabbing Meralda roughly by the shoulder and spinning her toward the house. Dohni shoved her along, then turned on Jaka, who put his hands up defensively in front of his face and darted about, trying to escape.

"Don't hit him, Da!" the young woman cried, and that plea alone stopped Dohni.

"Stay far from my girl," Dohni warned Jaka.

"I love—" Jaka started to reply.

"They'll find yer body washing on the beach," Dohni said.

When Meralda cried out again, the imposing man turned on her viciously. "Home!" he commanded. Meralda ran off at full speed, not even bothering to retrieve the shoe she had dropped when Dohni had shoved her.

Donny turned on Jaka, his eyes, red from anger and nights of restless sleep, as menacing as any sight the young man had ever witnessed. Jaka turned on his heel and ran away. He started to, anyway, for before he had gone three steps Dohni hit him with a flying tackle across the back of his knees, dropping him face down on the ground.

"Meralda begged you not to hit me!" the terrified young man pleaded.

Dohni climbed atop him, roughly pulling the young man over. "Meralda's not knowing what's best for Meralda," Dohni answered with a growl and a punch that jerked Jaka's head to the side.

The young man began to cry and to flail his arms wildly, trying to fend off Dohni. The blows got through, though, one after another, swelling Jaka's pretty eyes and fattening both his lips, knocking one tooth out of his perfect smile and bringing blue bruises to his normally rosy cheeks. Jaka finally had the sense to bring his arms down across his battered face, but Dohni, his rage not yet played out, only aimed his blows lower, pounding,

pounding Jaka about the chest. Every time Jaka dropped one arm down lower to block there, Dohni cunningly slipped a punch in around his face again.

Finally, Dohni leaped off the man, grabbed him by the front of the shirt, and hoisted him to his feet with a sudden, vicious jerk. Jaka held his palms out in front of him in a sign of surrender. That cowardly act only made Dohni slug him one more time, a brutal hook across the jaw that sent the young man flying to the ground again. Dohni pulled him upright, and he cocked his arm once more. Jaka's whimper made Dohni think of Meralda, of the inevitable look upon her face when he walked in, his knuckles all bloody. He grabbed Jaka in both hands and whipped him around, sending him running on his way.

"Get yourself gone!" the man growled at Jaka. "And don't be sniffing about my girl again!"

Jaka gave a great wail and stumbled off into the darkness.

9

THE BARREL'S BOTTOM

Robillard scratched his chin when he saw the pair, Wulfgar and Morik, moving down the alley toward the front door of the Cutlass. Deudermont was still inside, a fact that did not sit well with the divining wizard, given all the activity he had seen outside the tavern's door. Robillard had watched a seedy character come out and pay off a street urchin. The wizard understood the uses of such children. That same character, an unusual figure indeed, had exited the Cutlass again and moved off into the shadows.

Wulfgar appeared with a small, swarthy man. Robillard was not surprised when the same street urchin peeked out from an alley some distance away, no doubt waiting for his opportunity to return to his chosen place of business.

Robillard realized the truth after putting the facts together and adding a heavy dose of justifiable suspicion. He turned to the door and chanted a simple spell, grabbing at the air and using it to blast open the portal. "Mister Micanty!" he called, amplifying his voice with yet another spell.

"Go out with a pair of crewmen and alert the town guard," Robillard demanded. "To the Cutlass on Half-Moon Street with all speed."

With a growl the wizard reversed his first spell and slammed the door shut again, then fell back intently into the images within the crystal ball, focusing on the front door of the Cutlass. He moved inside to find Deudermont leaning calmly against the bar.

A few uneventful moments passed, and Robillard shifted his gaze back outside just long enough to note Wulfgar and his small friend lurking in the shadows, as if waiting for something.

Even as the wizard's roving magical eye moved back through the tavern's door, he found Deudermont approaching the exit.

"Hurry, Micanty," Robillard mouthed quietly, but he knew that the town guard, well-drilled as they were, wouldn't likely arrive in time and that he would have to take some action. The wizard plotted his course quickly: a dimensional door to the other end of the docks, and a second to the alley that ran beside the Cutlass. One final look into the crystal ball showed Deudermont walking out and Wulfgar and the other man moving toward him. Robillard let go his mental connection with the ball and brought up the first dimensional door.

⚔ ⚔ ⚔ ⚔ ⚔

Creeps Sharky and Tee-a-nicknick crouched in the shadows on the rooftop. The tattooed man brought the blowgun up to his lips the second Deudermont exited the tavern.

"Not yet," Creeps instructed, grabbing the barrel and pulling the weapon low. "Let him talk to Wulfgar and Morik, and get near to my stone that'll kill any magical protections he might be wearin'. And let others see 'em together, afore and when Deudermont falls dead."

The wretched pirate licked his lips in anticipation. "They gets the blame, we gets the booty," he said.

⚔ ⚔ ⚔ ⚔ ⚔

"Wulfgar," Captain Deudermont greeted him when the barbarian and his sidekick shifted out of the shadows and steadily approached. "My men said you came to *Sea Sprite*."

"Not from any desire," Wulfgar muttered, drawing an elbow from Morik.

"You said you want your warhammer back," the little man quietly reminded him.

What Morik was really thinking, though, was that this might be the perfect time for him to learn more about Deudermont, about the man's protections and, more importantly, his weaknesses. The street urchin had found the barbarian and the rogue down by the docks, handing over the small bag and its curious contents and explaining that Captain Deudermont desired their presence in front of the Cutlass on Half-Moon Street. Again, Morik had spoken to Wulfgar about the potential gain here, but he backed off immediately as soon as he recognized that dangerous scowl. If Wulfgar would not go along with the assassination, then Morik meant to find a way to do it on his own. He had nothing against Deudermont, of course, and wasn't usually a murderer, but the payoff was just too great to ignore. Good enough for Wulfgar, Morik figured, when he was living in luxury, the finest rooms, the finest food, the finest booze, and the finest whores.

Wulfgar nodded and strode right up to stand before Deudermont, though he did not bother accepting the man's offered hand. "What do you know?" he asked.

"Only that you came to the docks and looked up at Waillan

Micanty," Deudermont replied. "I assumed that you wished to speak with me."

"All that I want from you is information concerning Aegis-fang," he said sourly.

"Your hammer?" Deudermont asked, and he looked curiously at Wulfgar, as if only then noticing that the barbarian was not wearing the weapon.

"The boy said you had information," Morik clarified.

"Boy?" the confused captain asked.

"The boy who gave me this," Morik explained, holding up the bag.

Deudermont moved to take it but stopped, seeing Robillard rushing out of the alley to the side.

"Hold!" the wizard cried.

Deudermont felt a sharp sting on the side of his neck. He reached up instinctively with his hand to grab at it, but before his fingers closed around the cat's claw, a great darkness overcame him, buckling his knees. Wulfgar leaped ahead to grab him.

Robillard yelled and reached out magically for Wulfgar, extending a wand and blasting the huge barbarian square in the chest with a glob of sticky goo that knocked him back against the Cutlass and held him there. Morik turned and ran.

"Captain! Captain!" Robillard cried, and he let fly another glob for Morik, but the agile thief was too quick and managed to dodge aside as he skittered down another alley. He had to reverse direction almost immediately, for entering the other end came a pair of city guard, brandishing flaming torches and gleaming swords. He did keep his wits about him enough to toss the satchel the boy had given him into a cubby at the side of the alley before he turned away.

All of Half-Moon Street seemed to erupt in a frenzy then, with guardsmen and crewmen of *Sea Sprite* exiting from every conceivable angle.

Against the wall of the Cutlass, Wulfgar struggled mightily to draw breath. His mind whirled back to the grayness of the Abyss, back to some of the similar magic the demon Errtu had put on him to hold him so, helpless in the face of diabolical minions. That vision lent him rage, and that rage lent him strength. The frantic barbarian got his balance and pulled hard, tearing planking from the side of the building.

Robillard, howling with frustration and fear as he knelt over the scarcely breathing Deudermont, hit Wulfgar with another glob, pasting him to the wall again.

"They've killed him," the wizard yelled to the guardsmen. "Catch the little rat!"

✠ ✠ ✠ ✠ ✠

"We go," Tee-a-nicknick said as soon as Deudermont's legs buckled.

"Hit him again," Creeps begged.

The tattooed man shook his head. "One enough. We go."

Even as he and Creeps started to move, the guards descended upon Half-Moon Street and all the other avenues around the area. Creeps led his friend to the shadows by a dormer on the building, where they deposited the blowgun and poison. They moved to another dormer across the way and sat down with their backs against the wall. Creeps took out a bottle, and the pair started drinking, pretending to be oblivious, happy drunks.

Within a few moments, a trio of guardsmen came over the lip of the roof and approached them. After a cursory inspection and a cry from below revealing that one of the assassins had been captured and the other was running loose through the streets, the guards turned away in disgust.

⚔ ⚔ ⚔ ⚔ ⚔

Morik spun and darted one way, then another, but the noose was closing around him. He found a shadow in the nook of a building and thought he might wait the pursuit out, when he began glowing with magical light.

"Wizards," the rogue muttered. "I hate wizards!"

Off he ran to a building and started to climb, but he was caught by the legs and hauled down, then beaten and kicked until he stopped squirming.

"I did nothing!" he protested, spitting blood with every word as they hauled him roughly to his feet.

"Shut your mouth!" one guard demanded, jamming the hilt of his sword into Morik's gut, doubling the rogue over in pain. He half-walked and was half-dragged back to where Robillard worked feverishly over Deudermont.

"Run for a healer," the wizard instructed, and a guard and a pair of crewmen took off.

"What poison?" the wizard demanded of Morik.

Morik shrugged as if he did not understand.

"The bag," said Robillard. "You held a bag."

"I have no—" Morik started to say, but he lost the words as the guard beside him slammed him hard in the belly yet again.

"Retrace his steps," Robillard instructed the other guards. "He carried a small satchel. I want it found."

"What of him?" one of the guards asked, motioning to the mound of flesh that was Wulfgar. "Surely he can't breath under that."

"Cut his face free, then," Robillard hissed. "He should not die as easily as that."

"Captain!" Waillan Micanty cried upon seeing Deudermont.

He ran to kneel beside his fallen captain. Robillard put a comforting hand on the man's shoulder, turning a violent glare on Morik.

"I am innocent," the little thief declared, but even as he did a cry came from the alley. A moment later a guardsman ran out with the satchel in hand.

Robillard pulled open the bag, first lifting the stone from it and sensing immediately what it might be. He had lived through the Time of Troubles after all, and he knew all about dead magic regions and how stones from such places might dispel any magic near them. If his guess was right, it would explain how Morik and Wulfgar had so easily penetrated the wards he'd placed on the captain.

Next Robillard lifted a cat's claw from the bag. He led Morik's gaze and the stares of all the others from that curious item to Deudermont's neck, then produced another, similar claw, the one he had pulled from the captain's wound.

"Indeed," Robillard said dryly, eyebrows raised.

"I hate wizards," Morik muttered under his breath.

A sputter from Wulfgar turned them all around. The big man was coughing out pieces of the sticky substance. He started roaring in rage almost immediately and began tugging with such ferocity that all the Cutlass shook from the thrashing.

Robillard noted then that Arumn Gardpeck and several others had exited the place and stood staring incredulously at the scene before them. The tavernkeeper walked over to consider Wulfgar, then shook his head.

"What have ye done?" he asked.

"No good, as usual," remarked Josi Puddles.

Robillard walked over to them. "You know this man?" he asked Arumn, jerking his head toward Wulfgar.

"He's worked for me since he came to Luskan last spring,"

Arumn explained. "Until—" the tavernkeeper hesitated and stared at the big man yet again, shaking his head.

"Until?" Robillard prompted.

"Until he got too angry with all the world," Josi Puddles was happy to put in.

"You will be summoned to speak against him before the magistrates," Robillard explained. "Both of you."

Arumn nodded dutifully, but Josi's head bobbed eagerly. Perhaps too eagerly, Robillard observed, but he had to privately admit his gratitude to the little wretch.

A host of priests came running soon after, their numbers and haste alone a testament to the great reputation of the pirate-hunting Captain Deudermont. In mere moments, the stricken man was born away on a litter.

On a nearby rooftop, Creeps Sharky smiled as he handed the empty bottle to Tee-a-nicknick.

⚔ ⚔ ⚔ ⚔ ⚔

Luskan's gaol consisted of a series of caves beside the harbor, winding and muddy, with hard and jagged stone walls. Perpetually stoked fires kept the place brutally hot and steamy. Thick veils of moisture erupted wherever the hot air collided with the cold, encroaching waters of the Sword Coast. There were a few cells, reserved for political prisoners mostly, threats to the ruling families and merchants who might grow stronger if they were made martyrs. Most of the prisoners, though, didn't last long enough to be afforded cells, soon to be victims of the macabre and brutally efficient Prisoner's Carnival.

This revolving group's cell consisted of a pair of shackles set high enough on the wall to keep them on the tips of their toes, dangling agonizingly by their arms. Compounding that torture were the mindless gaolers, huge and ugly thugs, half-ogres mostly, walking slowly and methodically through the complex with glowing pokers in their hands.

"This is all a huge mistake, you understand," Morik complained to the most recent gaoler to move in his and Wulfgar's direction.

The huge brute gave a slow chuckle that sounded like stones grating together and casually jabbed the orange end of a poker at Morik's belly. The nimble thief leaped sidelong, pulling hard with his chained arm but still taking a painful burn on the side. The ogre gaoler just kept on walking, approaching Wulfgar, and chuckling slowly.

"And what've yerself?" the brute said, moving his smelly breath close to the barbarian. "Yerself as well, eh? Ne'er did nothin' deservin' such imprisonin'?"

Wulfgar, his face blank, stared straight ahead. He barely winced when the powerful brute slugged him in the gut or when that awful poker slapped against his armpit, sending wispy smoke from his skin.

"Strong one," the brute said and chuckled again. "More fun's all." He brought the poker up level with Wulfgar's face and began moving it slowly in toward the big man's eye.

"Oh, but ye'll howl," he said.

"But we have not yet been tried!" Morik complained.

"Ye're thinkin' that matters?" the gaoler replied, pausing long enough only to turn a toothy grin on Morik. "Ye're all guilty for the fun of it, if not the truth."

That struck Wulfgar as a profound statement. Such was justice. He looked at the gaoler as if acknowledging the ugly creature for the first time, seeing simple wisdom there, a viewpoint come from observation. From the mouths of idiots, he thought.

The poker moved in, but Wulfgar set the gaoler with such

a calm and devastating stare, a look borne of the barbarian's supreme confidence that this man—that all these foolish mortal men—could do nothing to him to rival the agonies he had suffered at the clawed hands of the demon Errtu.

The gaoler apparently got that message, or a similar one, for he hesitated, even backed the poker up so he could more clearly view Wulfgar's set expression.

"Ye think ye can hold it?" the brutal torturer asked Wulfgar. "Ye think ye can keep yer face all stuck like that when I pokes yer eye?" And on he came again.

Wulfgar gave a growl that came from somewhere very, very deep within, a feral, primal sound that stole the words from Morik's mouth as the little thief was about to protest. A growl that came from his torment in the pits of the Abyss.

The barbarian swelled his chest mightily, gathered his strength, and drove one shoulder forward with such ferocity and speed that the shackle anchor exploded from the wall, sending the stunned gaoler skittering back.

"Oh, but I'll kill ye for that!" the half-ogre cried, and he came ahead brandishing the poker like a club.

Wulfgar was ready for him. The barbarian coiled around, almost turning to face the wall, then swung his free arm wide, the chain and block of metal and stone fixed to its other end swishing across to clip the glowing poker and tear it from the gaoler's hand. Again the brute skittered back, and this time Wulfgar turned back on the wall fully, running his legs right up it so that he had his feet planted firmly, one on either side of the remaining shackle.

"Knock all the walls down!" Morik cheered.

The gaoler turned and ran.

Another growl came from Wulfgar, and he pulled with all his strength, every muscle in his powerful body straining. This anchor was more secure than the last, the stone wall more solid around it, but so great was Wulfgar's pull that a link in the heavy chain began to separate.

"Pull on!" Morik cried.

Wulfgar did, and he was sailing out from the wall, spinning into a back somersault. He tumbled down, unhurt, but then it hit him, a wave of anguish more powerful than any torture the sadistic gaoler might bring. In his mind he was no longer in the dungeon of Luskan but back in the Abyss, and though no shackles now held him he knew there could be no escape, no victory over his too-powerful captors. How many times had Errtu played this trick on him, making him think he was free only to snare him and drag him back to the stench and filth, only to beat him, then heal him, and beat him some more?

"Wulfgar?" Morik begged repeatedly, pulling at his own shackles, though with no results at all. "Wulfgar!"

The barbarian couldn't hear him, couldn't even see him, so lost was he in the swirling fog of his own thoughts. Wulfgar curled up on the floor, trembling like a babe when the gaoler returned with a dozen comrades.

A short while later, the beaten Wulfgar was hanging again from the wall, this time in shackles meant for a giant, thick and solid chains that had his feet dangling several feet from the floor and his arms stretched out straight to the side. As an extra precaution a block of sharpened spikes had been set behind the barbarian so if he pulled hard he would impale himself rather than tug the chains from their anchors. He was in a different chamber now, far removed from Morik. He was all alone with his memories of the Abyss, with no place to hide, no bottle to take him away.

"It should be working," the old woman grumbled. "Right herbs fer de poison."

Three priests walked back and forth in the room, one muttering prayers, another going from one side of Captain Deudermont to the other, listening for breath, for a heartbeat, checking for a pulse, while the third just kept rubbing his hand over his tightly cropped hair.

"But it is not working," Robillard argued, and he looked to the priests for some help.

"I don't understand," said Camerbunne, the ranking cleric among the trio. "It resists our spells and even a powerful herbal antidote."

"And wit some o' de poison in hand, it should be workin'," said the old woman.

"If that is indeed some of the poison," Robillard remarked.

"You yourself took it from the little one called Morik," Camerbunne explained.

"That does not necessarily mean . . ." Robillard started to reply. He let the thought hang in the air. The expressions on the faces of his four companions told him well enough that they had caught on. "What do we do, then?" the wizard asked.

"I can'no be promisin' anything," the old woman claimed, throwing up her hands dramatically. "Wit none o' de poison, me herbs'll do what dey will."

She moved to the side of the room, where they had placed a small table to act as her workbench, and began fiddling with different vials and jars and bottles. Robillard looked to Camerbunne. The man returned a defeated expression. The clerics had worked tirelessly over Deudermont in the day he had been in their care, casting spells that should have neutralized the vicious poison flowing through him. Those spells had provided temporary relief only, slowing the poison and allowing the captain to breath more easily and lowering his fever a bit, at least. Deudermont had not opened his eyes since the attack. Soon after, the captain's breathing went back to raspy, and he began bleeding again from his gums and his eyes. Robillard was no healer, but he had seen enough death to understand that if they did not come up with something soon, his beloved Captain Deudermont would fade away.

"Evil poison," Camerbunne remarked.

"It is an herb, no doubt," Robillard said. "Neither evil nor malicious. It just is what it is."

Camerbunne shook his head. "There is a touch of magic about it, do not doubt, good wizard," he declared. "Our spells will defeat any natural poison. No, this one has been specially prepared by a master and with the help of dark magic."

"Then what can we do?" the wizard asked.

"We can keep casting our spells over him to try and offer as much comfort as possible and hope that the poison works its way out of him," Camerbunne explained. "We can hope that old Gretchen finds the right mixture of herbs."

"Easier it'd be if I had a bit o' the poison," old Gretchen complained.

"And we can pray," Camerbunne finished.

The last statement brought a frown to the atheistic Robillard. He was a man of logic and specified rules and did not indulge in prayer.

"I will go to Morik the Rogue and learn more of the poison," Robillard said with a snarl.

"He has been tortured already," Camerbunne assured the wizard. "I doubt that he knows anything at all. It is merely something he purchased on the street, no doubt."

"Tortured?" Robillard replied skeptically. "A thumbscrew, a rack? No, that is not torture. That is a sadistic game and nothing more. The art of torture becomes ever more exquisite when magic is applied." He started for the door, but Camerbunne caught him by the arm.

"Morik will not know," he said again, staring soberly into the outraged wizard's hollowed eyes. "Stay with us. Stay with your captain. He may not survive the night, and if he does come out of the sleep before he dies, it would be better if he found a friend waiting for him."

Robillard had no argument against that heavy-handed comment, so he sighed and moved back to his chair, plopping down.

A short while later, a city guardsman knocked and entered the room, the routine call from the magistrate.

"Tell Jerem Boll and old Jharkheld that the charge against Wulfgar and Morik will likely be heinous murder," Camerbunne quietly explained.

Robillard heard the priest, and the words sank his heart even lower. It didn't matter much to Wulfgar and Morik what charge was placed against them. Either way, whether it was heinous murder or intended murder, they would be executed, though with the former the process would take much longer, to the pleasure of the crowd at the Prisoner's Carnival.

Watching them die would be of little satisfaction to Robillard, though, if his beloved captain did not survive. He put his head in his hands, considering again that he should go to Morik and punish the man with spell after spell until he broke down and revealed the type of poison that had been used.

Camerbunne was right, Robillard knew, for he understood city thieves like Morik the Rogue. Certainly Morik hadn't brewed the poison but had merely gotten some of it from a well-paid source.

The wizard lifted his head from his hands, a look of revelation on his haggard face. He remembered the two men who had been in the Cutlass before Wulfgar and Morik had arrived, the two men who had gone to the boy who had subsequently run off to find Wulfgar and Morik, the grimy sailor and his exotic, tattooed companion. He remembered *Leaping Lady,* sailing out fast from Luskan's harbor. Had Wulfgar and Morik traded the barbarian's marvelous warhammer for the poison to kill Deudermont?

Robillard sprang up from his chair, not certain of where to begin, but thinking now that he was on to something important. Someone, either the pair who had signaled Deudermont's arrival, the street urchin they had paid to go get Wulfgar and Morik, or someone on *Leaping Lady,* knew the secrets of the poison.

Robillard took another look at his poor, bedraggled captain, so obviously near to death. He stormed out of the room, determined to get some answers.

10

PASSAGE

Meralda walked tentatively into the kitchen the next morning, conscious of the stare her father leveled her way. She looked to her mother as well, seeking some indication that her father had told the woman about her indiscretion with Jaka the previous night. But Biaste was beaming, oblivious.

"Oh, the garden!" Biaste cried, all smiles. "Tell me about the garden. Is it as pretty as Gurdy Harkins says?"

Meralda glanced at her father. Relieved to find him smiling as well, she took her seat and moved it right beside Biaste's chair. "Prettier," she said, her grin wide. "All the colors, even in the late sun! And under the moon, though it's not shining so bright, the smells catch and hold you.

"That's not all that caught my fancy," Meralda said, forcing a cheerful voice as she launched into the news they were all waiting to hear. "Lord Feringal has asked me to marry him."

Biaste squealed with glee. Tori let out a cry of surprise, and a good portion of her mouthful of food, as well. Dohni Ganderlay slammed his hands upon the table happily.

Biaste, who could hardly get out of bed the tenday before, rushed about, readying herself, insisting that she had to go out at once and tell all of her friends, particularly Gurdy Harkins, who was always acting so superior because she sometimes sewed dresses for Lady Priscilla.

"Why'd you come in last night so flustered and crying?" Tori asked Meralda as soon as the two were alone in their room.

"Just mind what concerns you," Meralda answered.

"You'll be living in the castle and traveling to Hundelstone and Fireshear, and even to Luskan and all the wondrous places," pressed Tori, insisting, "but you were crying. I heard you."

Eyes moistening again, Meralda glared at the girl then went back to her chores.

"It's Jaka," Tori reasoned, a grin spreading across her face. "You're still thinking about him."

Meralda paused in fluffing her pillow, moved it close to her for a moment—a gesture that revealed to Tori her guess was true—then spun suddenly and launched the pillow into Tori's face, following it with a tackle that brought her sister down on the small bed.

"Say I'm the queen!" the older girl demanded.

"You just might be," stubborn Tori shot back, which made Meralda tickle her all the more. Soon Tori could take it no more and called out "Queen! Queen!" repeatedly.

"But you are sad about Jaka," Tori said soberly a few moments later, when Meralda had gone back to fixing the bedclothes.

"I saw him last night," Meralda admitted. "On my way home. He's gone sick thinking about me and Lord Feringal."

Tori gasped and swayed, then leaned closer, hanging on every word.

"He kissed me, too."

"Better than Lord Feringal?"

Meralda sighed and nodded, closing her eyes as she lost herself in the memory of that one brief, tender moment with Jaka.

"Oh, Meralda, what're you to do?" Tori asked.

"Jaka wants me to run away with him," she answered.

Tori moaned and hugged her pillow. "And will you?"

Meralda stood straighter then and flashed the young girl a brave smile. "My place is with Lord Feringal," she explained.

"But Jaka—"

"Jaka can't do nothing for Ma, and nothing for the rest of you," Meralda went on. "You can give your heart to whomever you want, but you give your life to the one who's best for you and for the ones you love."

Tori started to protest again, but Dohni Ganderlay entered the room. "You got work," he reminded them, and he put a look over Meralda that told the young woman that he had, indeed, overheard the conversation. He even gave a slight nod of approval before exiting the room.

Meralda walked through that day in a fog, trying to align her heart with acceptance of her responsibility. She wanted to do what was right for her family, she really did, but she could not ignore the pull of her heart, the desire to learn the ways of love in the arms of a man she truly loved.

Out in the fields higher on the carved steps of the mountain, Dohni Ganderlay was no less torn. He saw Jaka Sculi that morning, and the two didn't exchange more than a quick glance—one-eyed for Jaka, whose left orb was swollen shut. As much as Dohni wanted to throttle the young man for jeopardizing his family, he could not deny his own memories of young love, memories that made him feel guilty looking at the beaten Jaka. Something more insistent than responsibility had pulled Jaka and Meralda together the previous night, and Dohni reminded himself pointedly not to hold a grudge, either against his daughter or against Jaka, whose only crime, as far as Dohni knew, was to love Meralda.

⚔ ⚔ ⚔ ⚔ ⚔

The house was quiet and perfectly still in the darkness just after dusk, which only amplified the noise made by every one of Meralda's movements. The family had retired early after a long day of work and the excitement of Meralda receiving yet another invitation to the castle, three days hence, accompanied by the most beautiful green silk gown the Ganderlay women had ever seen. Meralda tried to put the gown on quietly and slowly, but the material ruffled and crackled.

"What're you doing?" came a sleepy whisper from Tori.

"Shh!" Meralda replied, moving right beside the girl's bed and kneeling so that Tori could hear her whispered reply. "Go back to sleep and keep your mouth shut," she instructed.

"You're going to Jaka," Tori exclaimed, and Meralda slapped her hand over the girl's mouth.

"No such thing," Meralda protested. "I'm just trying it out."

"No you're not!" said Tori, coming fully awake and sitting up. "You're going to see Jaka. Tell me true, or I'll yell for Da."

"Promise me that you'll not say," Meralda said, sitting on the bed beside her sister. Tori's head bobbed excitedly. "I'm hoping to find Jaka out there in the dark," Meralda explained. "He goes out every night to watch the moon and the stars."

"And you're running away to be married?"

Meralda gave a sad chuckle. "No, not that," she replied. "I'm giving my life to Lord Feringal for the good of Ma and Da and yourself," she explained. "And not with regrets," she added quickly, seeing her sister about to protest. "No, he'll give me a good life at the castle, of that I'm sure. He's not a bad man, though he has much to learn. But I'm taking tonight for my own heart. One night with Jaka to say good-bye." Meralda patted Tori's arm as she stood to leave. "Now, go back to sleep."

"Only if you promise to tell me everything tomorrow," Tori replied. "Promise, or I'll tell."

"You won't tell," Meralda said with confidence, for she understood that Tori was as enchanted by the romance of it all as she was. More, perhaps, for the young girl didn't understand the lifelong implications of these decisions as much as Meralda did.

"Go to sleep," Meralda said softly again as she kissed Tori on the forehead. Straightening the dress with a nervous glance toward the curtain door of the room, Meralda headed for the small window and out into the night.

⚔ ⚔ ⚔ ⚔ ⚔

Dohni Ganderlay watched his eldest daughter disappear into the darkness, knowing full well her intent. A huge part of him wanted to follow her, to catch her with Jaka and kill the troublesome boy once and for all, but Dohni also held faith that his daughter would return, that she would do what was right for the family as she had said to her sister that morning.

It tore at his heart, to be sure, for he understood the allure and insistence of young love. He decided to give her this one night, without question and without judgment.

⚔ ⚔ ⚔ ⚔ ⚔

Meralda walked through the dark in fear. Not of any monsters that might leap out at her—no, this was her home and the young woman had never been afraid of such things—but of the reaction of her parents, particularly her father, if they discovered her missing.

Soon enough, though, the woman left her house behind and fell into the allure of the sparkling starry sky. She came to a field and began spinning and dancing, enjoying the touch of the wet grass on her bare feet, feeling as if she were stretching up to the heavens above to join with those magical points of light. She sang softly to herself, a quiet tune that sounded spiritual and surely fit her feelings out here, alone, at peace, and as one with the stars.

She hardly thought of Lord Feringal, of her parents, of her responsibility, even of her beloved Jaka. She wasn't thinking at all, was just existing in the glory of the night and the dance.

"Why are you here?" came a question from behind her, Jaka's lisping voice.

The magic vanished, and Meralda slowly turned around to face the young man. He stood, hands in pockets, head down, curly brown hair flopping over his brow so that she couldn't even see his eyes. Suddenly another fear gripped the young woman, the fear of what she anticipated would happen this night with this man.

"Did Lord Feringal let you out?" Jaka asked sarcastically.

"I'm no puppet of his," Meralda replied.

"Are you not to be his wife?" Jaka demanded. He looked up and stared hard at the woman, taking some satisfaction in the moisture that glistened in her eyes. "That's what the villagers are saying," he went on, then he changed his voice. "Meralda Ganderlay," he cackled, sounding like an old gnome woman. "Oh, but what a lucky one, she is! To think that Lord Feringal himself'd come a-calling for her."

"Stop it," Meralda begged softly.

Jaka only went on more forcefully, his voice shifting timbre. "And what's he thinking, that fool, Feringal?" he said, now in the gruff tones of a village man. "He'll bring disgrace to us all, marrying so low as that. And what, with a hunnerd pretty and rich merchant girls begging for his hand. Ah, the fool!"

Meralda turned away and suddenly felt more silly than beautiful in her green gown. She also felt a hand on her shoulder, and Jaka was there, behind her.

"You have to know," he said softly. "Half of them think Lord Feringal a fool, and the other half are too blind by the false hopes of it all, like they're reliving their own courtships through you, wishing that their own miserable lives could be more like yours."

"What're you thinking?" Meralda said firmly, turning around to face the man, and starting as she did to see more clearly the bruises on his face, his fat lip and closed eye. She composed herself at once, though, understanding well enough where Jaka had found that beating.

"I think that Lord Feringal believes himself to be above you," Jaka answered bluntly.

"And so he is."

"No!" The retort came out sharply, making Meralda jump back in surprise. "No, he is not your better," Jaka went on quietly, and he lifted his hand to gently stroke Meralda's wet cheek. "Rather, you are too good for him, but he will not view things that way. Nay, he will use you at his whim, then cast you aside."

Meralda wanted to argue, but she wasn't sure the young man was wrong. It didn't matter, though, for whatever Lord Feringal had in mind for her, the things he could do for her family remained paramount.

"Why did you come out here?" Jaka asked again, and it seemed to Meralda as if he only then noticed her gown, for he ran the material of one puffy sleeve through his thumb and index finger, feeling its quality.

"I came out for a night for Meralda," the young woman explained. "For a night when my desires would outweigh me responsibility. One night . . ."

She stopped when Jaka put a finger over her lips, holding it there for a long while. "Desires?" he asked slyly. "And do you include me among them? Did you come out here, all finely dressed, just to see me?"

Meralda nodded slowly and before she had even finished, Jaka was against her, pressing his lips to hers, kissing her hungrily, passionately. She felt as if she were floating, and then she realized that Jaka was guiding her down to the soft grass, holding the kiss all the way. His hands continued to move about her, and she didn't stop them, didn't even stiffen when they brushed her in private places. No, this was her night, the night she would become a woman with the man of her choosing, the man of her desires and not her responsibilities.

Jaka reached down and pulled the gown halfway up her legs and wasted no time in putting his own legs between hers.

"Slower, please," Meralda said softly, taking his face in both her hands and holding him very close to her, so that he had to look in her eyes. "I want it to be perfect," she explained.

"Meralda," the young man breathed, seeming desperate. "I cannot wait another minute."

"You don't have to," the young woman assured him, and she pulled him close and kissed him gently.

Soon after, the pair lay side by side, naked on the wet grass, the chill ocean air tickling their bodies as they stared up at the starry canopy. Meralda felt different, giddy and lightheaded almost, and somehow spiritual, as if she had just gone through something magical, some rite of passage. A thousand thoughts swirled in her mind. How could she go back to Lord Feringal after this wondrous lovemaking with Jaka? How could she turn her back on these feelings of pure joy and warmth? She felt wonderful at that moment, and she wanted the moment to last and last for the rest of her life. The rest of her life with Jaka.

But it would not, the woman knew. It would be gone with the break of dawn, never to return. She'd had her one moment. A lump caught in her throat.

For Jaka Sculi, the moment was a bit different, though certainly no less satisfying. He had taken Meralda's virginity, had beaten the lord of Auckney himself to that special place. He, a lowly peasant in Lord Feringal's eyes, had taken something from Feringal that could never be replaced, something more valuable than all the gold and gems in Castle Auck.

Jaka liked that feeling, but he feared, as did Meralda, that this afterglow would not last. "Will you marry him?" he asked suddenly.

Beautiful in the moonlight, Meralda turned a sleepy eye his way. "Let's not be talking about such things tonight," the woman implored him. "Nothing about Lord Feringal or anyone else."

"I must know, Meralda," Jaka said firmly, sitting up to stare down at her. "Tell me."

Meralda gave the young man the most plaintive look he had ever seen. "He can do for my ma and da," she tried to explain. "You must understand that the choice is not mine to make," an increasingly desperate Meralda finished lamely.

"Understand?" Jaka echoed incredulously, leaping to his feet and walking away. "Understand! How can I after what we just did? Oh, why did you come to me if you planned to marry Lord Feringal?"

Meralda caught up to him and grabbed him by the shoulders. "I came out for one night where I might choose," she explained. "I came out because I love you and wish with all my heart that things could be different."

"We had just one brief moment," Jaka whined, turning back to face her.

Meralda came up on her tiptoes and kissed him gently. "We've more time," she explained, an offer Jaka couldn't resist. A short while later, Jaka was lying on the grass again, while Meralda stood beside him, pulling on her clothes.

"Deny him," Jaka said unexpectedly, and the young woman stopped and stared down at him. "Deny Lord Feringal," Jaka said again, as casually as if it were the most simple decision. "Forget him and run away with me. To Luskan, or even all the way to Waterdeep."

Meralda sighed and shook her head. "I'm begging you not to ask it of me," she started to say, but Jaka would not relent.

"Think of the life we might find together," he said. "Running through the streets of Waterdeep, magical Waterdeep! Running and laughing and making love. Raising a family together—how beautiful our children shall be."

"Stop it!" Meralda snapped so forcefully that she stole the words from Jaka's mouth. "You know I want to, and you also know I can't." Meralda sighed again profoundly. It was the toughest thing she had ever done in her entire life, but she bent to kiss Jaka's angry mouth one last time, then started toward home.

Jaka lay on the field for a long while, his mind racing. He had achieved his conquest, and it had been as sweet as he had expected. Still, it would not hold. Lord Feringal would marry Meralda, would beat him in the end. The thought of it made him sick. He stared up at the moon, now shaded behind lines of swift-moving clouds. "Fie this life," he grumbled.

There had to be something he could do to beat Lord Feringal, something to pull Meralda back to him.

A confident smile spread over Jaka's undeniably handsome face. He remembered the sounds Meralda had made, the way her body had moved in harmony with his own.

He wouldn't lose.

All Hands Joined

Y ou will tell me of the poison," said Prelate Vohltin, an associate of Camerbunne. He was sitting in a comfortable chair in the middle of the brutally hot room, his frame outlined by the glow of the huge, blazing hearth behind him.

"Never good," Morik replied, drawing another twist of the thumbscrew from the bulky, sadistic, one-eyed (and he didn't even bother to wear an eye patch) gaoler. This one had more orcish blood than human. "Poison, I mean," the rogue clarified, his voice going tight as waves of agony shot up his arm.

"It was not the same as the poison in the vial," Vohltin explained, and he nodded to the gaoler, who walked around the back of Morik. The rogue tried to follow the half-orc's movements, but both his arms were pulled outright, shackled tight at the wrists. One hand was in a press, the other in a framework box of strange design, its panels holding the hand open, fingers extended so that the gaoler could "play" with them one at a time.

The prelate shrugged, held his hands up, and when Morik

didn't immediately reply a cat-o'-nine-tails switched across the rogue's naked back, leaving deep lines that hurt all the more for the sweat.

"You had the poison," Vohltin logically asserted, "and the insidious weapons, but it was not the same poison in the vial we recovered. A clever ruse, I suspect, to throw us off the correct path in trying to heal Captain Deudermont's wounds."

"A ruse indeed," Morik said dryly. The gaoler hit him again with the whip and raised his arm for a third strike. However, Vohltin raised his arm to hold the brutal thug at bay.

"You admit it?" Vohltin asked.

"All of it," Morik replied. "A ruse perpetrated by someone else, delivering to me and Wulfgar what you consider the evidence against us, then striking out at Deudermont when he came over to speak—"

"Enough!" said an obviously frustrated Vohltin, for he and all of the other interrogators had heard the same nonsense over and over from both Morik and Wulfgar. The prelate rose and turned to leave, shaking his head. Morik knew what that meant.

"I can tell you other things," the rogue pleaded, but Vohltin just lifted his arm and waved his hand dismissively.

Morik started to speak out again, but he lost his words and his breath as the gaoler slugged him hard in the kidney. Morik yelped and jumped, which only made the pain in his hand and thumb all the more exquisite. Still, despite all self-control, he jumped again when the gaoler struck him another blow, for the thug was wearing a metal strip across his knuckles, inlaid with several small pins.

Morik thought of his drow visitors that night long ago in the small apartment he kept near the Cutlass. Did they know what was happening? Would they come and rescue Wulfgar, and if they did, would they rescue Morik as well? He had almost told

Wulfgar about them in those first hours when they had been chained in the same room, hesitating only because he feared that Wulfgar, so obviously lost in agonizing memories, wouldn't even hear him and that somebody else might.

Wouldn't it be wonderful if the magistrates could pin on him, as well a charge that he was an associate of dark elves? Not that it mattered. Another punch slammed in, then the gaoler went for the whip again to cut a few new lines on his back.

If those drow didn't come, his fate, Morik knew, was sealed in a most painful way.

⚔ ⚔ ⚔ ⚔ ⚔

Robillard had only been gone for a few moments, but when he returned to Deudermont's room he found half a dozen priests working furiously on the captain. Camerbunne stood back, directing the group.

"He is on fire inside," the priest explained, and even from this distance Robillard could see the truth of that statement from the color of the feverish Deudermont and the great streaks of sweat that trailed down his face. Robillard noticed, too, that the room was growing colder, and he realized that a pair of the six working on Deudermont were casting spells, not to heal, but to create cold.

"I have spells that will do the same," Robillard offered. "Powerful spells on scrolls back at *Sea Sprite*. Perhaps my captain would be better served if your priests were able to focus on healing."

"Run," Camerbunne said, and Robillard did him one better, using a series of dimensional doors to get back to *Sea Sprite* in a matter of moments. The wizard fished through his many components and scroll tubes, magical items and finely crafted pieces he meant to enchant when he found the time, at last coming upon a scroll with a trio of spells for creating ice, along with the necessary components. Cursing himself for not being better prepared and vowing that he would devote all his magical energies the next day to memorizing such spells, Robillard gated back to the chamber in the chapel. The priests were still working frenetically, and the old herb woman was there as well, rubbing a creamy, white salve all over Deudermont's wet chest.

Robillard prepared the components—a vial of ice troll blood, a bit of fur from the great white bear—and unrolled the scroll, flattening it on a small table. He tore his gaze from the dying Deudermont, focusing on the task at hand, and with the discipline only a wizard might know he methodically went to work, chanting softly and waggling his fingers and hands. He poured the cold ice troll blood on his thumb and index finger, then clasped the fur between them and blew onto it, once, twice, thrice, then cast the fur to the floor along a bare wall at the side of the room. A tap-tapping began there, hail bouncing off the floor, louder as the chunks came larger and larger, until, within a matter of moments, Captain Deudermont was laid upon a new bed, a block of ice.

"This is the critical hour," Camerbunne explained. "His fever is too great, and I fear he may die of it. Blood as thin as water pours from his orifices. I have more priests waiting to step in when this group has exhausted their healing spells, and I have sent several to other chapels, even of rival gods, begging aid." Camerbunne smiled at the wizard's surprised expression. "They will come," he assured Robillard. "All of them."

Robillard was not a religious man, mainly because in his days of trying to find a god that fit his heart, he found himself distressed at the constant bickering and rivalries of the many varied churches. So he understood the compliment Camerbunne had just paid to the captain. What a great reputation Deudermont had built among the honest folk of the northern Sword Coast that all would put aside rivalries and animosity to join in for his sake.

They did come as Camerbunne promised, priests of nearly every persuasion in Luskan, flocking in six at a time to expend their healing energies over the battered captain.

Deudermont's fever broke around midnight. He opened a weary eye to find Robillard asleep next to him. The wizard's head was cradled on his folded arms on the captain's small bed, next to Deudermont's side.

"How many days?" the weak captain asked, for he recognized that something was very wrong here, very strange, as if he had just awakened from a long and terrible nightmare. Also, though he was wrapped in a sheet, he knew that he was on no normal bed, for it was too hard and his backside was wet.

Robillard jumped up at the sound, eyes wide. He put his hand to Deudermont's forehead, and his smile widened considerably when he felt that the man was cool to the touch.

"Camerbunne!" he called, drawing a curious look from the confused captain.

It was the most beautiful sight Robillard had ever seen.

⚔ ⚔ ⚔ ⚔ ⚔

"Three circuits," came the nasally voice of Jharkheld the Magistrate, a thin old wretch who took far too much pleasure in his tasks for Morik's liking.

Every day the man walked through the dungeon caverns, pointing out those whose time had come for Prisoner's Carnival and declaring, based on the severity of their crime, or, perhaps, merely from his own mood, the preparation period for each. A "circuit," according to the gaoler who regularly beat Morik, was the time it took for a slow walk around the plaza where the Prisoner's Carnival was held. So the man Jharkheld had just labeled for three circuits would be brought up to carnival and tortured by various means for about half an hour before Jharkheld even began the public hearing. It was done to rouse the crowd, Morik understood, and the old wretch Jharkheld liked the hearty cheers.

"So you have come to beat me again," Morik said when the brutish gaoler walked into the natural stone chamber where the rogue was chained to the wall. "Have you brought the holy man with you? Or the magistrate, perhaps? Is he to join us to order me up to the carnival?"

"No beatin' today, Morik the Rogue," the gaoler said. "They're not wantin' anything more from ye. Captain Deudermont's not needin' ye anymore."

"He died?" Morik asked, and he couldn't mask a bit of concern in his tone. If Deudermont had died, the charge against Wulfgar and Morik would be heinous murder, and Morik had been around Luskan long enough to witness more than a few executions of people so charged, executions by torture that lasted the better part of a day, at least.

"Nah," the gaoler said with obvious sadness in his tone. "Nah, we're not so lucky. Deudermont's livin' and all the better, so it looks like yerself and Wulfgar'll get killed quick and easy."

"Oh, joy," said Morik.

The brute paused for a moment and looked around, then waded in close to Morik and hit him a series of wicked blows about the stomach and chest.

"I'm thinkin' that Magistrate Jharkheld'll be callin' ye up to carnival soon enough," the gaoler explained. "Wanted to get in a few partin's, is all."

"My thanks," the ever-sarcastic rogue replied, and that got him a left hook across the jaw that knocked out a tooth and filled his mouth with warm blood.

⚔ ⚔ ⚔ ⚔ ⚔

Deudermont's strength was fast returning, so much so that the priests had a very difficult task in keeping the man in his bed. Still they prayed over him, offering spells of healing, and the old herbalist woman came in with pots of tea and another soothing salve.

"It could not have been Wulfgar," Deudermont protested to Robillard, who had told him the entire story since the near tragedy in front of the Cutlass.

"Wulfgar and Morik," Robillard said firmly. "I watched it, Captain, and a good thing for you that I was watching!"

"It makes no sense to me," Deudermont replied. "I know Wulfgar."

"Knew," Robillard corrected.

"But he is a friend of Drizzt and Catti-brie, and we both know that those two would have nothing to do with an assassin— nothing good, at least."

"*Was* a friend," Robillard stubbornly corrected. "Now Wulfgar makes friends the likes of Morik the Rogue, a notorious street thug, and another pair, I believe, worse by far."

"Another pair?" Deudermont asked, and even as he did, Waillan Micanty and another crewman from *Sea Sprite* entered the room. They went to the captain first, bowed and saluted, both smiling widely, for Deudermont seemed even better than he had earlier in the day when all the crew had come running to Robillard's joyous call.

"Have you found them?" the wizard asked impatiently.

"I believe we have," a smug-looking Waillan replied. "Hiding in the hold of a boat just two berths down from *Sea Sprite*."

"They haven't come out much of late," the other crewman offered, "but we talked to some men at the Cutlass who thought they knew the pair and claimed that the one-eyed sailor was dropping gold coins without regard."

Robillard nodded knowingly. So it was a contracted attack, and those two were a part of the plan.

"With your permission, Captain," the wizard said, "I should like to take *Sea Sprite* out of dock."

Deudermont looked at him curiously, for the captain had no idea what this talk might be about.

"I sent Mister Micanty on a search for two other accomplices in the attack against you," Robillard explained. "It appears that we may have located them."

"But Mister Micanty just said they were in port," Deudermont reasoned.

"They're aboard *Bowlegged Lady,* as paying passengers. When I put *Sea Sprite* behind them, all weapons to bear, they will likely turn the pair over without a fight," Robillard reasoned, his eyes aglow.

Now Deudermont managed a chuckle. "I only wish that I could go with you," he said. The three took that as their cue and turned immediately for the door.

"What of Magistrate Jharkheld?" Deudermont asked quickly before they could skitter away.

"I bade him to hold on the justice for the pair," Robillard replied, "as you requested. We shall need them to confirm that these newest two were in on the attack, as well."

Deudermont nodded and waved the trio away, falling into his own thoughts. He still didn't believe that Wulfgar could be involved, though he had no idea how he might prove it. In Luskan, as in most of the cities of Faerûn, even the appearance of criminal activity could get a man hanged, or drawn and quartered, or whatever unpleasant manner of death the presiding magistrate could think up.

✖ ✖ ✖ ✖ ✖

"An honest trader, I be, and ye got no proof otherways," Captain Pinnickers of *Bowlegged Lady* declared, leaning over the taffrail and calling out protests against the appearance of the imposing *Sea Sprite*, catapult, ballista, and ranks of archers trained on his decks.

"As I have already told you, Captain Pinnickers, we have come not for your ship, nor for you, but for a pair you harbor," Robillard answered with all due respect.

"Bah! Go away with ye, or I'll be callin' out the city guard!" the tough, old sea dog declared.

"No difficult task," Robillard replied smugly, and he motioned to the wharves beside *Bowlegged Lady*. Captain Pinnickers turned to see a hundred city soldiers or more lining the dock, grim-faced and armed for battle.

"You have nowhere to run or hide," Robillard explained. "I ask your permission one more time as a courtesy to you. For your own sake, allow me and my crew to board your ship and find the pair we seek."

"My ship!" Pinnickers said, poking a finger into his chest.

"Or I shall order my gunners to have at it," Robillard explained, standing tall and imposing at *Sea Sprite's* rail, all pretense of politeness flown. "I shall join in with spells of destruction you cannot even begin to imagine. Then we will search the wreckage for the pair ourselves."

Pinnickers seemed to shrink back just a bit, but he held fast his grim and determined visage.

"I offer you the choice one last time," Robillard said, his mock politeness returning.

"Fine choice," Pinnickers grumbled. He gave a helpless little wave, indicating that Robillard and the others should cross to his deck.

They found Creeps Sharky and Tee-a-nicknick in short order, with Robillard easily identifying them. They also found an interesting item on a beam near the tattooed man-creature: a hollow tube.

"Blowgun," Waillan Micanty explained, presenting it to Robillard.

"Indeed," said the wizard, examining the exotic weapon and quickly confirming its use from the design. "What might someone shoot from it?"

"Something small with an end shaped to fill the tube," Micanty explained. He took the weapon back, pursed his lips, and blew through the tube. "It wouldn't work well if too much wind escaped around the dart."

"Small, you say. Like a cat's claw?" Robillard asked, eyeing the captured pair. "With a pliable, feathered end?"

Following Robillard's gaze at the miserable prisoners, Waillan Micanty nodded grimly.

⚔ ⚔ ⚔ ⚔ ⚔

Wulfgar was lost somewhere far beyond pain, hanging limply from his shackled wrists, both bloody and torn. The muscles on the back of his neck and shoulders had long ago knotted, and even if he had been released and dropped to the floor, only gravity would have changed his posture.

The pain had pushed too far and too hard and had released Wulfgar from his present prison. Unfortunately for the big man, that escape had only taken him to another prison, a darker place by far, with torments beyond anything these mortal men could inflict upon him. Tempting, naked, and wickedly beautiful succubae flew around him. The great pincer-armed glabrezu came at him repeatedly, snapping, snapping, nipping pieces of his body away. All the while he heard the demonic laughter of Errtu the conqueror. Errtu the great balor who hated Drizzt Do'Urden above all other mortals and played out that anger continually upon Wulfgar.

"Wulfgar?" The call came from far away, not a throaty, demonic voice like Errtu's, but gentle and soft.

Wulfgar knew the trap, the false hopes, the feigned friendship. Errtu had played this one on him countless times, finding him in his moments of despair, lifting him from the emotional valleys, then dropping him even deeper into the pit of black hopelessness.

"I have spoken with Morik," the voice went on, but Wulfgar was no longer listening.

"He claims innocence," Captain Deudermont stubbornly continued, despite Robillard's huffing doubts at his side. "Yet the dog Sharky has implicated you both."

Trying to ignore the words, Wulfgar let out a low growl, certain that it was Errtu come again to torment him.

"Wulfgar?" Deudermont asked.

"It is useless," Robillard said flatly.

"Give me something, my friend," Deudermont went on, leaning heavily on a cane for support, for his strength had far from returned. "Some word that you are innocent so that I might tell Magistrate Jharkheld to release you."

No response came back other than the continued growl.

"Just tell me the truth," Deudermont prodded. "I don't believe that you were involved, but I must hear it from you if I am to demand a proper trial."

"He can't answer you, Captain," Robillard said, "because there is no truth to tell that will exonerate him."

"You heard Morik," Deudermont replied, for the two had just come from Morik's cell, where the little thief had vehemently proclaimed his and Wulfgar's innocence. He explained that Creeps Sharky had offered quite a treasure for Deudermont's head, but that he and Wulfgar had flatly refused.

"I heard a desperate man weave a desperate tale," Robillard replied.

"We could find a priest to interrogate him," Deudermont said. "Many of them have spells to detect such lies."

"Not allowed by Luskan law," Robillard replied. "Too many priests bring their own agendas to the interrogation. The magistrate handles his questioning in his own rather successful manner."

"He tortures them until they admit guilt, whether or not the admission is true," Deudermont supplied.

Robillard shrugged. "He gets results."

"He fills his carnival."

"How many of those in the carnival do you believe to be innocent, Captain?" Robillard asked bluntly. "Even those innocent of the particular crime for which they are being punished have no doubt committed many other atrocities."

"That is a rather cynical view of justice, my friend," Deudermont said.

"That is reality," Robillard answered.

Deudermont sighed and looked back to Wulfgar, hanging and growling, not proclaiming his innocence, not proclaiming anything at all. Deudermont called to the man again, even moved over and tapped him on the side. "You must give me a reason to believe Morik," he said.

Wulfgar felt the gentle touch of a succubus luring him into

emotional hell. With a roar, he swung his hips and kicked out, just grazing the surprised captain, but clipping him hard enough to send him staggering backward to the floor.

Robillard sent a ball of sticky goo from his wand, aiming low to pin Wulfgar's legs against the wall. The big man thrashed wildly, but with his wrists firmly chained and his legs stuck fast to the wall, the movement did little but reinvigorate the agony in his shoulders.

Robillard was before him, hissing and sneering, whispering some chant. The wizard reached up, grabbed Wulfgar's groin, and sent a shock of electricity surging into the big man that brought a howl of pain.

"No!" said Deudermont, struggling to his feet. "No more."

Robillard gave a sharp twist and spun away, his face contorted with outrage. "Do you need more proof, Captain?" he demanded.

Deudermont wanted to offer a retort but found none. "Let us leave this place," he said.

"Better that we had never come," Robillard muttered.

Wulfgar was alone again, hanging easier until Robillard's wand material dissipated, for the goo supported his weight. Soon enough, though, he was hanging by just the shackles again, his muscles bunching in renewed pain. He fell away, deeper and darker than ever before.

He wanted a bottle to crawl into, needed the burning liquid to release his mind from the torments.

12

TO HER FAMILY TRUE

Merchant Banci to speak with you," Steward Temigast announced as he stepped into the garden. Lord Feringal and Meralda had been standing quiet, enjoying the smells and the pretty sights, the flowers and the glowing orange sunset over the dark waters.

"Bring him out," the young man replied, happy to show off his newest trophy.

"Better that you come to him," Temigast said. "Banci is a nervous one, and he's in a rush. He'll not be much company to dear Meralda. I suspect he will ruin the mood of the garden."

"Well, we cannot allow that," Lord Feringal conceded. With a smile to Meralda and a pat of her hand, he started toward Temigast.

Feringal walked past the steward, and Temigast offered Meralda a wink to let her know he had just saved her from a long tenure of tedium. The young woman was far from insulted at being excluded. Also, the ease with which Feringal had agreed to go along surprised her.

Now she was free to enjoy the fabulous gardens alone, free to touch the flowers and take in their silky texture, to bask in their aromas without the constant pressure of having an adoring man following her every movement with his eyes and hands. She savored the moment and vowed that after she was lady of the castle she would spend many such moments out in this garden alone.

But she was not alone. She spun around to find Priscilla watching her.

"It is *my* garden, after all," the woman said coldly, moving to water a row of bright blue bachelor buttons.

"So Steward Temigast told me," Meralda replied.

Priscilla didn't respond, didn't even look up from her watering.

"It surprised me to learn of it," Meralda went on, her eyes narrowing. "It's so beautiful, after all."

That brought Priscilla's eyes up in a flash. The woman was very aware of insults. Scowling mightily, she strode toward Meralda. For a moment the younger woman thought Priscilla might try to strike her, or douse her, perhaps, with the bucket of water.

"My, aren't you the pretty one?" Priscilla remarked. "And only a pretty one like you could make so beautiful a garden, of course."

"Pretty inside," Meralda replied, not backing down an inch. She recognized that her posture had, indeed, caught the imposing Priscilla off guard. "And yes, I'm knowing enough about flowers to understand that the way you talk to them and the way you're touching them is what makes them grow. Begging your pardon, Lady Priscilla, but you're not for showing me any side of yourself that's favoring to flowers."

"Begging my pardon?" Priscilla echoed. She stood straight, her eyes wide, stunned by the peasant woman's bluntness. She stammered over a couple of replies before Meralda cut her off.

"By my own eyes, it's the most beautiful garden in all of Auckney," she said, breaking eye contact with Priscilla to take in the view of the flowers, emphasizing her words with a wondrous look of approval. "I thought you hateful and all."

She turned back to face the woman directly, but Meralda was not scowling. Priscilla's frown, too, had somewhat abated. "Now I'm knowing better, for anyone who could make a garden so delightful is hiding delights of her own." She ended with a disarming grin that even Priscilla could not easily dismiss.

"I have been working on this garden for years," the older woman explained. "Planting and tending, finding flowers to come to color every tenday of every summer."

"And the work's showing," Meralda sincerely congratulated her. "I'll wager there's not a garden to match it in Luskan or even Waterdeep."

Meralda couldn't suppress a bit of a smile to see Priscilla blushing. She'd found the woman's weak spot.

"It is a pretty garden," the woman said, "but Waterdeep has gardens the size of Castle Auck."

"Bigger then, but sure to be no more beautiful," the unrelenting Meralda remarked.

Priscilla stammered again, so obviously off guard from the unexpected flattery from this peasant girl. "Thank you," she managed to blurt out, and her chubby face lit up with as wide a smile as Meralda could ever have imagined. "Would you like to see something special?"

Meralda was at first wary, for she certainly had a hard time trusting Priscilla, but she decided to take a chance. Priscilla grabbed her by the hand and tugged her back into the castle, through a couple of small rooms, down a hidden stairway, and to a small open-air courtyard that seemed more like a hole in the castle design, an empty space barely wide enough for the two of them to stand side by side. Meralda laughed aloud at the sight, for while the walls were naught but cracked and weathered gray stone, there, in the middle of the courtyard, stood a row of poppies, most the usual deep red, but several a delicate pink variety that Meralda didn't recognize.

"I work with the plants in here," Priscilla explained, guiding Meralda to the pots. She knelt before the red poppies first, stroking the stem with one hand while pushing down the petals to reveal the dark core of the flower with the other. "See how rough the stem is?" she asked. Meralda nodded as she reached out to touch the solid plant.

Priscilla abruptly stood and guided Meralda to the other pots containing lighter colored poppies. Again she revealed the core of the flower, this time showing it to be white, not dark. When Meralda touched the stem of this plant she found it to be much more delicate.

"For years I have been using lighter and lighter plants," Priscilla explained. "Until I achieved this, a poppy so very different from its original stock."

"Priscilla poppies!" Meralda exclaimed. She was delighted to see surly Priscilla Auck actually break into a laugh.

"But you've earned the name," Meralda went on. "You should be taking them to the merchants when they come in on their trek between Hundelstone and Luskan. Wouldn't the ladies of Luskan pay a high price for so delicate a poppy?"

"The merchants who come to Auckney are interested only in trading for practical things," Priscilla replied. "Tools and weapons, food and drink, always drink, and perhaps a bit of Ten-Towns scrimshaw. Lord Feri has quite a collection of that."

"I'd love to see it."

Priscilla gave her a rather strange look then. "You will, I suppose," she said somewhat dryly, as if only remembering then that this was no ordinary peasant servant but the woman who would soon be the lady of Auckney.

"But you should be selling your flowers," Meralda continued encouragingly. "Take them to Luskan, perhaps, to the open air markets I've heard are so very wonderful."

The smile returned to Priscilla's face, at least a bit. "Yes, well, we shall see," she replied, a haughty undercurrent returning to her tone. "Of course, only village peasants hawk their wares."

Meralda wasn't too put off. She had made more progress with Priscilla in this one day than she ever expected to make in a lifetime.

"Ah, there you are." Steward Temigast stood in the doorway to the castle. As usual, his timing couldn't have been better. "Pray forgive us, dear Meralda, but Lord Feringal will be caught in a meeting all the night, I fear, for Banci can be a demon in bartering, and he has actually brought a few pieces that have caught Lord Feringal's eye. He bade me to inquire if you would like to visit tomorrow during the day."

Meralda looked to Priscilla, hoping for some clue, but the woman was tending her flowers again as if Meralda and Temigast weren't even there.

"Tell him that surely I will," Meralda replied.

"I pray that you are not too angry with us," said Temigast. Meralda laughed at the absurd notion. "Very well, then. Perhaps you should be right away, for the coach is waiting and I fear a storm will come up tonight," Temigast said as he moved aside.

"Your Priscilla poppies are as beautiful a flower as I've ever seen," Meralda said to the woman who would soon be kin. Priscilla caught her by the pleat of her dress, and when she turned back, startled, she grew even more surprised, for Priscilla held a small pink poppy out to her.

The two shared a smile, and Meralda swept past Temigast into the castle proper. The steward hesitated in following, though, turning his attention to Lady Priscilla. "A friend?" he asked.

"Hardly," came the cold reply. "Perhaps if she has her own flower, she will leave mine in peace."

Temigast chuckled, drawing an icy stare from Priscilla. "A friend, a *lady* friend, might not be so bad a thing as you seem to believe," the steward remarked. He turned and hastened to catch up to Meralda, leaving Priscilla kneeling in her private garden with some very curious and unexpected thoughts.

⚔ ⚔ ⚔ ⚔ ⚔

Many budding ideas rode with Meralda on the way back to her house from Castle Auck. She had handled Priscilla well, she thought, and even dared to hope that she and the woman might become real friends one day.

Even as that notion crossed her mind, it brought a burst of laughter from the young woman's lips. In truth, she couldn't imagine ever having a close friendship with Priscilla, who would always, always, consider herself Meralda's superior.

But Meralda knew better now, and not because of that day's interaction with the woman but rather, because of the previous night's interaction with Jaka Sculi. How much better Meralda understood the world now, or at least her corner of it. She had used the previous night as a turning point. It had taken that one moment of control, by Meralda and for Meralda, to accept the wider and less appealing responsibility that had been thrown her way. Yes, she would play Lord Feringal now, bringing him on her heel to the wedding chapel of Castle Auck. She, and more importantly, her family, would get from him what they required. While such gains would come at a cost to Meralda, it was a cost

193

that this new woman, no more a girl, would pay willingly and with some measure of control.

She was glad she hadn't seen much of Lord Feringal tonight, though. No doubt he would have tried to force himself on her, and Meralda doubted she could have maintained the self—control necessary to not laugh at him.

Smiling, satisfied, the young woman stared out the coach's window as the twisting road rolled by. She saw him, and suddenly her smile disappeared. Jaka Sculi stood atop a rocky bluff, a lone figure staring down at the place where the driver normally let Meralda out.

Meralda leaned out the coach window opposite Jaka so she would not be seen by him. "Good driver, please take me all the way to my door this night."

"Oh, but I hoped you'd ask me that this particular ride, Miss Meralda," Liam Woodgate replied. "Seems one of my horses is having a bit of a problem with a shoe. Might your father have a straight bar and a hammer?"

"Of course he does," Meralda replied. "Take me to my house, and I'm sure that me da'll help you fix that shoe."

"Good enough, then!" the driver replied. He gave the reins a bit of a snap that sent the horses trotting along more swiftly.

Meralda fell back in her seat and stared out the window at the silhouette of a slender man she knew to be Jaka from his forlorn posture. In her mind she could see his expression clearly. She almost reconsidered her course and told the driver to let her out. Maybe she should go to Jaka again and make love under the stars one more time, be free for yet another night. Perhaps she should run away with him and live her life for her sake and no one else's.

No, she couldn't do that to her mother, or her father, or Tori. Meralda was a daughter her parents could depend upon to do the right thing. The right thing, Meralda knew, was to put her affections for Jaka Sculi far behind her.

The coach pulled up before the Ganderlay house. Liam Woodgate, a nimble fellow, hopped down and pulled open Meralda's door before she could reach for the latch.

"You're not needing to do that," the young woman stated as the gnome helped her out of the carriage.

"But you're to be the lady of Auckney," the cheery old fellow replied with a smile and a wink. "Can't be having you treated like a peasant, now can we?"

"It's not so bad," Meralda replied, adding, "being a peasant, I mean." Liam laughed heartily. "Gets you out of the castle at night."

"And gets you back in, whenever you're wanting," Liam replied. "Steward Temigast says I'm at your disposal, Miss Meralda. I'm to take you and your family, if you so please, wherever you're wanting to go."

Meralda smiled widely and nodded her thanks. She noticed then that her grim-faced father had opened the door and was standing just within the house.

"Da!" Meralda called. "Might you help my friend . . ." The woman paused and looked to the driver. "Why, I'm not even knowing your proper name," she remarked.

"Most noble ladies don't take the time to ask," he replied, and both he and Meralda laughed again. "Besides, we all look alike to you big folks." He winked mischievously, then bowed low. "Liam Woodgate, at your service."

Dohni Ganderlay walked over. "A short stay at the castle this night," he remarked suspiciously.

"Lord Feringal got busy with a merchant," Meralda replied. "I'm to return on the morrow. Liam here's having a bit of trouble with a horseshoe. Might you help him?"

Dohni looked past the driver to the team and nodded. "'Course," he answered. "Get yourself inside, girl," he instructed Meralda. "Your ma's taken ill again."

Meralda bolted for the house. She found her mother in bed, hot with fever again, her eyes sunken deep into her face. Tori was kneeling beside the bed, a mug of water in one hand, a wet towel in the other.

"She got the weeps soon after you left," Tori explained, a nasty affliction that had been plaguing Biaste off and on for several months.

Looking at her mother, Meralda wanted to fall down and cry. How frail the woman appeared, how unpredictable her health. It was as if Biaste Ganderlay had been walking a fine line on the edge of her own grave day after day. Good spirits alone had sustained the woman these last days, since Lord Feringal had come calling, Meralda knew. Desperately, the young woman grasped at the only medication she had available.

"Oh, Ma," she said, feigning exasperation. "Aren't you picking a fine time to fall ill again?"

"Meralda," Biaste Ganderlay breathed, and even that seemed a labor to her.

"We'll just have to get you better and be quick about it," Meralda said sternly.

"Meralda!" Tori complained.

"I told you about Lady Priscilla's garden," Meralda went on, ignoring her sister's protest. "Get better, and be quick, because tomorrow you're to join me at the castle. We'll walk the garden together."

"And me?" Tori pleaded. Meralda turned to regard her and noticed that she had another audience member. Dohni Ganderlay stood at the door, leaning on the jamb, a surprised expression on his strong but weary face.

"Yeah, Tori, you can join us," Meralda said, trying hard to ignore her father, "but you must promise that you'll behave."

"Oh, Ma, please get better quickly!" Tori implored Biaste, clutching the woman's hand firmly. It did seem as if the sickly woman showed a little bit more life at that moment.

"Go, Tori," Meralda instructed. "Run to the coach driver—Liam's his name—and tell him that we three'll be needing a ride to the castle at midday tomorrow. We can't have Ma walking all the way."

Tori ran off as instructed, and Meralda bent low over her mother. "Get well," she whispered, kissing the woman on the forehead. Biaste smiled and nodded her intent to try.

Meralda walked out of the room under the scrutinizing gaze of Dohni Ganderlay. She heard the man pull the curtain closed to her parents' room, then follow her to the middle of the common room.

"Will he let you bring them both?" Dohni asked, softly so that Biaste would not hear.

She shrugged. "I'm to be his wife, and that's his idea. He'd be a fool to not grant me this one favor."

Dohni Ganderlay's face melted into a grateful smile as he fell into his daughter, hugging her closely. Though she couldn't see his face, Meralda knew that he was crying.

She returned that hug tenfold, burying her face in her father's strong shoulder, a not so subtle reminder to her that, though she was being the brave soldier for the good of her family, she was still, in many ways, a scared little girl.

How warm it felt to her, a reassurance that she was doing the right thing, when her father kissed her on top of her head.

⚔ ⚔ ⚔ ⚔ ⚔

Up on the hill a short distance away, Jaka Sculi watched Dohni Ganderlay help the coachman fix the horseshoe, the two of them talking and chuckling as if they were old friends. Considering the treatment Dohni Ganderlay had given him the previous night, the sight nearly leveled poor, jealous Jaka. Didn't Dohni understand that Lord Feringal wanted the same things for which Dohni had chastised him? Couldn't the man see that Jaka's intentions were better than Lord Feringal's, that he was more akin to Meralda's class and background and would therefore be a better choice for her?

Dohni went back into the house then, and Meralda's sister soon emerged, jumping for joy as she rushed over to speak with the coachman.

"Have I no allies?" Jaka asked quietly, chewing on his bottom lip petulantly. "Are they all against me, blinded by the unearned wealth and prestige of Feringal Auck? Damn you, Meralda! How could you betray me so?" he cried, heedless if his wail carried down to Tori and the driver.

He couldn't look at them anymore. Jaka clenched his fists and smacked them hard against his eyes, falling on his back to the hard ground. "What justice is this life?" he cried. "O fie, to have been born a pauper, I, when the mantle of a king would better suit! What justice allows that fool Feringal to claim the prize? What universal order so decrees that the purse is stronger than the loins? O fie this life! And damn Meralda!"

Long after Liam Woodgate had repaired the shoe, shared a drink with Dohni Ganderlay, and departed; long after Meralda's mother had fallen into a comfortable sleep at last; long after Meralda had confided to Tori all that had happened with Jaka, Feringal, Priscilla and Temigast; and long after the storm Temigast had predicted arrived with all its fury, pelting the prone Jaka with drenching rain and buffeting him with cold ocean winds; he lay there, muttering curses and mewling like a trapped cat.

He still lay upon the hill when the clouds were swept away, making room for a brilliant sunrise, when the workers made their way to the fields. One worker, the only dwarf among the group, moved over to the young man and nudged him with the toe of one boot.

"You dead or dead drunk?" the gnarly creature asked.

Jaka rolled away from him, stifling the groan that came from the stiffness in his every muscle and joint. Too wounded in pride to respond, too angry to face anyone, the young man scrambled up to his feet and ran off.

"Strange bird, that one," the dwarf remarked, and those around him nodded.

Much later that morning, when his clothes had dried and with the chill of the night's wind and rain still deep under his skin, Jaka returned to the fields for his workday, suffering the berating of the field boss and the teasing of the other workers. He fought hard to tend to his work properly but it was a struggle, for his thoughts remained jumbled, his spirit sagged, and his skin felt clammy under the relentless sun.

It only got worse for him when he saw Lord Feringal's coach roll by on the road below, first heading toward Meralda's house, then back again, loaded with more than one passenger.

They were all against him.

⚔ ⚔ ⚔ ⚔ ⚔

Meralda enjoyed that day at Castle Auck more than any of her previous visits, though Lord Feringal did little to hide his disappointment that he would not have Meralda to himself. Priscilla boiled at the thought of three peasants in her wondrous garden.

Still, Feringal got over it soon enough, and Priscilla, with some coughing reminders from Steward Temigast, remained outwardly polite. All that mattered to Meralda was to see her mother smiling and holding her frail face up to the sunlight, basking in the warmth and the sweet scents. The scene only strengthened Meralda's resolve and gave her hope for the future.

They didn't remain at the castle for long, just an hour in the garden, a light lunch, then another short stroll around the flowers. At Meralda's bidding, an apology of sorts to Lord Feringal for the unexpected additions, the young lord rode in the coach back to the Ganderlay house, leaving a sour Priscilla and Temigast at the castle door.

"Peasants," Priscilla muttered. "I should batter that brother of mine about the head for bringing such folk to Castle Auck."

Temigast chuckled at the woman's predictability. "They are uncultured, indeed," the steward admitted. "Not unpleasant, though."

"Mud-eaters," said Priscilla.

"Perhaps you view this situation from an errant perspective," Temigast said, turning a wry smile on the woman.

"There is but one way to view peasants," Priscilla retorted. "One must look down upon them."

"But the Ganderlays are to be peasants no more," Temigast couldn't resist reminding her.

Priscilla scoffed doubtfully.

"Perhaps you should view this as a challenge," suggested Temigast. He paused until Priscilla turned a curious eye upon him. "Like coaxing a delicate flower from a bulb."

"Ganderlays? Delicate?" Priscilla remarked incredulously.

"Perhaps they could be with the help of Lady Priscilla Auck," said Temigast. "What a grand accomplishment it would be for Priscilla to enlighten them so, a feat that would make her brother brag to every merchant who passed through, an amazing accomplishment that would no doubt reach the ears of Luskan society. A plume in Priscilla's bonnet."

Priscilla snorted again, her expression unconvinced, but she said no more, not even her usual muttered insults. As she walked away, her expression changed to one of thoughtful curiosity, in the midst of some planning, perhaps.

Temigast recognized that she had taken his bait, or nibbled it, at least. The old steward shook his head. It never ceased to amaze him how most nobles considered themselves so much better than the people they ruled, even though that rule was always no more than an accident of birth.

13
PRISONER'S CARNIVAL

It was an hour of beatings and taunting, of eager peasants throwing rotten food and spitting in their faces.

It was an hour that Wulfgar didn't even register. The man was so far removed from the spectacle of Prisoner's Carnival, so well hidden within a private emotional place, a place created through the mental discipline that had allowed him to survive the torments of Errtu, that he didn't even see the twisted, perverted faces of the peasants or hear the magistrate's assistant stirring up the mob for the real show when Jharkheld joined them on the huge stage. The barbarian was bound, as were the other three, with his hands behind his back and secured to a strong wooden post. Weights were chained around his ankles and another one around his neck, heavy enough to bow the head of powerful Wulfgar.

He had recognized the crowd with crystalline clarity. The drooling peasants, screaming for blood and torture, the excited, almost elated, ogre guards working the crowd, and the unfortunate prisoners. He'd seen them for what they were, and his mind had transformed them into something else, something demonic, the twisted, leering faces of Errtu's minions, slobbering over him with their acidic drool, nipping at him with their sharpened fangs and horrid breath. He smelled the fog of Errtu's home again, the sulfuric Abyss burning his nostrils and his throat, adding an extra sting to all of his many, many wounds. He felt the itching of the centipedes and spiders crawling over and inside his skin. Always on the edge of death. Always wishing for it.

As those torments had continued, day after tenday after month, Wulfgar had found his escape in a tiny corner of his consciousness. Locked inside, he was oblivious to his surroundings. Here at the carnival he went to that place.

One by one the prisoners were taken from the posts and paraded around, sometimes close enough to be abused by the peasants, other times led to instruments of torture. Those included cross ties for whipping; a block and tackle designed to hoist victims into the air by a pole lashed under their arms locked behind their back; and ankle stocks to hang prisoners upside down in buckets of filthy water, or, in the case of unfortunate Creeps Sharky, a bucket of urine. Creeps cried through most of it, while Tee-a-nicknick and Wulfgar stoically accepted whatever punishment the magistrate's assistant could dish out without a sound other than the occasional, unavoidable gasp of air being blasted from their lungs. Morik took it all in stride, protesting his innocence and throwing witty comments around, which only got him beaten all the worse.

Magistrate Jharkheld appeared, entering to howls and cheers, wearing a thick black robe and cap, and carrying a silver scroll tube. He moved to the center of the stage, standing between the prisoners to eye them deliberately one by one.

Jharkheld stepped out front. With a dramatic flourish he presented the scroll tube, the damning documents, bringing eager shouts and cheers. Each movement distinct, with an appropriate response mounting to a crescendo, Jharkheld popped the cap from the tube's end and removed the documents. Unrolling them, the magistrate showed the documents to the crowd one at a time, reading each prisoner's name.

The magistrate surely seemed akin to Errtu, the carnival barker, ordering the torments. Even his voice sounded to the barbarian like that of the balor: grating, guttural, inhuman.

"I shall tell to you a tale," Jharkheld began, "of treachery and deceit, of friendship abused and murder attempted for profit. That man!" he said powerfully, pointing to Creeps Sharky, "that man told it to me in full, and the sheer horror of it has stolen my sleep every night since." The magistrate went on to detail the crime as Sharky had presented it. All of it had been Morik's idea, according to the wretch. Morik and Wulfgar had lured Deudermont into the open so that Tee-a-nicknick could sting him with a poisoned dart. Morik was supposed to sting the honorable captain, too, using a different variety of poison to ensure that the priests could not save the man, but the city guard had arrived too quickly for that second assault. Throughout the planning, Creeps Sharky had tried to talk them out of it, but he'd said nothing to anyone else out of fear of Wulfgar. The big man had threatened to tear his head from his shoulders and kick it down every street in Luskan.

Enough of those gathered in the crowd had fallen victim to Wulfgar's enforcer tactics at the Cutlass to find that last part credible.

"You four are charged with conspiracy and intent to heinously murder goodman Captain Deudermont, a visitor in excellent standing to our fair city," Jharkheld said when he completed the story and let the howls and jeers from the crowd die away. "You four are charged with the infliction of serious harm to the same.

In the interest of justice and fairness, we will hear your answers to these charges."

He walked over to Creeps Sharky. "Did I relate the tale as you told it to me?" he asked.

"You did sir, you did," Creeps Sharky eagerly replied. "They done it, all of it!"

Many in the crowd yelled out their doubts about that, while others merely laughed at the man, so pitiful did he sound.

"Mister Sharky," Jharkheld went on, "do you admit your guilt to the first charge?"

"Innocent!" Sharky protested, sounding confident that his cooperation had allowed him to escape the worst of the carnival, but the jeers of the crowd all but drowned out his voice.

"Do you admit your guilt to the second charge against you?"

"Innocent!" the man said defiantly, and he gave a gap-toothed smile to the magistrate.

"Guilty!" cried an old woman. "Guilty he is, and deserving to die horrible for trying to blame the others!"

A hundred cries arose agreeing with the woman, but Creeps Sharky held fast his smile and apparent confidence. Jharkheld walked out to the front of the platform and patted his hands in the air, trying to calm the crowd. When at last they quieted he said, "The tale of Creeps Sharky has allowed us to convict the others. Thus, we have promised leniency to the man for his cooperation." That brought a rumble of boos and derisive whistles. "For his honesty and for the fact that he, by his own words—undisputed by the others—was not directly involved."

"I'll dispute it!" Morik cried, and the crowd howled. Jharkheld merely motioned to one of the guards, and Morik got the butt of a club slammed into his belly.

More boos erupted throughout the crowd, but Jharkheld

denied the calls and a smile widened on the face of clever Creeps Sharky.

"We promised him leniency," Jharkheld said, throwing up his hands as if there was nothing he could do about it. "Thus, we shall kill him quickly."

That stole the smile from the face of Creeps Sharky and turned the chorus of boos into roars of agreement.

Sputtering protests, his legs failing him, Creeps Sharky was dragged to a block and forced to kneel before it.

"Innocent I am!" he cried, but his protest ended abruptly as one of the guards forced him over the block, slamming his face against the wood. A huge executioner holding a monstrous axe stepped up to the block.

"The blow won't fall clean if you struggle," a guard advised him.

Creeps Sharky lifted his head. "But ye promised me!"

The guards slammed him back down on the block. "Quit yer wiggling!" one of them ordered. The terrified Creeps jerked free and fell to the platform, rolling desperately. There was pandemonium as the guards grabbed at him. He kicked wildly, the crowd howled and laughed, and cries of "Hang him!" "Keel haul!" and other horrible suggestions for execution echoed from every corner of the square.

✕ ✕ ✕ ✕ ✕

"Lovely gathering," Captain Deudermont said sarcastically to Robillard. They stood with several other members of *Sea Sprite* among the leaping and shouting folk.

"Justice," the wizard stated firmly.

"I wonder," the captain said pensively. "Is it justice, or entertainment? There is a fine line, my friend, and considering this almost daily spectacle, it's one I believe the authorities in Luskan long ago crossed."

"You were the one who wanted to come here," Robillard reminded him.

"It is my duty to be here in witness," Deudermont answered.

"I meant here in Luskan," Robillard clarified. "You wanted to come to this city, Captain. I preferred Waterdeep."

Deudermont fixed his wizard friend with a stern stare, but he had no rebuttal to offer.

⚔ ⚔ ⚔ ⚔ ⚔

"Stop yer wiggling!" the guard yelled at Creeps, but the dirty man fought all the harder, kicking and squealing desperately. He managed to evade their grasps for some time to the delight of the onlookers who were thoroughly enjoying the spectacle. Creeps's frantic movements brought his gaze in line with Jharkheld. The magistrate fixed him with a glare so intense and punishing that Creeps stopped moving.

"Draw and quarter him," Jharkheld said slowly and deliberately.

The gathering reached a new level of joyous howling.

Creeps had witnessed that ultimate form of execution only twice in his years, and that was enough to steal the blood from his face, to send him into a fit of trembling, to make him, right there in front of a thousand onlookers, wet himself.

"Ye promised," he mouthed, barely able to draw breath, but loud enough for the magistrate to hear and come over to him.

"I did promise leniency," Jharkheld said quietly, "and so I will honor my word to you, but only if you cooperate. The choice is yours to make."

Those in the crowd close enough to hear groaned their protests, but Jharkheld ignored them.

"I have four horses in waiting," Jharkheld warned.

Creeps started crying.

"Take him to the block," the magistrate instructed the guards. This time Creeps made no move against them, offered no resistance at all as they dragged him back, forced him into a kneeling position, and pushed his head down.

"Ye promised," Creeps softly cried his last words, but the cold magistrate only smiled and nodded. Not to Creeps, but to the large man standing beside him.

The huge axe swept down, the crowd gasped as one, then broke into howls. The head of Creeps Sharky tumbled to the platform and rolled a short distance. One of the guards rushed to it and held it up, turning it to face the headless body. Legend had it that with a perfect, swift cut and a quick guard the beheaded man might still be conscious for a split second, long enough to see his own body, his face contorted into an expression of the purest, most exquisite horror.

Not this time, though, for Creeps Sharky wore the same sad expression.

✕ ✕ ✕ ✕ ✕

"Beautiful," Morik muttered sarcastically at the other end of the platform. "Yet, it's a better fate by far than the rest of us will find this day."

Flanking him on either side, neither Wulfgar nor Tee-a-nicknick offered a reply.

"Just beautiful," the doomed rogue said again. Morik was not unaccustomed to finding himself in rather desperate situations, but this was the first time he ever felt himself totally without options. He shot Tee-a-nicknick a look of utter contempt then turned his attention to Wulfgar. The big man seemed so impassive and distanced from the mayhem around them that Morik envied him his oblivion.

The rogue heard Jharkheld's continuing banter as he worked up the crowd. He apologized for the rather unentertaining execution of Creeps Sharky, explaining the occasional need for such mercy. Else, why would anyone ever confess?

Morik drowned out the magistrate's blather and willed his mind to a place where he was safe and happy. He thought of Wulfgar, of how, against all odds, they had become friends. Once they had been rivals, the new barbarian rising in reputation on Half-Moon Street, particularly after he had killed the brute, Tree Block Breaker. The only remaining operator with a reputation to protect, Morik had considered eliminating Wulfgar, though murder had never really been the rogue's preferred method.

Then there had come the strangest of encounters. A dark elf—a damned drow!—had come to Morik in his rented room, had just walked in without warning, and had bade Morik to keep a close watch over Wulfgar but not to hurt the man. The dark elf had paid Morik well. Realizing that gold coins were better payment than the sharpened edge of drow weapons, the rogue had gone along with the plan, watching Wulfgar more and more closely as the days slipped past. They'd even becoming drinking partners, spending late nights, often until dawn, together at the docks.

Morik had never heard from that dark elf again. If the order had come from for him to eliminate Wulfgar, he doubted he would have accepted the contract. He realized now that if he heard the dark elves were coming to kill the barbarian, Morik would have stood by Wulfgar.

Well, the rogue admitted more realistically, he might not have stood beside Wulfgar, but he would have warned the barbarian, then run far, far away.

Now there was nowhere to run. Morik wondered briefly again if those dark elves would show up to save this human in whom they had taken such an interest. Perhaps a legion of drow warriors would storm Prisoner's Carnival, their fine blades slicing apart the macabre onlookers as they worked their way to the platform.

The fantasy could not hold, for Morik knew they would not be coming for Wulfgar. Not this time.

"I am truly sorry, my friend," he apologized to Wulfgar, for Morik could not dismiss the notion that this situation was largely his fault.

Wulfgar didn't reply. Morik understood that the big man had not even heard his words, that his friend was already gone from this place, fallen deep within himself.

Perhaps that was the best course to take. Looking at the sneering mob, hearing Jharkheld's continuing speech, watching the headless body of Creeps Sharky being dragged across the platform, Morik wished that he, too, could so distance himself.

⚔ ⚔ ⚔ ⚔ ⚔

The magistrate again told the tale of Creeps Sharky, of how these other three had conspired to murder that most excellent man, Captain Deudermont. Jharkheld made his way over to Wulfgar. He looked at the doomed man, shook his head, then turned back to the mob, prompting a response.

There came a torrent of jeers and curses.

"You are the worst of them all!" Jharkheld yelled in the barbarian's face. "He was your friend, and you betrayed him!"

"Keel haul 'im on Deudermont's own ship!" came one anonymous demand.

"Draw and quarter 'im, and feed 'im to the fishes!" yelled another.

Jharkheld turned to the crowd and lifted his hand, demanding silence, and after a bristling moment they obeyed. "This one," the magistrate said, "I believe we shall save for last."

That brought another chorus of howls.

"And what a day we shall have," said Jharkheld, the showman barker. "Three remaining, and all of them refusing to confess!"

"Justice," Morik whispered under his breath.

Wulfgar stared straight ahead, unblinkingly, and only thoughts of poor Morik held him from laughing in Jharkheld's ugly old face. Did the magistrate really believe that he could do anything to Wulfgar worse than the torments of Errtu? Could Jharkheld produce Catti-brie on the stage and ravish her, then dismember her in front of Wulfgar, as Errtu had done so many times? Could he bring in an illusionary Bruenor and bite through the dwarf's skull, then use the remaining portion of the dwarf's head as a bowl for brain stew? Could he inflict more physical pain upon Wulfgar than the demon who had practiced such torturing arts for millennia? At the end of it all, could Jharkheld bring Wulfgar back from the edge of death time and again so that it would begin anew?

Wulfgar realized something profound and actually brightened. This was where Jharkheld and his stage paled against the Abyss. He would die here. At last he would be free.

⚔ ⚔ ⚔ ⚔ ⚔

Jharkheld ran from the barbarian, skidding to a stop before Morik and grabbing the man's slender face in his strong hand, turning Morik roughly to face him. "Do you admit your guilt?" he screamed.

Morik almost did it, almost screamed out that he had indeed conspired to kill Deudermont. Yes, he thought, a quick plan formulating in his mind. He would admit to the conspiracy, but with the tattooed pirate only, trying to somehow save his innocent friend.

His hesitation cost him the chance at that time, for Jharkheld gave a disgusted snort and snapped a backhanded blow across Morik's face, clipping the underside of the rogue's nose, a stinging technique that brought waves of pain shifting behind Morik's eyes. By the time the man blinked away his surprise and pain, Jharkheld had moved on, looming before Tee-a-nicknick.

"Tee-a-nicknick," the magistrate said slowly, emphasizing every syllable, his method reminding the gathering of how strange, how foreign, this half-man was. "Tell me, Tee-a-nicknick, what role did you play?"

The tattooed half-qullan pirate stared straight ahead, did not blink, and did not speak.

Jharkheld snapped his fingers in the air, and his assistant ran out from the side of the platform, handing Jharkheld a wooden tube.

Jharkheld publicly inspected the item, showing it to the crowd. "With this seemingly innocent pole, our painted friend here can blow forth a dart as surely as an archer can launch an arrow," he explained. "And on that dart, the claw of a small cat, for instance, our painted friend can coat some of the most exquisite poisons. Concoctions that can make blood leak from your eyes, bring a fever so hot as to turn your skin the color of fire, or fill your nose and throat with enough phlegm to make every breath a forced and wretched-tasting labor are but a sampling of his vile repertoire."

The crowd played on every word, growing more disgusted and angry. Master of the show, Jharkheld measured their response and played to them, waiting for the right moment.

"Do you admit your guilt?" Jharkheld yelled suddenly in Tee-a-nicknick's face.

The tattooed pirate stared straight ahead, did not blink, and did not speak. Had he been full-blooded qullan, he might have cast a confusion spell at that moment, sending the magistrate stumbling away, baffled and forgetful, but Tee-a-nicknick was not pure blooded and had none of the innate magical abilities of his race. He did have qullan concentration, though, a manner, much like Wulfgar's, of removing himself from the present scene before him.

"You shall admit all," Jharkheld promised, wagging his finger angrily in the man's face, unaware of the pirate's heritage and discipline, "but it will be too late."

The crowd went into a frenzy as the guards pulled the pirate free of his binding post and dragged him from one instrument of torture to another. After about half an hour of beating and whipping, pouring salt water over the wounds, even taking one of Tee-a-nicknick's eyes with a hot poker, the pirate still showed no signs of speaking. No confession, no pleading or begging, hardly even a scream.

Frustrated beyond endurance, Jharkheld went to Morik just to keep things moving. He didn't even ask the man to confess. In fact he slapped Morik viciously and repeatedly every time the man tried to say a word. Soon they had Morik on the rack, the torturer giving the wheel a slight, almost imperceptible—except to the agonized Morik—turn every few moments.

Meanwhile, Tee-a-nicknick continued to bear the brunt of the torment. When Jharkheld went to him again, the pirate couldn't stand, so the guards pulled him to his feet and held him.

"Ready to tell me the truth?" Jharkheld asked.

Tee-a-nicknick spat in his face.

"Bring the horses!" the magistrate shrieked, trembling with rage. The crowd went wild. It wasn't often that the magistrate went to the trouble of a drawing and quartering. Those who had witnessed it boasted it was the greatest show of all.

Four white horses, each trailing a sturdy rope, were ridden into the square. The crowd was pushed back by the city guard as the horses approached the platform. Magistrate Jharkheld guided his men through the precise movements of the show. Soon Tee-a-nicknick was securely strapped in place, wrists and ankles bound one to each horse.

On the magistrate's signal, the riders nudged their powerful beasts, one toward each point on the compass. The tattooed pirate instinctively bunched up his muscles, fighting back, but resistance was useless. Tee-a-nicknick was stretched to the limits of his physical coil. He grunted and gasped, and the riders and their well-trained mounts kept him at the very limits. A moment later, there came the loud popping of a shoulder snapping out of joint; soon after one of Tee-a-nicknick's knees exploded.

Jharkheld motioned for the riders to hold steady, and he walked over to the man, a knife in one hand and a whip in the other. He showed the gleaming blade to the groaning Tee-a-nicknick, rolling it over and over before the man's eyes. "I can end the agony," the magistrate promised. "Confess your guilt, and I will kill you swiftly."

The tattooed half-qullan grunted and looked away. On Jharkheld's wave, the riders stepped their horses out a bit more.

The man's pelvis shattered, and how he howled at last! How the crowd yelled in appreciation as the skin started to rip!

"Confess!" Jharkheld yelled.

"I stick him!" Tee-a-nicknick cried. Before the crowd could

even groan its disappointment Jharkheld yelled, "Too late!" and cracked his whip.

The horses jumped away, tearing Tee-a-nicknick's legs from his torso. Then the two horses bound to the man's wrists had him out straight, his face twisted in the horror of searing agony and impending death for just an instant before quartering that portion as well.

Some gasped, some vomited, and most cheered wildly.

"Justice," Robillard said to the growling, disgusted Deudermont. "Such displays make murder an unpopular profession."

Deudermont snorted. "It merely feeds the basest of human emotions," he argued.

"I don't disagree," Robillard replied. "I don't make the laws, but unlike your barbarian friend, I abide by them. Are we any more sympathetic to pirates we catch out on the high seas?"

"We do as we must," Deudermont argued. "We do not torture them to sate our twisted hunger."

"But we take satisfaction in sinking them," Robillard countered. "We don't cry for their deaths, and often, when we are in pursuit of a companion privateer, we do not stop to pull them from the sharks. Even when we do take them as prisoners, we subsequently drop them at the nearest port, often Luskan, for justice such as this."

Deudermont had run out of arguments, so he just stared ahead. Still, to the civilized and cultured captain's thinking, this display in no way resembled justice.

Jharkheld went back to work on Morik and Wulfgar before the many attendants had even cleared the blood and grime from the square in front of the platform.

"You see how long it took him to admit the truth?" the magistrate said to Morik. "Too late, and so he suffered to the end. Will you be as much a fool?"

Morik, whose limbs were beginning to pull past the breaking point, started to reply, started to confess, but Jharkheld put a finger over the man's lips. "Now is not the time," he explained.

Morik started to speak again, so Jharkheld had him tightly gagged, a dirty rag stuffed into his mouth, another tied around his head to secure it.

The magistrate moved around the back of the rack and produced a small wooden box, the rat box it was called. The crowd howled its pleasure. Recognizing the horrible instrument, Morik's eyes popped wide and he struggled futilely against the unyielding bonds. He hated rats, had been terrified of them all of his life.

His worst nightmare was coming true.

Jharkheld came to the front of the platform again and held the box high, turning it slowly so that the crowd could see its ingenious design. The front was a metal mesh cage, the other three walls and the ceiling solid wood. The bottom was wooden as well, but it had a sliding panel that left an exit hole. A rat would be pushed into the box, then the box would be put on Morik's bared belly and the bottom door removed. Then the box would be lit on fire.

The rat would escape through the only means possible—through Morik.

A gloved man came out holding the rat and quickly got the boxed creature in place atop Morik's bared belly. He didn't light it then, but rather, let the animal walk around, its feet tapping on flesh, every now and then nipping. Morik struggled futilely.

Jharkheld went to Wulfgar. Given the level of excitement and enjoyment running through the mob, the magistrate wondered how he would top it all, wondered what he might do to this stoic behemoth that would bring more spectacle than the previous two executions.

"Like what we're doing to your friend Morik?" the magistrate asked.

Wulfgar, who had seen the bowels of Errtu's domain, who had been chewed by creatures that would terrify an army of rats, did not reply.

⚔ ⚔ ⚔ ⚔ ⚔

"They hold you in the highest regard," Robillard remarked to Deudermont. "Rarely has Luskan seen so extravagant a multiple execution."

The words echoed in Captain Deudermont's mind, particularly the first sentence. To think that his standing in Luskan had brought this about. No, it had provided sadistic Jharkheld with an excuse for such treatment of fellow human beings, even guilty ones. Deudermont remained unconvinced that either Wulfgar or Morik had been involved. The realization that this was all done in his honor disgusted Deudermont profoundly.

"Mister Micanty!" he ordered, quickly scribbling a note he handed to the man.

"No!" Robillard insisted, understanding what Deudermont had in mind and knowing how greatly such an action would cost *Sea Sprite,* both with the authorities and the mob. "He deserves death!"

"Who are you to judge?" Deudermont asked.

"Not I!" the wizard protested. "Them," he explained, sweeping his arm out to the crowd.

Deudermont scoffed at the absurd notion.

"Captain, we'll be forced to leave Luskan, and we'll not be welcomed back soon," Robillard pointed out.

"They will forget as soon as the next prisoners are paraded out for their enjoyment, likely on the morrow's dawn." He gave a wry, humorless smile. "Besides, you don't like Luskan anyway."

Robillard groaned, sighed, and threw up his hands in defeat as Deudermont, too civilized a man, gave the note to Micanty and bade him to rush it to the magistrate.

⚔ ⚔ ⚔ ⚔ ⚔

"Light the box!" Jharkheld called from the stage after the guards had brought Wulfgar around so that the barbarian could witness Morik's horror.

Wulfgar could not distance himself from the sight of setting the rat cage on fire. The frightened creature scurried around, and then began to burrow.

The scene of such pain inflicted on a friend entered into Wulfgar's private domain, clawed through his wall of denial, even as the rat bit through Morik's skin. The barbarian loosed a growl so threatening, so preternaturally feral, that it turned the eyes of those near him from the spectacle of Morik's horror. Huge muscles bunched and flexed, and Wulfgar snapped his torso out to the side, launching the man holding him there away. The barbarian lashed out with one leg, swinging the iron ball and chain so that it wrapped the legs of the other man holding him. A sharp tug sent the guard to the ground.

Wulfgar pulled and pulled as others slammed against him, as clubs battered him, as Jharkheld, angered by the distraction, yelled for Morik's gag to be removed. Somehow, incredibly, powerful Wulfgar pulled his arms free and lurched for the rack.

Guard after guard slammed into him. He threw them aside as if they were children, but so many rushed the barbarian that he couldn't beat a path to Morik, who was screaming in agony now.

"Get it off me!" cried Morik.

Suddenly Wulfgar was facedown. Jharkheld got close enough to snap his whip across the man's back with a loud *crack!*

"Admit your guilt!" the frenzied magistrate demanded as he beat Wulfgar viciously.

Wulfgar growled and struggled. Another guard tumbled away, and another got his nose splattered all over his face by a heavy slug.

"Get it off me!" Morik cried again.

The crowd loved it. Jharkheld felt certain he'd reached a new level of showmanship.

"Stop!" came a cry from the audience that managed to penetrate the general howls and hoots. "Enough!"

The excitement died away fast as the crowd turned and recognized the speaker as Captain Deudermont of *Sea Sprite*. Deudermont looked haggard and leaned heavily on a cane.

Magistrate Jharkheld's trepidation only heightened as Waillan Micanty pushed past the guards to climb onto the stage. He rushed to Jharkheld's side and presented him with Deudermont's note.

The magistrate pulled it open and read it. Surprised, stunned even, he grew angrier by the word. Jharkheld looked up at Deudermont, casually motioned for one of the guards to gag the screaming Morik again, and for the others to pull the battered Wulfgar up to his feet.

Unconcerned for himself and with no comprehension of what was happening beyond the torture of Morik, Wulfgar bolted from their grasp. He staggered and tripped over the swinging balls and chains but managed to dive close enough to reach out and slap the burning box and rat from Morik's belly.

He was beaten again and hauled before Jharkheld.

"It will only get worse for Morik now," the sadistic magistrate promised quietly, and he turned to Deudermont, a look of outrage clear on his face. "Captain Deudermont!" he called. "As the victim and a recognized nobleman, you have the authority to pen such a note, but are you *sure?* At this late hour?"

Deudermont came forward, ignoring the grumbles and protests, even threats, and stood tall in the midst of the bloodthirsty crowd. "The evidence against Creeps Sharky and the tattooed pirate was solid," he explained, "but plausible, too, is Morik's tale of being set up with Wulfgar to take the blame, while the other two took only the reward."

"But," Jharkheld argued, pointing his finger into the air, "plausible, too, is the tale that Creeps Sharky told, one of conspiracy that makes them all guilty."

The crowd, confused but suspecting that their fun might soon be at an end, seemed to like Magistrate Jharkheld's explanation better.

"And plausible, too, is the tale of Josi Puddles, one that further implicates both Morik the Rogue and Wulfgar," Jharkheld went on. "Might I remind you, Captain, that the barbarian hasn't even denied the claims of Creeps Sharky!"

Deudermont looked then to Wulfgar, who continued his infuriating, expressionless stance.

"Captain Deudermont, do you declare the innocence of this man?" Jharkheld asked, pointing to Wulfgar and speaking slowly and loudly enough for all to hear.

"That is not within my rights," Deudermont replied over the shouts of protest from the bloodthirsty peasants. "I cannot determine guilt or innocence but can only offer that which you have before you."

Magistrate Jharkheld stared at the hastily penned note again, then held it up for the crowd to see. "A letter of pardon for Wulfgar," he explained.

The crowd hushed as one for just an instant, then began jostling and shouting curses. Both Deudermont and Jharkheld feared that a riot would ensue.

"This is folly," Jharkheld snarled.

"I am a visitor in excellent standing, by your own words, Magistrate Jharkheld," Deudermont replied calmly. "By that standing I ask the city to pardon Wulfgar, and by that standing I expect you to honor that request or face the questioning of your superiors."

There it was, stated flatly, plainly, and without any wriggle room at all. Jharkheld was bound, Deudermont and the magistrate knew, for the captain was, indeed, well within his rights to offer such a pardon. Such letters were not uncommon, usually given at great expense to the family of the pardoned man, but never before in such a dramatic fashion as this. Not at the Prisoner's Carnival, at the very moment of Jharkheld's greatest show!

"Death to Wulfgar!" someone in the crowd yelled, and others joined in, while Jharkheld and Deudermont looked to Wulfgar in that critical time.

Their expressions meant nothing to the man, who still thought that death would be a relief, perhaps the greatest escape possible from his haunting memories. When Wulfgar looked to Morik, the man stretched near to breaking, his stomach all bloody and the guards bringing forth another rat, he realized it wasn't an option, not if the rogue's loyalty to him meant anything at all.

"I had nothing to do with the attack," Wulfgar flatly declared. "Believe me if you will, kill me if you don't. It matters not to me."

"There you have it, Magistrate Jharkheld," Deudermont said.

"Release him, if you please. Honor my pardon as a visitor in excellent standing to Luskan."

Jharkheld held Deudermont's stare for a long time. The old man was obviously disapproving, but he nodded to the guards, and Wulfgar was immediately released from their grasp. Tentatively, and only after further prompting from Jharkheld, one of the men brought a key down to Wulfgar's ankles, releasing the ball and chain shackles.

"Get him out of here," an angry Jharkheld instructed, but the big man resisted the guards' attempts to pull him from the stage.

"Morik is innocent," Wulfgar declared.

"What?" Jharkheld exclaimed. "Drag him away!"

Wulfgar, stronger than the guards could ever imagine, held his ground. "I proclaim the innocence of Morik the Rogue!" he cried. "He did nothing, and if you continue here, you do so only for your own evil pleasures and not in the name of justice!"

"How much you two sound alike," an obviously disgusted Robillard whispered to Deudermont, coming up behind the captain.

"Magistrate Jharkheld!" the captain called above the cries of the crowd.

Jharkheld eyed him directly, knowing what was to come. The captain merely nodded. Scowling, the magistrate snapped up his parchments, waved angrily to his guards, and stormed off the stage. The frenzied crowd started pressing forward, but the city guard held them back.

Smiling widely, sticking his tongue out at those peasants who tried to spit at him, Morik was half dragged, half carried from the stage behind Wulfgar.

Morik spent most of the walk through the magistrate offices talking soothingly to Wulfgar. The rogue could tell from the big man's expression that Wulfgar was locked into those awful memories again. Morik feared that he would tear down the walls and kill half the magistrate's assistants. The rogue's stomach was still bloody, and his arms and legs ached more profoundly than anything he had ever felt. He had no desire to go back to Prisoner's Carnival.

Morik thought they would be brought before Jharkheld. That prospect, given Wulfgar's volatile mood, scared him more than a little. To his relief, the escorting guards avoided Jharkheld's office and turned into a small, nondescript room. A nervous little man sat behind a tremendous desk littered with mounds of papers.

One of the guards presented Deudermont's note to the man. He took a quick look at it and snorted, for he had already heard of the disappointing show at Prisoner's Carnival. The little man quickly scribbled his initials across the note, confirming that it had been reviewed and accepted.

"You are not innocent," he said, handing the note to Wulfgar, "and thus are not declared innocent."

"We were told that we would be free to go," Morik argued.

"Indeed," said the bureaucrat. "Not really free to go, but rather compelled to go. You were spared because Captain Deudermont apparently had not the heart for your execution, but understand that in the eyes of Luskan you are guilty of the crime charged. Thus, you are banished for life. Straightaway to the gate with you, and if you are ever caught in our city again, you'll face Prisoner's Carnival one last time. Even Captain Deudermont will not be able to intervene on your behalf. Do you understand?"

"Not a difficult task," Morik replied.

The wormy bureaucrat glared at him, to which Morik only shrugged.

"Get them out of here," the man commanded. One guard grabbed Morik by the arm, the other reached for Wulfgar, but a shrug and a look from the barbarian had him thinking better of it. Still, Wulfgar went along without argument, and soon the pair were out in the sunshine, unshackled and feeling free for the first time in many days.

To their surprise, though, the guards did not leave them there, escorting them all the way to the city's eastern gate.

"Get out, and don't come back," one of them said as the gates slammed closed behind them.

"Why would I want to return to your wretched city?" Morik cried, making several lewd and insulting gestures at those soldiers staring down from the wall.

One lifted a crossbow and leveled it Morik's way. "Looky," he said. "The little rat's already trying to sneak back in."

Morik knew that it was time to leave, and in a hurry. He turned and started to do just that, then looked back to see the soldier, a wary look upon the man's grizzled face, quickly lower the bow. When Morik looked back, he understood, for Captain Deudermont and his wizard sidekick were fast approaching.

For a moment, it occurred to Morik that Deudermont might have saved them from Jharkheld only because he desired to exact a punishment of his own. That fear was short-lived, for the man strode right up to Wulfgar, staring hard but making no threatening moves. Wulfgar met his stare, neither blinking nor flinching.

"Did you speak truly?" Deudermont asked.

Wulfgar snorted, and it was obvious it was all the response the captain would get.

"What has happened to Wulfgar, son of Beornegar?" Deudermont said quietly. Wulfgar turned to go, but the captain rushed around to stand before him. "You owe me this, at least," he said.

"I owe you nothing," Wulfgar replied.

Deudermont considered the response for just a moment, and Morik recognized that the seaman was trying to see things from Wulfgar's point of view.

"Agreed," the captain said, and Robillard huffed in displeasure. "You claimed your innocence. In that case, you owe nothing to me, for I did nothing but what was right. Hear me out of past friendship."

Wulfgar eyed him coldly but made no immediate move to walk away.

"I don't know what has caused your fall, my friend, what has led you away from companions like Drizzt Do'Urden and Catti-brie, and your adoptive father, Bruenor, who took you in and taught you the ways of the world," the captain said. "I only pray that those three and the halfling are safe and well."

Deudermont paused, but Wulfgar said nothing.

"There is no lasting relief in a bottle, my friend," the captain said, "and no heroism in defending a tavern from its customary patrons. Why would you surrender the world you knew for this?"

Having heard enough, Wulfgar started to walk away. When the captain stepped in front of him again, the big man just pushed on by without slowing, with Morik scrambling to keep up.

"I offer you passage," Deudermont unexpectedly—unexpectedly even to Deudermont—called after him.

"Captain!" Robillard protested, but Deudermont brushed him away and scrambled after Wulfgar and Morik.

"Come with me to *Sea Sprite*," Deudermont said. "Together we shall hunt pirates and secure the Sword Coast for honest sailors. You will find your true self out there, I promise!"

"I would hear only your definition of me," Wulfgar clarified, spinning back and hushing Morik, who seemed quite enthralled by the offer, "and that's one I don't care to hear." Wulfgar turned and started away.

Jaw hanging open, Morik watched him go. By the time he turned back, Deudermont had likewise retreated into the city. Robillard, though, held his ground and his sour expression.

"Might I?" Morik started to ask, walking toward the wizard.

"Be gone and be fast about it, rogue," Robillard warned. "Else you will become a stain on the ground, awaiting the next rain to wash you away."

Clever Morik, the ultimate survivor, who hated wizards, didn't have to be told twice.

PART THREE

A WILD LAND MADE WILDER

The course of events in my life have often made me examine the nature of good and evil. I have witnessed the purest forms of both repeatedly, particularly evil. The totality of my early life was spent living among it, a wickedness so thick in the air that it choked me and forced me away.

Only recently, as my reputation has begun to gain me some acceptance among the human populations—a tolerance, at least, if not a welcome—have I come to witness a more complex version of what I observed in Menzoberranzan, a shade of gray varying in lightness and darkness. So many humans, it seems, a vast majority, have within their makeup a dark side, a hunger for the macabre, and the ability to dispassionately dismiss the agony of another in the pursuit of the self.

Nowhere is this more evident than in the Prisoner's Carnival at Luskan and other such pretenses of justice. Prisoners, sometimes guilty, sometimes not—it hardly matters—are paraded before the blood-hungry mob, then beaten, tortured, and finally executed in grand fashion. The presiding magistrate works very hard to exact the most exquisite screams of the purest agony. His job is to twist the expressions of those prisoners into the epitome of terror, the ultimate horror reflected in their eyes.

Once, when in Luskan with Captain Deudermont of the *Sea Sprite*, I ventured to the carnival to witness the "trials" of several pirates we had fished from the sea after sinking their ship. Witnessing the spectacle of a thousand people crammed around a grand stage, yelling and squealing with delight as these miserable pirates were literally cut into pieces, almost made me walk away from Deudermont's ship, almost made me forego a life as a pirate hunter and retreat to the solitude of the forest or the mountains.

Of course, Catti-brie was there to remind me of the truth of it, to point out that these same pirates often exacted equal tortures upon innocent prisoners. While she admitted that such a truth did not justify the Prisoner's Carnival—Catti-brie was so horrified by the mere thought of the place that she would not go anywhere near it—she argued that such treatment of pirates was preferable to allowing them free run of the high seas.

But why? Why any of it?

The question has bothered me for all these years, and in seeking its answer I have come to explore yet another facet of these incredibly complex creatures called humans. Why would common, otherwise decent folk, descend to such a level as the spectacle of Prisoner's Carnival? Why would some of the *Sea Sprite*'s own crew, men and women I knew to be honorable and decent, take pleasure in viewing such a macabre display of torture?

The answer, perhaps—if there is a more complicated answer than the nature of evil itself—lies in an examination of the attitudes of other races. Among the goodly races, humans alone "celebrate" the executions and torments of prisoners. Halfling societies would have no part of such a display—halfling prisoners have been known to die of overeating. Nor would dwarves, as aggressive as they can be. In dwarven society, prisoners are dealt with efficiently and tidily, without spectacle and out of public view. A murderer among dwarves would be dealt a single blow to the neck. Never did I see any elves at Prisoner's Carnival, except on one occasion when a pair ventured by, then quickly left, obviously disgusted. My understanding is that in gnome society there are no executions, just a lifetime of imprisonment in an elaborate cell.

So why humans? What is it about the emotional construct of the human being that brings about such a spectacle as Prisoner's Carnival? Evil? I think that too simple an answer.

Dark elves relish torture—how well I know!—and their actions are, indeed, based on sadism and evil, and an insatiable desire to satisfy the demonic hunger of the spider queen, but with humans, as with everything about humans, the answer becomes a bit more complex. Surely there is a measure of sadism involved, particularly on the part of the presiding magistrate and his torturer assistants, but for the common folk, the powerless paupers cheering in the audience, I believe their joy stems from three sources.

First, peasants in Faer n are a powerless lot, subjected to the whims of unscrupulous lords and landowners, and with the ever-present threat of some invasion or another by goblins, giants, or fellow humans, stomping flat the lives they have carved. Prisoner's Carnival affords these unfortunate folk a taste of power, the power over life and death. At long last they feel some sense of control over their own lives.

Second, humans are not long-lived like elves and dwarves. Even halflings will usually outlast them. Peasants face the possibility of death daily. A mother fortunate enough to survive two or three births will likely witness the death of at least one of her children. Living so intimately with death obviously breeds a curiosity and fear, even terror. At Prisoner's Carnival these folk witness death at its most horrible, the worst that death can give, and take solace in the fact that their own deaths, unless they become the accused brought before the magistrates, will not likely be nearly as terrible. I have witnessed your worst, grim Death, and I fear you not.

The third explanation for the appeal of Prisoner's Carnival lies in the necessity of justice and punishment in order to maintain order in a society. This was the side of the debate held up by Robillard the wizard upon my return to the *Sea Sprite* after witnessing the horror. While he took no pleasure in viewing the carnival and rarely attended, Robillard defended it as vigorously as I might expect from the magistrate himself. The public humiliation of these men, the public display of their agony, would keep other folk on an honest course, he believed. Thus, the cheers of the peasant mob were no more than a rousing affirmation of their belief in the law and order of their society.

It is a difficult argument to defeat, particularly concerning the effectiveness of such displays in dissuading future criminals, but is it truly justice?

Armed with Robillard's arguments, I went to some minor magistrates in Luskan on the pretense of deciding better protocol for the *Sea Sprite* to hand over captured pirates, but in truth to get them talking about Prisoner's Carnival. It became obvious to me, and very quickly, that the carnival itself had little to do with justice. Many innocent men and women had found their way to the stage in Luskan, forced into false confession by sheer brutality, then punished publicly for those crimes. The magistrates knew this and readily admitted it by citing their relief that at least the prisoners we brought to them were assuredly guilty!

For that reason alone I can never come to terms with the Prisoner's Carnival. One measure of any society is the way it deals with those who have walked away from the course of community and decency, and an indecent treatment of these criminals decreases the standards of morality to the level of the tortured.

Yet the practice continues to thrive in many cities in Faer n and in many, many rural communities, where justice, as a matter of survival, must be even more harsh and definitive.

Perhaps there is a fourth explanation for the carnival. Perhaps the crowds gather around eagerly merely for the excitement of the show. Perhaps there is no underlying cause or explanation other than the fun of it. I do not like to consider this a possibility, for if humans on as large a scale are capable of eliminating empathy and sympathy so completely as to actually enjoy the spectacle of watching another suffer horribly, then that, I fear, is the truest definition of evil.

After all of the hours of investigation, debate, and interrogation, and many, many hours of contemplation on the nature of these humans among whom I live, I am left without simple answers to travesties such as the Prisoner's Carnival.

I am hardly surprised. Rarely do I find

a simple answer to anything concerning humans. That, perhaps, is the reason I find little tedium in my day-to-day travels and encounters. That, perhaps, is the reason I have come to love them.

–Drizzt Do'Urden

14
STOLEN SEED

Wulfgar stood outside of Luskan, staring back at the city where he had been wrongly accused, tortured, and publicly humiliated. Despite all of that, the barbarian held no anger toward the folk of the town, even toward the vicious magistrate. If he happened upon Jharkheld, he would likely twist the man's head off, but out of a need for closure on that particular incident and not out of hatred. Wulfgar was past hatred, had been for a long time. As it was when Tree Block Breaker had come hunting him at the Cutlass, and he had killed the man. As it was when he happened upon the Sky Ponies, a barbarian tribe akin to his own. He had taken vengeance upon their wicked shaman, an oath of revenge he had sworn years before. It was not for hatred, not even for unbridled rage, but simply Wulfgar's need to try to push forward in a life where the past was too horrible to contemplate.

Wulfgar had come to realize that he wasn't moving forward, and that point seemed obvious to him now as he stared back at the city. He was going in circles, small circles, that left him in the same place over and over, a place made tolerable only through use of the bottle, only by blurring the past into oblivion and putting the future out of mind.

Wulfgar spat on the ground, trying for the first time since he had come to Luskan months before to figure out how he had entered this downward spiral. He thought of the open range to the north, his homeland of Icewind Dale, where he had shared such excitement and joy with his friends. He thought of Bruenor, who had beaten him in battle when he was but a boy, but had shown him such mercy. The dwarf had taken him in as his own, then brought Drizzt to train him in the true ways of the warrior. What a friend Drizzt had been, leading him on grand adventures, standing by him in any fight, no matter the odds. He'd lost Drizzt.

He thought again of Bruenor, who had given Wulfgar his greatest achievement in craftsmanship, the wondrous Aegis-fang. The symbol of Bruenor's love for him. And now he'd lost not only Bruenor, but Aegis-fang as well.

He thought of Catti-brie, perhaps the most special of all to him, the woman who had stolen his heart, the woman he admired and respected above all. Perhaps they could not be lovers, or husband and wife. Perhaps she would never bear his children, but she was his friend, honest and true. When he thought of their last encounter he came to understand the truth of that friendship. Catti-brie would have given anything to help him, would have shared with him her most intimate moments and feelings, but Wulfgar understood that her heart was truly for another.

The fact didn't bring anger or jealousy to the barbarian. He felt only respect, for despite her feelings, Catti-brie would have given all to help him. Now Cattie-brie was lost to him, too.

Wulfgar spat again. He didn't deserve them, not Bruenor, Drizzt, nor Catti-brie. Not even Regis, who, despite his diminutive size and lack of fighting prowess, would leap in front of Wulfgar in time of crisis, would shield the barbarian, as much as he could, from harm. How could he have thrown all that away?

His attention shifted abruptly back to the present as a wagon rolled out of Luskan's western gate. Despite his foul mood, Wulfgar could not hold back a smile as the wagon approached. The driver, a plump elderly woman, came into view.

Morik. The two had been banished only days before, but they had hung around the city's perimeter. The rogue explained that he was going to have to secure some supplies if he was to survive on the open road, so he'd reentered the city alone. Judging from the way the pair of horses labored, judging from the fact that Morik had a wagon and horses at all, Wulfgar knew his sneaky little friend had succeeded.

The rogue turned the wagon off the wide road and onto a small trail that wove into the forest where Wulfgar waited. He came right up to the bottom of the bluff where Wulfgar sat, then stood up and bowed.

"Not so difficult a thing," he announced.

"The guards didn't notice you?" Wulfgar asked.

Morik snorted, as if the notion were preposterous. "They were the same guards as when we were escorted out," he explained, his tone full of pride.

Their experience at the hands of Luskan's authorities had reminded Wulfgar that he and Morik were just big players in a small pond, insignificant when measured against the larger pond that was the backdrop of the huge city—but what a large player Morik was in their small corner! "I even lost a bag of food at the gate," Morik went on. "One of the guards ran to catch up to me so that he could replace it on the wagon."

Wulfgar moved down the bluff to the side of the wagon and pulled aside the canvas that covered the load. There were bags of food at the back, along with rope and material for shelter, but most prominent to Wulfgar's sensibilities were the cases of bottles, full bottles of potent liquor.

"I thought you would be pleased," Morik remarked, moving beside the big man as he stared at the haul. "Leaving the city doesn't have to mean leaving our pleasures behind. I was thinking of dragging Delly Curtie along as well."

Wulfgar snapped an angry glare at Morik. The mention of the woman in such a lewd manner profoundly offended him.

"Come," Morik said, clearing his throat and obviously changing the subject. "Let us find a quiet place where we may quench our thirst." The rogue pulled off his disguise slowly, wincing at the pain that still permeated his joints and his ripped stomach. Those wounds, particularly in his knees, would be slow to heal. He paused again a moment later, holding up the wig to admire his handiwork, then climbed onto the driving bench, taking the reins in hand.

"The horses are not so fine," Wulfgar noted. The team seemed an old, haggard pair.

"I needed the gold to buy the drink," Morik explained.

Wulfgar glanced back at the load, thinking that Morik should have spent the funds on a better team of horses, thinking that his days in the bottle had come to an end. He started up the bluff again, but Morik stopped him with a call.

"There are bandits on the road," the rogue announced, "or so I was informed in town. Bandits on the road north of the forest, and all the way to the pass through the Spine of the World."

"You fear bandits?" Wulfgar asked, surprised.

"Only ones who've never heard of me," Morik explained, and Wulfgar understood the deeper implications. In Luskan, Morik's reputation served him well by keeping most thugs at bay.

"Better that we are prepared for trouble," the rogue finished.

Morik reached under the driver's bench and produced a huge axe. "Look," he said with a grin, obviously quite proud of himself as he pointed to the axe head. "It's still stained with Creeps Sharky's blood."

The headsman's own axe! Wulfgar started to ask Morik how in the Nine Hells he'd managed to get his hands on that weapon but decided he simply didn't want to know.

"Come along," Morik instructed, patting the bench beside him. The rogue pulled a bottle from the closest case. "Let's ride and drink, and plot our defense."

Wulfgar stared long and hard at that bottle before climbing onto the bench. Morik offered him the bottle, but he declined with gritted teeth. Shrugging, the rogue took a healthy swallow and offered it again. Again Wulfgar declined. That brought a puzzled look to Morik's face, but it fast turned into a smile as he decided that Wulfgar's refusal would leave more for him.

"We needn't live like savages just because we're on the road," Morik stated.

The irony of that statement from a man guzzling so potent a drink was not lost on Wulfgar. The barbarian managed to resist the bottle throughout the afternoon, and Morik happily drained it. Keeping the wagon at a swift pace, Morik tossed the empty bottle against a rock as they passed, then howled with delight when it shattered into a thousand pieces.

"You make a lot of noise for one trying to avoid highwaymen," Wulfgar grumbled.

"Avoid?" Morik asked with a snap of his fingers. "Hardly that. Highwaymen often have well-equipped campsites where we might find some comfort."

"Such well-equipped campsites must belong to successful highwaymen," Wulfgar reasoned, "and successful highwaymen are likely very good at what they do."

"As was Tree Block Breaker, my friend," Morik reminded. When Wulfgar still didn't seem convinced, he added, "Perhaps they will accept our offer to join with them."

"I think not," said Wulfgar.

Morik shrugged, then nodded. "Then we must chase them off," he said matter-of-factly.

"We'll not even find them," Wulfgar muttered.

"Oh?" Morik asked, and he turned the wagon down a side trail so suddenly that it went up on two wheels and Wulfgar nearly tumbled off.

"What?" the barbarian growled as they bounced along. He just barely ducked a low branch, then got a nasty scratch as another whipped against his arm. "Morik!"

"Quiet, my large friend," the rogue said. "There's a river up ahead with but one bridge across it, a bridge bandits would no doubt guard well." They burst out of the brush, bouncing to the banks of the river. Morik slowed the tired horses to a walk, and they started across a rickety bridge. To the rogue's dismay they crossed safely with no bandits in sight.

"Novices," a disappointed Morik grumbled, vowing to go a few miles, then turn back and cross the bridge again." Morik abruptly stopped the wagon. A large and ugly man stepped onto the road up ahead, pointing a sword their way.

"How interesting that such a pair as yourselves should be walking in my woods without my permission," the thug remarked, bringing the sword back and dropping it across his shoulder.

"Your woods?" Morik asked. "Why, good sir, I had thought this forest open for travel." Under his breath to Wulfgar, he added, "Half-orc."

"Idiot," Wulfgar replied so that only Morik could hear. "You, I mean, and not the thief. To look for this trouble. . . ."

"I thought it would appeal to your heroic side," the rogue

replied. "Besides, this highwayman has a camp filled with comforts, no doubt."

"What're you talking about?' the thug demanded.

"Why, you, good sir," Morik promptly replied. "My friend here was just saying that he thought you might be a thief and that you do not own this forest at all."

The bandit's eyes widened, and he stuttered over several responses unsuccessfully. He wound up spitting on the ground. "I'm saying it's my wood!" he declared, poking his chest. "Togo's wood!"

"And the cost of passage through, good Togo?" Morik asked.

"Five gold!" the thug cried and after a pause, he added, "Each of you!"

"Give it to him," Wulfgar muttered.

Morik chuckled, then an arrow zipped past, barely an inch in front of his face. Surprised that this band was so well organized, the rogue abruptly changed his mind and started reaching for his purse.

However, Wulfgar had changed his mind as well, enraged that someone had nearly killed him. Before Morik could agree on the price, the barbarian leaped from the wagon and rushed at Togo barehanded, then suddenly changed his mind and direction. A pair of arrows cut across his initial path. He turned for the monstrous archer he'd spotted perched high in a tree a dozen feet back from the road. Wulfgar crashed through the first line of brush and slammed hard into a fallen log. Hardly slowing, he lifted the log and threw it into the face of another crouching human, then continued his charge.

He made it to the base of the tree just as an arrow thunked into the ground beside him, a near miss Wulfgar ignored. Leaping to a low branch, he caught hold and hauled himself upward with tremendous strength and agility, nearly running up it. Bashing back small branches, scrambling over others, he came level with the archer. The creature, a gnoll bigger than Wulfgar, was desperately trying to set another arrow.

"Keep it!" the cowardly gnoll yelled, throwing the bow at Wulfgar and stepping off the branch, preferring the twenty-foot drop to Wulfgar's rage.

Escape wasn't that easy for the gnoll. Wulfgar thrust out a hand and caught the falling creature by the collar. Despite all the wriggling and punching, the awkward position and the gnoll's weight, Wulfgar had no trouble hauling it up.

Then he heard Morik's cry for help.

✂ ✂ ✂ ✂ ✂

Standing on the driver's bench, the rogue worked furiously with his slender sword to fend off the attacks from both Togo and another human swordsman who had come out from the brush. Worse, he heard a third approaching from behind, and worse still, arrows regularly cut the air nearby.

"I'll pay!" he cried, but the monstrous thugs only laughed.

Out of the corner of his eye Morik spotted an archer taking aim. He leaped backward as the missile came on, dodging both it and the thrust from the surprisingly deft swordsman in front of him. The move cost him, though, for he tumbled over the back of the bench, crashing into a case of bottles, shattering them. Morik leaped up and shrieked his outrage, smashing his sword impotently across the chair back.

On came Togo, gaining the bench position, but angry Morik matched his movements, coming ahead powerfully without regard for the other swordsman or archers. Togo retracted his arm for a swing, but Morik, quick with the blade, stabbed first, scoring a hit on Togo's hand that cost the thug his grip. Even as Togo's sword clanged against the wooden bench Morik closed in, turning his sword out to fend off the attacks from Togo's partner. He produced a dagger from his belt, a blade he promptly and repeatedly drove into Togo's belly. The half-orc tried desperately to fend off the attacks, using his bare hands, but Morik was too quick and too clever, stabbing around them even as his sword worked circles around Togo's partner's blade.

Togo fell back from the bench to the ground. He managed only a single running step before he collapsed, clutching his torn guts.

Morik heard the third attacker coming in around the side of the wagon. He heard a terrified scream from above, then another from the approaching enemy. The rogue glanced that way just in time to see Wulfgar's captured gnoll archer flying down from on high, arms flailing, screaming all the way. The humanoid missile hit the third thug, a small human woman, squarely, smashing both hard against the wagon in a heap. Groaning, the woman began trying to crawl away. The archer lay very still.

Morik pressed the attack on the remaining swordsman, as much to get down from the open driver's bench as to continue the fight. The swordsman, though, apparently had little heart remaining in the battle with his friends falling all around him. He parried Morik's thrust, backing all the while as the man leaped down to the road.

On Morik came, his sword working the thug's blade over and under. He thrust ahead and retracted quickly when the swordsman blocked, then came forward after a subtle roll of his slender sword that disengaged the thug's blade. Staggering, the man retreated, blood running from one shoulder. He started to turn and flee, but Morik kept pace, forcing him to work defensively.

Morik heard another cry of alarm behind him, followed by

the crack of breaking branches. He smiled with the knowledge that Wulfgar continued to clear out the archers.

"Please, mister," Morik's prey grunted as more and more of the rogue's attacks slipped through with stinging results and it became clear that Morik was the superior swordsman. "We was just needing your coin."

"Then you wouldn't have harmed me and my friend after you took our coin?" Morik asked cynically.

The man shook his head vigorously, and Morik used the distraction to slip through yet again, drawing a line of red on the man's cheek. Morik's prey fell to his knees with a yelp and tossed his sword to the ground, begging for mercy.

"I am known as a merciful sort," Morik said with mock sympathy, hearing Wulfgar approaching fast, "but my friend, I fear, is not."

Wulfgar stormed by and grabbed the kneeling man by the throat, hoisting him into the air and running him back into a tree. With one arm—the other tucked defensively with a broken arrow shaft protruding from his shoulder—Wulfgar held the highwayman by the throat off the ground, choking the life out of him.

"I could stop him," Morik explained, walking over and putting his hand on his huge friend's bulging forearm. Only then did he notice Wulfgar's serious wound. "You must lead us to your camp."

"No camp!" the man gasped. Wulfgar pressed and twisted.

"I will! I will!" the thug squealed, his voice going away as Wulfgar tightened his grip, choking all sounds and all air. His face locked in an expression of the purest rage, the barbarian pressed on.

"Let him go," Morik said.

No answer. The man in Wulfgar's grasp wriggled and slapped but could neither break the hold nor draw breath.

"Wulfgar!" Morik called, and he grabbed at the big man's arm with both hands, tugging fiercely. "Snap out of it, man!"

Wulfgar wasn't hearing any of it, didn't even seem to notice the rogue.

"You will thank me for this," Morik vowed, though he was not so sure as he balled up his fist and smashed Wulfgar on the side of the head.

Wulfgar did let go of the thug, who slumped unconscious at the base of the tree, but only to backhand Morik, a blow that sent the rogue staggering backward, with Wulfgar coming in pursuit. Morik lifted his sword, ready to plunge it through the big man's heart if necessary, but at the last moment Wulfgar stopped, blinking repeatedly, as if he had just come awake. Morik recognized that Wulfgar had returned from wherever he had gone to this time and place.

"He'll take us to the camp now," the rogue said.

Wulfgar nodded dumbly, his gaze still foggy. He looked dispassionately at the broken arrow shaft poking from his wounded shoulder. The barbarian blanched, looked to Morik in puzzlement, then collapsed face down in the dirt.

⚔ ⚔ ⚔ ⚔ ⚔

Wulfgar awoke in the back of the wagon on the edge of a field lined by towering pines. He lifted his head with some effort and nearly panicked. A woman walking past was one of the thugs from the road. What happened? Had they lost? Before full panic set in, though, he heard Morik's lighthearted voice, and he forced himself up higher, wincing with pain as he put some weight on his injured arm. Wulfgar looked at that shoulder curiously. The arrow shaft was gone, the wound cleaned and dressed.

Morik sat a short distance away, chatting amiably and sharing a bottle with another of the gnoll highwaymen as if they were old friends. Wulfgar slid to the end of the wagon and rolled his legs over, climbing unsteadily to his feet. The world swam before his eyes, black spots crossing his field of vision. The feeling passed quickly, though, and Wulfgar gingerly but deliberately made his way over to Morik.

"Ah, you're awake. A drink, my friend?" the rogue asked, holding out the bottle.

Frowning, Wulfgar shook his head.

"Come now, ye gots to be drinkin'," the dog-faced gnoll sitting next to Morik slurred. He spooned a glob of thick stew into his mouth, half of it falling to the ground or down the front of his tunic.

Wulfgar glared at Morik's wretched new comrade.

"Rest easy, my friend," Morik said, recognizing that dangerous look. "Mickers here is a friend, a loyal one now that Togo is dead."

"Send him away," Wulfgar said, and the gnoll dropped his jaw in surprise.

Morik came up fast, moving to Wulfgar's side and taking him by the good arm. "They are allies," he explained. "All of them. They were loyal to Togo, and now they are loyal to me. And to you."

"Send them away," Wulfgar repeated fiercely.

"We're out on the road," Morik argued. "We need eyes, scouts to survey potential territory and swords to help us hold it fast."

"No," Wulfgar said flatly.

"You don't understand the dangers, my friend," Morik said reasonably, hoping to pacify his large friend.

"Send them away!" Wulfgar yelled suddenly. Seeing he'd make no progress with Morik, he stormed up to Mickers. "Be gone from here and from this forest!"

Mickers looked past the big man. Morik gave a resigned shrug.

Mickers stood up. "I'll stay with him," he said, pointing to the rogue.

Wulfgar slapped the stew bowl from the gnoll's hand and grabbed the front of his shirt, pulling him up to his tiptoes. "One last chance to leave of your own accord," the big man growled as he shoved Mickers back several steps.

"Mister Morik?" Mickers complained.

"Oh, be gone," Morik said unhappily.

"And the rest of us, too?" asked another one of the humans of the bandit band, standing amidst a tumble of rocks on the edge of the field. He held a strung bow.

"Them or me, Morik," Wulfgar said, his tone leaving no room for debate. The barbarian and the rogue both glanced back to the archer to see that the man had put an arrow to his bowstring.

Wulfgar's eyes flared with simmering rage, and he started toward the archer. "One shot," he called steadily. "You will get one shot at me. Will you hit the mark?"

The archer lifted his bow.

"I don't think you will," Wulfgar said, smiling. "No, you will miss because you know."

"Know what?" the archer dared ask.

"Know that even if your arrow strikes me, it will not kill me," Wulfgar replied, and he continued his deliberate stalk. "Not right away, not before I get my hands around your throat."

The man drew his bowstring back, but Wulfgar only smiled more confidently and continued forward. The archer glanced around nervously, looking for support, but there was none to be found. Realizing he had taken on too great a foe, the man eased his string, turned, and ran off.

Wulfgar turned back. Mickers, too, had sprinted away.

"Now we'll have to watch out for them," Morik observed glumly when Wulfgar returned to him. "You cost us allies."

"I'll not ally myself with murdering thieves!" Wulfgar said simply.

Morik jumped back from him. "What am I, if not a thief?"

Wulfgar's expression softened. "Well, perhaps just one," he corrected with a chuckle.

Morik laughed uneasily. "Here, my big and not so smart friend," he said, reaching for another bottle. "A drink to the two of us. Highwaymen!"

"Will we find the same fate as our predecessors?" Wulfgar wondered aloud.

"Our predecessors were not so smart," Morik explained. "I knew where to find them because they were too predictable. A good highwayman strikes and runs on to the next target area. A good highwayman seems like ten separate bands, always one step ahead of the city guards, ahead of those who ride into the cities with information enough to find and defeat him."

"You sound as if you know the life well."

"I have done it from time to time," Morik admitted. "Just because we're on the wild road doesn't mean we must live like savages," the rogue repeated what was fast becoming his mantra. He held the bottle out toward Wulfgar.

It took all the willpower he could muster for Wulfgar to refuse that drink. His shoulder ached, and he was still agitated about the thugs. Retreat into a swirl of semi consciousness was very inviting at that moment.

But he did refuse by walking away from a stunned Morik. Moving to the other end of the field, he scrambled up a tree, settled into a comfortable niche, and sat back to survey the outlying lands.

His gaze was drawn repeatedly to the mountains in the north, the Spine of the World, the barrier between him and that other world of Icewind Dale, that life he might have known and might still know. He thought of his friends again, mostly of Catti-brie. The barbarian fell asleep to dreams of her close in his arms, kissing him gently, a respite from the pains of the world.

Suddenly Catti-brie backed away, and as Wulfgar watched, small ivory horns sprouted from her forehead and great bat wings extended behind her. A succubus, a demon of the Abyss, tricking him again in the hell of Errtu's torments, assuming the guise of comfort to seduce him.

Wulfgar's eyes popped open wide, his breath coming in labored gasps. He tried to dismiss the horrible images, but they wouldn't let him go. Not this time. So poignant and distinct were they that the barbarian wondered if all of this, his last months of life, had been but a ruse by Errtu to bring him hope again so that the demon might stomp it. He saw the succubus, the horrid creature that had seduced him . . .

"No!" Wulfgar growled, for it was too ugly a memory, too horrible for him to confront it yet again.

I stole your seed, the succubus said to his mind, and he could not deny it. They had done it to him several times in the years of his torment, had taken his seed and spawned alu-demons, Wulfgar's children. It was the first time Wulfgar had been able to consciously recall the memory since his return to the surface, the first time the horror of seeing his demonic offspring had forced itself through the mental barriers he had erected.

He saw them now, saw Errtu bring to him one such child, a crying infant, its mother succubus standing behind the demon. He saw Errtu present the infant high in the air, and then, right before Wulfgar's eyes, right before its howling mother's eyes, the great demon bit the child's head off. A spray of blood showered Wulfgar, who was unable to draw breath, unable to comprehend that Errtu had found a way to get at him yet again, the worst way of all.

Wulfgar half scrambled and half tumbled out of the tree, landing hard on his injured shoulder, reopening the wound. Ignoring the pain, he sprinted across the field and found Morik resting beside the wagon. Wulfgar went right to the crates and frantically tore one open.

His children! The offspring of his stolen seed!

The potent liquid burned all the way down, the heat of it spreading, spreading, dulling Wulfgar's senses, blurring the horrid images.

15
A Child No More

You must give love time to blossom, my lord," Temigast whispered to Lord Feringal. He'd ushered the young lord to the far side of the garden, away from Meralda, who was staring out over the sea wall. The steward had discovered the amorous young man pressuring Meralda to marry him the very next tenday. The flustered woman was making polite excuse after polite excuse, with stubborn Feringal defeating each one.

"Time to blossom?" Feringal echoed incredulously. "I am going mad with desire. I can think of nothing but Meralda!"

He said the last loudly, and both men glanced to see a frowning Meralda looking back at them.

"As it should be," Steward Temigast whispered. "Let us discover if the feeling holds strong over the course of time. The duration of such feelings is the true meaning of love, my lord."

"You doubt me still?" a horrified Lord Feringal replied.

"No, my lord, not I," Temigast explained, "but the villagers must see your union to a woman of Meralda's station as true love and not infatuation. You must consider her reputation."

That last statement gave Lord Feringal pause. He glanced back at the woman, then at Temigast, obviously confused. "If she is married to me, then what harm could come to her reputation?"

"If the marriage is quickly brought, then the peasants will assume she used her womanly tricks to bewitch you," Temigast explained. "Better for her, by far, if you spend the tendays showing your honest and respectful love for her. Many will resent her in any case, my lord, out of jealousy. Now you must protect her, and the best way to do that is to take your time with the engagement."

"How much time?" the eager young lord asked.

"The spring equinox," Temigast offered, bringing another horrified look from Feringal. "It is only proper."

"I shall die," wailed Feringal.

Temigast frowned at the overwrought lord. "We can arrange a meeting with another woman if your needs become too great."

Lord Feringal shook his head vigorously. "I cannot think of passion with another woman."

Smiling warmly, Temigast patted the young man on the shoulder. "That is the correct answer for a man who is truly in love," he said. "Perhaps we can arrange the wedding for the turn of the year."

Lord Feringal's face brightened, then he frowned again. "Five months," he grumbled.

"But think of the pleasure when the time has passed."

"I think of nothing else," said a glum Feringal.

"What were you speaking of?" Meralda asked when Feringal joined her by the wall after Temigast excused himself from the garden.

"The wedding, of course," the lord replied. "Steward Temigast believes we must wait until the turn of the year. He believes love to be a growing, blossoming thing," said Feringal, his voice tinged with doubt.

"And so it is," Meralda agreed with relief and gratitude to Temigast.

Feringal grabbed her suddenly and pulled her close. "I cannot believe that my love for you could grow any stronger," he explained. He kissed her, and Meralda returned it, and glad she was that he didn't try to take it any further than that, as had been his usual tactics.

Instead, Lord Feringal pushed her back to arms' length. "Temigast has warned me to show my respect for you," he admitted. "To show the villagers that our love is a real and lasting thing. And so I shall by waiting. Besides, that will give Priscilla the time she needs to prepare the event. She has promised a wedding such as Auckney—as the whole of the North—has never before seen."

Meralda's smile was genuine indeed. She was glad for the delay, glad for the time she needed to put her feelings for Lord Feringal and Jaka in the proper order, to come to terms with her decision and her responsibility. Meralda was certain she could go through with this, and not as a suffering woman. She could marry Lord Feringal and act as lady of Auckney for the sake of her mother and her family. Perhaps it would not be such a terrible thing.

The woman looked with a glimmer of affection at Feringal, who stood watching the dark waves. Impulsively she put an arm around the man's waist and rested her head on his shoulder and was rewarded with a chaste but grateful smile from her husband-to-be. He said nothing, didn't even try to take the touch further. Meralda had to admit it was . . . pleasant.

⚔ ⚔ ⚔ ⚔ ⚔

"Oh, tell me everything!" Tori whispered, scrambling to Meralda's bed when the older girl at last returned home that night. "Did he touch you?"

"We talked and watched the waves," Meralda replied noncommittally.

"Do you love him yet?"

Meralda stared at her sister. Did she love Lord Feringal? No, she could say for certain she did not, at least not in the heated manner in which she longed for Jaka, but perhaps that was all right. Perhaps she would come to love the generous lord of Auckney. Certainly Lord Feringal wasn't an ugly man—far from it. As their relationship grew, as they began to move beyond the tortured man's desperate groping, Meralda was starting to see his many good qualities, qualities she could indeed grow to love.

"Don't you still love Jaka?" Tori asked.

Meralda's contented smile dissipated at once with the painful reminder. She didn't answer, and for once Tori had the sense to let it drop as Meralda turned over, curled in upon herself, and tried hard not to cry.

It was a night of torrid dreams that left her tangled in her blankets. Still, Meralda's mood was better that next morning, and it improved even more when she entered the common room to hear her mother talking with Mam Gardener, one of their nosier neighbors—the little gnome had a beak that could shame a vulture—happily telling the visitor about her stroll in the castle garden.

"Mam Gardener brought us some eggs," Biaste Ganderlay explained, pointing to a skillet of scrambled eggs. "Help yourself, as I'm not wanting to get back up."

Meralda smiled at the generous gnome, then moved to the pan. Inexplicably, the young woman felt her stomach lurch at the sight and the smell and had to rush from the house to throw up beside the small bush outside the door.

Mam Gardener was there beside her in an instant. "Are you all right, girl?" she asked.

Meralda, more surprised than sick, stood back up. "The rich food at the castle," she explained. "They're feeding me too good, I fear."

Mam Gardener howled with laughter. "Oh, but you'll be getting used to that!" she said. "All fat and plump you'll get, living easy and eating well."

Meralda returned her smile and went back into the house.

"You still got to eat," Mam Gardener said, guiding her toward the eggs.

Even the thought of the eggs made Meralda's stomach turn again. "I'm thinking that I need to go and lay down," she explained, pulling away to head back to her room.

She heard the older ladies discussing her plight, with Mam telling Biaste about the rich food. Biaste, no stranger to illness, hoped that to be all it was.

Privately, Meralda wasn't so sure. Only then did she consider the timeline since her encounter with Jaka two tendays before. It was true she'd not had her monthly, but she hadn't thought much about it, for she'd never been regular in that manner anyway. . . .

The young woman clutched at her belly, both overwhelmed with joy and fear.

She was sick again the next morning, and the next after that, but she was able to hide her condition by going nowhere near the smell or sight of eggs. She felt well after throwing up in the morning and was not troubled with it after that, and so it became clear to her that she was, indeed, with child.

In her fantasies, the thought of having Jaka Sculi's babe was not terrible. She could picture herself married to the young rogue, living in a castle, walking in the gardens beside him, but the reality of her situation was far more terrifying.

She had betrayed the lord of Auckney, and worse, she had betrayed her family. Stealing that one night for herself, she had likely condemned her mother to death and branded herself a whore in the eyes of all the village.

Would it even get that far? she wondered. Perhaps when her father learned the truth he would kill her—he'd beaten her for far less. Or perhaps Lord Feringal would have her paraded through the streets so that the villagers might taunt her and throw rotten fruit and spit upon her. Or perhaps in a fit of rage Lord Feringal would cut the baby from her womb and send soldiers out to murder Jaka.

What of the baby? What might the nobles of Auckney do to a child who was the result of the cuckolding of their lord? Meralda had heard stories of such instances in other kingdoms, tales of potential threats to the throne, tales of murdered infants.

All the possibilities whirled in Meralda's mind one night as she lay in her bed, all the terrible possibilities, events too wicked for her to truly imagine, and too terrifying for her to honestly face. She rose and dressed quietly, then went in to see her mother, sleeping comfortably, curled up in her father's arms.

Meralda silently mouthed a heartsick apology to them both, then stole out of the house. It was a wet and windy night. To the woman's dismay, she didn't find Jaka in his usual spot in the fields above the houses, so she went to his house. Trying not to wake his kin, Meralda tossed pebbles against the curtain screening his glassless window.

The curtain was abruptly yanked to the side, and Jaka's handsome face poked through the opening.

"It's me, Meralda," she whispered, and the young man's face

brightened in surprise. He held his hand out to her, and when she clenched it, he pulled it close to his face through the opening, his smile wide enough to take in his ears.

"I must talk with you," Meralda explained. "Please come outside."

"It's warmer in here," Jaka replied in his usual sly, lewd tone.

Knowing it unwise but shivering in the chill night air, Meralda motioned to the front door and scurried to it. Jaka was there in a moment, stripped bare to the waist and holding a single candle. He put his finger over his pursed lips and took Meralda by the arm, walking her quietly through the curtained doorway that led to his bedchamber. Before the young woman could begin to explain, Jaka was against her, kissing her, pulling her down beside him.

"Stop!" she hissed, pulling away. "We must talk."

"Later," Jaka said, his hands roaming.

Meralda rolled off the side of the bed and took a step away. "Now," she said. " 'Tis important."

Jaka sat up on the edge of the bed, grinning still but making no move to pursue her.

"I'm running too late," Meralda explained bluntly.

Jaka's face screwed up as though he didn't understand.

"I am with child," the woman blurted softly. "Your child."

The effect of her words would have been no less dramatic if she had smashed Jaka across the face with a cudgel. "How?" he stammered after a long, trembling pause. "It was only once."

"I'm guessing that we did it right, then," the woman returned dryly.

"But—" Jaka started, shaking his head. "Lord Feringal? What are we to do?" He paused again, then turned a sharp eye upon Meralda. "Have you and he—?"

"Only yourself," Meralda firmly replied. "Only that once in all my life."

"What are we to do?" Jaka repeated, pacing nervously. Meralda had never seen him so agitated.

"I was thinking that I had to marry Lord Feringal," Meralda explained, moving over and taking hold of the man to steady him. "For the sake of my family, if not my own, but now things are changed," she said, looking Jaka in the eyes. "I cannot bring another man's child into Castle Auck, after all."

"Then what?" asked Jaka, still appearing on the very edge of desperation.

"You said you wanted me," Meralda said softly, hopefully. "So, with what's in my belly you've got me, and all my heart."

"Lord Feringal will kill me."

"We'll not stay, then," Meralda replied. "You said we'd travel the Sword Coast to Luskan and to Waterdeep, and so we shall, and so I must."

The thought didn't seem to sit very well with Jaka. He said "But . . ." and shook his head repeatedly. Finally, Meralda gave him a shake to steady him and pushed herself up against him.

"Truly, this is for the better," she said. "You're my love, as I'm your own, and now fate has intervened to put us together."

"It's crazy," Jaka replied, pulling back from her. "We can't run away. We no coin. We have nothing. We shall die on the road before we ever get near Luskan."

"Nothing?" Meralda echoed incredulously, starting to realize that this was more than shock speaking. "We've each other. We've our love, and our child coming."

"You think that's enough?" Jaka asked in the same incredulous tone. "What life are we to find under such circumstances as this? Paupers forever, eating mud and raising our child in mud?"

"What choice have we?"

"We?" Jaka bit back the word as soon as it left his mouth, realizing too late that it had not been wise to say aloud.

Meralda fought back tears. "Are you saying that you lied to get me to lay down with you? Are you saying that you do not love me?"

"That's not what I'm saying," Jaka reassured her, coming over to put a hand on her shoulder, "but what chance shall we have to survive? You don't really believe that love is enough, do you? We shall have no food, no coin, and three to feed. And how will it be when you get all fat and ugly, and we have not even our lovemaking to bring us joy?"

The woman blanched and fell back from his reach. He came for her, but she slapped him away. "You said you loved me," she said.

"I did," Jaka replied. "I do."

She shook her head slowly, eyes narrowing in a moment of clarity. "You lusted for me but never loved me." Her voice quivered, but the woman was determined to hold strong her course. "You fool. You're not even knowing the difference." With that she turned and ran out of the house. Jaka didn't make a move to go after her.

Meralda cried all through the night on the rainy hillside and didn't return home until early in the morning. The truth was there before her now, whatever might happen next. What a fool she felt for giving herself to Jaka Sculi. For the rest of her life, when she would look back on the moment she became a woman, the moment she left her innocent life as a girl behind her, it would not be the night she lost her virginity. No, it would be this night, when she first realized she had given her most secret self to a selfish, uncaring, shallow man. No, not a man—a boy. What a fool she had been.

16
HOME SWEET HOME

They sat huddled under the wagon as the rain pelted down around them. Rivulets of water streamed in, and the ground became muddy even in their sheltered little place.

"This is not the life I envisioned," a glum Morik remarked. "How the mighty have fallen."

Wulfgar smirked at his friend and shook his head. He was not as concerned with physical comforts as Morik, for the rain hardly bothered him. He had grown up in Icewind Dale, after all, a climate more harsh by far than anything the foothills on this side of the Spine of the World could offer.

"Now I've ruined my best breeches," Morik grumbled, turning around and slapping the mud from his pants.

"The farmers would have offered us shelter," Wulfgar reminded him. Earlier that day, the pair had passed clusters of farmhouses, and Wulfgar had mentioned several times that the folk within would likely offer them food and a warm place to stay.

"Then the farmers would know of us," Morik said by way of

explanation, the same answer he had given each time Wulfgar had brought up the possibility. "If or when we have someone looking for us, our trail would be easier to follow."

A bolt of lightning split a tree a hundred yards away, bringing a startled cry from Morik.

"You act as though you expect half the militias of the region to be chasing us before long," Wulfgar replied.

"I have made many enemies," Morik admitted, "as have you, my friend, including one of the leading magistrates of Luskan."

Wulfgar shrugged. He hardly cared.

"We'll make more, I assure you," Morik went on.

"Because of the life you have chosen for us."

The rogue cocked an eyebrow. "Are we to live as farmers, tilling dirt?"

"Would that be so terrible?"

Morik snorted, and Wulfgar only chuckled again helplessly.

"We need a base," Morik announced suddenly as another rivulet found its way to his bottom. "A house . . . or a cave."

"There are many caves in the mountains," Wulfgar offered. The look on Morik's face, both hopeful and fearful, told him he needn't speak the thought. Mountain caves were almost always occupied.

The sun was up the next morning, shining bright in a blue sky, but that did little to change Morik's complaining mood. He grumbled and slapped at the dirt, then stripped off his clothes and washed them when the pair came across a clear mountain stream.

Wulfgar, too, washed his clothes and his dirty body. The icy water felt good against his injured shoulder. Lying on a sunny rock waiting for their clothes to dry, Wulfgar spotted some smoke drifting lazily into the air.

"More houses," the barbarian remarked. "Friendly folk to those who come as friends, no doubt."

"You never stop," Morik replied dryly, and he reached behind the rock and pulled out a bottle of wine he had cooling in the water. He took a drink and offered it to Wulfgar, who hesitated, then accepted.

Soon after, their clothes still wet, and both a bit lightheaded, the pair started off along the mountain trails. They couldn't take their wagon, so they stashed it under some brush and let the horses graze nearby, with Morik noting the irony of how easy it would be for someone to rob them.

"Then we would just have to steal them back," Wulfgar replied, and Morik started to laugh, missing the barbarian's sarcasm.

He stopped abruptly, though, noting the suddenly serious expression on his large friend's face. Following Wulfgar's gaze to the trail ahead, Morik began to understand, for he spotted a broken sapling, recently snapped just above the trunk. Wulfgar went to the spot and bent low, studying the ground around the sapling.

"What do you think broke the tree?" Morik asked from behind him.

Wulfgar motioned for the rogue to join him, then pointed out the heel print of a large, large boot.

"Giants?" Morik asked, and Wulfgar looked at him curiously. Already Wulfgar recognized the signs of Morik becoming unhinged, as the rogue had over the rat in the cage at Prisoner's Carnival.

"You don't like giants, either?" Wulfgar asked.

Morik shrugged. "I have never seen one," he admitted, "but who truly likes them?"

Wulfgar stared at him incredulously. Morik was a seasoned veteran, skilled as a thief and warrior. A significant portion of Wulfgar's own training had come at the expense of giants. To think one as skilled as Morik had never even seen one surprised the barbarian.

"I saw an ogre once," Morik said. "Of course, our gaoler friends had more than a bit of ogre blood in them."

"Bigger," Wulfgar said bluntly. "Giants are much bigger."

Morik blanched. "Let us return the way we came."

"If there are giants about, they'll very likely have a lair," Wulfgar explained. "Giants would not suffer rain and hot sun when there are comfortable caves in the region. Besides, they prefer their meals cooked, and they try not to advertise their presence with campfires under the open sky."

"Their meals," Morik echoed. "Are barbarians and thieves on their menu of cooked meals?"

"A delicacy," Wulfgar said earnestly, nodding.

"Let us go and speak with the farmers," said Morik, turning around.

"Coward," Wulfgar remarked quietly. The word had Morik spinning back to face him. "The trail is easy enough to follow," Wulfgar explained. "We don't even know how many there are. Never would I have expected Morik the Rogue to run from a fight."

"Morik the rogue fights with this," Morik countered, poking his finger against his temple.

"A giant would eat that."

"Then Morik the Rogue runs with his feet," the thief said.

"A giant would catch you," Wulfgar assured him. "Or it would throw a rock at you and squash you from afar."

"Pleasant choices," said Morik cynically. "Let us go and speak with the farmers."

Wulfgar settled back on his heels, studying his friend and making no move to follow. He couldn't help but contrast Morik to Drizzt at that moment. The rogue was turning to leave, while the drow would, and often had, eagerly rushed headlong into such adventure as a giant lair. Wulfgar recalled the time he and

Drizzt had dispatched an entire lair of verbeeg, a long and brutal fight but one that Drizzt had entered laughing. Wulfgar thought of the last fight he had waged beside his ebon-skinned friend, against another band of giants. That time they'd chased them into the mountains after learning that the brutes had set their eyes on the road to Ten-Towns.

It seemed to Wulfgar that Morik and Drizzt were similar in so many way, but in the most important ways they were nothing alike. It was a contrast that continually nagged at Wulfgar, a reminder of the startling differences in his life now, the difference between that world north of the Spine of the World and this world south of it.

"There may only be a couple of giants," Wulfgar suggested. "They rarely gather in large numbers."

Morik pulled out his slender sword and his dagger. "A hundred hits to fell one?" he asked. "Two hundred? And all the time I spend sticking the behemoth two hundred times, I'll be comforted by the thought that one strike from the giant will crush me flat."

Wulfgar's grin widened. "That's the fun of it," he offered. The barbarian hoisted the headman's axe over one shoulder and started after the giant, having little trouble in discerning the trail.

Crouching on the backside of a wide boulder by mid-afternoon, Wulfgar and Morik had the giants and their lair in sight. Even Morik had to admit that the location was perfect, an out-of-the-way cave nestled among rocky crests, yet less than half a day's march to one of two primary mountain passes, the easternmost of the pair, separating Icewind Dale from the southlands.

They watched for a long while and noted only a pair of giants, then a third appeared. Even so, Wulfgar was not impressed.

"Hill giants," he remarked disparagingly, "and only a trio. I have battled a single mountain giant who could fell all three."

"Well, let us see if we can find that mountain giant and prompt him to come and evict this group," said Morik.

"That mountain giant is dead," Wulfgar replied. "As these three shall soon be." He took up the huge axe in hand and glanced around, finally deciding on a roundabout trail that would bring him to the lair.

"I have no idea of how to fight them," Morik whispered.

"Watch and learn," Wulfgar replied, and off he went.

Morik didn't know whether he should follow or not, so he stayed put on the rock, noting his friend's progress, watching the trio of giants disappear into the cave. Wulfgar crept up to that dark entrance soon after, slipping to the edge and peering in. Glancing back Morik's way, he went spinning into the gloom.

"You don't even know if there are others inside," Morik muttered to himself, shaking his head. He wondered if coming out here with Wulfgar had been a wise idea after all. The rogue could get back into Luskan easily, he knew, with a new identity as far as the authorities were concerned, but with the same old position of respect on the streets. Of course, there remained the not-so-little matter of the dark elves who had come calling.

Still, given the size of those giants, Morik was thinking that he just might have to return to Luskan. Alone.

⚔ ⚔ ⚔ ⚔ ⚔

The initial passageway inside the cave was not very high or open, at least for giants. Wulfgar took comfort in the knowledge that his adversaries would have to stoop very low, perhaps even crawl, to get under one overhanging boulder. Pursuit would not be swift if Wulfgar were forced to retreat.

The tunnel widened and heightened considerably beyond that curving walk of about fifty feet. After that it opened into a wide, high chamber where a tremendous bonfire reflected enough orange light down the tunnel so that Wulfgar was not walking in darkness.

He noted that the walls were broken and uneven, a place of shadows. There was one particularly promising perch about ten feet off the ground. Wulfgar crept along a bit farther, hoping to catch a glimpse of the entire giant clan within. He wanted to make sure that there were only three and that they didn't have any of the dangerous pets giants often harbored, like cave bears or huge wolves. The barbarian had to backtrack, though, before he even got near the chamber entrance, for he heard one of the giants approaching, belching with every booming step. Wulfgar went up the wall to the perch and melted back into the shadows to watch.

Out came the giant, rubbing its belly and belching yet again. It stooped and bent in preparation for the tight stretch of corridor ahead. Caution dictated that Wulfgar hold his attack, that he scout further and discern the exact strength of his enemy, but Wulfgar wasn't feeling cautious.

Down he came with a great roar and a tremendous overhead chop of the headsman's axe, his pure strength adding to the momentum of the drop.

The startled giant managed a slight dodge, enough so that the axe didn't sheer through its neck. Despite its great size, Wulfgar's power would have decapitated the behemoth. Still, the axe drove through the giant's shoulder blade, tearing skin and muscle and crushing bone, knocking the giant into a howling, agonized stagger that left it crouched on one knee.

But in the process, Wulfgar's weapon snapped at mid-shaft. Ever one to improvise, the barbarian hit the ground in a roll, came right back to his feet, and rushed in on the wounded, kneeling giant, stabbing it hard in the throat with the pointed, broken end of the shaft. As the gurgling behemoth reached for him with huge, trembling hands, Wulfgar tore the shaft free, tightened his grip on the end, and smashed the giant across the face.

He left the giant there on one knee, knowing that its friends would soon come out. Looking for a defensible position, he noticed then that the action of his attack, or perhaps the landing on the floor, had reopened his shoulder wound, his tunic already growing wet with fresh blood.

Wulfgar didn't have time to think about it. He made it back to his high perch as the other two entered the area below him. He found his next weapon in the form of a huge rock. With a stifled grunt, Wulfgar brought it up overhead and waited.

The last giant in line, the smallest of the three, heard that grunt and looked up just as Wulfgar brought the rock smashing down—and how that giant howled!

Wulfgar scooped his club and leaped down, once again using his momentum to heighten the strike as he smashed this one across the face. The barbarian hit the floor and pivoted back at the behemoth, rushing past its legs to smash at its kneecaps. Altering his grip, he stabbed hard at the tender hamstrings on the back of the giant's legs, just as Bruenor had taught him.

Still holding its smashed face and howling in pain, the giant tumbled to the ground behind Wulfgar, where it fell in the way of the last of the group, the only one who had not yet felt the sting of Wulfgar's weapons.

⚔ ⚔ ⚔ ⚔ ⚔

Outside the cave, Morik winced as he heard the cries, groans, and howls, and the unmistakable sound of boulder against bone.

Curious despite himself, the rogue moved up closer to the entrance, trying to get a look inside, though he feared and honestly believed that his friend was already dead.

"You should be well on your way to Luskan," Morik scolded himself under his breath. "A warm bed for Morik tonight."

⚔ ⚔ ⚔ ⚔ ⚔

He'd hit them as hard as he could both times, yet he hadn't killed a single one of the trio, probably hadn't even knocked one of them out of the fight for long. Here he was, exposed and running into the main chamber without even knowing if the place had another exit.

But memories of Errtu weren't with the barbarian now. He was temporarily free of that emotional bondage, on the very edge of present desperation, and he loved it.

For once luck was with him. Inside the lair proper Wulfgar found the spoils of the giants' last raid, including the remains of a trio of dwarves, one of whom had carried a small, though solid hammer and another with several hand axes set along a bandolier.

Roaring, the giant rushed in, and Wulfgar let fly one, two, three, with the hand axes, scoring two gouging hits. Still the brute came on, and it was only a single running stride away when a desperate Wulfgar, thinking he was about to get squished into the wall, spun the hammer right into its thigh.

Wulfgar dived desperately, for the staggering giant couldn't begin to halt its momentum. It slammed headlong into the stone wall, dropping more than a bit of dust and pebbles from the cave ceiling. Somehow Wulfgar managed to avoid the crunch, but he had left his new weapons behind and couldn't possibly get to them in time as the giant Wulfgar had smashed with the rock came limping into the chamber.

Wulfgar went for the snapped axe shaft instead. Scooping it up, he dived aside in another roll as the behemoth stomped down with a heavy boot. Wulfgar was already in motion, charging for those vulnerable knees, smashing one repeatedly, then spinning around the trunklike leg, out of the giant's grasp. Turning his weapon point out as he pivoted, he stabbed again at the back of the bloodied leg. The giant lying against the wall kicked out, clipping Wulfgar's wounded shoulder and launching the man away to slam hard against the far wall.

Wulfgar was in his warrior rage now. He came out of the slam with a bellow, charging right back at the limping behemoth too fast for it to recognize the movement. His relentless club went at the knees again, and though the giant slapped at him, Wulfgar took hope in finally hearing the bone crunch apart. Down went the behemoth, clutching its broken knee, the sheer volume of its cries shaking the entire cave. Shaking off the dull ache of that slap, Wulfgar taunted it with laughter.

The one against the wall tried to rise, but Wulfgar was there in an instant, standing on its back, his club battering it about the back of the head. He scored several thunderous hits and had the behemoth flat down and trying to cover. Wulfgar dared hope he might finally finish one off.

Then the huge hand of the other giant tightened around his leg.

⚔ ⚔ ⚔ ⚔

Morik could hardly believe his movements, felt as if his own feet were betraying him, as he crept right up to the cave entrance and peered inside.

He saw the first of the giant group, standing bent over at the waist under the overhanging rock, one arm extended against the wall to lend support as it coughed up the last remnants of blood from its mouth.

Before his own good sense could overrule him, Morik was on the move, silently creeping into the gloom of the cave along the wall. He got by the giant with hardly a whisper of sound, his small noises easily covered by the giant's hacking and wheezing, then climbed to a ledge several feet from the ground.

The sounds of battle rang out from the inner chamber, and he could only hope that Wulfgar was doing well, both for his friend's sake and because he realized that if the other giants came out now he would be in a difficult position indeed.

The rogue held his nerve, and waited, poised, dagger in hand, lining up his strike. He considered the attack from the perspective of those backstabs he knew from his experiences fighting men, but he looked at his puny dagger doubtfully.

The giant began to turn around. Morik was out of time. Knowing he had to be perfect, figuring that this was going to hurt more than a little, and wondering why in the Nine Hells he had come in here after foolish Wulfgar, Morik went with his instinct and leaped for the giant's torn throat.

His dagger flashed. The giant howled and leaped up—and slammed its head on the overhanging boulder. Groaning, it tried to straighten, flailing its arms, and Morik flew aside, his breath blasted away. Half-tumbling, half-running, and surely screaming, Morik exited the cave with the gasping, grasping giant right behind.

He felt the giant closing, step by step. At the last instant Morik dived aside and the behemoth stumbled past, one hand clutching its throat, wheezing horribly, its face blue, eyes bulging.

Morik sprinted back the other way, but the giant didn't pursue. The huge creature was down on its knees now, gasping for air.

"Going home to Luskan," Morik mumbled over and over, but he kept moving for the cave entrance as he spoke.

⚔ ⚔ ⚔ ⚔ ⚔

Wulfgar spun and stabbed with all his strength, then drove ahead ferociously, twisting and pulling at the giant's leg. The giant was on one knee, its broken leg held out straight as it struggled to maintain some balance. The other meaty hand came at Wulfgar, but he slipped under it and pulled on furiously, breaking free and leaping to the giant's shoulder.

He scrambled behind the behemoth's head and wrapped his hands back around, lining up the point of his axe shaft with the creature's eye. Wulfgar locked his hands around that splintered pole and pushed hard. The giant's hands grabbed at him to stop his progress, but he growled and pulled on.

The terrified giant tried to wriggle away, pulled with its huge hands with all its strength, bunched muscle that would stop nearly any human cold.

But Wulfgar had the angle and was possessed of a strength beyond that of nearly any human. He saw the other giant climbing back to its feet, but reminded himself to take the fight one at a time. Wulfgar felt the tip of his axe shaft sink into the giant's eye. It went into a frenzy, even climbing back to its feet, but Wulfgar held on. Driving, driving.

The giant ran blindly for the wall and turned around, going in hard, trying to crush the man. Wulfgar growled away the pain and pressed on with all his strength until the spear slipped in deeper to the behemoth's brain.

The other giant came in then. Wulfgar fell away, scrambling across the chamber, using the spasms of the dying giant to cover his retreat. The butt end of Wulfgar's impromptu spear remained visible within the folds of the dying brute's closed eyelid. Wulfgar scarcely had time to notice as he dived headlong across the way to retrieve the hammer and one of the bloody hand axes.

The giant threw its dead companion aside and strode forward, then staggered back with a hand axe embedded deep into its forehead.

Wulfgar continued to press in with a mighty overhead chop that slammed the hammer hard into the behemoth's chest. He hit it again, and a third time, then went down under the flailing fists and struck a brutal blow against the giant's knee. Wulfgar skittered past and ran behind the brute to the wall, leaping upward two full strides, then springing off with yet another wicked, downward smash as the turning giant came around.

The hammer's head cracked through the giant's skull. The behemoth dropped straight down and lay very still on the floor.

Morik entered the chamber at that moment and gaped at the battered Wulfgar. The barbarian's shoulder was soaked with blood, his leg bruised from ankle to thigh, and his knees and hands were skinned raw.

"You see?" Wulfgar said with a triumphant grin. "No trouble at all. Now we have a home."

Morik looked past his friend to the gruesome remains of the half-eaten dwarves and the two dead giants oozing blood throughout the chamber. "Such as it is," he answered dryly.

⚔ ⚔ ⚔ ⚔ ⚔

They spent the better part of the next three days cleaning out their cave, burying the dwarves, chopping up and disposing of the giants, and retrieving their supplies. They even managed to get the horses and the wagon up to the place along a roundabout route, though they simply let the horses run free after the great effort, figuring that they would never be very useful as a pulling team.

A full pack on his back, Morik took Wulfgar out along the trails. The pair finally came to a spot overlooking a wide pass, the one true trail through this region of the Spine of the World. It was the same trail that Wulfgar and his former friends had used whenever they'd ventured out of Icewind Dale. There was another pass to the west that ran through Hundelstone, but this was the most direct route, though more dangerous by far.

"Many caravans will roll through this place before winter," Morik explained. "They'll be heading north with varied goods and south with scrimshaw knucklehead carvings."

More familiar with the routine than Morik would ever understand, Wulfgar merely nodded.

"We should hit them both ways," the rogue suggested. "Secure our provisions from those coming from the south and our future monies from those coming from the north."

Wulfgar sat down on a slab and stared north along the pass, beyond it to Icewind Dale. He was reminded again of the sharp contrast between his past and his present. How ironic it would be if his former friends were the ones to track down the highwaymen.

He pictured Bruenor, roaring as he charged up the rocky slope, agile Drizzt skipping past him, scimitars in hand. Guenhwyvar would already be above them, Wulfgar knew, cutting off any retreat. Morik would likely flee, and Catti-brie would cut him down with a single, blazing arrow.

"You look a thousand miles away. What's on your mind?" Morik inquired. As usual, he was holding an open bottle he'd already begun sampling.

"I'm thinking I need a drink," Wulfgar replied, taking the bottle and lifting it to his lips. Burning all the way down, the huge swallow helped calm him somewhat, but he still couldn't reconcile himself to his present position. Perhaps his friends would come after him, as he, Drizzt and Guenhwyvar, and the others following, had gone after the giant band they suspected to be highwaymen in Icewind Dale.

Wulfgar took another long drink. He didn't like the prospects if they came after him.

17

COERCION

I cannot wait until the spring, I fear," Meralda said coyly to Feringal after dinner one night at Auckney Castle. At Meralda's request the pair was walking the seashore this evening, instead of their customary stroll in the garden.

The young lord stopped in his tracks, eyes wider than Meralda had ever seen them. "The waves," he said, drawing closer to Meralda. "I fear I did not hear you correctly."

"I said that I cannot wait for the spring," Meralda repeated. "For the wedding, I mean."

A grin spread from ear to ear across Feringal's face, and he seemed as if he were about to dance a jig. He took her hand gently, brought it up to his lips, and kissed it. "I would wait until the end of time, if you so commanded," he said solemnly. To her great surprise—and wasn't this man always full of surprises?—Meralda found that she believed him. He had never betrayed her.

As thrilled as Meralda was, however, she had pressing problems. "No, my lord, you'll not be waiting long," she replied, pulling her hand from his and stroking his cheek. "Suren I'm glad that you'd wait for me, but I can no longer wait for the spring for my own desires." She moved in close and kissed him, and felt him melting against her.

Feringal pulled away from her for the first time. "You know we cannot," he said, though it obviously pained him. "I have given my word to Temigast. Propriety, my love. Propriety."

"Then make it proper, and soon," Meralda replied, stroking the man's cheek gently. She thought that Feringal might collapse under her tender touch, so she moved in close again and added breathlessly, "I simply can't wait."

Feringal lost his thin resolve and wrapped her in his arms, burying her in a kiss.

Meralda didn't want this, but she knew what she had to do. She feared too much time had passed already. The young woman started to pull the man down to the sand with her, setting her mind firmly that she would seduce him and be done with it, but there came a call from the castle wall—Priscilla's shrill voice: *"Feri!"*

"I detest it when she calls me that!" With great effort, the young lord jumped back from Meralda and cursed his sister under his breath. "Can I never escape her?"

"Feri, is that you?" Priscilla called again.

"Yes, Priscilla," the man replied with barely concealed irritation.

"Do come back to the castle," the woman beckoned. "It grows dark, and Temigast says there are reports of thieves about. He wants you within the walls."

Brokenhearted Feringal looked to Meralda and shook his head. "We must go," he said.

"I can't wait for spring," the woman said determinedly.

"And you shan't," Lord Feringal replied, "but we shall do it properly, in accordance with etiquette. I will move the wedding day forward to the winter solstice."

"Too long," Meralda replied.

"The autumn equinox then."

Meralda considered the timeline. The autumn equinox was four tendays away, and she was already more than a month pregnant. Her expression revealed her dismay.

"I cannot possibly move it up more than that," Lord Feringal explained. "As you know, Priscilla is doing the planning, and she will already howl with anger when she hears that I wish to move it up at all. Temigast desires that we wait until the turn of the year, at least, but I will convince him otherwise."

He was talking more to himself than to Meralda, and so she let him ramble, falling within her own thoughts as the pair made their way back to the castle. She knew that the man's fears of his sister's rage were, if anything, an underestimation. Priscilla would fight their plans for a change of date. Meralda was certain the woman was hoping the whole thing would fall apart.

It *would* fall apart before the wedding if anyone suspected she was carrying another man's child.

"You should know better than to go out without guards in the night," Priscilla scolded as soon as the pair entered the foyer. "There are thieves about."

She glared at Meralda, and the woman knew the truth of Priscilla's ire. Feringal's sister didn't fear thieves on her brother's account. Rather, she was afraid of what might happen between Feringal and Meralda, of what had nearly happened between them on the beach.

"Thieves?" Feringal replied with a chuckle. "There are no thieves in Auckney. We have had no trouble here in many years, not since before I became lord."

"Then we are overdue," Priscilla replied dryly. "Would you have it that the first attack in Auckney in years happen upon the lord and his future wife? Have you no sense of responsibility toward the woman you say you love?"

That set Feringal back on his heels. Priscilla always seemed able to do that with just a few words. She made a mental note to remedy that situation as soon as she had a bit of power behind her.

" 'Twas my own fault," Meralda interrupted, moving between the siblings. "I'm often walking the night, my favorite time."

"You are no longer a common peasant," Priscilla scolded bluntly. "You must understand the responsibility that will accompany your ascent into the family."

"Yes, Lady Priscilla," Meralda replied, dipping a polite curtsey, head bowed.

"If you wish to walk at night, do so in the garden," Priscilla added, her tone a bit less harsh.

Meralda, head still bowed so that Priscilla could not see her face, smiled knowingly. She was beginning to figure out how to get to the woman. Priscilla liked a feisty target, not an agreeable, humble one.

Priscilla turned to leave with a frustrated huff.

"We have news," Lord Feringal said suddenly, stopping the woman short. Meralda's head shot up, her face flush with surprise and more than a little anger. She wanted to choke her intended's words back at that moment. The time for the announcement had not yet come.

"We have decided that we cannot wait until the spring to marry," the oblivious Feringal went on. "The wedding shall be on the day of the autumn equinox."

As expected, Priscilla's face turned bright red. It was obviously taking all of the woman's willpower to keep her from shaking.

"Indeed," she said through clenched teeth. "And have you shared your news with Steward Temigast?"

"You're the first," Lord Feringal replied. "Out of courtesy, and since you are the one making the wedding preparations."

"Indeed," Priscilla said again with ice in her voice. "Do go tell him, Feri," she bade. "He is in the library. I will see that Meralda is escorted home."

That brought Lord Feringal rushing back to Meralda. "Not so long now, my love," he said. Gently kissing her knuckles, he strode away eagerly to find the steward.

"What did you do to him out there?" Priscilla snapped at Meralda as soon as her brother was gone.

Meralda pursed her lips. "Do?"

"You, uh, worked your charms upon him, didn't you?"

Meralda laughed out loud at Priscilla's efforts to avoid coarse language, a response the imposing Priscilla certainly did not expect. "Perhaps I should have," she replied. "Put a calming on the beast, we call it, but no, I didn't. I love him, you know, but my ma didn't raise a slut. Your brother's to marry me, and so we'll wait. Until the autumn equinox, by his own words."

Priscilla narrowed her eyes threateningly.

"You hate me for it," Meralda accused her bluntly. Priscilla was not prepared for that. Her eyes widened, and she fell back a step. "You hate me for taking your brother and disrupting the life you had set out for yourself, but I'm finding that to be a bit selfish, if I might be saying so. Your brother loves me and I him, and so we're to marry, with or without your blessings."

"How dare you—"

"I dare tell the truth," cut in Meralda, surprised at her own forwardness but knowing she could not back down. "My ma won't live the winter in our freezing house, and I'll not let her die. Not for the sake of what's proper, and not for your own troubles. I know you're doing the planning, and so I'm grateful to you, but do it faster."

"That is what this is all about, then?" Priscilla asked, thinking she had found a weakness here. "Your mother?"

" 'Tis about your brother," Meralda replied, standing straight, shoulders squared. "About Feringal and not about Priscilla, and that's what's got you so bound up."

Priscilla was so overwrought and surprised that she couldn't even force an argument out of her mouth. Flustered, she turned and fled, leaving Meralda alone in the foyer.

The young woman spent a long moment considering her own words, hardly able to believe that she had stood her ground with Priscilla. She considered her next move and thought it prudent to be leaving. She'd spotted Liam with the coach out front when she and Feringal had returned, so she went to him and bade him to take her home.

⚔ ⚔ ⚔ ⚔ ⚔

He watched the coach travel down the road from the castle, as he did every time Meralda returned from another of her meetings with the lord of Auckney.

Jaka Sculi didn't know what to make of his own feelings. He kept thinking back to the moment when Meralda had told him about the child, about *his* child. He had rebuffed her, allowing his guard to slip so that his honest feelings showed clearly on his face. Now this was his punishment, watching her come back down the road from Castle Auck, from *him*.

What might Jaka have done differently? He surely didn't want the life Meralda had offered. Never that! The thought of marrying the woman, of her growing fat and ugly with a crying baby about, horrified him, but perhaps not as much as the thought of Lord Feringal having her.

That was it, Jaka understood now, though the rationalization did little to change what he felt in his heart. He couldn't bear the notion of Meralda lying down for the man, of Lord Feringal raising Jaka's child as if it were his own. It felt as if the man were stealing from him outright, as every lord in every town did to the peasants in more subtle ways. Yes, they always took from the peasants, from honest folk like Jaka. They lived in comfort, surrounded by luxury, while honest folk like Jaka broke their fingernails in the dirt and ate rotten food. They took the women of their choice, offering nothing of character, only wealth against which peasants like Jaka could not compete. Feringal took his woman, and now he would take Jaka's child.

Trembling with rage, Jaka impulsively ran down to the road waving his arms, bidding the coach to stop.

"Be gone!" Liam Woodgate called down from above, not slowing one bit.

"I must speak with Meralda," Jaka cried. "It is about her ma."

That made Liam slow the coach enough so that he could glance down and get Meralda's thoughts. The young woman poked her head out the coach window to learn the source of the commotion. Spotting an obviously agitated Jaka, she blanched but did not retreat.

"He wants me to stop so he can speak with you. Something about your ma," the coachman explained.

Meralda eyed Jaka warily. "I'll speak with him," she agreed. "You can stop and let me out here, Liam."

"Still a mile to your home," the gnome driver observed, none too happy about the disturbance. "I could be taking you both there," he offered.

Meralda thanked him and waved him away. "A mile I'll walk easy," she answered and was out the door before the coach had even stopped rolling, leaving her alone on the dark road with Jaka.

"You're a fool to be out here," Meralda scolded as soon as Liam had turned the coach around and rambled off. "What are you about?"

"I had no choice," Jaka replied, moving to hug her. She pushed him away.

"You know what I'm carrying," the woman went on, "and so will Lord Feringal soon enough. If he puts you together with my child he'll kill us both."

"I'm not afraid of him," Jaka said, pressing toward her. "I know only how I feel, Meralda. I had no choice but to come to you tonight."

"You've made your feelings clear enough," the woman replied coldly.

"What a fool I was," Jaka protested. "You must understand what a shock the news was, but I'm over that. Forgive me, Meralda. I cannot live without your charity."

Meralda closed her eyes, her body swaying as she tried to digest it all. "What're you about, Jaka Sculi?" she asked again quietly. "Where's your heart?"

"With you," he answered softly, coming closer.

"And?" she prompted, opening her eyes to stare hard at him. He didn't seem to understand. "Have you forgotten the little one already then?" she asked.

"No," he blurted, catching on. "I'll love the child, too, of course."

Meralda found that she did not believe him, and her expression told him so.

"Meralda," he said, taking her hands and shaking his head. "I can't bear the thought of Lord Feringal raising my—our child as his own."

Wrong answer. All of Meralda's sensibilities, her eyes still wide open from her previous encounter with this boy, screamed the truth at her. It wasn't about his love for the child, or even his love for her. No, she realized, Jaka didn't have the capacity for such emotions. He was here now, pleading his love, because he couldn't stand the thought of being bested by Lord Feringal.

Meralda took a deep and steadying breath. Here was the man she thought she had loved saying all the things she'd once longed to hear. The two of them would be halfway to Luskan by now if Jaka had taken this course when she'd come to him. Meralda Ganderlay was a wiser woman now, a woman thinking of her own well-being and the welfare of her child. Jaka would never give them a good life. In her heart she knew he'd come to resent her and the child soon enough, when the trap of poverty held them in its inescapable grip. This was a competition, not love. Meralda deserved better.

"Be gone," she said to Jaka. "Far away, and don't you come back."

The man stood as if thunderstruck. "But—"

"There are no answers you can give that I'll believe," the woman went on. "There's no life for us that would keep you happy."

"You're wrong."

"No, I'm not, and you know it, too," Meralda said. "We had a moment, and I'll hold it dear for all of my life. Another moment revealed the truth of it all. You've no room in your life for me or the babe. You never will." What she really wanted to tell him was to go away and grow up, but he didn't need to hear that from her.

"You expect me to stand around quietly and watch Lord Feringal—"

Clapping her hands to her ears, Meralda cut him off. "Every word you speak takes away from my good memories. You've made your heart plain to me."

"I was a fool," Jaka pleaded.

"And so you still are," Meralda said coldly. She turned and walked away.

Jaka called after her, his cries piercing her as surely as an arrow, but she held her course and didn't look back, reminding herself every step of the truth of this man, this boy. She broke into a run and didn't stop until she reached her home.

A single candle burned in the common room. To her relief, her parents and Tori were all asleep, a merciful bit of news for her because she didn't want to talk to anyone at that time. She had resolved her feelings about Jaka at last, could accept the pain of the loss. She tried hard to remember the night of passion and not the disappointments that had followed, but those disappointments, the revelations about who this boy truly was, were the thing of harsh reality, not the dreamy fantasies of young lovers. She really did want him to just go away.

Meralda knew that she had another more pressing problem. The autumn equinox was too far away, but she understood that she would never convince Lord Feringal, let alone Priscilla and Temigast, to move the wedding up closer than that.

Perhaps she wouldn't have to, she thought as an idea came to her. The fiefdom would forgive them if they were married in the fall and it was somehow revealed that they had been making love beforehand. Auckney was filled with "seven month babies."

Lying in her dark room, Meralda nodded her head, knowing what she had to do. She would seduce Feringal again, and very soon. She knew his desires and knew, too, that she could blow them into flame with a simple kiss or brush of her hand.

Meralda's smile dissipated almost immediately. She hated

herself for even thinking such a thing. If she did soon seduce Feringal he would think the child his own, the worst of all lies, for Feringal and for the child.

She hated the plan and herself for devising it, but then, in the other chamber, her mother coughed. Meralda knew what she had to do.

18

THE HEART FOR IT

"Our first customers," Morik announced. He and Wulfgar stood on a high ridge overlooking the pass into Icewind Dale. A pair of wagons rolled down the trail, headed for the break in the mountains, their pace steady but not frantic.

"Travelers or merchants?" Wulfgar asked, unconvinced.

"Merchants, and with wealth aboard," the rogue replied. "Their pace reveals them, and their lack of flanking guardsmen invites our presence."

It seemed foolish to Wulfgar that merchants would make such a dangerous trek as this without a heavy escort of soldiers, but he didn't doubt Morik's words. On his own last journey from the dale beside his former friends, they had come upon a single merchant wagon, riding alone and vulnerable.

"Surprised?" Morik asked, noting his expression.

"Idiots always surprise me," Wulfgar replied.

"They cannot afford the guards," Morik explained. "Few who make the run to Icewind Dale can, and those who can usually take the safer, western pass. These are minor merchants, you see, trading pittances. Mostly they rely on good fortune, either in finding able warriors looking for a ride or an open trail to get them through."

"This seems too easy."

"It is easy!" Morik replied enthusiastically. "You understand, of course, that we are doing this caravan a favor." Wulfgar didn't appear convinced of that.

"Think of it," prompted the rogue. "Had we not killed the giants, these merchants would likely have found boulders raining down on them," Morik explained. "Not only would they be stripped of their wealth, but their skin would be stripped from their bones in a giant's cooking pot." He grinned. "So do not fret, my large friend," he went on. "All we want is their coin, fair payment for the work we have done for them."

Strangely, it made a bit of sense to Wulfgar. In that respect, the work to which Morik referred was no different than Wulfgar had been doing for many years with Drizzt and the others, the work of bringing justice to a wild land. The difference was that never before had he asked for payment, as Morik was obviously thinking to do now.

"Our easiest course would be to show them our power without engaging," the rogue explained. "Demand a tithe in payment for our efforts, some supplies and a perhaps a bit of gold, then let them go on their way. With only two wagons, though, and no other guards evident, we might be able to just knock them off completely, a fine haul, if done right, with no witnesses." His smile as he explained that latter course disappeared when he noted Wulfgar's frown.

"A tithe then, no more," Morik compromised. "Rightful payment for our work on the road."

Even that sat badly with the barbarian, but he nodded his head in agreement.

✕ ✕ ✕ ✕ ✕

He picked a section of trail littered with rocks where the wagons would have to slow considerably or risk losing a wheel or a horse. A single tree on the left side of the trail provided Wulfgar with the prop he would need to carry out his part of the attack, if it came to that.

Morik waited in clear view along the trail as the pair of wagons came bouncing along.

"Greetings!" he called, moving to the center of the trail, his arms held high. Morik shrank back just a bit, seeing the man on the bench seat beside the driver lifting a rather large crossbow his way. Still, he couldn't back up too much, for he had to get the wagon to stop on the appropriate mark.

"Out o' the road, or I'll shoot ye dead!" the crossbowman yelled.

In response, Morik reached down and lifted a huge head, the head of a slain giant, into the air. "That would be ill-advised," he replied, "both morally and physically."

The wagon bounced to a stop, forcing the one behind it to stop as well.

Morik used his foot, nearly straining his knee in the process, to move a second severed giant head out from behind a rock. "I am happy to inform you that the trail ahead is now clear."

"Then get outta me way," the driver of the first wagon replied, "or he'll shoot ye down, and I'll run ye into ruts."

Morik chuckled and moved aside the pack he had lain on the trail, revealing the third giant head. Despite their bravado, he saw that those witnessing the spectacle of the heads were more than a little impressed—and afraid. Any man who could defeat three giants was not one to take lightly.

"My friends and I have worked hard all the tenday to clear the trail," Morik explained.

"Friends?"

"You think I did this alone?" Morik said with a laugh. "You flatter me. No, I had the help of many friends." Morik cast his gaze around the rocky outcroppings of the pass as if acknowledging his countless "friends." "You must forgive them, for they are shy."

"Ride on!" came a cry from inside the wagon, and the two men on the bench seat looked at each other.

"Yer friends hide like thieves," the driver yelled at Morik. "Clear the way!"

"Thieves?" Morik echoed incredulously. "You would be dead already, squashed flat under a giant's boulder, were it not for us."

The wagon door creaked open and an older man leaned out, standing with one foot inside and the other on the running board. "You're demanding payment for your actions," he remarked, obviously knowing this routine all too well—as did most merchants of the northern stretches of Faerûn.

"Demand is such a nasty word," Morik replied.

"Nasty as your game, little thief," the merchant replied.

Morik narrowed his eyes threateningly and glanced pointedly down at the three giant heads.

"Very well, then," the merchant conceded. "What is the price of your heroism?"

"We need supplies that we might maintain our vigil and keep the pass safe," Morik explained reasonably. "And a bit of gold, perhaps, as a reward for our efforts." It was the merchant's turn to scowl. "To pay the widows of those who did not survive our raid on the giant clan," Morik improvised.

"I'd hardly call three a clan," the merchant replied dryly, "but I'll not diminish your efforts. I offer you and your hiding friends a fine meal, and if you agree to accompany us to Luskan as guards, I will pay each of you a gold piece a day," the merchant added, proud of his largesse and obviously pleased with himself for having turned the situation to his advantage.

Morik's eyes narrowed at the weak offer. "We have no desire to return to Luskan at this time."

"Then take your meal and be happy with that," came the curt response.

"Idiot," Morik remarked under his breath. Aloud he countered the merchant's offer. "We will accept no less than fifty gold pieces and enough food for three fine meals for seven men."

The merchant laughed. "You will accept our willingness to let you walk away with your life," he said. He snapped his fingers, and a pair of men leaped from the second wagon, swords drawn. The driver of that wagon drew his as well.

"Now be gone!" he finished, and he disappeared back into the coach. "Run him down," he cried to his driver.

"Idiots!" Morik screamed, the cue for Wulfgar.

The driver hesitated, and that cost him. Holding the end of a strong rope, Wulfgar leaped from his concealment along the left-hand rock wall and swooped in a pendulum arc with a bloodcurdling howl. The crossbowman spun and fired but missed badly. Wulfgar barreled in at full speed, letting go of the rope and swinging his mighty arms out wide to sweep both crossbowman and driver from the bench, landing atop them in a pile on the far side. An elbow to the face laid the driver low. Reversing his swing, Wulfgar slammed the crossbowman on the jaw, surely breaking it as blood gushed forth.

The three swordsmen from the trailing wagon came on, two to the left of the first wagon, the third going to the right. Morik went right, a long and slender sword in one hand, a dagger in the other, intercepting the man before he could get to Wulfgar.

The man came at the rogue in a straightforward manner. Morik put his sword out beside the thrusting blade but rolled it around, disengaging. He stepped ahead, looping his dagger over the man's sword and pulling it harmlessly aside while he countered with a thrust of his own sword, heading for the man's throat. He had him dead, or would have, except that Morik's arm was stopped as surely as if he were trying to poke his sword through solid stone.

"What are you doing?" he demanded of Wulfgar as the barbarian stepped up and slugged the guard, nearly losing his ear to the thrashing sword and dagger. The man got his free hand up to block, but Wulfgar's heavy punch went right through the defense, planting his fist and the man's own forearm into his face and launching him away. But it was a short-lived victory.

Though staggered by Wulfgar's elbow, the driver was up again with blade in hand. Worse still, the other two swordsmen had found strong positions, one atop the bench, the other in front of the wagon. If that weren't bad enough, the merchant burst from the door, a wand in hand.

"Now we are the idiots!" Morik yelled to Wulfgar, cursing and spinning out from the attack of the swordsman on the bench. From the man's one thrust-and-cut routine, Morik could tell that this one was no novice to battle.

Wulfgar went for the merchant. Suddenly he was flying backward, his hair dancing on end, his heart palpitating wildly.

"So that's what the wand does," Morik remarked after the flash. "I hate wizards."

He went at the swordsman on the ground, who defeated his initial attempt at a quick kill with a circular parry that almost had the rogue overbalancing. "Do hurry back!" Morik called to Wulfgar, then he ducked and thrust his sword up frantically as the swordsman from the bench leaped atop the horse team and stabbed at his head.

The driver came at Wulfgar, as did the man he had just slugged, and the barbarian worked fast to get the hammer off his back. He started to meet the driver's charge but stopped fast and reversed his grip and direction, spinning the hammer the merchant's way instead, having no desire to absorb another lightning bolt.

The hammer hit the mark perfectly, not on the merchant, but against the coach door, slamming it on the man's extended arm just as he was about to loose yet another blast. Fire he did, though, a sizzling bolt that just missed the other man rushing Wulfgar.

"All charge!" Morik called, looking back to the rocky cliff on the left. The bluff turned his opponents' heads for just an instant. When they turned back, they found the rogue in full flight, and Morik was a fast runner indeed when his life was on the line.

The driver came in hesitantly, respectful of Wulfgar's strength. The other man, though, charged right in, until the barbarian turned toward him with a leap and a great bellow. Wulfgar reversed direction almost immediately, going back for the driver, catching the man by surprise with his uncanny agility. He accepted a stinging cut along the arm in exchange for grabbing the man's weapon hand. Pulling him close with a great tug, Wulfgar bent low, clamped his free hand on the man's belt, and hoisted the flailing fool high over his head. A turn and a throw sent the driver hard into his charging companion.

Wulfgar paused, to note Morik skittering by in full flight. A reasonable choice, given the course of the battle, but the barbarian's blood was up, and he turned back to the wagons and the two swordsmen, just in time to get hammered by another lightning stroke. With his long legs, Wulfgar passed Morik within fifty yards up the rocky climb.

Another bolt slammed in near to the pair, splintering rocks. A crossbow quarrel followed soon after, accompanied by taunts and threats, but there came no pursuit, and soon the pair were running up high along the cliffs. When they dared to stop and catch their breath, Wulfgar looked down at the two scars on his tunic, shaking his head.

"We would have won if you had gone straight for the merchant after your sweep of the driver and crossbowman as planned," Morik scolded.

"And you would have cut out that man's throat," charged Wulfgar.

Morik scowled. "What of it? If you've not the heart for this life, then why are we out here?"

"Because you chose to deal with murderers in Luskan," Wulfgar reminded him, and they shared icy stares. Morik put his hand on his blade, thinking that the big man might attack him.

Wulfgar thought about doing just that.

They walked back to the cave separately. Morik beat him there and started in. Wulfgar changed his mind and stayed outside, moving to a small stream nearby where he could better tend his wounds. He found that his chest wasn't badly scarred, just the hair burned away from what was a minor lightning strike. However, his shoulder wound had reopened rather seriously. Only then, with his heavy tunic off, did the barbarian understand how much blood he had lost.

Morik found him out there several hours later, passed out on a flat rock. He roused the barbarian with a nudge. "We did not fare well," the rogue remarked, holding up a pair of bottles, "but we are alive, and that is cause for celebration."

"We need cause?" Wulfgar replied, not smiling, and he turned away.

"First attacks are always disastrous," Morik explained reasonably. "We must become accustomed to each other's fighting style, is all."

Wulfgar considered the words in light of his own experience, in light of the first true battle he and Drizzt had seen together. True, at one point, he had almost clobbered the drow with a low throw of Aegis-fang, but from the start there had been a symbiosis with Drizzt, a joining of heart that had brought them to a joining of battle routines. Could he say the same with Morik? Would he ever be able to?

Wulfgar looked back at the rogue, who was smiling and holding out the bottles of potent liquor. Yes, he would come to terms with Morik. They would become of like heart and soul. Perhaps that was what bothered Wulfgar most of all.

"The past no longer exists, and the future does not yet exist," Morik reasoned. "So live in the present and enjoy it, my friend. Enjoy every moment."

Wulfgar considered the words, a common mantra for many of those living day-to-day on the streets. He took the bottle.

19

THE CHANCE

We've not much time! What am I to wear?" Biaste Ganderlay wailed when Meralda told her the wedding had been moved up to the autumn equinox.

"If we're to wear anything more than we have, Lord Feringal will be bringing it by," Dohni Ganderlay said, patting the woman's shoulder. He gave Meralda a look of pride, and mostly of appreciation, and she knew that he understood the sacrifice she was making here.

How would that expression change, she wondered, if her father learned of the baby in her belly?

She managed a weak smile in reply despite her thoughts and went into her room to dress for the day. Liam Woodgate had arrived earlier to inform Meralda that Lord Feringal had arranged for her to meet late that same day with the seamstress who lived on the far western edge of Auckney, some two hours' ride.

"No borrowed gowns for the great day." Liam had proclaimed. "If you don't mind my saying so, Biaste, your daughter will truly be the most beautiful bride Auckney's ever known."

How Biaste's face had glowed and her eyes sparkled! Strangely, that also pained Meralda, for though she knew that she was doing right by her family, she could not forgive herself for her stupidity with Jaka. Now she had to seduce Lord Feringal, and soon, perhaps that very night. With the wedding moved up, she could only hope that others, mostly Priscilla and Temigast, would forgive her for conceiving a child before the official ceremony. Worst of all, Meralda would have to take the truth of the child with her to her grave.

What a wretched creature she believed herself to be at that moment. Madam Prinkle, a seamstress renowned throughout the lands, would no doubt make her a most beautiful gown with gems and rich, colorful fabrics, but she doubted she would be wearing the glowing face to go with it.

Meralda got cleaned up and dressed, ate a small meal, and was all smiles when Liam Woodgate returned for her, guiding her into the coach. She sat with her elbow propped on the sill, staring at the countryside rolling by. Men and gnomes worked in the high fields, but she neither looked for nor spotted Jaka Sculi among them. The houses grew sparse, until only the occasional cottage dotted the rocky landscape. The carriage went through a small wood, where Liam stopped briefly to rest and water the horses.

Soon they were off again, leaving the small woods and traveling into rocky terrain again. On Meralda's right was the sea. Sheer rock cliffs rose on the north side of the path, some reaching down so close to the water's edge that Meralda wondered how Liam would get the coach through.

She wondered, too, how any woman could live out here alone. Meralda resolved to ask Liam about it later. Now she spied an outpost, a stone keep flying Lord Feringal's flag. Only then did she begin to appreciate the power of the lord of Auckney. The slow-moving coach had only traveled about ten miles, but it seemed as if they had gone halfway around the world. For some reason she couldn't understand, the sight of Feringal's banner in this remote region made Meralda feel better, as if powerful Lord Feringal Auck would protect her.

Her smile was short lived as she remembered he would only protect her if she lied.

The woman sank back into her seat, sighed, and felt her still-flat belly, as if expecting the baby to kick right then and there.

⚔ ⚔ ⚔ ⚔ ⚔

"The flag is flying, so there are soldiers within," Wulfgar reasoned.

"Within they shall stay," Morik answered. "The soldiers rarely leave the shelter of their stones, even when summoned. Their lookout, if they have one, is more concerned with those attacking the keep and not with anything down on the road. Besides, there can't be more than a dozen of them this far out from any real supply towns. I doubt there are even half that number."

Wulfgar thought to remind Morik that far fewer men had routed them just a couple of days before, but he kept quiet.

After the disaster in the pass, Morik had suggested they go out from the region, in case the merchant alerted Luskan guards, true to his belief that a good highwayman never stays long in one place, particularly after a failed attack. Initially, Morik wanted to go north into Icewind Dale, but Wulfgar had flatly refused.

"West, then," the rogue had offered. "There's a small fiefdom squeezed between the mountains and the sea southwest of the Hundelstone pass. Few go there, for it's not on most maps, but the merchants of the northern roads know of it, and sometimes they travel there on their way to and from Ten-Towns. Perhaps we will even meet up with our friend and his lightning wand again."

The possibility didn't thrill Wulfgar, but his refusal to go back into Icewind Dale had really left them only two options. They'd be deeper into the unaccommodating Spine of the World if they went east to the realm of goblins and giants and other nasty, unprofitable monsters. That left south and west, and given their relationship with the authorities of Luskan in the south, west seemed a logical choice.

It appeared as if that choice would prove to be a good one, for the pair watched as a lone wagon, an ornate carriage such as a nobleman might ride, rambled down the road.

"It could be a wizard," Wulfgar reasoned, painfully recalling the lightning bolts he'd suffered.

"I know of no wizards of any repute in this region," Morik replied.

"You haven't been in this region for years," Wulfgar reminded him. "Who would dare travel in such an elaborate carriage alone?" he wondered aloud.

"Why not?" Morik countered. "This area south of the mountains sees little trouble, and there are outposts along the way, after all," he added, waving his hand at the distant stone keep. "The people here are not trapped in their homes by threats of goblins."

Wulfgar nodded, but it seemed too easy. He figured that the coach driver must be a veteran fighter, at least. It was likely there would be others inside, and perhaps they held nasty wands or other powerful magical items. One look at Morik, though, told the barbarian that he'd not dissuade his friend. Morik was still smarting from the disaster in the pass. He needed a successful hit.

The road below made a great bend around a mountain spur. Morik and Wulfgar took a more direct route, coming back to the road far ahead of the coach, out of sight of the stone outpost.

Wulfgar immediately began laying out his rope, looking for some place he might tie it off. He found one slender tree, but it didn't look promising.

"Just jump in," Morik reasoned, pointing to an overhang. The rogue rushed down to the road, taking out a whip as he went, for the coach appeared, rambling around the southern bend.

"Clear the way!" came Liam Woodgate's call a moment later.

"I must speak with you, good sir!" Morik cried, holding his ground in the middle of the narrow trail. The gnome slowed the coach and brought it to a halt a safe distance from the rogue—and too far, Morik noted, for Wulfgar to make the leap.

"By order of Lord Feringal of Auckney, clear the way," Liam stated.

"I am in need of assistance, sir," Morik explained, watching out of the corner of his eye as Wulfgar scrambled into position. Morik took a step ahead then, but Liam warned him back.

"Keep your distance, friend," the gnome said. "I've an errand for my lord, and don't doubt that I'll run you down if you don't move aside."

Morik chuckled. "I think not," he said.

Something in Morik's tone, or perhaps just a movement along the high rocks caught the corner of Liam's eye. Suddenly the gnome understood the imminent danger and spurred his team forward.

Wulfgar leaped out at that moment, but he hit the side of the carriage behind the driver, his momentum and the angle of the rocky trail putting the thing up on two wheels. Inside the coach a woman screamed.

Purely on instinct, Morik brought forth his whip and gave a great *crack* right in front of the horses. The beasts cut left against the lean, and before the driver could control them, before

Wulfgar could brace himself, before the passenger inside could even cry out again, the coach fell over on its side, throwing both the driver and Wulfgar.

Dazed, Wulfgar forced himself to his feet, expecting to be battling the driver or someone else climbing from the coach, but the driver was down among some rocks, groaning, and no sounds came from within the coach. Morik rushed to calm the horses, then leaped atop the coach, scrambling to the door and pulling it open. Another scream came from within.

Wulfgar went to the driver and gently lifted the gnome's head. He set it back down, secure that this one was out of the fight but hoping he wasn't mortally wounded.

"You must see this," Morik called to Wulfgar. He reached into the coach, offering his hand to a beautiful young woman, who promptly backed away. "Come out, or I promise I will join you in there," Morik warned, but still the frightened woman curled away from him.

"Now that is the way true highwaymen score their pleasures," Morik announced to Wulfgar as the big man walked over to join him. "And speaking of pleasures. . . ." he added, then dropped into the coach.

The woman screamed and flailed at him, but she was no match for the skilled rogue. Soon he had her pinned against the coach's ceiling, which was now a wall, her arms held in place, his knee blocking her from kicking his groin, his lips close to hers. "A kiss for the winner?"

Morik rose suddenly, caught by the collar and hoisted easily out of the coach by a fuming Wulfgar. "You cross a line," Wulfgar replied, dropping the rogue on the ground.

"She is fairly caught," Morik argued, not understanding his friend's problem. "We have our way, and we let her go. What's the harm?"

Wulfgar glared at him. "Go tend the driver's wounds," he said. "Then find what treasures you may about the wagon."

"The girl—"

"—does not count as a treasure," Wulfgar growled at him.

Morik threw his hands up in defeat and moved to check on the fallen gnome.

Wulfgar reached into the coach, much as Morik had done, offering his huge paw to the frightened young woman. "Come out," he bade her. "I promise you won't be harmed."

Stunned and sore, the woman dodged his hand.

"We can't turn your wagon upright with you in it," Wulfgar explained reasonably. "Don't you wish to be on your way?"

"I want you to be on your way," the woman snarled.

"And leave you here alone?"

"Better alone than with thieves," Meralda shot back.

"It would be better for your driver if you got out. He'll die if we leave him lying on the rocks," Wulfgar was trying very hard to comfort the woman, or at least frighten her into action. "Come. I'll not hurt you. Rob you, yes, but not hurt you."

She timidly lifted her hand. Wulfgar took hold and easily hoisted her out of the coach. Setting her down, he stared at her for a long moment. Despite a newly forming bruise on the side of her face she was truly a beautiful young woman. He could understand Morik's desire, but he had no intention of forcing himself on any woman, no matter how beautiful, and he certainly wasn't going to let Morik do so.

The two thieves spent a few moments going through the coach, finding, to Morik's delight, a purse of gold. Wulfgar searched about for a log to use as a lever.

"You don't intend to upright the carriage, do you?" Morik asked incredulously.

"Yes, I do," Wulfgar replied.

"You can't do that," the rogue argued. "She'll drive right up to the stone keep and have a host of soldiers pursuing us within the hour."

Wulfgar wasn't listening. He found some large rocks and placed them near the roof of the fallen carriage. With a great tug, he brought the thing off the ground. Seeing no help forthcoming from Morik, he braced himself and managed to free one hand to slide a rock into place under the rim.

The horses snorted and tugged, and Wulfgar almost lost the whole thing right there. "At least go and calm them," he instructed Morik. The rogue made no move. Wulfgar looked to the woman, who ran to the team and steadied them.

"I can't do this alone," Wulfgar called again to Morik, his tone growing more angry.

Blowing out a great, long-suffering sigh, the rogue ambled over. Studying the situation briefly, he trotted off to where Wulfgar had left the rope, which he looped about the tree then brought one end back to tie off the upper rim of the coach. Morik passed by the woman, who jumped back from him, but he scarcely noticed.

Next, Morik took the horses by their bridle and pulled them around, dragging the coach carefully and slowly so that its wheels were equidistant from the tree. "You lift, and I will set the rope to hold it," he instructed Wulfgar. "Then brace yourself and lift it higher, and soon we will have it upright."

Morik was a clever one, Wulfgar had to admit. As soon as the rogue was back in place at the rope and the woman had a hold of the team again, Wulfgar bent low and gave a great heave, and up the carriage went.

Morik quickly took up the slack, tightening the rope around the tree, allowing Wulfgar to reset his position. A moment later, the barbarian gave another heave, and again Morik held the coach in place at its highest point. The third pull by Wulfgar brought it over bouncing onto its four wheels.

The horses nickered nervously and stamped the ground, tossing their heads in protest so forcefully that the woman couldn't hold on. Wulfgar was beside her instantly, though, grabbing the bridles and pulling hard, steadying the beasts. Then, using the same rope, he tied them off to the tree and went to the fallen driver.

"What's his name?" he asked of the woman. Seeing her hesitation he said, "We can't do anything worse to you than we have already, just by knowing your name. I feel strange helping him but not knowing what to call him."

The woman's expression lightened as she saw the sense of his remark. "His name's Liam." Apparently having found some courage, she came over and crouched next to her driver, concern replacing fear on her face. "Is he going to be all right?"

"Don't know yet."

Poor Liam seemed far from consciousness, but he was alive, and upon closer inspection his injuries didn't appear too serious. Wulfgar lifted him gently and brought him to the coach, laying him on the bench seat inside. The barbarian went back to the woman, taking her arm and pulling her along behind him.

"You said you wouldn't hurt me," she protested and tried to fight back. She would have had an easier time holding back the two horses.

Morik's smile grew wide when Wulfgar dragged her by. "A change of heart?" the rogue asked.

"She's coming with us for a while," Wulfgar explained.

"No!" the young woman protested. Balling up her fist, she leaped up and smacked Wulfgar hard across the back of his head.

He stopped and turned to her, his expression amused and a little impressed at her spunk. "Yes," he answered, pinning her

303

arm as she tried to hit him again. "You'll come with us for just a mile," he explained. "Then I'll let you loose to return to the coach and the driver, and you may go wherever you please."

"You won't hurt me?"

"Not I," Wulfgar answered. He glowered at Morik. "Nor him."

Realizing she had little choice in the matter, the young woman went along without further argument. True to his word, Wulfgar released her a mile or so from the coach. Then he and Morik and their purse of gold melted into the mountains.

⚔ ⚔ ⚔ ⚔ ⚔

Meralda ran the whole way back to poor Liam. Her side was aching by the time she found the old gnome. He was awake but hardly able to climb out of the coach, let alone drive it.

"Stay inside," the woman bade him. "I'll turn the team around and get us back to Castle Auck."

Liam protested, but Meralda just shut the door and went to work. Soon she had them moving back west along the road, a bumpy and jostling ride, for she was not experienced in handling horses and the road was not an easy one. Along the way, the miles and the hours rolling out behind her, an idea came to the woman, a seemingly simple solution to all her troubles.

It was long after sunset when they pulled back into Auckney proper at the gates of Castle Auck. Lord Feringal and Priscilla came out to greet them, and their jaws dropped when they saw the bedraggled woman and the battered coachman within.

"Thieves on the road," Meralda explained. Priscilla climbed to her side, uncharacteristically concerned. In a voice barely above a whisper, Meralda added, "He hurt me." With that, she broke into sobs in Priscilla's arms.

⚔ ⚔ ⚔ ⚔ ⚔

The wind moaned around him, a sad voice that sang to Wulfgar about what had been and what could never be again, a lost time, a lost innocence, and friends he sorely missed yet could not seek out.

Once more he sat on the high bluff at the northern end of the pass through the Spine of the World, overlooking Icewind Dale, staring out to the northeast. He saw a sparkle out there. It might have been a trick of the light, or maybe it was the slanted rays of late afternoon sunlight reflecting off of Maer Dualdon, the largest of the three lakes of the Ten-Towns region. Also, he thought he saw Kelvin's Cairn, the lone mountain north of the range.

It was probably just his imagination, he told himself again or a trick of the light, for the mountain was a long way from him. To Wulfgar, it seemed like a million miles.

"They have camped outside the southern end of the pass," Morik announced, moving to join the big man. "There are not so many. It should be a clean take."

Wulfgar nodded. After the success along the shore road to the west, the pair had returned to the south, the region between Luskan and the pass, and had even bought some goods from one passing merchant with their ill-found gold. Then they had come back to the pass and had hit another caravan. This time it went smoothly, with the merchant handing over a tithe and no blood spilled. Morik had spotted their third group of victims, a caravan of three wagons heading north out of Luskan, bound for Icewind Dale.

"Always you are looking north," the rogue remarked, sitting next to Wulfgar, "and yet you will not venture there. Have you enemies in Ten-Towns?"

"I have friends who would stop us if they knew what we were about," Wulfgar explained.

"Who would *try* to stop us?" cocky Morik replied.

Wulfgar looked him right in the eye. "They *would* stop us," he insisted, his grave expression offering no room for argument. He let that look linger on Morik for a moment, then turned back to the dale, the wistfulness returning as well to his sky-blue eyes.

"What life did you leave behind there?" Morik asked.

Wulfgar turned back, surprised. He and Morik didn't often talk about their respective pasts, at least not unless they were drinking.

"Will you tell me?" Morik pressed. "I see so much in your face. Pain, regret, and what else?"

Wulfgar chuckled at that observation. "What did I leave behind?" he echoed. After a moment's pause, he answered, "Everything."

"That sounds foolish."

"I could be a king," Wulfgar went on, staring out at the dale again as if speaking to himself . Perhaps he was. "Chieftain of the combined tribes of Icewind Dale, with a strong voice on the council of Ten-Towns. My father—" He looked at Morik and laughed. "You would not like my father, Morik. Or at least, he would not like you."

"A proud barbarian?"

"A surly dwarf," Wulfgar countered. "He's my adoptive father," he clarified as Morik sputtered over that one. "The Eighth King of Mithral Hall and leader of a clan of dwarves mining in the valley before Kelvin's Cairn in Icewind Dale."

"Your father is a dwarven king?" Wulfgar nodded. "And you are out on the road beside me, sleeping on the ground?" Again the nod. "Truly you are a bigger fool than I had believed."

Wulfgar just stared out at the tundra, hearing the sad song

of the wind. He couldn't disagree with Morik's assessment, but neither did he have the power to change things. He heard Morik reaching for his pack, then heard the familiar clink of bottles.

PART FOUR

We think we understand those around us. The people we have come to know reveal patterns of behavior, and as our expectations of that behavior are fulfilled time and again we begin to believe that we know the person's heart and soul.

BIRTH

I consider that to be an arrogant perception, for one cannot truly understand the heart and soul of another, one cannot truly appreciate the perceptions another might hold toward similar or recounted experiences. We all search for truth, particularly within our own sphere of existence, the home we have carved and those friends with whom we choose to share it. But truth, I fear, is not always evident where individuals, so complex and changing, are concerned.

If ever I believe that the foundations of my world are rooted in stone, I think of Jarlaxle and I am humbled. I have always recognized that there is more to the mercenary than a simple quest for personal gain—he let me and Catti-brie walk away from Menzoberranzan, after all, and at a time when our heads would have brought him a fine price, indeed. When Catti-brie was his prisoner and completely under his power, he did not take advantage of her, though he has admitted, through actions if not words, that he thinks her quite attractive. So always have I seen a level of character beneath the cold mercenary clothing, but despite that knowledge my last encounter with Jarlaxle has shown me that he is far more complex, and certainly more compassionate, than ever I could have guessed. Beyond that, he called himself a friend of Zaknafein, and though I initially recoiled at such a notion, now I consider it to be not only believable, but likely.

Do I now understand the truth of Jarlaxle? And is it the same truth that those around him, within Bregan D'aerthe, perceive? Certainly not, and though I believe my current assessment to be correct, I'll not be as arrogant as to claim certainty, nor do I even begin to believe that I know more of him than my surface reasoning.

What about Wulfgar, then? Which Wulfgar is the true Wulfgar? Is he the proud and honorable man Bruenor raised, the man who fought beside me against Biggrin and in so many subsequent battles? The man who saved the barbarian tribes from certain extermination and the folk of Ten-Towns from future disasters by uniting the groups diplomatically? The man who ran across Faer n for the sake of his imprisoned friend? The man who helped Bruenor reclaim his lost kingdom?

Or is Wulfgar the man who harmed Catti-brie, the haunted man who seems destined, in the end, to fail utterly?

He is both, I believe, a compilation of his experiences, feelings, and perceptions, as are we all. It is the second of that composite trio, feelings, brought on by experiences beyond his ability to cope, that control Wulfgar now. The raw emotion of those feelings alter his perceptions to the negative. Given that reality, who is Wulfgar now, and more importantly, if he survives this troubled time, who will he become?

How I long to know. How I wish that I could walk beside him on this perilous journey, could speak with him and influence him, perhaps. That I could remind him of who he was, or at least, who we perceived him to be.

But I cannot, for it is the heart and soul of Wulfgar, ultimately, and not his particular daily actions, that will surface in the end. And I, and anyone else, could no more influence that heart and soul as I could influence the sun itself.

Curiously, it is in the daily rising of that celestial body that I take my comfort now when thinking about Wulfgar. Why watch the dawn? Why then, why that particular time, instead of any other hour of daylight?

Because at dawn the sun is more brilliant by far. Because at dawn, we see the resurgence after the darkness. There is my hope, for as with the sun, so it can be true of people. Those who fall can climb back up, then brighter will they shine in the eyes of those around them.

I watch the dawn and think of the man I thought I knew, and pray that my perceptions were correct.

— Drizzt Do'Urden

THE LAST GREAT ACT
OF SELFISHNESS

He kicked at the ground, splashing mud, then jammed his toe hard against an unyielding buried rock that showed only one-hundredth of its actual size. Jaka didn't even feel the pain, for the tear in his heart—no, not in his heart, but in his pride—was worse by far. A thousand times worse.

The wedding would take place at the turn of the season, the end of this very tenday. Lord Feringal would have Meralda, would have Jaka's own child.

"What justice, this?" he cried. Reaching down to pick up the rock he learned the truth of its buried size. Jaka grabbed another and came back up throwing, narrowly missing a pair of older farmers leaning on their hoes.

The pair, including the old long-nosed dwarf, came storming over, spitting curses, but Jaka was too distracted by his own problems, not understanding that he had just made another problem, and didn't even notice them.

Until, that is, he spun around to find them standing right

behind him. The surly dwarf leaped up and launched a balled fist right into Jaka's face, laying him low.

"Damn stupid boy," the dwarf grumbled, then turned to walk away.

Humiliated and hardly thinking, Jaka kicked at his ankles, tripping him up.

In an instant, the slender young man was hauled to his feet by the other farmer. "Are you looking to die then?" the man asked, giving him a good shake.

"Perhaps I am," Jaka came back with a great, dramatic sigh. "Yes, all joy has flown from this coil."

"Boy's daft," the farmer holding Jaka said to his companion. The dwarf was coming back over, fists clenched, jaw set firm under his thick beard. As he finished, the man whipped Jaka around and shoved him backward toward the other farmer. The dwarf didn't catch Jaka but instead shoved him back the other way, high up on the back so that the young man went face down in the dirt. The dwarf stepped on the small of Jaka's back, pressing down with his hard-soled boots.

"You watch where you're throwing stones," he said, grinding down suddenly and for just an instant, blowing the breath out of Jaka.

"The boy's daft," the other farmer said as he and his companion walked away.

Jaka lay on the ground and cried.

⚔ ⚔ ⚔ ⚔ ⚔

"All that good food at the castle," remarked Madam Prinkle, an old, gray woman with a smiling face. The woman's skin, hanging in wrinkled folds, seemed too loose for her bones. She grabbed Meralda's waist and gave a pinch. "If you change your size every tenday, how's my dress ever to fit you? Why, girl, you're three fingers bigger."

Meralda blushed and looked away, not wanting to meet the stare of Priscilla, who was standing off to the side, watching and listening intently.

"Truly I've been hungry lately," Meralda replied. "Been eating everything I can get into my mouth. A bit on the jitters, I am." She looked anxiously at Priscilla, who had been working hard with her to help her lose her peasant accent.

Priscilla nodded, but hardly seemed convinced.

"Well, you best find a different way for calming," Madam Prinkle replied, "or you'll split the dress apart walking to Lord Feringal's side." She laughed riotously then, one big, bobbing ball of too-loose skin. Meralda and Priscilla both laughed self-consciously as well, though neither seemed the least bit amused.

"Can you alter it correctly?" Priscilla asked.

"Oh, not to fear," replied Madam Prinkle. "I'll have the girl all beautiful for her day." She began to gather up her thread and sewing tools. Priscilla moved to help her while Meralda quickly removed the dress, gathered up her own things, and rushed out of the room.

Away from the other two, the woman put her hand on her undeniably larger belly. It was over two and a half months now since her encounter with Jaka in the starlit field, and though she doubted that the baby was large enough to be pushing her belly out so, she certainly had been eating volumes of late. Perhaps it was nerves, perhaps it was because she was nourishing two, but whatever the cause, she would have to be careful for the rest of the tenday so as not to draw more attention to herself.

"She will have the dress back to us on the morrow," Priscilla said behind her, and the young woman nearly jumped out of her boots. "Is something wrong, Meralda?" the woman asked, moving beside her and dropping a hand on her shoulder.

"Would you not be scared if you were marrying a lord?"

Priscilla arched a finely plucked brow. "I would not be frightened, because I would not be in such a situation," she replied.

"But if ye—you, were?" Meralda pressed. "If you were born a peasant, and the lord—"

"Preposterous," the woman interrupted. "If I had been born a peasant, I would not be who I am, and so your whole question makes little sense."

Meralda stared at her, obviously confused.

"I am not a peasant because I've not the soul nor blood of a peasant," Priscilla explained. "You people think it an accident that you were born of your family, and we of nobility born of ours, but that is not the case, my dear. Station comes from within, not without."

"So you're better, then?" Meralda asked bluntly.

Priscilla smiled. "Not better, dear," she answered condescendingly. "Different. We each have our place."

"And mine's not with your brother," the younger woman posited.

"I do not approve of mixing blood," Priscilla stated, and the two stared at each other for a long and uncomfortable while.

Then you should marry him yourself, Meralda thought, but bit back.

"However, I shall honor my brother's choice," Priscilla went on in that same denigrating tone. "It is his own life to ruin as he pleases. I will do what I may do to bring you as close to his level as possible. I do like you, my dear," she added, reaching out to pat Meralda's shoulder.

You'd let me clean your commode then, Meralda silently fumed. She wanted to speak back against Priscilla's reasoning, truly she did, but she wasn't feeling particularly brave at that moment. No, given the child, Jaka's child, growing within her womb, she was vulnerable now, and feeling no match for the likes of vicious Priscilla Auck.

⚔ ⚔ ⚔ ⚔ ⚔

It was late in the morning when Meralda awoke. She could tell from the height of the sun beaming through her window. Worried, she scrambled out of bed. Why hadn't her father awakened her earlier for chores? Where was her mother?

She pushed through the curtain into the common room and calmed immediately, for there sat her family, gathered around the table. Her mother's chair was pulled back, and the woman sat facing the ceiling. A curious man, dressed in what seemed to be religious garments, chanted softly and patted her forehead with sweet-smelling oil.

"Da?" she started to ask, but the man held his hand up to quiet her, motioning her to move near him.

"Watcher Beribold," he explained. "From the Temple of Helm in Luskan. Lord Feringal sent him to get your ma up and strong for the wedding."

Meralda's mouth dropped open. "You can heal her then?"

"A difficult disease," Watcher Beribold replied. "Your mother is strong to have fought on with such resilience." Meralda started to press him, but he answered her with a reassuring smile. "Your mother will be on the mend and free of the wilting before I and High Watcher Risten depart Auckney," he promised.

Tori squealed, and Meralda's heart leaped with joy. She felt her father's strong arm go around her waist, pulling her in close. She could hardly believe the good news. She had known that Lord Feringal would heal her mother, but never had she imagined that the man would see to it before the wedding. Her mother's illness was like a huge sword Feringal had hanging over her head, and yet he was removing it.

She considered the faith Lord Feringal was showing in her to send a healer unbidden to her family door. Jaka would never have relinquished such an obvious advantage. Not for her, not for anyone. Yet here was Feringal—and the man was no fool—holding enough faith in Meralda to take the sword away.

The realization brought a smile to Meralda's face. For so long, she had considered the courtship with Feringal to be a sacrifice for her family, but now, suddenly, she was recognizing the truth of it all. He was a good man, a handsome man, a man of means who loved her honestly. The only reason she'd been unable to return his feeling was because of her unhealthy infatuation with a selfish boy. Strange, but she, too, had been cured of her affliction by the arrival of Feringal's healer.

The young woman went back into her room to dress for the day. She could hardly wait for her next visit with Lord Feringal, for she suspected—no, she knew—that she would see the man a bit differently now.

She was with him that very afternoon for what would be their last meeting before the wedding. Feringal, excited about the arrangements and the guest list, said nothing at all about the healer's visit to Meralda's house.

"You sent your healer to my house today," she blurted, unable to contain the thoughts any longer. "Before the wedding. With my ma sick and you alone the power to heal her, you could have made me your slave."

Feringal looked as if he simply couldn't digest her meaning. "Why would I desire such a thing?"

That honest and innocent question confirmed that which she had already known. A smile wreathed her beautiful face, and she leaped up impulsively to plant a huge kiss on Feringal's cheek. "Thank you for healing my ma, for healing my family."

Her thanks filled his heart and face with joy. When she tried to kiss him again on the cheek, he turned so that his lips met hers. She returned it tenfold, confident that her life with this kind and wonderful man would be more than tolerable. Far more.

Pondering the scene on the ride back to her home, Meralda's emotions took a downward swing as her thoughts shifted back to the baby and the lie she would have to tell for the rest of her days. How much more awful her actions seemed now! Meralda believed she was guilty of nothing more than poor judgment, but the reality would make it much more than that, would elevate her errant longing for one night of love to the status of treason.

And so it was with fear and hope and joy combined that Meralda stepped into the garden early the next morning to where every one of Auckney's nobles and important witnesses, her own family, Lord Feringal's sister and Steward Temigast included, stood smiling and staring at her. There was Liam Woodgate dressed in his finery, holding the door and beaming from ear to ear, and at the opposite end of the garden from her stood High Watcher Kalorc Risten, a more senior priest of Helm, Feringal's chosen god, in his shining armor and plumed, open-faced helmet.

What a day and what a setting for such an event! Priscilla had replaced her summer flowers with autumn-blooming mums, kaphts, and marigolds, and though they weren't as brilliant as the previous batch, the woman had supplemented their hues with bright banners. It had rained before the dawn, but the clouds had flown, leaving a clean smell in the air. Puddles atop the low wall and droplets on petals caught the morning sunlight in a sparkling display. Even the wind off the ocean smelled clean this day.

Meralda's mood brightened. About to be married, she couldn't be vulnerable any longer. She was not afraid of anything more than tripping over her own feet as she made her way to the ceremonial stand, a small podium bedecked on top by a war gauntlet and with a tapestry depicting a blue eye set on its front. That confidence was only bolstered when Meralda looked upon the shining face of her mother, for Kalorc Risten's young assistant had, indeed, worked a miracle upon the woman. Meralda had feared that her mother would not be healthy enough to attend the ceremony, but now her face was aglow, her eyes sparkling with health she had not enjoyed in years.

Beaming herself, all fears about her secret put away, the young woman began her walk to the podium. She didn't trip. Far from it. Those watching thought Meralda seemed to float along the garden path, the perfect bride, and if she was a bit thicker in the middle, they all believed it a sign that the young woman was at last eating well.

Standing beside the prefect, Meralda turned to watch Lord Feringal's entrance. He stepped out in his full Auckney Castle Guard Commander's uniform, a shining suit of mail crossed in gold brocade, a plumed helmet on his head, and a great sword belted to his hip. Many in the crowd gasped, women tittered, and Meralda thought again that her union with the man might not be such a bad thing. How handsome Feringal seemed to her, even more so now because she knew the truth of his gentle heart. His dashing soldiery outfit was little more than show, but he did cut a grand and impressive figure.

All smiles, Feringal joined her beside the High Watcher. The clergyman began the ceremony, solemnly appointing all gathered as witnesses to the sacred joining. Meralda focused her gaze not on Lord Feringal but on her family. She scarcely heard Kalorc Risten as he preached through the ceremony. At one point she was given a chalice of wine to sip, then to hand to Lord Feringal.

The birds were singing around them, the flowers were

spectacular, the couple handsome and happy—it was the wedding that all the women of Auckney envied. Everyone not in attendance at the ceremony was invited to greet the couple afterward outside the castle's front gate. To those of lesser fortune, the spectacle evoked vicarious pleasure. Except from one person.

"*Meralda!*"

The cry cut the morning air and sent a flock of gulls rushing out from the cliffs east of the castle. All eyes turned toward the voice from high on a cliff. There stood a lone figure, the unmistakable, saggy-shouldered silhouette of Jaka Sculi.

"Meralda!" the foolish young man cried again, as if the name had been torn from his heart.

Meralda looked to her parents, to her fretting father, then to the face of her soon-to-be husband.

"Who is that?" Lord Feringal asked in obvious agitation.

Meralda sputtered and shook her head, her expression one of honest disgust. "A fool," she finally managed to say.

"You cannot marry Lord Feringal! Run away with me, I beg you, Meralda!" Jaka took a step precariously close to edge of the cliff.

Lord Feringal, and everyone else, it seemed, stared hard at Meralda.

"A childhood friendship," she explained hastily. "A fool, I tell you, a little boy, and nothing to be concerned with." Seeing that her words were having little effect, she put her hand on Feringal's forearm and moved very close. "I'm here to marry you because we found a love I never dreamed possible," she said, trying desperately to reassure him.

"*Meralda!*" Jaka wailed.

Lord Feringal scowled up at the cliff. "Someone shut the fool up," he demanded. He looked to High Watcher Risten. "Drop a globe of silence on his foolish head."

"Too far," Risten replied, shaking his head, though in truth, he hadn't even prepared such a spell.

At the other end of the garden, Steward Temigast feared where this interruption could lead, so he hustled guards off to silence the loudmouthed young man.

Like Temigast, Meralda was truly afraid, wondering how stupid Jaka would prove to be. Would the idiot say something that could cost Meralda the wedding, that might cost them both their reputations and perhaps their very lives?

"Run away with me, Meralda," Jaka yelled. "I am your true love."

"Who is that bastard?" Lord Feringal demanded again, past agitated.

"A field worker who thinks he is in love with me," she whispered while the crowd watched the couple. Meralda recognized the danger here, the volatile fires simmering in Feringal's eyes. She looked at him directly and stated flatly, without room for debate, "If you and I were not to be married, if we hadn't found love together, I'd still have nothing to do with that fool."

Lord Feringal stared at her a while longer, but he couldn't stay angry after hearing Meralda's honest assessment.

"Shall I continue, my lord?" High Watcher Risten asked.

Lord Feringal held up his hand. "When the fool is dragged away," he replied.

"Meralda! If you do not come out to me, I shall throw myself to the rocks below!" Jaka yelled suddenly, and he stepped forward to the rim of the cliff.

Several people in the garden gasped, but not Meralda. She stood eyeing Jaka coldly, so angry that she cared little if the fool went through with his threat, because she was certain he wouldn't. He hadn't the courage to kill himself. He wanted only to torture and humiliate her publicly to show up Lord Feringal. This was petty revenge, not love.

"Hold!" cried a guard, fast approaching Jaka on the cliff.

The young man spun around at the call, but as he did so his foot slipped out from under him, dropping him to his belly. He clawed with his hands but slid farther out so that he was hanging in air from the chest down, a hundred-foot drop to jagged rocks below him.

The guard lunged for him, but he was too late.

"*Meralda!*" came Jaka's last cry, a desperate, wailing howl as he dropped from sight.

Stunned as she was by the sudden, dramatic turn, Meralda was torn between disbelieving grief for Jaka and awareness that Feringal's scrutinizing gaze was upon her, watching and measuring her every reaction. She immediately understood that any failure on her part now would be held against her when the truth of her condition became evident.

"By the gods!" she gasped, slapping her hand over her mouth. "Oh, the poor fool!" She turned to Lord Feringal and shook her head, seeming very much at a loss.

And surely she was, her heart a jumble of hatred, horror, and remembered passion. She hated Jaka—how she hated him—for his reaction to the knowledge that she was pregnant, and hated him even more for his stupidity on this day. Still, she could not deny those remembered feelings, the way the mere sight of Jaka had put such a spring in her skip just a few short months before. Meralda knew that Jaka's last cry would haunt her for the rest of her life.

She hid all of that and reacted as those around her did to the gruesome sight—with shock and horror.

They postponed the wedding. Three days later they would complete the ceremony on a gray and thickly overcast morning. It seemed fitting.

⚔ ⚔ ⚔ ⚔ ⚔

Meralda felt the hesitance in her husband's movements for the rest of the day during the grand celebration that was open to all of Auckney. She tried to approach Feringal about it, but he would not reveal himself. Meralda understood he was afraid. And why wouldn't Feringal be afraid? Jaka had died crying out to Feringal's wife-to-be.

But still, as the wine flowed and the merriment continued, Lord Feringal managed more than a few smiles. How those smiles widened when Meralda whispered into his ear that she could hardly wait for their first night together, the consummation of their love.

In truth, the young woman was excited by the prospect, if not a bit fearful. He would recognize, of course, that her virginity wasn't intact, but that was not such an uncommon thing among women living in the harsh farming environment, working hard, often riding horses, and could be explained away. She wondered if perhaps it might be better to reveal the truth of her condition and the lie she had concocted to explain it.

No, she decided, even as she and her husband ascended the staircase to their private quarters. No, the man had been through enough turmoil in the last few days. This would be a night for his pleasure, not his pain.

She would see to that.

⚔ ⚔ ⚔ ⚔ ⚔

It was a grand first tenday of marriage, full of love and smiles, and those of Biaste Ganderlay touched Meralda most of all. Her family had not come to live with her at Castle Auck. She wouldn't dare suggest such a thing to Priscilla, not yet, but High Watcher Risten had worked tirelessly with Meralda's mother and had declared the woman completely cured. Meralda could see the truth of it painted clearly on Biaste's beaming face.

She could see, too, that though still shaken by Jaka's act upon the cliff, Feringal would get by the event. The man loved her, of that she was sure, and he fawned over her constantly.

Meralda had come to terms with her own feelings for Jaka. She was sorry for what had happened, but she carried no guilt for the man's death. Jaka had done it to himself, and for himself and surely not for her. Meralda understood now that Jaka had done everything for himself. There would always be a tiny place in her heart for the young man, for the fantasies that would never be, but it was more than compensated for by the knowledge that her family would be better off than any of them could ever have hoped. Eventually, she'd move Biaste and Dohni into the castle or a proper estate of their own, and she'd help Tori find a suitable husband, a wealthy merchant perhaps, when the girl was ready.

There remained only one problem. Meralda feared that Priscilla was catching on to her condition, for the woman, though outwardly pleasant, had cast her a few unmistakable glances. Suspicious glances, like those of Steward Temigast. They knew of her condition or suspected it. In any case they would all know soon enough, which brought a measure of desperation creeping into Meralda's otherwise perfect existence.

Meralda had even thought of going to High Watcher Risten to see if there was some magic that might rid her of the child. She had dismissed that thought almost immediately, however, and not for any fears that Risten would betray her. While she wanted no part of Jaka Sculi, she couldn't bring herself to destroy the life that was growing within her.

By the end of the first tenday of her marriage, Meralda had

determined the only course open to her, and by end of the second tenday she had mustered the courage to initiate her plan. She asked the cook to prepare eggs for breakfast and waited at the table with Feringal, Priscilla, and Temigast. Better to get it over with all of them at once.

Even before the cook came out with the eggs the smell of the food drifted in to Meralda and brought that usual queasy feeling to her. She bent over and clutched at her belly.

"Meralda?" Feringal asked with concern.

"Are you all right, child?" Temigast added.

Meralda looked across the table to Priscilla and saw suspicion there.

She came up fast with a wail and began crying immediately. It was not hard for Meralda to bring forth those tears.

"No, I am not all right!" she cried.

"What is it, dearest?" Lord Feringal asked, leaping up and running to her side.

"On the road," Meralda explained between sobs, "to Madam Prinkle's . . ."

"When you were attacked?" Steward Temigast supplied gently.

"The man, the big one," Meralda wailed. "He ravished me!"

Lord Feringal fell back as if struck.

"Why did you not tell us?" Temigast demanded after a hesitation that seemed to hit all three of them. Indeed, the cook, entering with Meralda's breakfast plate, dropped it to the floor in shock.

"I feared to tell you," Meralda wailed, looking to her husband. "I feared you'd hate me."

"Never!" Feringal insisted, but he was obviously shaken to the core, and he made no move to come back to his wife's side.

"And you're telling us now because . . . ?" Priscilla's tone and

Temigast's wounded expression revealed to the young woman that they both knew the answer.

"Because I'm with child, I fear," Meralda blurted. Overwhelmed by her own words and the smell of those damned eggs, she leaned to the side and vomited. Meralda heard Feringal's cry of despair through her own coughs, and it truly hurt the woman to wound him so.

Then there came only silence.

Meralda, finished with the sickness, feared to sit up straight, feared to face the three. She didn't know what they would do, though she had heard of a village woman who had become pregnant through rape. That woman had not been held to blame.

A comforting hand gripped her shoulder and eased her out of the chair. Priscilla hugged Meralda close and whispered softly into her ear that it would be all right.

"What am I to do?" Lord Feringal stuttered, hardly able to speak through the bile in his throat. His tone made Meralda think that he might banish her from the castle, from his life, then and there.

Steward Temigast moved to support the young man. "This is not without precedence, my lord," the old man explained. "Even in your own kingdom." All three stared at the steward.

"There is no betrayal here, of course," Temigast went on. "Except that Meralda did not immediately tell us. For that, you may punish her as you see fit, though I pray you will be generous toward the frightened girl."

Feringal looked at Meralda hard, but he nodded just a bit.

"As for the child," Temigast went on, "it must be announced openly and soon. It will be made clear and binding that this child will not be heir to your throne."

"I will slay the babe as it is born!" Lord Feringal said with a growl. Meralda wailed, as did Priscilla, to Meralda's absolute surprise.

"My lord," said Steward Temigast. Feringal punched his fists

327

against the sides of his legs in utter frustration. Meralda noted his every movement then, and recognized that his claim of murder was pure bluster.

Steward Temigast just shook his head and walked over to pat Lord Feringal's shoulder. "Better to give the babe to another," he said. "Let it be gone from your sight and from your lives."

Feringal stared questioningly at his wife.

"I'm not wanting it," Meralda answered that look with an honest answer. "I'm not wanting to think at all of that night, er, time." She bit her lip as she finished, hoping that her slip of the tongue had not been detected.

To her relief and continued surprise it was Priscilla who stayed close to her, who escorted her to her room. Even when they were out of earshot of Temigast and Lord Feringal, the older woman's gentle demeanor did not waver in the least.

"I cannot guess your pain," Priscilla said.

"I'm sorry I didn't tell you sooner."

Priscilla patted her cheek. "It must have been too painful," she offered, "but you did nothing wrong. My brother was still your first lover, the first man to whom you gave yourself willingly, and a husband can ask no more than that."

Meralda swallowed the guilt she felt, swallowed it and pushed it aside with the justification that Feringal was, indeed, her first true lover, the first man she'd lain with who had honest feelings for her.

"Perhaps we will come to some agreement when the child is born," Priscilla said unexpectedly.

Meralda looked at her strangely, not quite catching on.

"I was thinking that perhaps it would be better if I found another place to live," Priscilla explained. "Or took a wing of the castle for myself, perhaps, and made it my own."

Meralda squinted in puzzlement, then it hit her. She was so

shocked that her previous peasant dialect came rushing back. "Ye're thinking o' taking the babe for yerself," she blurted.

"Perhaps, if we could agree," Priscilla said hesitantly.

Meralda had no idea of how to respond but suspected she wouldn't know until after the child was born. Would she be able to have the baby anywhere near her? Or would she find that she could not part with an infant that was hers, after all?

No, she decided, not that. She would not, could not, keep the child, however she might feel after its birth.

"We plan too far ahead," Priscilla remarked as if reading Meralda's mind. "For now we must make sure you eat well. You are my brother's wife now and will give him heirs to the throne of Auckney. We must keep you healthy until then."

Meralda could hardly believe the words, the genuine concern. She had never expected this level of success with her plan, which only made her feel even more guilty about it all.

And so it went for several days, with Meralda believing that things were on a steady course. There were a few rough spots, particularly in the bedroom, where she had to constantly assuage her husband's pride, insisting that the barbarian who had savaged her had given her no pleasure at all. She even went to the extent of claiming that she was practically unconscious throughout the ordeal and wasn't even sure it had happened until she came to realize that she was with child.

Then one day, Meralda encountered an unexpected problem with her plan.

"Highwaymen do not travel far," she heard Lord Feringal tell Temigast as she joined the two in the drawing room.

"Certainly the scoundrels are nowhere near Auckney," the steward replied.

"Close enough," Feringal insisted. "The merchant Galway has a powerful wizard for hire."

"Even wizards must know what to look for," Temigast remarked.

"I don't remember his face," Meralda blurted, hurrying to join them.

"But Liam Woodgate does," said Feringal, wearing the smug smile of one who intended to find his revenge.

Meralda worked very hard to not appear distressed.

21

THE BANE OF ANY THIEF

The little creature scrambled over the rocks, descending the steep slope as if death itself were chasing it. With an outraged Wulfgar close behind, roaring in pain from his reopened shoulder wound, the goblin would've had better odds against death.

The trail ended at a fifteen-foot drop, but the goblin's run didn't end there as it leaped with hardly a thought. Landing with a thump and a rather sorry attempt at a roll, it got back up, bloody but still moving.

Wulfgar didn't follow. He couldn't afford to take himself so far from the cave entrance where Morik was still battling. The barbarian skidded to a stop and searched about for a rock. Snatching one up, he heaved it at the fleeing goblin. He missed, the goblin too far away, but satisfied that it wouldn't return, Wulfgar turned and sprinted back to the cave.

Long before he arrived there, though, he saw that the battle had ended. Morik was perched on a rock at the base of a jagged spur of stones, huffing and puffing. "The little rats run fast," Morik remarked.

Wulfgar nodded and fell into a sitting position on the ground. They had gone out to scout the pass earlier. Upon returning, they'd found a dozen goblins determined to take the cave home as their own. Twelve against two—the goblins hadn't had a chance.

Only one of the goblins was dead, one Wulfgar had caught first by the throat and squeezed. The others had been sent running to the four winds, and both men knew that none of the cowardly creatures would return for a long, long time.

"I did get its purse, if not its heart," Morik remarked holding up a little leather bag. He blew into his empty hand for luck—and also because the mountain wind whistled chilly that day—then emptied the bag, his eyes wide. Wulfgar, too, leaned in eagerly. A pair of silver pieces, several copper, and three shiny stones—not gemstones, just stones—tumbled out.

"Our luck that we did not encounter a merchant on the path," Wulfgar muttered sarcastically, "for this is a richer haul by far."

Morik flung the meager treasure to the ground. "We still have plenty of gold from the raid on the coach in the west," he remarked.

"So nice to hear you admit it," came an unexpected voice from above. The pair looked up the rocky spur to see a man in flowing blue robes and holding a tall oaken staff staring down at them. "I would hate to believe I'd found the wrong thieves, after all."

"A wizard," Morik muttered with disgust, tensing. "I hate wizards."

The robed man lifted his staff and began chanting. Wulfgar moved quicker, skidding down to scoop a fair-sized stone, then coming up fast and launching it. His aim proved perfect. The rock crashed against the wizard's chest, though it harmlessly bounced away. If the man even noticed it, he showed no sign.

"I hate wizards!" Morik yelled again, diving out of the way. Wulfgar started to move, but he was too late, for the lightning bolt firing from the staff clipped him and sent him flying.

Up came Wulfgar, rolling and cursing, a rock in each hand. "How many hits can you take?" he cried to the wizard, letting fly one that narrowly missed. The second one went spinning into the obviously amused wizard's blocking arm and bounced away as surely as if it had hit solid stone.

"Does everybody in all of Faerûn have access to a wizard?" Morik cried, picking his trail from cover to cover as he tried to ascend the spur. Morik believed he could get away from, outwit, or outfight—particularly with Wulfgar beside him—any bounty hunter or warrior lord in the area. However, wizards were an entirely different manner, as he had learned so many painful times before, most recently in his capture on the streets of Luskan.

"How many can you take?" Wulfgar yelled again, hurling another stone that also missed its mark.

"One!" the wizard replied. "I can take but one."

"Then hit him!" Morik yelled to Wulfgar, misunderstanding. The wizard was not talking about taking hits on his magical stoneskin, but about taking prisoners. Even as Morik cried out, the robed man pointed at Wulfgar with his free hand. A black tendril shot from his extended fingers, snaking down the spur at tremendous speed to wrap around Wulfgar, binding him fast to the mage.

"I'll not leave the other unscathed!" the wizard cried to no one present. He clenched his fist, his ring sparkled, and he stamped his staff on the stone. A blinding light, a puff of smoke, and Wulfgar and the mage were gone amid a thunderous rumble along the spur.

"Wizards," Morik spat with utter contempt, just before the spur, with Morik halfway up it, collapsed.

✗ ✗ ✗ ✗ ✗

He was in the audience hall of a castle. The incessant black tendril continued to wrap him stubbornly in its grip, looping his torso several times, trying to pin his powerful arms. Wulfgar punched at it, but it was a pliable thing, and it merely bent under the blows, absorbing all the energy. He grabbed at the tendril, tried to twist and tear it, but even as his hands worked one area, the long end of the tendril, released from the wizard's hand, looped his legs and tripped him up, bringing him crashing to the hard floor. Wulfgar rolled and squirmed and wriggled to no avail. He was caught.

The barbarian used his arms to keep the thing from wrapping his neck, and when he was at last sure that it could not harm him, he turned his attention more fully to the area around him. There stood the wizard before a pair of chairs, wherein sat a man in his mid-twenties and a younger, undeniably beautiful woman—a woman Wulfgar recognized all too well.

Beside them stood an old man, and in a chair to the side sat a plump woman of perhaps forty winters. Wulfgar also noted that several soldiers lined the room, grim-faced and well-armed.

"As I promised," the wizard said, bowing before the man on the throne. "Now, if you please, there is the small matter of my payment."

"You will find the gold awaiting you in the quarters I provided," the man replied. "I never doubted you, good sir. Your merchant mentor Galway recommended you most highly."

The wizard bowed again. "Are my services further required?" he asked.

"How long will it last?" the man asked, indicating the tendril holding Wulfgar.

"A long time," the wizard promised. "Long enough for you to question and condemn him, certainly, then to drag him down to your dungeon or kill him where he lies."

"Then you may go. Will you dine with us this night?"

"I fear that I have pressing business at the Hosttower," the wizard replied. "Well met, Lord Feringal." He bowed again and walked out, chuckling as he passed the prone barbarian.

To everyone's surprise, Wulfgar growled and grabbed the tendril in both hands and tore it apart. He had just managed to gain his feet, many voices screaming around him, when a dozen soldiers descended, pounding him with mailed fists and heavy clubs. Still fighting against the tendril, Wulfgar managed to free his hand for one punch, sending a soldier flying, and to grab another by the neck and slam him facedown on the floor. Wulfgar went down, dazed and battered. As the wizard magically dispelled the remnants of the tendril, the barbarian's arms were brought behind him and looped with heavy chains.

"If it were just me and you, wizard, would you have anything left with which to stop me?" the stubborn barbarian growled.

"I would have killed you out in the mountains," snapped the mage, obviously embarrassed by the failure of his magic.

Wulfgar launched a ball of spit that struck the man in the face. "How many can you take?" he asked.

The enraged wizard began waggling his fingers, but before he could get far Wulfgar plowed through the ring of soldiers and shoulder-slammed the man, sending him flying away. The barbarian was subdued again almost immediately, but the shaken wizard climbed up from the floor and skittered out of the room.

"Impressive display," Lord Feringal said sarcastically, scowling. "Am I to applaud you before I castrate you?"

That got Wulfgar's attention. He started to respond, but a guard slugged him to keep him quiet.

Lord Feringal looked to the young woman seated beside him. "Is this the man?" he asked, venom in every word.

Wulfgar stared hard at the woman, at the woman he had stopped Morik from harming on the road, at the woman he had released unscathed. He saw something there in her rich, green eyes, some emotion he could not quite fathom. Sorrow, perhaps? Certainly not anger.

"I . . . don't think so," the woman said and looked away.

Lord Feringal's eyes widened, indeed. The old man standing beside him gasped openly, as did the other woman.

"Look again, Meralda," Feringal commanded sharply. "Is it him?"

No answer, and Wulfgar could clearly see the pain in the woman's eyes.

"Answer me!" the lord of Auckney demanded.

"No!" the woman cried, refusing to meet any gaze.

"Fetch Liam," Lord Feringal yelled. Behind Wulfgar, a soldier rushed out of the room, returning a moment later with an old gnome.

"Oh, be sure it is," the gnome said, coming around to stare Wulfgar right in the eye. "You thinking I won't know you?" he asked. "You got me good, with your little rat friend distracting my eyes and you swinging down. I know you, thieving dog, for I seen you afore you hit me!" He turned to Lord Feringal. "Aye," he said. "He's the one."

Feringal eyed the woman beside him for a long, long time. "You are certain?" he asked Liam, his eyes still on the woman.

"I've not been bested often, my lord," Liam replied. "You've named me as the finest fighter in Auckney, which's why you entrusted me with your lady. I failed you, and I'm not taking that lightly. He's the one, I say, and oh, but what I'd pay you to let me fight him fairly."

He turned back and glared into Wulfgar's eyes. Wulfgar matched that stare, and though he had no doubt he could snap this gnome in half with hardly an effort, he said nothing. Wulfgar couldn't escape the fact that he had wronged the diminutive fellow.

"Have you anything to say for yourself?" Lord Feringal asked Wulfgar. Before the barbarian could begin to reply, the young lord rushed forward, brushing Liam aside to stand very close. "I have a dungeon for you," he whispered harshly. "A dark place, filled with the waste and bones of the previous occupants. Filled with rats and biting spiders. Yes, fool, I have a place for you to rot until I decide the time has come to kill you most horribly."

Wulfgar knew the procedure well by this point in his life and merely heaved a heavy sigh. He was promptly dragged away.

In the corner of the audience hall, Steward Temigast watched it all very carefully, shifting his gaze from Wulfgar to Meralda and back again. He noted Priscilla, sitting quietly, no doubt taking it all in, as well.

He noted the venom on Priscilla's face as she regarded Meralda. She was thinking that the woman had enjoyed being ravished by the barbarian, Temigast realized. She was thinking that, perhaps, it hadn't really been a rape.

Given the size of the man, Temigast couldn't agree with that assessment.

The cell was everything Lord Feringal had promised, a wretched, dark, damp place filled with the awful stench of death. Wulfgar couldn't see a thing, not his own hand if he held it an inch in front of his face. He scrabbled around in the mud and worse, pushing past sharp bones in a futile attempt to find some piece of dry ground upon which he might sit. And all the while he slapped at the spiders and other crawling things that scurried in to learn what new meal had been delivered to them.

To most, this dungeon would have seemed worse than Luskan's prison tunnels, mostly because of its purest sense of emptiness and solitude, but Wulfgar feared neither rats nor spiders. His terrors ran much deeper than that. Here in the dark he found he was somewhat able to fend off those horrors.

And so the day passed. Sometime during the next one, the barbarian awoke to torchlight and the sound of a guard slipping a plate of rotten food through the small slit in the half-barred, half-metal hatch that sealed the filthy burrow cell from the wet tunnels beyond. Wulfgar started to eat but spat it out, thinking he might be better off trying to catch and skin a rat.

That second day a turmoil of emotions found the barbarian. Mostly he was angry at all the world. Perhaps he deserved punishment for his highwayman activities—he could accept responsibility for that—but this went beyond justice concerning his actions on the road with Lord Feringal's coach.

Also, Wulfgar was angry at himself. Perhaps Morik had been right all along. Perhaps he did not have the heart for this life. A true highwayman would have let the gnome die or at least finished him quickly. A true highwayman would have taken his pleasures with the woman, then dragged her along either to be sold as a slave or kept as a slave of his own.

Wulfgar laughed aloud. Yes, indeed, Morik had been right. Wulfgar hadn't the heart for any of it. Now here he was, the wretch of wretches, a failure at the lowest level of civilized society, a fool too incompetent to even be a proper highwayman.

He spent the next hour not in his cell, but back in the Spine of the World, that great dividing line between who he once was and what he had become, that physical barrier that seemed such an appropriate symbol of the mental barrier within him, the wall he had thrown up like an emotional mountain range to hold back the painful memories of Errtu.

In his mind's eye he was there now, sitting on the Spine of the World, staring out over Icewind Dale and the life he once knew, then turning around to face south and the miserable existence he now suffered. He kept his eyes closed, though he wouldn't have seen much in the dark anyway, ignored the many crawling things assaulting him, and got more than a few painful spider bites for his inattentiveness.

Sometime later that day, a noise brought him from his trance. He opened his eyes to see the flickers of another torch in the tunnel beyond his door.

"Living still?" came a question from the voice of an old man.

Wulfgar shifted to his knees and crawled to the door, blinking repeatedly as his eyes adjusted to the light. After a few moments he recognized the man holding the torch as the advisor Wulfgar had seen in the audience hall, a man who physically reminded him of Magistrate Jharkheld of Luskan.

Wulfgar snorted and squeezed one hand through the bars. "Burn it with your torch," he offered. "Take your perverted pleasures where you will find them."

"Angry that you were caught, I suppose," the man called Temigast replied.

"Twice imprisoned wrongly," Wulfgar replied.

"Are not all prisoners imprisoned wrongly by their own recounting?" the steward asked.

"The woman said that it wasn't me."

"The woman suffered greatly," Temigast countered. "Perhaps she cannot face the truth."

"Or perhaps she spoke correctly."

"No," Temigast said immediately, shaking his head. "Liam remembered you clearly and would not be mistaken." Wulfgar snorted again. "You deny that you were the thief who knocked over the carriage?" Temigast asked bluntly.

Wulfgar stared at him unblinking, but his expression spoke clearly that he did not deny the words.

"That alone would cost you your hands and imprison you for as many years as Lord Feringal decided was just," Temigast explained. "Or that alone could cost you your life."

"Your driver, Liam, was injured," Wulfgar replied, his voice a growl. "Accidentally. I could have let him die on the road. The girl was not harmed in any way."

"Why would she say differently?" Temigast asked calmly.

"Did she?" Wulfgar came back, and he tilted his head, beginning to catch on, beginning to understand why the young lord had been so completely outraged. At first he had thought mere pride to be the source—the man had failed to properly protect his wife, after all—but now, in retrospect, Wulfgar began to suspect there had been something even deeper there, some primal outrage. He remembered Lord Feringal's first words to him, a threat of castration.

"I pray that Lord Feringal has a most unpleasant death prepared for you, barbarian," Temigast remarked. "You cannot know the agony you have brought to him, to Lady Meralda, or to the folk of Auckney. You are a scoundrel and a dog, and justice will be served when you die, whether in public execution or down here alone in the filth."

"You came down here just to deliver this news?" Wulfgar asked sarcastically. Temigast struck him in the hand with the lit torch, forcing Wulfgar to quickly retract his arm.

With that the old man turned and stormed away, leaving Wulfgar alone in the dark and with some very curious notions swirling around in his head.

X X X X X

Despite his final outburst and genuine anger, Temigast didn't walk away with his mind made up about anything. He had gone to see the barbarian because of Meralda's reaction to the man in the audience hall, because he had to learn the truth. Now that truth, seemed fuzzier by far. Why wouldn't Meralda identify Wulfgar if she had, indeed, recognized him? How could she not? The man was remarkable, after all, being near to seven feet in height and with shoulders as broad as a young giant's.

Priscilla was wrong, Temigast knew, for he recognized that she was thinking that Meralda had enjoyed the rape. "Ridiculous," the steward muttered, verbalizing his thoughts that he might make some sense of them. "Purely and utterly ridiculous.

"But would Meralda protect her rapist?" he asked himself quietly.

The answer hit him as clearly as the image of an idiotic young man slipping off a cliff.

22

Good Lord Brandeburg

I hate wizards," Morik muttered, crawling out of the rubble of the slide, a dozen cuts and bruises decorating his body. "Not really a fair fight. I must learn this spellcasting business!"

The rogue spent a long while surveying the area, but of course, Wulfgar was nowhere to be found. The wizard's choice in taking Wulfgar seemed a bit odd to Morik. Likely the man thought Wulfgar the more dangerous of the two foes, probably the leader. But it had been Morik, and surely not Wulfgar, who had made an attempt at the lady in the carriage. Wulfgar was the one who had insisted that they let her go, and quickly enough to save the wounded driver. Obviously, the wizard had not come well informed.

Now where was Morik to turn? He went back to the cave first, tending his wounds and collecting the supplies he would need for the road. He didn't want to stay here, not with an angry band of goblins nearby and Wulfgar gone from his side. But where to go?

The choice seemed obvious after but a moment's serious thought—back to Luskan. Morik had always known he would venture back to the streets he knew so well. He'd concoct a new identity as far as most were concerned, but he'd remain very much the same intimidating rogue to those whose alliance he needed. The snag in his plans thus far had been Wulfgar. Morik couldn't walk into Luskan with the huge barbarian beside him and hope to maintain secrecy for any length of time.

Of course, there was also the not-so-little matter of dark elves.

Even that potential problem didn't hold up, though, for Morik had done his best to remain with Wulfgar, as he had been instructed. Now Wulfgar was gone, and the way was left open. Morik took the first steps out of the Spine of the World, heading back for the place he knew so well.

But something very strange happened just then to Morik's sensibilities. The rogue found himself taking two steps westward for every one south. It was no trick of the wizard but a spell cast by his own conscience, a spell of memory that whispered the demands Wulfgar had placed on Captain Deudermont at Prisoner's Carnival that Morik, too, must be set free. Bound by friendship for the first time in his miserable life, Morik the Rogue was soon trotting along the road, sorting out his plan.

He camped on the side of a mountain that night and spotted the campfire of a group of circled wagons. He wasn't far from the main northern pass. The wagons had come from Ten-Towns, no doubt, and were on the road to the south, thus wouldn't go anywhere near to the fiefdom in the west. It was unlikely these merchants had even heard of the place.

"Greetings!" Morik called to the lone sentry later that night.

"Stand fast!" the man called back. Behind him, the others scrambled.

"I am no enemy," Morik explained. "I'm a wayward

adventurer separated from my group, wounded a bit, but more angry than hurt."

After a short discussion, which Morik could not hear, another voice announced that he could approach, but it warned that a dozen archers were trained on his heart and he would be wise to keep his palms showing empty.

Wanting no part of a fight, Morik did just that, walking through twin lines of armed men into the firelight to stand before two middle-aged merchants, one a great bear of a man, the other leaner, but still quite sturdy.

"I am Lord Brandeburg of Waterdeep," Morik began, "returning to Ten-Towns, to Maer Dualdon, where I hope to find some remaining sport fishing for knucklehead. Fun business that!"

"You are a long way from anywhere, Lord Brandeburg," the heavier merchant replied.

"Late in the year to be out on Maer Dualdon," the other replied, suspicious.

"Yet that is where I am going, if I find my playful, wandering friends," Morik replied with a laugh. "Perchance have you seen them? A dwarf, Bruenor Battlehammer by name, his human daughter Catti-brie—oh, but the sun itself bows before her beauty!—a rather fat halfling, and . . ." Morik hesitated and appeared somewhat nervous suddenly, though the smiles of recognition on the faces of the merchants were exactly what he had hoped to see.

"And a dark elf," the heavy man finished for him. "Go ahead and speak openly of Drizzt Do'Urden, Lord Brandeburg. Well known, he is, and no enemy of any merchant crossing into the dale."

Morik sighed with feigned relief and silently thanked Wulfgar for telling him so much of his former friends during their drinking binges over the last few days.

"Well met, I say to you," the heavy man continued. "I am Petters, and my associate Goodman Dawinkle." On a motion from Petters, the guards behind Morik relaxed, and the trio settled into seats around the fire, where Morik was handed a bowl of thick stew.

"Back to Icewind Dale, you say?" Dawinkle asked. "How have you lost that group? No trouble, I pray."

"More a game," Morik answered. "I joined them many miles to the south, and perhaps in my ignorance I got a little forward with Catti-brie." Both merchants scowled darkly

"Nothing serious, I assure you," Morik quickly added. "I was unaware that her heart was for another, an absent friend, nor did I realize that grumbling Bruenor was her father. I merely requested a social exchange, but that, I fear was enough to make Bruenor wish to pay me back."

The merchants and guards laughed now. They had heard of surly and overprotective Bruenor Battlehammer, as had anyone who spent time in Icewind Dale.

"I fear that I bragged of some tracking, some ranger skills," Morik continued, "and so Bruenor decided to test me. They took my horse, my fine clothes, and disappeared from the road—so well into the brush, led by Drizzt, that one not understanding the dark elf's skills would think they had magical aid." The merchants bobbed their heads, laughing still.

"So now I must find them, though I know they are already nearing Icewind Dale." He chuckled at himself. "I'm sure they'll laugh when I arrive on foot, wearing soiled and tattered clothing."

"You look as if you've had a fight," Dawinkle remarked, noticing the signs of the landslide and the goblin battle.

"A row with a few goblins and a single ogre, nothing serious," the rogue replied nonchalantly. The men raised their eyebrows, but not in doubt—never that for someone who had traveled with those powerful companions. Morik's charm and skill was such that he understood how to weave tales beneath tales beneath tales, that the basic premise became quickly accepted as fact.

"You are welcome to spend the night, good sir," merchant Petters offered, "or as many nights as you choose. We are returning to Luskan, though, the opposite direction from your intended path."

"I will accept the bed this night," Morik replied, "and perhaps . . ." He let the words hang in the air, bringing his fingers to his lips in a pensive pose.

Both Petters and Dawinkle leaned forward in anticipation.

"Would you know where I might purchase a horse, a fine riding horse?" Morik asked. "Perhaps a fine set of clothing as well. My friends have left the easy road, and so I might still beat them to Ten-Towns. What wondrous expressions I might paint on their faces when they enter Lonelywood to find me waiting and looking grand, indeed."

The men around him howled.

"Why, *we* have both, horse and clothing," Petters roared, sliding over to slap Morik on the shoulder, which made him wince because he had been battered there by rocks. "A fine price we shall offer to Lord Brandeburg!"

They ate, they exchanged stories, and they laughed. By the time he finished with the group, Morik had procured their strongest riding horse and a wondrous set of clothing, two-toned green of the finest material with gold brocade, for a mere pittance, a fraction of the cost in any shop in Luskan.

He stayed with them through the night but left at first light, riding north and singing a song of adventure. When the caravan was out of sight he turned to the west and charged on, thinking that he should further alter his appearance before he, Lord Brandeburg of Waterdeep, arrived in the small fiefdom.

He hoped the wizard wouldn't be around. Morik hated wizards.

⚔ ⚔ ⚔ ⚔ ⚔

Errtu found him. There, in the darkness of his dungeon cell, Wulfgar could not escape the haunting memories, the emotional agony, twisted into his very being by the years of torment at the clawed hands of Errtu and his demonic minions.

The demon found him once again and held him, taunted him with alluring mistresses to tempt and destroy him, to destroy, too, the fruit of his seed.

He saw it all again so vividly, the demon standing before him, the babe—Wulfgar's child—in its powerful arms. He had been repulsed at the thought that he had sired such a creature, an alu-demon, but he remembered, too, his recognition of that child—innocent child?—as his own.

Errtu had opened wide his drooling maw, showing those awful canine teeth. The demon's face moved lower, pointed teeth hovering an inch above the head of Wulfgar's child, jaws wide enough to fit the babe's head inside. Errtu moved lower . . .

Wulfgar felt the succubae fingers tickling his body, and he woke with a start. He screamed, kicked, and batted, slapping away several spiders but taking bites from more. The barbarian scrambled to his feet and ran full out in the pitch darkness of his cell, nearly knocking himself unconscious as he barreled into the unyielding door.

He fell back to the dirt floor, sobbing, face buried in his hands, full of anger and frustration. Then he understood what had so startled him from his nightmare-filled sleep, for he heard footsteps out in the corridor. When he looked up he saw the flickers of a torch approaching his door.

Wulfgar moved back and sat up straight, trying to regain some measure of his dignity. He recalled that doomed men were often granted one last request. His would be a bottle of potent drink, a fiery liquid that would burn those memories from his mind for the last time.

The light appeared right outside his cell, and Lord Feringal's face stared in at him. "Are you prepared to admit your crime, dog?" he asked.

Wulfgar stared at him for a long, long moment.

"Very well, then," the unshaken lord continued. "You have been identified by my trusted driver, so by law I need only tell you your crime and punishment."

Still no response.

"For the robbery on the road, I shall take your hands," Lord Feringal explained matter-of-factly. "One at a time and slowly. For your worse crime—" He hesitated, and it seemed to Wulfgar, even in that meager light, as if the man was suddenly pained.

"My lord," prompted old Temigast behind him.

"For your worse crime," Lord Feringal began again, his voice was stronger, "for the ravishing of Lady Meralda you shall be publicly castrated, then chained for public spectacle for one day. And then, dog Wulfgar, you shall be burned at the stake."

Wulfgar's face screwed up incredulously at the reading of the last crime. He had saved the woman from such a fate! He wanted to yell that in Lord Feringal's face, to scream at the man and tear the door from its fitting. He wanted to do all of that, and yet, he did nothing, just sat there quietly, accepting the injustice.

Or was it injustice? Wulfgar asked himself. Did he not deserve such a fate? Did it even matter?

That was it, Wulfgar decided. It mattered to him not at all. He would find freedom in death. Let Lord Feringal kill him and be done with it, doing them both a favor. The woman had falsely accused him, and he could not understand why, but . . . no matter.

"Have you nothing to say?" Lord Feringal demanded.

"Will you grant a final request?"

The young man trembled visibly at the absurd notion. "I would give you *nothing!*" he screamed. "Nothing more than a night, hungry and wretched, to consider your horrid fate."

"My lord," Temigast said again to calm him. "Guard, lead Lord Feringal back to his chambers." The young man scowled one last time at Wulfgar through the opening in the door, then let himself be led away.

Temigast stayed, though, taking one of the torches and waving the remaining guards away. He stood at the cell door for a long while, staring at Wulfgar.

"Go away, old man," the barbarian said.

"You did not deny the last charge," Temigast said, "though you protested your innocence to me."

Wulfgar shrugged, but said nothing and did not meet the man's gaze. "What would be the point of repeating myself? You've already condemned me."

"You did not deny the rape," Temigast stated again.

Wulfgar's head swung up to return Temigast's stare. "Nor did you speak up for me," he replied.

Temigast looked at him as if slapped. "Nor shall I."

"So you would let an innocent man die."

Temigast snorted aloud. "Innocent?" he declared. "You are a thief and a dog, and I'll do nothing against Lady Meralda, nor against Lord Feringal, for your miserable sake."

Wulfgar laughed at him, at the ridiculousness of it all.

"But I offer you this," Temigast went on. "Say not a word against Lady Meralda, and I will ensure that your death will be quick. That is the best I can offer."

Wulfgar stopped laughing and stared hard at the complicated steward.

"Or else," Temigast warned, "I promise to drag the spectacle of your torture out for the length of a day and more, shall make you beg for your death a thousand thousand times before setting you free of the agony."

"Of the agony?" Wulfgar echoed hollowly. "Old man, you know nothing of agony."

"We shall see," Temigast growled, and he turned away, leaving Wulfgar along in the dark . . . until Errtu returned to him, as the demon always did.

✕ ✕ ✕ ✕

Morik rode as fast as his horse would take him, for as long as the poor beast would last. He crossed along the same road where he and Wulfgar had encountered the carriage, past the same spot where Wulfgar had overturned the thing.

He came into Auckney late one afternoon to the stares of many peasants. "Pray tell me the name of your lord, good sir," he called to one, accentuating his request with a tossed gold piece.

"Lord Feringal Auck," the man supplied quickly. "He lives with his new bride in Castle Auck, there," he finished, pointing a gnarly finger toward the coast.

"Many thanks!" Morik bowed his head, tossed another couple of silver coins, then kicked his horse's flanks, trotting down the last few hundred yards of road to the small bridge leading to Castle Auck. He found the gate open with a pair of bored-looking guards standing to either side.

"I am Lord Brandeburg of Waterdeep," he said to them, bringing his steed to a stop. "Pray announce me to your lord, for I've a long road behind me and a longer one ahead."

With that, the rogue dismounted and brushed off his fine pantaloons, going so far as to draw his slender sword from his belt, wiping clean the blade as he brought it forth, then launching into a sudden, dazzling display of swordsmanship before replacing it on his hip. He had impressed them, he realized, as one ran off for the castle and the other moved to tend his horse.

Within the span of a few moments, Morik, Lord Brandeburg, stood before Lord Feringal in the audience hall of Castle Auck. He dipped a low bow and introduced himself as a traveler who had lost his companions to a band of giants in the Spine of the World. He could see from Feringal's eyes that the minor nobleman was thrilled and proud to be visited by a lord of the great city of Waterdeep and would drop his guard in his efforts to please.

"I believe that one or two of my friends escaped," Morik finished his tale, "though on my word not a giant can say the same."

"How far away was this?" asked Lord Feringal. The man seemed somewhat distracted, but Morik's tale obviously alarmed him.

"Many miles, my lord," Morik supplied, "and no threat to your quiet kingdom. As I said, the giants are all dead." He looked around and smiled. "A pity it would be for such monsters to descend on such a quiet and safe place as this."

Lord Feringal took the bait. "Not so quiet, and not so safe," he growled through clenched teeth.

"Danger, here?" he said incredulously. "Pirates, perhaps?" Morik appeared surprised and looked to the old steward standing beside the throne. The man shook his head imperceptivity, which Morik took to mean he should not press the issue, but that was exactly the point.

"Highwaymen," Lord Feringal snarled.

Morik started to respond but held his tongue, and his breath, as a woman whom Morik surely recognized entered the room.

"My wife," Lord Feringal introduced her distractedly. "Lady Meralda Auck."

Morik bowed low, took her hand in his, and lifted it to his lips, pointedly staring her right in the eyes as he did. To his ultimate relief, and pride at his own clever disguise, he detected no flicker of recognition there.

"A most beautiful wife," Morik stated. "You have my envy, Lord Feringal."

That brought a smile at last to Feringal's face, but it quickly turned into a frown. "My wife was in the coach attacked by these highwaymen."

Morik gasped. "I would find them, Lord Feringal," he said. "Find them and slay them on the road. Or bring them back to you, if you would prefer."

Lord Feringal waved his hands, quieting the man. "I have the one I desire," he said. "The other was buried under a rockslide."

Morik's lips pursed at the painful thought. "A fitting fate," he said.

"More fitting is the fate I have planned for the captured barbarian," Feringal grimly replied. "A most horrible death, I assure you. You may witness it if you will stay in Auckney for the night."

"Of course, I shall," Morik said. "What have you planned for the scoundrel?"

"First, castration," Lord Feringal explained. "The barbarian will be killed properly two mornings hence."

Morik assumed a pensive pose. "A barbarian, you say?"

"A huge northerner, yes," Feringal replied.

"Strong of arm?"

"As strong as any man I have ever seen," the lord of Auckney replied. "It took a powerful wizard to bring him to justice, and even that man would have fallen to him had not my guards surrounded him and beat him down."

Morik almost choked over the mention of the wizard, but he held his calm.

"Killing a highwayman is surely an appropriate ending," Morik said, "but perhaps you would be better served in another manner." He waited, watching carefully as Lord Feringal eyed him closely.

"Perhaps I might purchase the man," Morik explained. "I am a man of no small means, I assure you, and could surely use a strong slave at my side as I begin the search for my missing companions."

"Not a chance," Feringal replied rather sharply.

"But if he is familiar with these parts . . ." Morik started to reason.

"He is going to die horribly for the harm he brought to my wife," Lord Feringal retorted.

"Ah, yes, my lord," Morik said. "The incident has distressed her."

"The incident has left her with child!" Feringal yelled, grabbing the arms of his chair so forcefully that his knuckles whitened.

"My lord!" the steward cried at the unwise announcement, and Meralda gasped. Morik was glad for their shock, as it covered his own.

Lord Feringal calmed quickly, forcing himself back into his seat and mumbling an apology to Meralda. "Lord Brandeburg, I beg your forgiveness," he said. "You understand my anger."

"I will castrate the dog for you," Morik replied, drawing forth his sword. "I assure you that I am skilled at such arts."

That broke the tension in the room somewhat. Even

Lord Feringal managed a smile. "We will take care of the unpleasantries," he replied, "but I would, indeed, enjoy your company at the execution of sentence. Will you stay as my guest for the two days?"

Morik bowed very low. "I am at your service, my lord."

Soon after, Morik was brought to an inn just beyond the castle bridge. He wasn't thrilled to learn that Lord Feringal kept guests outside the castle walls. That would make it all the harder for him to get near Wulfgar. He did learn from the escort, though, that Wulfgar was being kept in a dungeon beneath the castle.

Morik had to get to his friend, and fast, for, given the false accusations placed against Wulfgar, Lord Feringal would surely and horribly kill the man. A daring rescue had never been a part of Morik's plan. Many thieves were sold to adventuring lords, and so he had hoped Lord Feringal would part with this one for a handsome sum—and the lord's own gold, at that——but rapists, particularly men who ravished noblewomen, found only one, horrible fate.

Morik stared out the window of his small room, looking to Castle Auck and the dark waters beyond. He would try to find some way to get to Wulfgar, but he feared he would be returning to Luskan alone.

23

THE SECOND
ATTEMPTED JUSTICE

Here's your last meal, dog," said one of the two guards standing outside Wulfgar's cell. The man spat on the food and slipped the tray in through the slot.

Wulfgar ignored them and made no move for the food. He could hardly believe that he had escaped execution in Luskan, only to be killed in some nondescript fiefdom. It struck him, then, that perhaps he had earned this. No, he hadn't harmed the woman, of course, but his actions of the last months, since he had left Drizzt and the others in Icewind Dale—since he had slapped Catti-brie across the face—were not those of a man undeserving of such a grim fate. Hadn't Wulfgar and Drizzt killed monsters for the same crimes that Wulfgar had committed? Had the pair not gone into the Spine of the World in pursuit of a giant band that had been scouting out the trail, obviously planning to waylay merchant wagons? What mercy had they shown the giants? What mercy, then, did Wulfgar deserve?

Still, it bothered the big man more than a little, shook what little confidence he had left in justice and humanity, that both in Luskan and in Auckney he had been convicted of crimes for which he was innocent. It made no sense to him. If they wanted to kill him so badly, why not just do it for those crimes he had committed? There were plenty of those from which to chose.

He caught the last snatches of the guards' conversation as they walked away down the tunnel. "A wretched child it'll be, coming from such loins as that."

"It'll tear Lady Meralda apart, with its da so big!"

That gave Wulfgar pause. He sat in the dark for a long while, his mouth hanging open. Now it began to make a little more sense to him as he put the pieces of the puzzle together. He knew from the guards' previous conversations that Lord Feringal and Lady Meralda were only recently married, and now she was with child, but not by Lord Feringal.

Wulfgar nearly laughed aloud at the absurdity of it all. He had become a convenient excuse for an adulterous noblewoman, a balm against Lord Feringal's cuckolding.

"What luck," he muttered, but he understood that more than bad luck had caused his current predicament. A series of bad choices on his part had landed him here in the dark with the spiders and the stench and the visits of the demon.

Yes, he deserved this, he believed. Not for the crimes accused, but for those committed.

⚔ ⚔ ⚔ ⚔ ⚔

She couldn't sleep, couldn't even begin to close her eyes. Feringal had left her early and returned to his own room, for she had claimed discomfort and begged him to give her a reprieve from his constant amorous advances. It wasn't that she minded the man's attention. In fact, her lovemaking with Feringal was certainly pleasant, and were it not for the child and the thought of the poor man in the dungeon, it would go far beyond pleasant.

Meralda had come to know that her change of heart concerning Feringal was well founded, that he was a gentle and decent man. She had little trouble looking at Feringal in a fresh way, recognizing his handsome features and his charm, though that was somewhat buried by his years under the influences of his shrewish sister. Meralda could unearth that charm, she knew, could bring out the best in Feringal and live in bliss with the good man.

However, the woman found that she could not tolerate herself. How her foolishness had come back to haunt her in the form of the baby in her womb, in the simmering anger within her husband. Perhaps the most bitter blow of all to Meralda was the forthcoming execution of an innocent man, a man who had saved her from the very crime for which he was to be horribly killed.

After Wulfgar had been dragged away, Meralda tried to rationalize the sentence, reminding herself that the man was, indeed, a highwayman, going so far as to tell herself that the barbarian had victimized others, perhaps even raped other women.

But those arguments hadn't held water, for Meralda knew better. Though he had robbed her carriage, she'd gotten a fair glimpse into the man's character. Her lie had caused this. Her lie would bring the brutal execution to a man undeserving.

Meralda lay late into the night, thinking herself the most horrible person in all the world. She hardly realized that she was moving sometime later, padding barefoot along the castle's cold stone floor with the guiding light of a single candle. She went to Temigast's room, pausing at the door to hear the reassuring sounds of the old man's snoring, and in she crept. As the steward, Temigast kept the keys to every door in the castle on a large wrought iron ring.

Meralda found the ring on a hook above the steward's dresser, and she took it quietly, glancing nervously at Temigast with every little noise. Somehow she got out of the room without waking the man, then skittered across the audience hall, past the servant's quarters, and into the kitchen. There she found the trap door leading to the levels below, bolted and barred so strongly that no man, not even a giant, could hope to open it. Unless he had the keys.

Meralda fumbled with them, trying each until she had finally thrown every lock and shifted every bar aside. She paused, collecting herself, trying to form a more complete plan. She heard the guards then, laughing in a side room, and paced over to peer inside. They were playing bones.

Meralda went to the larder door, a hatch really, that led to the outside wall of the castle. There wasn't much room among the rocks out there, especially if the tide was in, which it was, but it would have to do. Unlocking it as well, the woman went to the trap door and gently pulled it open. Slipping down to the dirty tunnels, she walked barefoot in the slop, hiking her dressing gown up so that it would carry no revealing stains.

Wulfgar awoke to sounds of a key in the lock of his cell door, and a thin, flickering light outside in the corridor. Having lost all track of time in the dark, he thought the morning of his torture had arrived. How surprised he was to find Lady Meralda staring in at him though the bars of his locked cell.

"Can you forgive me?" she whispered, glancing over her shoulder nervously.

Wulfgar just gaped at her.

"I didn't know he'd come after you," the woman explained. "I thought he'd let it go, and I'd be—"

"Safe," he finished for her. "You thought that your child would be safe." Now it was Meralda's turn for an incredulous stare. "Why have you come?" Wulfgar asked.

"You could've killed us," she replied. "Me and Liam on the road, I mean. Or done as they said you done."

"As *you* said I did," Wulfgar reminded.

"You could've let your friend have his way on the road, could've let Liam die," Meralda went on. "I'm owing you this much at least." To Wulfgar's astonishment she turned the key in the lock. "Up the ladder and to the left, then through the larder," she explained. "The way's clear." She lit another candle and left it for him, then turned and ran off.

Wulfgar gave her a lead, not wanting to catch up to her, for he didn't want her implicated if he were caught. Outside his cell, he pulled a metal sconce from the wall and used it to batter the lock as quietly as he could to make it look as though he had broken out of his own accord. Then he moved down the corridors to the ladder and up into the kitchen.

He, too, heard the guards arguing and rolling bones in a nearby room, so he couldn't similarly destroy the locks and bars up here. He re-locked and barred the trap door. Let them think he'd found some magical assistance. Going straight through the larder, as Meralda had bade him, Wulfgar squeezed through the small door, a tight fit indeed, and found a precarious perch on wet rocks outside at the base of the castle. The stones were worn and smooth. Wulfgar couldn't hope to scale it, nor was there any apparent way around the corner, for the tide was crashing in.

Wulfgar leaped into the cold water.

⚔ ⚔ ⚔ ⚔ ⚔

Hiding in the kitchen, Meralda nodded as Wulfgar heightened her ruse by securing the trap door. She similarly locked the larder, washed all signs of her subterranean adventure from her feet, and padded quietly back to return the keys to Steward Temigast's room without further incident.

Meralda was back in her bed soon after, the terrible demons of guilt—some of them, at least—banished at last.

⚔ ⚔ ⚔ ⚔ ⚔

The breeze off the water was chill, but Morik was still sweating under the heavy folds of his latest disguise as an old washer-woman. He stood behind a stone wall near the entrance to the short bridge leading to Castle Auck.

"Why did they put the thing on an island?" the rogue muttered disgustedly, but of course, his own current troubles answered the question. A lone guard leaned on the wall above the huge castle gate. The man was very likely half asleep, but Morik could see no way to get near to him. The bridge was well lit, torches burning all the night long from what he had heard, and it offered no cover whatsoever. He would have to swim to the castle.

Morik looked at the dark waters doubtfully. He wouldn't have much of a disguise left after crossing through that, if he even made it. Morik wasn't a strong swimmer and didn't know the sea or what monsters might lurk beneath the dark waves.

Morik realized then and there that his time with Wulfgar was at its end. He would go to the place of torture in the morning, he decided, but probably only to say farewell, for it was unlikely he could rescue the man there without jeopardizing himself.

No, he decided, he wouldn't even attend. "What good might it bring?" he muttered. It could even bring disaster for Morik if the wizard who had caught Wulfgar was there and recognized him. "Better that I remember Wulfgar from our times of freedom.

"Farewell, my big friend," Morik said aloud sadly. "I go now back to Luskan—"

Morik paused as the water churned at the base of the wall. A large, dark form began crawling from the surf. The rogue's hand went to his sword.

"Morik?" Wulfgar asked, his teeth chattering from the icy water. "What are you doing here?"

"I could ask the same of you!" the rogue cried, delighted and astounded all at once. "I, of course, came to rescue you," the cocky rogue added, bending to take Wulfgar's arm and help pull the man up beside him. "This will require a lot of explaining, but come, let us be fast on our way."

Wulfgar wasn't about to argue.

✕ ✕ ✕ ✕ ✕

"I shall have every guard in this place executed!" Lord Feringal fumed when he learned of the escape the next morning, the morning he was planning to exact his revenge upon the barbarian.

The guard shrank back, fearing Lord Feringal would attack him then and there, and indeed, it seemed as if the young man would charge him from his chair. Meralda grabbed him by the arm, settling him. "Calm, my lord," she said.

"Calm?" Lord Feringal balked. "Who failed me?" he yelled at the guard. "Who shall pay in Wulfgar's stead?"

"None," Meralda answered before the stammering guard could begin to reply. Feringal looked at her incredulously. "Anyone you harm will be because of me," the woman explained. "I'll have no blood on my hands. You'd only be making things worse."

The young lord calmed somewhat and sat back, staring at his wife, at the woman he wanted, above all else, to protect. After a moment's thought, a moment of looking into that beautiful, innocent face, Feringal nodded his agreement. "Search all the lands," he instructed the guard, "and the castle again from dungeon to parapet. Return him to me alive."

Beads of sweat on his forehead, the guard bowed and ran out of the room.

"Fear not, my love," Lord Feringal said to Meralda. "I shall recall the wizard and begin the search anew. The barbarian shall not escape."

"Please, my lord," Meralda begged. "Don't summon the wizard again, or any other." That raised a few eyebrows, including Priscilla's and Temigast's. "I'm wanting it all done," she explained. "It's done, I say, and on the road behind me. I'm not wanting to look back ever again. Let the man go and die in the mountains, and let us look ahead to our own life, to when you might be siring children of our own."

Feringal continued to stare, unblinking. Slowly, very slowly, his head nodded, and Meralda relaxed back in her chair.

⚔ ⚔ ⚔ ⚔ ⚔

Steward Temigast watched it all with growing certainty. He knew, without doubt, that Meralda was the one who had freed the barbarian. The wise old man, suspicious since seeing the woman's reaction when Wulfgar had first been dragged before her, had little trouble in understanding why. He resolved to say nothing, for it was not his place to inflict unnecessary pain on his lord. In any event, the child would be put out of the way and in no line of ascension.

But Temigast was far from easy with it all, especially after he looked at Priscilla and saw her wearing an expression that might have been his own. She was always suspicious, that one, and Temigast feared she was harboring his same doubts about the child's heritage. Though Temigast felt it not his place to inflict unnecessary pain, Priscilla Auck seemed to revel in just that sort of thing. The road to which Meralda had referred was far from clear in either direction.

24

WINTER'S PAUSE

This is our chance," Wulfgar explained to Morik. The pair were crouched behind a shielding wall of stone on a mountainside above one of the many small villages on the southern side of the Spine of the World.

Morik looked at his friend and shook his head, giving a less-than-enthusiastic sigh. Not only had Wulfgar refrained from the bottle in the two tendays since their return from Auckney, but had forbidden either of them to engage in any more highwayman activities. The season was getting late, turning toward winter, which meant a nearly constant stream of caravans as the last merchants returned from Icewind Dale. The seasonal occupants of the northern stretches left then as well, the men and women who went to Ten-Towns to fish for the summers then rolled their wagons back to Luskan when the season ended.

Wulfgar had made it clear to Morik that their thieving days were over. So here they were, overlooking a small, incredibly boring village they'd learned was expecting some sort of orc or goblin attack.

"They will not attack from below," Wulfgar remarked, pointing to a wide field east of the village on the same height as the higher buildings. "From there," Wulfgar explained.

"That's where they've constructed their wall and best defenses," Morik replied, as if that should settle it all. They believed that the coming band of monsters numbered less than a score, and while there weren't more than half that number in the town, Morik didn't see any real problems here.

"More may come down from above," Wulfgar reasoned. "The villagers might be sorely pressed if attacked from two sides."

"You're looking for an excuse," Morik accused. Wulfgar stared at him curiously. "An excuse to get into the fight," the rogue clarified, which brought a smile to Wulfgar's face. "Unless it's against merchants," Morik glumly added.

Wulfgar held his calm and contented expression. "I wish to battle deserving opponents," he said.

"I know many peasants who would argue that merchants are more deserving than goblinkind," Morik replied.

Wulfgar shook his head, in no mood and with no time to sit and ponder the philosophical points. They saw the movement beyond the village, the approach of monsters Wulfgar knew, of creatures the barbarian could cut down without remorse or regard. A score of orcs charged wildly across the field, rushing past the ineffective arrow volleys from the villagers.

"Go and be done with it," Morik said, starting to rise.

Wulfgar, a student of such attacks, held him down and turned his gaze up the slopes to where a huge boulder soared down, smashing the side of one building.

"There's a giant above," Wulfgar whispered, already starting his circle up the mountain. "Perhaps more."

"So that is where we shall go," Morik grumbled with resignation, though he obviously doubted the wisdom of such a course.

Another rock soared down, then a third. The giant was lifting a fourth when Wulfgar and Morik turned a bend in the trail and slipped between a pair of boulders, spotting the behemoth from behind.

Wulfgar's hand axe bit into the giant's arm, and it dropped the boulder onto its own head. The giant bellowed and spun around to where Morik stood shrugging, slender sword in hand. Bellowing, the giant came at him in one long stride. Morik yelped and turned to flee back through the boulders. The giant came on in swift pursuit, but as it reached the narrow pass Wulfgar leaped atop one of the boulders and brought his ordinary hammer in hard against the side of the behemoth's head, sending it stagger-ing. By the time the dazed giant managed to look to the boulder Wulfgar was already gone. Back on the ground, the barbarian rushed at the giant's side to smash its kneecap hard, then dashed back into the boulders.

The giant ran in pursuit, clutching its bruised head, then its aching knee, then looking at the axe deep into its forearm. It changed direction suddenly, having had enough of this fight, and ran up the mountainside instead, back into the wilds of the Spine of the World.

Morik stepped from the boulders and offered his hand to Wulfgar. "A job well done," he congratulated him.

Wulfgar ignored the hand. "A job just begun," he corrected, sprinting down the mountainside toward the village and the battle being waged at the eastern barricade.

"You do love the fighting," Morik commented dryly after his friend. Sighing, he loped behind.

Below, the battle at the barricade was practically at a standoff, with no orcs yet breaching the shielding wall, but few had taken any solid hits, either. That changed abruptly when Wulfgar came down from on high, running full out across the field, howling at the top of his lungs. Leaping, soaring, arms outstretched, he crashed into four of the creatures, bearing them all to the ground. A frenzy of clubbing and stabbing, punching and kicking ensued. More orcs moved to join the fight but in the end, bloody, battered, but smiling widely, Wulfgar was the only one to emerge alive.

Rallied by his amazing assault and by the appearance of Morik, who had struck down another orc on his way down the slope, the villagers poured into the remaining raiding party. The routed creatures, the dozen who still could run, fled back the way they had come.

By the time Morik got near Wulfgar, the barbarian was surrounded by villagers, patting him, cheering him, promising eternal friendship, offering him a place to live for the coming winter.

"You see," Wulfgar said to Morik with a happy smile. "Easier than any work at the pass."

Wiping off his blade, the rogue eyed his friend skeptically. The fight had been easy, even more so than an optimistic Wulfgar had predicted. Morik, too, was quickly surrounded by appreciative villagers, including a couple of young and attractive women. A quiet winter of relaxation in front of a blazing hearth might not be so bad a thing. Perhaps he would hold off on his plans to return to Luskan after all.

✘ ✘ ✘ ✘ ✘

Meralda's first three months of married life had been wonderful. Not blissful, but wonderful, as she watched her mother grow strong and healthy for the first time in years. Even life at the castle was not as bad as she had feared. Priscilla was there, of course, never more than casually friendly and often glowering, but she'd made no move against Meralda. How could she with her brother so obviously enamored of his wife?

She, too, had grown to love her husband. That combined with the sight of her healthy mother had made it a lovely autumn for the young woman, a time of things new, a time of comfort, a time of hope.

But as winter deepened around Auckney, ghosts of the past began to creep into the castle.

Jaka's child growing large and kicking reminded Meralda in no uncertain terms of her terrible lie. She found herself thinking more and more about Jaka Sculi, of her own moments of foolishness regarding him, and there had been many. She pondered the last moments of Jaka's life when he had cried out her name, had risked his entire existence for her. At the time, Meralda had convinced herself that it was out of jealousy for Lord Feringal and not love. Now, with Jaka's child kicking in her womb and the inevitable haze brought by the passage of time, she wasn't so sure. Perhaps Jaka had loved her in the end. Perhaps the tingling they'd felt on their night of passion had also planted the seeds of deeper emotions that had only needed time to find their way through the harsh reality of a peasant's existence.

More likely her mood was just the result of winter's gloom playing on her thoughts, and on her new husband's as well. It didn't help that their lovemaking decreased dramatically as Meralda's belly increased in size. He came to her one morning when the snow was deep around the castle and the wind howled through the cracks in the stone. Even as he began kissing her, he stopped and stared hard at her, then he'd asked her an unthinkable question.

What had it been like with the barbarian?

If he had kicked her in the head, it would not have hurt so much, yet Meralda was not angry at her husband, could surely understand his doubts and fears given her distant mood and the tangible evidence that she had been with another man.

The woman told herself repeatedly that once the child was born and taken away, she and Feringal would settle into a normal existence. In that time when the obvious pressures were gone, they would come to love each other deeply. She could only hope that it all would not disintegrate in the months she had left carrying the child.

Of course, as the tension grew between Feringal and Meralda, so too did the scowls Priscilla shot Meralda's way. Power wrought of having Lord Feringal wrapped around her little finger had given Meralda the upper hand in the constant silent war Priscilla waged against her. Growing thick with another man's child, she found that power waning.

She didn't understand it, though, considering Priscilla's initial response to learning that she had been raped. Priscilla had even mentioned taking the child as her own, to raise away from the castle, as was often done in such situations.

"You are uncommonly large for so early in the pregnancy," Priscilla remarked to her on the same winter day that Feringal had asked her about Wulfgar. It occurred to Meralda that the shrewish woman had obviously sensed the palpable tension between the couple. Priscilla's voice was uncommonly thick with suspicion and venom, which told Meralda that her sister-in-law was keeping close track of the passage of time. There would be trouble, indeed, when Meralda delivered a healthy, full-term baby only seven months after the incident on the road. Yes, Priscilla would have questions.

Meralda deflected the conversation by sharing her fears about the barbarian's size, that perhaps the child would tear her apart. That had silenced Priscilla briefly, but Meralda knew the truce wouldn't last and the questions would return.

Indeed, as winter waned and Meralda's belly swelled, the whispers began throughout Auckney. Whispers about the child's due date. Whispers about the incident on the road. Whispers about the tragic death of Jaka Sculi. No fool, Meralda saw people counting on their fingers, saw the tension in her mother's face, though the woman wouldn't openly ask for the truth.

When the inevitable happened, predictably, Priscilla proved the source of it.

"You will birth the child in the month of Ches," the woman said rather sharply as she and Meralda dined with Steward Temigast one cold afternoon. The equinox was fast approaching, but winter hadn't released its grip on the land yet, a howling blizzard whipping the snow deep around the castle walls. Meralda looked at her skeptically.

"Mid-Ches," Priscilla remarked. "Or perhaps late in the month, or even early in the Month of the Storms."

"Do you sense a problem with the pregnancy?" Steward Temigast intervened.

Once again Meralda recognized that the man was her ally. He too knew, or at least he suspected as much as Priscilla, yet he'd shown no hostility toward Meralda. She'd begun to regard Temigast as a father figure, but the comparison seemed even more appropriate when she thought back to the morning after her night with Jaka, when Dohni Ganderlay had suspected the truth but had forgiven it in light of the larger sacrifice, the larger good.

"I sense a problem, all right," Priscilla replied, somehow managing to convey through her tone that she meant no problem with the physical aspects of the pregnancy. Priscilla looked at Meralda and huffed, then threw down her napkin and rushed away, heading right up the stairs.

"What's she about?" Meralda asked Temigast, her eyes fearful. Before he could respond, she had her answer, when shouts rang out from upstairs. Neither of them could make out any distinct words, but it was obvious Priscilla had gone to speak with her brother.

"What should I do—" Meralda started to say, but Temigast hushed her.

"Eat, my lady," he said calmly. "You must remain strong, for you've trials ahead." Meralda understood the double meaning in those words. "I'm certain you'll come through them as long as you keep your wits about you," the old steward added with a comforting wink. "When it is all past, you will find the life you desire."

Meralda wanted to run over and bury her head on the man's shoulder, or to run out of the castle altogether, down the road to the warm and comfortable house Lord Feringal had given to her family and bury her face on her father's shoulder. Instead, she took a deep breath to steady herself, then did as Temigast suggested and ate her meal.

⚔ ⚔ ⚔ ⚔ ⚔

The snow came early and deep that year. Morik would have preferred Luskan, but he'd come to see Wulfgar's point in bringing them to this village refuge. There was plenty of work to do, particularly after snowfalls when the grounds had to be cleared and defensible berm built, but Morik managed to avoid most of it by feigning an injury from the battle that had brought them here.

Wulfgar, though, went at the work with relish, using it to keep his body so occupied he hadn't time to think or dream. Still, Errtu found him in that village as he had in every place Wulfgar went, every place he would ever go. Now, instead of hiding in a bottle from the demon, the barbarian met those memories head-on, replayed the events, however horrible, and forced himself to admit that it had happened, all of it, and that he had faced moments of weakness and failure. Many times Wulfgar sat alone in the dark corner of the room he had been given, trembling, wet with cold sweat, and with tears he could hold back no longer. Many times he wanted to run to Morik's inexhaustible supply of potent liquor, but he did not.

He growled and he cried out, and yet he held fast his resolve to accept the past for what it was and to somehow move beyond it. Wulfgar didn't know where he had found the strength and determination, but he suspected it had laid dormant within him, summoned when he'd witnessed the courage Meralda had displayed to free him. She'd had so much more to lose than he, and yet she had rejuvenated his faith in the world. He knew now that his fight with Errtu would continue until he had honestly won, that he could hide in a bottle, but not forever.

They fought another battle around the turn of the year, a minor skirmish with another band of orcs. The villagers had seen the attack coming and had prepared the battlefield, pouring melted snow over the field of approach. When the orcs arrived they came skidding in on sheets of ice that left them floundering in the open while archers picked them off.

The unexpected appearance of a group of Luskan soldiers who had lost their way on patrol did more to distress Wulfgar and Morik and shatter their idyllic existence than that battle. Wulfgar was certain at least one of the soldiers recognized the pair from Prisoner's Carnival, but either the soldiers said nothing to the villagers or the villagers simply didn't care. The pair heard no tremors of unrest after the soldiers departed.

In the end, it was the quietest winter Wulfgar and Morik had ever known, a needed respite. The season turned to spring, though the snow remained thick, and the pair began to lay their future plans.

"No more highwaymen," Wulfgar reminded Morik one quiet night halfway through the month of Ches.

"No," the rogue agreed. "I don't miss the life."

"What, then, for Morik?"

"Back to Luskan, I'm afraid," the rogue said. "My home. Ever my home."

"And your disguise will keep you safe?" Wulfgar asked with genuine concern.

Morik smiled. "The folk have short memories, my friend," he explained, silently adding that he hoped that drow had short memories, as well, for returning to Luskan meant abandoning his mission to watch over Wulfgar. "Since we were . . . exported they have no doubt sated their blood thirst on a hundred unfortunates at Prisoner's Carnival. My disguise will protect me from the authorities, and my true identity will again grant me the respect needed on the streets."

Wulfgar nodded, not doubting Morik in the least. Out here in the wilds the rogue was not nearly as impressive as on the streets of Luskan, where few could match his wiles.

"And what for Wulfgar?" Morik asked, surprised by the honest concern on his own voice. "Icewind Dale?" Morik asked. "Friends of old?"

The barbarian shook his head, for he simply didn't know the road ahead of him. He would have dismissed that possibility with hardly a thought, but he considered it now. Was he ready to return to the side of the companions of the hall, as he, Drizzt, Bruenor, Catti-brie, Guenhwyvar, and Regis had once been called? Had he escaped the demon and the demon bottle? Had he come to terms with Errtu and the truth of his imprisonment?

"No," he answered, and left it at that, wondering if he would ever again meet the gazes of his former friends.

Morik nodded, though a bit dismayed for his own reasons. He

didn't want Wulfgar to return to Luskan with him. Disguising the huge man would be difficult enough, but it was more than that. Morik didn't want Wulfgar to be caught by the dark elves.

"She is playing you for a fool, and all of Auckney knows it, Feri!" Priscilla screamed at her brother

"Don't call me that!" he snapped, pushing past her, looking for distraction from the subject. "You know I hate it."

Priscilla would not let it go. "Can you deny the stage of her pregnancy?" she pressed. "She will give birth in a tenday."

"The barbarian was a large man," Feringal growled. "The child will be large, and that is what is deceiving you."

"The child will be average," Priscilla retorted, "as you shall learn within the month." Her brother started to walk away. "I'll wager he'll be a pretty thing with the curly brown hair of his father." That brought Feringal spinning around, glaring at her. "His dead father," the woman finished, not backing down an inch.

Lord Feringal crossed the few feet separating them in one stride and slapped his sister hard across the face. Horrified by his own actions, he fell back, holding his face in his hands.

"My poor cuckolded brother," Priscilla replied to that slap, glaring at him above the hand she had brought to her bruise. "You will learn." With that, she stalked from the room.

Lord Feringal stood there, motionless for a long, long time, trying hard to steady his breathing.

Three days after their discussion, the weather had warmed enough to bring about a thaw, allowing Morik and Wulfgar to depart the village. The villagers were unhappy to see them go, especially because the thaw signaled the time of renewed monster attacks. The pair, particularly impatient Morik, would hear none of their pleas.

"Perhaps I will return to you," Wulfgar remarked, and he was thinking that he might indeed, once he and Morik had gone their own ways outside of Luskan. Where else might the barbarian go, after all?

The road out of the foothills was slow and so muddy and treacherous that the pair often had to walk, leading their horses carefully. Once the mountains gave way to the flatter plain just north of Luskan they found the going relatively easy.

"You still have the wagon and the supplies we left at the cave," Morik remarked.

Wulfgar realized the rogue was beginning to feel a pang of guilt about leaving him. "The cave did not remain empty throughout the winter I'm sure," the barbarian remarked. "Not so many supplies left, I would guess."

"Then take the belongings of the present occupants," Morik replied with a wink. "Giants, perhaps, nothing for Wulfgar to fear." That brought a smile to both their faces, but they didn't hold.

"You should have stayed in the village," Morik reasoned. "You can't go back to Luskan with me, so the village seems as good a place as any while you decide your course."

They'd come to a fork in the road. One path headed south to Luskan, the other to the west. When Morik turned to regard Wulfgar, he found the man staring out that second course, back toward the small fiefdom where he had been imprisoned, where Morik—to hear Morik tell it—had rescued him from a torturous death.

"Plotting revenge?" the rogue asked.

Wulfgar looked at him curiously, then caught on. "Hardly," he replied. "I am wondering the fate of the lady of the castle."

"The one who wrongly accused you of raping her?" Morik asked.

Wulfgar shrugged, as if not wanting to concede that point. "She was with child," he explained, "and very much afraid."

"You believe she cuckolded her husband?" Morik asked.

Wulfgar wrinkled his lips and nodded.

"So she offered your head to protect her reputation," Morik said derisively. "Typical noble lady."

Wulfgar didn't reply, but he wasn't seeing things quite that way. The barbarian understood that she had never intended for him to be caught, but rather, that he should remain a distant and mysterious solution to her personal problems. It was understandable, if not honorable.

"She must have had the babe by now," he mumbled to himself. "I wonder how she faired when they saw it and realized the child couldn't be mine."

Morik recognized Wulfgar's tone, and it worried him. "I'll not have to wonder your fate if you go back to determine hers," Morik dryly remarked. "You couldn't get into that town without being recognized."

Wulfgar nodded, not disagreeing, but he was smiling all the while, a look that was not lost on Morik. "But you could," he said.

Morik spent a long while studying his friend. "If my road was not Luskan," he replied.

"A road of your own making, and with no appointments needing prompt attention," said Wulfgar.

"Winter is not yet gone. We took a chance in coming down from the foothills. Another storm might descend at any time, burying us deep." Morik continued to protest, but Wulfgar could tell by the rogue's tone that he was considering it.

"The storms are not so bad south of the mountains."

Morik scoffed.

"This last favor?" Wulfgar asked.

"Why do you care?" Morik argued. "The woman nearly had you killed, and in a manner horrible enough to have satisfied the crowd at Prisoner's Carnival."

Wulfgar shrugged, not honestly sure of that answer himself, but he wasn't about to back down. "A last act of friendship between us two," he prodded, "that we might properly part in the hopes of seeing each other again."

Morik scoffed again. "One last fight with me at your side is all you're after," he said half humorously. "Admit it, you're nothing as a fighter without me!" Even Wulfgar had to laugh at Morik's irony, but he followed it up with a plaintive expression.

"Oh, lead on," Morik grumbled, conceding as Wulfgar knew he would. "I will play the part of Lord Brandeburg yet again. I only hope that Brandeburg was not connected with your escape and that our common departure times were seen by Feringal as pure coincidence."

"If captured, I will honestly tell Lord Feringal that you played no part in my escape," Wulfgar said, a crooked smile showing under his thick winter beard.

"You have no idea how the promise comforts me," Morik said wryly as he pushed his friend ahead of him toward the west, toward trouble in Auckney.

25

EPIPHANY

Two days later, Morik's predicted snowstorm did come on, but its fury was somewhat tempered by the late season, leaving the road passable. The two riders plodded along, taking care to stay on the trail. They made good time, despite the foul weather, with Wulfgar driving them hard. Soon they came to a region of scattered farmhouses and stone cottages. Now the storm proved to be their ally, for few curious faces showed in the heavily curtained windows, and through the snow, wrapped in thick skins, the pair were hardly recognizable.

Soon after, Wulfgar waited in a sheltered overhang along the foothills, while Morik, Lord Brandeburg of Waterdeep, rode down into the village. The day turned late, the storm continued, but Morik didn't return. Wulfgar left his shelter to move to a vantage point that would afford him a view of Castle Auck. He wondered if Morik had been discovered. If so, should he rush down to find some way to aid his friend?

Wulfgar gave a chuckle. It was more likely that Morik had

stayed on at the castle for a fine meal and was warming himself before the hearth at that very moment. The barbarian retreated again to his shelter to brush down his horse, telling himself to be patient.

Finally Morik did return, wearing a grim expression indeed. "I was not met with friendly hugs," he explained.

"Your disguise did not hold?"

"It's not that," said the rogue. "They thought me Lord Brandeburg, but just as I feared they considered it a bit odd that I disappeared at the same time you did."

Wulfgar nodded. They had discussed that very possibility. "Why did they let you leave if they were suspicious?"

"I convinced them it was but a coincidence," he reported, "else why would I return to Auckney? Of course, I had to share a large meal to persuade them."

"Of course," Wulfgar agreed archly, his tone dry. "What of Lady Meralda and her child? Did you see her?" the barbarian prompted.

Morik pulled the saddle from his horse and began brushing his own beast down, as if preparing again for the road. "It is time for us to be gone," he replied flatly. "Far from here."

"What news?" Wulfgar pressed, now truly concerned.

"We have no allies here, and no acquaintances even, in any mood to entertain visitors," Morik replied. "Better for all that Wulfgar, Morik, and Lord Brandeburg, put this wretched little pretend fiefdom far behind their horses' tails."

Wulfgar leaned over and grabbed the rogue's shoulder, roughly turning him from his work on the horse. "The Lady Meralda?" he demanded.

"She birthed a child late last night," Morik admitted reluctantly. Wulfgar's eyes grew wide with trepidation. "Both survived," Morik quickly added, "for now." Pulling away, the rogue went back to his work with renewed vigor.

Feeling Wulfgar's eyes on him expectantly, Morik sighed and turned back. "Look, she told them that you had ravished her," he reminded his friend. "It seems likely that she was covering an affair," Morik reasoned. "She lied, condemning you, to hide her own betrayal of the young lord." Again, the knowing nod, for this was no news to Wulfgar.

Morik looked at him hard, surprised that he was not shaken somewhat by the blunt expression of all that had occurred, surprised that he was showing no anger at all despite the fact that, because of the woman, he had been beaten and nearly brutally executed.

"Well, now there is doubt concerning the heritage of the child," Morik explained. "The birth was too soon, considering our encounter with the girl on the road, and there are those within the village and castle who do not believe her tale."

Wulfgar gave a profound sigh. "I suspected as much would happen."

"I heard some talk of a young man who fell to his death on the day of the wedding between Lord Feringal and Meralda, a man who died crying out for her."

"Lord Feringal believes he's the one who cuckolded him?" Wulfgar asked.

"Not specifically," Morik replied. "Since the child was surely conceived before the wedding—even if it had been your child, that would have been so—but he knows, of course, that his wife once lay with another, and now he may be thinking that it was of her own volition and not something forced upon her on a wild road."

"A ravished woman is without blame," Wulfgar put in, for it all made sense.

"While a cheating woman. . . ." Morik added ominously.

Wulfgar gave another sigh and walked out of the shelter,

staring again at the castle. "What will happen to her?" he called back to Morik.

"The marriage will be declared invalid, surely," Morik answered, having lived in human cities long enough to understand such things.

"And the Lady Meralda will be sent from the castle," the barbarian said hopefully.

"If she's fortunate, she'll be banished from Feringal Auck's domain with neither coin nor title," Morik replied.

"And if she's *un*fortunate?" Wulfgar asked.

Morik winced. "Noblemen's wives have been put to death for such offenses," the worldly rogue replied.

"What of the child?" an increasingly agitated Wulfgar demanded. The images of his own horrible past experiences began edging in at the corners of his consciousness.

"If fortunate, banished," Morik replied, "though I fear such an action will take more good fortune than the banishment of the woman. It is very complicated. The child is a threat to Auck's domain, but also to his pride."

"They would kill a child, a helpless babe?" Wulfgar asked, his teeth clenched tightly as those awful memories began to creep ever closer.

"The rage of a betrayed lord cannot be underestimated," Morik answered grimly. "Lord Feringal cannot show weakness, else risk the loss of the respect of his people and the loss of his lands. Complicated and unpleasant business, all. Now let us be gone from this place."

Wulfgar was indeed gone, storming out from under the overhang and stalking down the trails. Morik was quick to catch him.

"What will you do?" the rogue demanded, recognizing Wulfgar's resolve.

"I don't know, but I've got to do something," Wulfgar said, increasing his pace with the level of his agitation while Morik struggled to keep up. As they entered the village, the storm again proved an ally, for no peasants were around. Wulfgar's eyes were set on the bridge leading to Castle Auck.

✕ ✕ ✕ ✕

"Give the child away, as you planned," Steward Temigast suggested to the pacing Lord Feringal.

"It is different now," the young man stammered, slapping his fists helplessly at his sides. He glanced over at Priscilla. His sister was sitting comfortably, her smug smile a reminder that she'd warned him against marrying a peasant in the first place.

"We don't know that anything has changed," Temigast said, always the voice of reason.

Priscilla snorted. "Can you not count?" she asked.

"The child could be early," Temigast protested.

"As well-formed a babe as ever I've seen," said Priscilla. "She was not early, Temigast, and you know it." Priscilla looked straight at her brother, reiterating the talk that had been buzzing around Castle Auck all day. "The child was conceived mid-summer," she said, "before the supposed attack on the road."

"How can I know for sure?" Lord Feringal wailed. His hands tore at the sides of his pants, an accurate reflection of the rending going on inside his mind.

"How can you not know?" Priscilla shot back. "You've been made a fool to the mirth of all the village. Will you compound that now with weakness?"

"You still love her," Steward Temigast cut in.

"Do I?" Lord Feringal said, so obviously torn and confused. "I don't know anymore."

"Send her away, then," the steward offered. "Banish her with the child."

"That would make the villagers laugh all the harder," Priscilla observed sourly. "Do you want the child to return in a score of years and take your kingdom from you? How many times have we heard of such tales?"

Temigast glared at the woman. Such things had occurred, but they were far from common.

"What am I to do, then?" Lord Feringal demanded of his sister.

"A trial of treason for the whore," Priscilla answered matter-of-factly, "and a swift and just removal of the result of her infidelity."

"Removal?" Feringal echoed skeptically.

"She wants you to kill the child," Temigast explained archly.

"Throw it to the waves," Priscilla supplied feverishly, coming right out of her chair. "If you show no weakness now, the folk will still respect you."

"They will hate you more if you murder an innocent child," Temigast said angrily, more to Priscilla than Lord Feringal.

"Innocent?" Priscilla balked as if the notion were preposterous.

"Let them hate you," she said to Lord Feringal, moving her face to within an inch of his. "Better that than to laugh at you. Would you suffer the bastard to live? A reminder, then, of he who lay with Meralda before you?"

"Shut your mouth!" Lord Feringal demanded, pushing her back.

Priscilla didn't back down. "Oh, but how she purred in the arms of Jaka Sculi," she said, and her brother was trembling so much that he couldn't even speak through his grinding teeth.

"I'll wager she arched that pretty back of hers for him," Priscilla finished lewdly.

Feral, sputtering sounds escaped the young lord. He grabbed his sister by the shoulders with both hands and flung her aside. She was smiling the whole time, satisfied, for the enraged lord shoved past Temigast and ran for the stairs. The stairs that led to Meralda and her bastard child.

✕ ✕ ✕ ✕ ✕

"It's guarded, you know," Morik reminded him, yelling though his voice sounded thin in the howling wind.

Wulfgar wouldn't have heeded the warning anyway. His eyes were set on Castle Auck, and his line to the bridge didn't waver. He pictured the mounds of snow as the Spine of the World, as that barrier between the man he had been and the victim he had become. Now, his mind free at last of all influence of potent liquor, his strength of will granting him armor against those awful images of his imprisonment, Wulfgar saw the choices clearly before him. He could turn back to the life he had found or he could press on, could cross that emotional barrier, could fight and claw his way back to the man he once was.

The barbarian growled and pressed on against the storm. He even picked up speed as he reached the bridge, a fast walk, a trot, then a full run as he picked his course, veering to the right, where the snow had drifted along the railing and the castle's front wall. Up the drift Wulfgar went, crunching into snow past his knees, but growling and plowing on, maintaining his momentum. He leaped from the top of the drift, reaching with an outstretched arm to hook his hammer's head atop the wall. Wulfgar heard a startled call from above as it caught loudly against the stone, but he hardly slowed, great muscles cording and tugging, propelling him upward, where he rolled around, slipping right over the crenellated barrier. He landed nimbly on his feet on the parapet within, right between two dumbfounded guards, neither of them holding a weapon as they tried to keep their hands warm.

Morik rushed up the same path as Wulfgar, using agile moves to scale the wall nearly as fast as his friend had done with brute strength. Still, by the time he got to the parapet Wulfgar was already down in the courtyard, storming for the main keep. Both guards were down, too, lying on the ground and groaning, one holding his jaw, the other curled up and clutching his belly.

"Secure the door!" one of the guards managed to cry out.

The main door cracked open then, a man peeking out. Seeing Wulfgar bearing in, he tried to close it fast. Wulfgar got there just before it slammed, pushing back with all his strength. He heard the man calling frantically for help, felt the greater push as another guard joined the first, both leaning heavily.

"I'm coming, too," Morik called, "though only the gods know why!"

His thoughts far away, in a dark and smoky place where his child's last terrified cry rent the air, Wulfgar didn't hear his friend, didn't need him. Bellowing, he shoved with all his strength until the door flew in, tossing the two guards like children against the back wall of the foyer.

"Where is she?" Wulfgar demanded, and even as he spoke the foyer's other door swung open. Liam Woodgate appeared, rushing in with sword in hand.

"Now you pay, dog!" the coachman cried, coming in fast and hard, stabbing, a feint. Pulling the blade back in, he sent it into a sudden twirl, then feigned a sidelong slice, turning it over again and coming straight in with a deadly thrust.

Liam was good, the best fighter in all of Auckney, and he knew it. That's why it was difficult to understand how Wulfgar's hammer came out so fast to hook over Liam's blade and take it safely wide of the mark. How could the huge barbarian turn so nimbly on his feet to get within reach of Liam's sword? How was he able to come around perfectly, sending his thick arm spiking up under Liam's sword arm? Liam knew his own skill, and so it was even harder for him to understand how his clever attack had been turned against him so completely. Liam knew only that his face was suddenly pressed against the stone wall, his arms pulled tight behind his back, and the snarling barbarian's breath was on his neck.

"Lady Meralda and the child," Wulfgar asked. "Where are they?"

"I'd die afore I'd tell you!" Liam declared. Wulfgar pressed in. The poor old gnome thought he surely *would* die, but Liam held his determined tongue and growled against the pain.

Wulfgar spun him around and slammed him once, then slammed him again when he managed somehow to hold his feet, launching him over to the floor. Liam nearly tripped up Morik, who skipped right on by through the other door and into the castle proper.

Wulfgar was right behind him. They heard voices, and Morik led the way, crashing through a set of double doors and into a comfortable sitting room.

"Lord Brandeburg?" Lady Priscilla asked.

She squealed in fright and fell back in her chair as Wulfgar followed the rogue into the room. "Where is Lady Meralda and the child?" he roared.

"Haven't you caused enough harm?" Steward Temigast demanded, moving to stand boldly before the huge man.

Wulfgar looked him right in the eye. "Too much," he admitted, "but none here."

That set Temigast back on his heels.

"Where are they?" Wulfgar demanded, rushing up to Priscilla.

"Thieves! Murderers!" Priscilla cried, swooning.

Wulfgar locked stares with Temigast. To Wulfgar's surprise, the old steward nodded and motioned toward the staircase.

Even as he did, Priscilla Auck ran full-out up the staircase.

☒ ☒ ☒ ☒ ☒

"Do you have any idea what you've done to me?" Feringal asked Meralda, standing by the edge of her bed, the infant girl lying warm beside her. "To us? To Auckney?"

"I beg you to try to understand, my lord," the woman pleaded.

Feringal winced, pounding his fists into his eyes. His visage steeled, and he reached down and plucked the babe from her side. Meralda started up toward him, but she hadn't the strength and fell back on the bed. "What're you about?"

Feringal strode over to the window and pulled the curtain aside. "My sister says I should toss it to the waves upon the rocks," he said through teeth locked in a tight grimace, "to rid myself of the evidence of your betrayal."

"Please, Feringal, do not—" Meralda began.

"It's what they're all saying, you know," Feringal said as if she hadn't spoken. He blinked his eyes and wiped his nose with his sleeve. "The child of Jaka Sculi."

"My lord!" she cried, her red-rimmed eyes fearful.

"How could you?" Feringal yelled, then looked from the baby in his hands to the open window. Meralda started to cry.

"The cuckold, and now the murderer," Feringal muttered to himself as he moved closer to the window. "You have damned me, Meralda!" he cursed. Holding out his arms, he moved the crying baby to the opening, then he looked down at the innocent little girl and pulled her back close, his tears mixing with the baby's. "Damned me, I say!" he cried, and the breath came in labored, forced gasps.

Suddenly the door to the room flew open, and Lady Priscilla burst in. She slammed it shut and secured the bolt behind her. Surveying the scene quickly, she ran to her brother, her voice shrill. "Give it to me!"

Lord Feringal rolled his shoulder between the child and Priscilla's grasping hands.

"Give it to me!" the woman shrieked again, and a tussle for the baby ensued.

✖ ✖ ✖ ✖ ✖

Wulfgar went in fast pursuit, taking the curving staircase four steps at a stride. He came to a long hallway lined with rich tapestries where he ran into yet another bumbling castle guard. The barbarian slapped the prone man's sword away, caught him by the throat, and lifted him into the air.

Morik skittered past him, going from door to door, ear cocked, then he stopped abruptly at one. "They're in here," he announced. He grabbed the handle only to find it locked.

"The key?" Wulfgar demanded, giving the guard a shake.

The man grabbed the barbarian's iron arm. "No key," he gasped breathlessly. Wulfgar looked about to strangle him, but the thief intervened.

"Don't bother, I'll pick the lock," he said, going fast to his belt pouch.

"Don't bother, I have a key," Wulfgar cried. Morik looked up to see the barbarian bearing down on him, the guard still dangling at the end of one arm. Seeing his intent, Morik skittered out of the way as Wulfgar hurled the hapless man through the wooden door. "A key," the barbarian explained.

"Well thrown," Morik commented.

"I have had practice," explained Wulfgar, thundering past the dazed guard to leap into the room.

Meralda sat up on the bed, sobbing, while Lord Feringal and his sister stood by the open window, the babe in Feringal's arms. He was leaning toward the opening as if he meant to throw the child out. Both siblings and Meralda turned stunned expressions Wulfgar's way, and their eyes widened even more when Morik crashed in behind the barbarian.

"Lord Brandeburg!" Feringal cried.

Lady Priscilla shouted at her brother, "Do it now, before they ruin every—"

"The child is mine!" Wulfgar declared. Priscilla bit off the end of her sentence in surprise. Feringal froze as if turned to stone.

"What?" the young lord gasped.

"What?" Lady Priscilla gasped.

"What?" gasped Morik, at the same time.

"What?" gasped Meralda, quietly, and she coughed quickly to cover her surprise.

"The child is mine," Wulfgar repeated firmly, "and if you throw her out the window, then you shall follow so quickly that you'll pass her by and your broken body will pad her fall."

"You are so eloquent in emergencies," Morik remarked. To Lord Feringal, he added, "The window is small, yes, but I'll wager that my big friend can squeeze you through it. And your plump sister, as well."

"You can't be the father," Lord Feringal declared, trembling so violently that it seemed as if his legs would just buckle beneath him. He looked to Priscilla for an answer, to his sister who was

389

always hovering above him with all of the answers. "What trick is this?"

"Give it to me!" Priscilla demanded. Taking advantage of her brother's paralyzing confusion, she moved quickly and tore the child from Feringal's grasp. Meralda cried out, the baby cried, and Wulfgar started forward, knowing that he could never get there in time, knowing that the innocent was surely doomed.

Even as Priscilla turned for the window, her brother leaped before her and slugged her in the face. Stunned, she staggered back a step. Feringal snatched the child from her arms and shoved her again, sending his sister stumbling to the floor.

Wulfgar eyed the man for a long and telling moment, understanding then beyond any doubt that despite his obvious anger and revulsion, Feringal would not hurt the child. The barbarian strode across the room, secure in his observations, confident that the young man would take no action against the babe.

"The child is mine," the barbarian said with a growl, reaching over to gently pull the wailing baby from Feringal's weakening grasp. "I meant to wait another month before returning," he explained, turning to face Meralda. "But it's good you delivered early. A child of mine come to full term would likely have killed you in birthing."

"Wulfgar!" Morik cried suddenly.

Lord Feringal, apparently recovering some of his nerve and most of his rage, produced a dagger from his belt and came in hard at the barbarian. Morik needn't have worried, though, for Wulfgar heard the movement. Lifting the babe high with one arm to keep her from harm's way, he spun and slapped the dagger aside with his free hand. As Feringal came in close, Wulfgar brought his knee up hard into the man's groin. Down Lord Feringal went, curling into a mewling heap on the floor.

"I think my large friend can make it so that you never

have children of your own," Morik remarked with a wink to Meralda.

Meralda didn't even hear the words, staring dumbfounded at Wulfgar, at the child he had proclaimed as his own.

"For my actions on the road, I truly apologize, Lady Meralda," the barbarian said, and he was playing to a full audience now, as Liam Woodgate, Steward Temigast and the remaining half dozen castle guards appeared at the door, staring in wide-eyed disbelief. On the floor before Wulfgar, Lady Priscilla looked up at him, confusion and unbridled anger simmering in her eyes.

"It was the bottle and your beauty that took me," Wulfgar explained. He turned his attention to the child, his smile wide as he lifted the infant girl into the air for his sparkling blue eyes to behold. "But I'll not apologize for the result of that crime," he said. "Never that."

"I will kill you," Lord Feringal growled, struggling to his knees.

Wulfgar reached down with one hand and grabbed him by the collar. Helping him up with a powerful jerk, he spun the lord around into a choke hold. "You will forget me, and the child," Wulfgar whispered into his ear. "Else the combined tribes of Icewind Dale will sack you and your wretched little village."

Wulfgar pushed the young lord, spinning him into Morik's waiting grasp. Staring at Liam and the other dangerous guards, the rogue wasted no time in putting a sharp dagger to the man's throat.

"Secure us supplies for the road," Wulfgar instructed. "We need wrappings and food for the babe." Everyone in the room, save Wulfgar and the baby, wore incredulous expressions. "Do it!" the barbarian roared. Frowning, Morik pushed toward the door with Lord Feringal, waving a scrambling Priscilla out ahead of him.

"Fetch!" the rogue instructed Liam and Priscilla. He glanced back and saw Wulfgar moving toward Meralda then, so he pushed out even further, backing them all away.

"What made you do such a thing?" Meralda asked when she was alone with Wulfgar and the child.

"Your problem was not hard to discern," Wulfgar explained.

"I falsely accused you."

"Understandably so," Wulfgar replied. "You were trapped and scared, but in the end you risked everything to free me from prison. I could not let that deed go unpaid."

Meralda shook her head, too overwhelmed to even begin to sort this out. So many thoughts and emotions whirled in her mind. She had seen the look of despair on Feringal's face, had thought he would, indeed, drop the baby to the rocks. Yet, in the end he hadn't been able to do it, hadn't let his sister do it. She did love this man—how could she not? And yet, she could hardly deny her unexpected feelings for her child, though she knew that never, ever, could she keep her.

"I am taking the babe far from here," Wulfgar said determinedly, as if he had read her mind. "You are welcome to come with us."

Meralda laughed softly, without humor, because she knew she would be crying soon enough. "I can't," she explained, her voice a whisper. "I've a duty to my husband, if he'll still have me, and to my family. My folks would be branded if I went with you."

"Duty? Is that the only reason you're staying?" Wulfgar asked her, apparently sensing something more.

"I love him, you know," Meralda replied, tears streaming down her beautiful face. "I know what you must think of me, but truly, the babe was made before I ever—"

Wulfgar held up his hand. "You owe me no explanation," he said, "for I am hardly in a position to judge you or anyone else. I came to understand your . . . problem, and so I returned to repay your generosity, that is all." He looked to the door through which Morik held Lord Feringal. "He does love you," he said. "His eyes and the depth of his pain showed that clearly."

"You think I'm right in staying?"

Wulfgar shrugged, again refusing to offer any judgments.

"I can't leave him," Meralda said, and she reached up and tenderly stroked the child's face, "but I cannot keep her, either. Feringal would never accept her," she admitted, her tone empty and hollow, for she realized her time with her daughter was nearing its end. "But perhaps he'd give her over to another family in Auckney now that he's thinking I didn't betray him," she suggested faintly.

"A reminder to him of his pain, and to you of your lie," Wulfgar said softly, not accusing the woman, but surely reminding her of the truth. "And within the reach of his shrewish sister."

Meralda lowered her gaze and accepted the bitter truth. The baby was not safe in Auckney.

"Who better to raise her than me?" Wulfgar asked suddenly, resolve in his voice. He looked down at the little girl, and his mouth turned up into a warm smile.

"You'd do that?"

Wulfgar nodded. "Happily."

"You'd keep her safe?" Meralda pressed. "Tell her of her ma?"

Wulfgar nodded. "I don't know where my road now leads," he explained, "but I suspect I'll not venture too far from here. Perhaps someday I will return, or at least she will, to glimpse her ma."

Meralda was shaking with sobs, her face gleaming with tears. Wulfgar glanced to the doorway to make sure that he was not being watched, then bent down and kissed her on the cheek. "I think it best," he said quietly. "Do you agree?"

After she studied the man for a moment, this man who had risked everything to save her and her child though they had done nothing to deserve his heroism, Meralda nodded.

The tears continued to flow freely. Wulfgar could appreciate the pain she was feeling, the depth of her sacrifice. He leaned in, allowing Meralda to stroke and kiss her baby girl one last time, but when she moved to take her away, Wulfgar pulled back. Meralda's smile of understanding was bittersweet.

"Farewell, little one," she said through her sobs and looked away. Wulfgar bowed to Meralda one last time, then, with the baby cradled in his big arms, he turned and left the room.

He found Morik in the hallway, barking commands for plenty of food and clothing—and gold, for they'd need gold to properly situate the child in warm and comfortable inns. Barbarian, baby, and thief, made their way through the castle, and no one made a move to stop them. It seemed as if Lord Feringal had cleared their path, wanting the two thieves and the bastard child out of his castle and out of his life as swiftly as possible.

Priscilla, however, was a different issue. They ran into her on the first floor, where she came up to Wulfgar and tried to take the baby, glaring at him defiantly all the while. The barbarian held her at bay, his expression making it clear that he would break her in half if she tried to harm the child. Priscilla huffed her disgust, threw a thick wool wrap at him, and with a final growl of protest, turned on her heel.

"Stupid cow," Morik muttered under his breath.

Chuckling, Wulfgar tenderly wrapped the baby in the warm blanket, finally silencing her crying. Outside, the daylight was fast on the wane, but the storm had faded, the last clouds breaking apart and rushing across the sky on swift winds. The gate was lowered. Across the bridge they saw Steward Temigast waiting for them with a pair of horses, Lord Feringal at his side.

Feringal stood staring at Wulfgar and the baby for a long moment. "If you ever come back . . ." he started to say.

"Why would I?" the barbarian interrupted. "I have my child now, and she will grow up to be a queen in Icewind Dale. Entertain no thoughts of coming after me, Lord Feringal, to the ruin of all your world."

"Why would I?" Feringal returned in the same grim tone, facing up to Wulfgar boldly. "I have my wife, my beautiful wife. My innocent wife, who gives herself to me willingly. I do not have to force myself upon her."

That last statement, a recapture of some measure of manly pride, told Wulfgar that Feringal had forgiven Meralda, or that he soon enough would. Wulfgar's desperate, unconsidered and purely improvised plan had somehow, miraculously, worked. He bit back any semblance of a chuckle at the ridiculousness of it all, let Feringal have his needed moment. He didn't even blink as the lord of Auckney composed himself, squared his shoulders, and walked back across the bridge through the lowered gate to his home and his wife.

Steward Temigast handed the reins to the pair. "She isn't yours," the steward said unexpectedly. Starting to pull himself and the babe up into the saddle, Wulfgar pretended not to hear him.

"Fear not, for I'll not tell, nor will Meralda, whose life you have truly saved this day," the steward went on. "You are a fine man, Wulfgar, son of Beornegar, of the Tribe of the Elk of Icewind Dale." Wulfgar blinked in amazement, both at the compliment and at the simple fact that the man knew so much of him.

"The wizard who caught you told him," Morik reasoned. "I hate wizards."

"There will be no pursuit," said Temigast. "On my word."

And that word held true, for Morik and Wulfgar rode without

incident back to the overhang, where they retrieved their own horses, then continued down the east road and out of Auckney for good.

"What is it?" Wulfgar asked Morik later that night, seeing the rogue's amused expression. They were huddled around a blazing fire, keeping the child warm. Morik smiled and held up a pair of bottles, one with warm goat's milk for the child, the other with their favored potent drink. Wulfgar took the one with the goat's milk.

"I will never understand you, my friend," Morik remarked.

Wulfgar smiled, but did not respond. Morik could never truly know of Wulfgar's past, of the good times with Drizzt and the others, and of the very worst times with Errtu and the offspring of his stolen seed.

"There are easier ways to make gold," Morik remarked, and that brought Wulfgar's steely gaze over him. "You mean to sell the child, of course," Morik reasoned.

Wulfgar scoffed.

"A fine price," Morik argued, taking a healthy swig from the bottle.

"Not fine enough," said Wulfgar, turning back to the babe. The little girl wriggled and cooed.

"You cannot plan to keep her!" Morik argued. "What place has she with us? With you, wherever you plan to go? Have you lost all sensibility?"

Scowling, Wulfgar spun on him, slapped the bottle from his hands, then shoved him back to the ground, as determined an answer as Morik the Rogue had ever heard.

"She's not even yours!" Morik reminded him.

The rogue could not have been more wrong.

EPILOGUE

Morik looked at Wulfgar's disguise one more time and sighed helplessly. There was only so much one could do to change the appearance of a nearly seven-foot-tall, three hundred pound, blond-haired barbarian.

Wulfgar was clean shaven again for the first time since his return from the Abyss. Morik had taught him to walk in a way that would somewhat lessen his height, with shoulders drooped but arms crooked so that they did not hang to his knees. Also, Morik had procured a large brown robe such as a priest might wear, with a bunched collar that allowed Wulfgar to scrunch down his neck without being obvious about it.

Still, the rogue was not entirely happy with the disguise, not when so much was riding on it. "You should wait out here," he offered, for perhaps the tenth time since Wulfgar had told him his wishes.

"No," Wulfgar said evenly. "They would not come at your word alone. This is something I must do."

"Get us both killed?" the rogue asked sarcastically.

"Lead on," Wulfgar said, ignoring him. When Morik tried to argue, the barbarian slapped a hand over the smaller man's mouth and turned him around to face the distant city gate.

With one last sigh and a shake of his head, Morik led the way back into Luskan. To the great relief of both of them, for Wulfgar surely did not wish to be discovered while carrying the baby, they were not recognized, were not detained at all, but merely strode into the city where the spring festival was on in full.

They had come in late in the day by design. Wulfgar went straight to Half-Moon Street, arriving at the Cutlass as one of the evening's first patrons. He moved to the bar, right beside Josi Puddles.

"What're ye drinking?" Arumn Gardpeck asked, but the question caught in his throat and his eyes went wide as he looked more carefully at the big man. "Wulfgar," he gasped.

Behind the barbarian a tray dropped, and Wulfgar turned to see Delly Curtie standing there, stunned. Josi Puddles gave a squeal and leaned away.

"Well met, Arumn," Wulfgar said to the tavernkeeper. "I drink only water."

"What're ye doing here?" the tavernkeeper gasped, suspicious and more than a little fearful.

Josi hopped off his stool and started for the door, but Wulfgar caught him by the arm and held him in place. "I came to apologize," the barbarian offered. "To you, and to you," he added, turning to Josi.

"Ye tried to kill me," Josi sputtered.

"I was blind with anger, and likely drink," Wulfgar replied.

"He took yer hammer," Arumn reminded.

"Out of rightful fear that I would use it against you," the

barbarian answered. "He acted as a friend, which is much more than I can say for Wulfgar."

Arumn shook his head, hardly believing any of this. Wulfgar released Josi, but the man made no move to continue for the door, just stood there, dumbfounded.

"You took me in, gave me food, a paying job, and friendship when I needed it most," Wulfgar continued to Arumn alone. "I wronged you, terribly so, and can only hope that you will find it in your heart to forgive me."

"Are ye looking to live here again?" Arumn asked.

Wulfgar smiled sadly and shook his head. "I risk my life by even entering the city," he replied. "I'll be gone within the hour, but I had to come, to apologize to you two, and mostly," he turned around, facing Delly, "to you."

Delly Curtie blanched as Wulfgar approached, as if she didn't know how to react to the man's words, to the mere sight of him again.

"I am most humbly sorry for any pain that I ever caused you, Delly," he said. "You were as true a friend as any man could ever have desired."

"More than a friend," Wulfgar quickly added, seeing her frown.

Delly eyed the bundle in his arms. "Ye've a little one," the woman said, her voice thick with emotion.

"Mine by chance and not by heritage," Wulfgar replied. He handed the little girl over to her. Delly took her, smiling tenderly, playing with the child's fingers and bringing a smile to that innocent little face.

"I wish ye might be stayin' again," Arumn offered, and he sounded sincere, though Josi's eyes widened in doubt at the mere mention.

"I cannot," Wulfgar replied. Smiling at Delly, he leaned over and took the babe back, then kissed Delly on the forehead. "I pray you find all the happiness you deserve, Delly Curtie," he said, and with a look and a nod at Arumn and Josi, he started for the door.

Delly, too, looked hard at Arumn, so much her father. The man understood and nodded once again. She caught up to Wulfgar before he reached the exit.

"Take me with ye," she said, her eyes sparkling with hope—something few had seen from the woman in a long, long time.

Wulfgar looked puzzled. "I did not return to rescue you," he explained.

"Rescue?" Delly echoed incredulously. "I'm not needin' yer rescue, thank ye very much, but you're needin' help with the little one, I can see. I'm good with tykes—spent most o' me young life raisin' me brothers and sisters—and I've grown more than a bit bored with me life here."

"I don't know where my road shall lead," Wulfgar argued.

"Safe enough, I'm guessing," Delly replied. "Since ye've the little one to care for, I mean."

"Waterdeep, perhaps," said Wulfgar.

"A place I've always wanted to see," she said, her smile growing with every word, for it seemed obvious that Wulfgar was becoming more than a little intrigued by her offer.

The barbarian looked curiously to Arumn, and the tavern-keeper nodded his head yet again. Even from that distance Wulfgar could see a bit of moisture rimming the man's eyes.

He gave the child back to Delly, bade her wait there, and moved back to the bar with Arumn and Josi. "I'll not hurt her ever again," Wulfgar promised Arumn.

"If ye do, I'll hunt ye down and kill ye," Josi growled.

Wulfgar and Arumn looked at the man, Arumn doubtfully, but Wulfgar working hard to keep his expression serious. "I know that, Josi Puddles," he replied without sarcasm, "and your wrath is something I would truly fear."

When he got past his own surprise, Josi puffed up his little chest with pride. Wulfgar and Arumn exchanged stares.

"No drinking?" Arumn asked.

Wulfgar shook his head. "I needed the bottle to hide in," he answered honestly, "but I have learned it to be worse than what haunts me."

"And if ye get bored with the girl?"

"I didn't come here for Delly Curtie," Wulfgar replied. "Only to apologize. I didn't think she would accept my apology so completely, but glad I am that she did. We'll find a good road to travel, and I'll protect her as best I can, from myself most of all."

"See that ye do," Arumn replied. "I'll expect ye back."

Wulfgar shook Arumn's hand, patted Josi on the shoulder, and moved to take Delly's arm, leading her out of the Cutlass. Together they walked away from a significant part of their lives.

⚔ ⚔ ⚔ ⚔ ⚔

Lord Feringal and Meralda walked along the garden, hand in hand, enjoying the springtime fragrance and beauty. Wulfgar's ploy had worked. Feringal and all the fiefdom believed Meralda the wronged party again, freeing her from blame and the young lord from ridicule.

Truly the woman felt pain at the loss of her child, but it, like her marriage, seemed well on the mend. She kept telling herself over and over that the babe was with a good and strong man, a better father than Jaka could ever have been. Many were the times Meralda cried for the lost child, but always she repeated her logical litany and remembered that her life, given her mistakes and station by birth, was better by far than she could ever have imagined. Her mother and father were healthy, and Tori visited her every day, bobbing happily among the flowers and proving more of a thorn to Priscilla than Meralda had ever been.

Now the couple was simply enjoying the splendor of spring, the woman adjusting to her new life. Feringal snapped his fingers suddenly and pulled away. Meralda regarded him curiously.

"I have forgotten something," her husband replied. Feringal motioned for her to wait, then ran back into the castle, nearly running down Priscilla, who was coming out the garden door.

Of course, Priscilla still didn't believe any of Wulfgar's tale. She scowled at Meralda, but the younger woman just turned away and moved to the wall, staring out over the waves.

"Watching for your next lover to arrive?" Priscilla muttered under her breath as she moved by. She often launched verbal jabs Meralda's way, and Meralda often just let them slide down her shoulders.

Not this time, though. Meralda stepped in front of her sister-in-law, hands on her hips. "You've never felt an honest emotion in your miserable life, Priscilla Auck, which is why you're so bitter." she said. "Judge me not."

Priscilla's eyes widened with shock and she trembled, unused to being spoken to in such a forward manner. "You ask—"

"I'm not asking you, I'm telling you," Meralda said curtly.

Priscilla stood up and grimaced, then slapped Meralda across the face.

Feeling the sting, Meralda slapped her back harder. "Judge me not, or I'll whisper the truth of your wretchedness into your brother's ear," Meralda warned, so calm and calculating that her words alone made Priscilla's face burn hot. "You can't doubt that I have his ear," Meralda finished. "Have you thought of what a life in the village among the peasants might be like for you?"

Even as she finished her husband bounded back out, a huge bouquet of flowers in his hand, flowers for his dear Meralda. Priscilla took one look at her fawning brother, gave a great cry, and ran into the castle.

Feringal watched her go, confused, but so little did he care what Priscilla thought or felt these days that he didn't even bother to ask Meralda about it.

Meralda, too, watched the wretched woman depart. Her smile was wrought from more than delight at her husband's thoughtful present. Much more.

⚔ ⚔ ⚔ ⚔

Morik said his farewells to Wulfgar and to Delly, then began at once to reestablish himself on Luskan's streets. He took a room at an inn on Half-Moon Street but spent little time there, for he was out working hard, telling the truth of his identity to those who needed to know, establishing a reputation as a completely different man, Burglar Brandeburg, to those who did not.

By the end of the tenday many nodded in deference as he passed them on the streets. By the end of the month, the rogue no longer feared retribution from the authorities. He was home again, and soon things would be as they had been before Wulfgar had ever come to Luskan.

He was leaving his room one night with just that in mind when he stepped out of his bedroom door into the inn's upper hallway. Instead he found himself sliding through a dizzying tunnel, coming to rest in a crystalline room whose circular walls gave the appearance of one level in a tower.

Dazed, Morik started to reach for his dagger, but he saw the ebon-skinned forms and changed his mind, wise enough not to resist the dark elves.

"You know me, Morik," said Kimmuriel Oblodra, moving close to the man.

Morik did, indeed, recognize the drow as the messenger who had come to him a year before, bidding him to keep a watch over Wulfgar.

"I give you my friend, Rai-guy," Kimmuriel said politely, indicating the other dark elf in the room, one wearing a sinister expression.

"Did we not ask you to watch over the one named Wulfgar?" Kimmuriel asked.

Morik stuttered, not knowing what to say.

"And have you not failed us?" Kimmuriel went on.

"But . . . but that was a year ago," Morik protested. "I have heard nothing since."

"Now you are in hiding, in disguise, knowing your crime against us," said Kimmuriel.

"My supposed crimes are of another matter," Morik stuttered, feeling as if the very walls were tightening around him. "I hide from the Luskan authorities, not from you."

"From them you hide?" said the other drow. "Help you, I can!" He strode over to Morik and lifted his hands. Sheets of flame erupted from his fingertips, burning Morik's face and lighting his hair on fire. The rogue howled and fell to the floor, slapping at his singed skin.

"Now you appear different," Kimmuriel remarked, and both dark elves chuckled wickedly. They dragged him up the tower stairs into another room, where a bald-headed drow holding a great plumed purple hat sat comfortably in a chair.

"My apologies, Morik," he said. "My lieutenants are an excitable lot."

"I was with Wulfgar for months," Morik claimed, obviously on the edge of hysteria. "Circumstance forced us apart and forced him from Luskan. I can find him for you—"

"No need," said the drow in the chair, holding up his hand to calm the groveling man. "I am Jarlaxle, of Menzoberranzan, and I forgive you in full."

Morik rubbed one hand over what was left of his hair, as if to say that he wished Jarlaxle had been so beneficent earlier.

"I had planned for Wulfgar to be my primary trading partner in Luskan, my representative here." Jarlaxle explained. "Now, with him gone, I ask you to assume the role."

Morik blinked, and his heart skipped a beat.

"We will make you wealthy and powerful beyond your dreams," the mercenary leader explained, and Morik believed him. "You'll not need to hide from the authorities. Indeed, many will invite you to their homes almost daily, for they will desperately want to remain in good standing with you. If there are any you wish . . . eliminated, that, too, can be easily arranged."

Morik licked what was left of his lips.

"Does this sound like a position Morik the Rogue would be interested in pursuing?" Jarlaxle asked, and Morik returned the dark elf's sly look tenfold.

"I warn you," Jarlaxle said, coming forward in his chair, his dark eyes flashing, "if you ever fail me, my friend Rai-guy will willingly alter your appearance yet again."

"And again," the wizard happily added.

"I hate wizards," Morik muttered under his breath.

⚔ ⚔ ⚔ ⚔ ⚔

Wulfgar and Delly looked down on Waterdeep, the City of Splendors. The most wondrous and powerful city on the Sword Coast, it was a place of great dreams and greater power.

"Where are ye thinkin' we'll be staying?" the happy woman asked, gently rocking the child.

Wulfgar shook his head. "I have coins," he replied, "but I don't know how long we'll remain in Waterdeep."

"Ye're not thinkin' to make our lives here?"

The barbarian shrugged, for he hadn't given it much thought. He had come to Waterdeep with another purpose. He hoped to find Captain Deudermont and *Sea Sprite* in port, or hoped that they would come in soon, as they often did.

"Have you ever been to sea?" he asked the woman, his best friend and partner now, with a wide smile.

It was time for him to get Aegis-fang back.